MARCO POLO

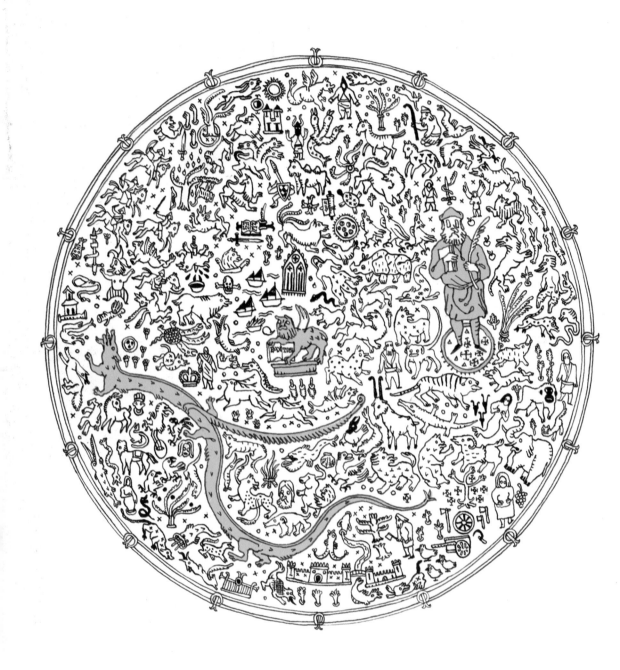

Marco Polo
Dangers and Visions

Marco Tabilio

Translation by Kerstin Schwandt

Graphic Universe™ • Minneapolis

First American edition published in 2017 by Graphic Universe™

Published in arrangement with AMBook (www.ambook.ch)

Translation by Kerstin Schwandt

Graphic Universe™
A division of Lerner Publishing Group, Inc.
241 First Avenue North
Minneapolis, MN 55401 USA

For reading levels and more information, look up this title at
www.lernerbooks.com.

Main body text set in King George Bold Clean 9/9.
Typeface provided by Chank.

Library of Congress Cataloging-in-Publication Data

Names: Tabilio, Marco, author.
Title: Marco Polo : dangers and visions / Marco Tabilio; translated by
    Kerstin Schwandt.
Description: First North American edition. | Minneapolis : Graphic Universe,
    2017. | Includes bibliographical references.
Identifiers: LCCN 2016006055 (print) | LCCN 2016010077 (ebook) | ISBN
    9781512411829 (lb : alk. paper) | ISBN 9781512427028 (eb pdf)
Subjects: LCSH: Polo, Marco, 1254-1323?—Juvenile literature. | Explorers-
    -Italy—Biography—Juvenile literature. | Travel, Medieva—Juvenile
    literature. | Asia—Description and trave—Juvenile literature.
Classification: LCC G370.P9 T34 2017 (print) | LCC G370.P9 (ebook) | DDC
    915.04/2092 [B] —dc23

LC record available at https://lccn.loc.gov/2016006055

Manufactured in the United States of America
1-39682-21295-1/9/2017

少小離家老大回
鄉音無改鬢毛衰
兒童相見不相識
笑問客從何處來

I was young when I left home.

I came back older but carefree.

My accent has not changed much,

but my hair much thinner be.

Now those I meet know not my face.

They ask, "From whence come thee?"

He Zhizhang (ca. 659–744), *Coming Home*

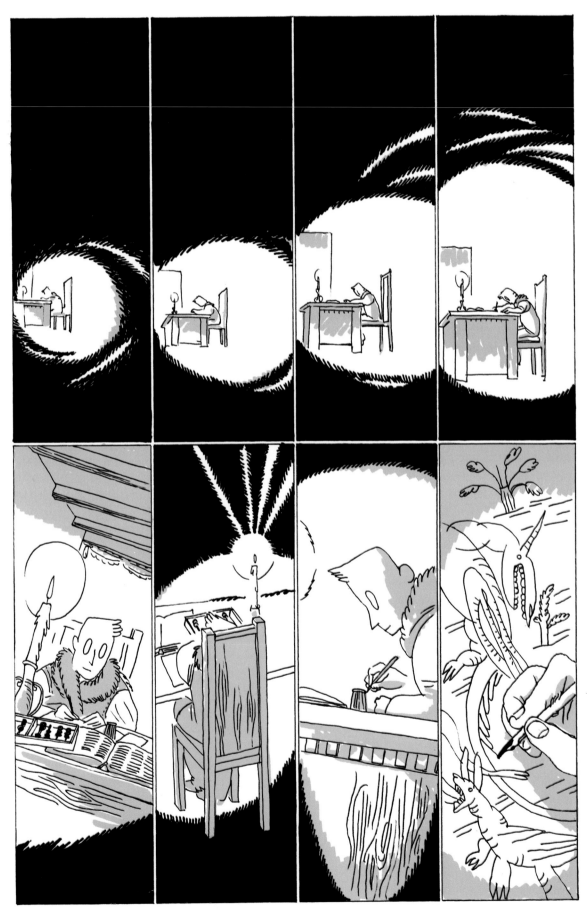

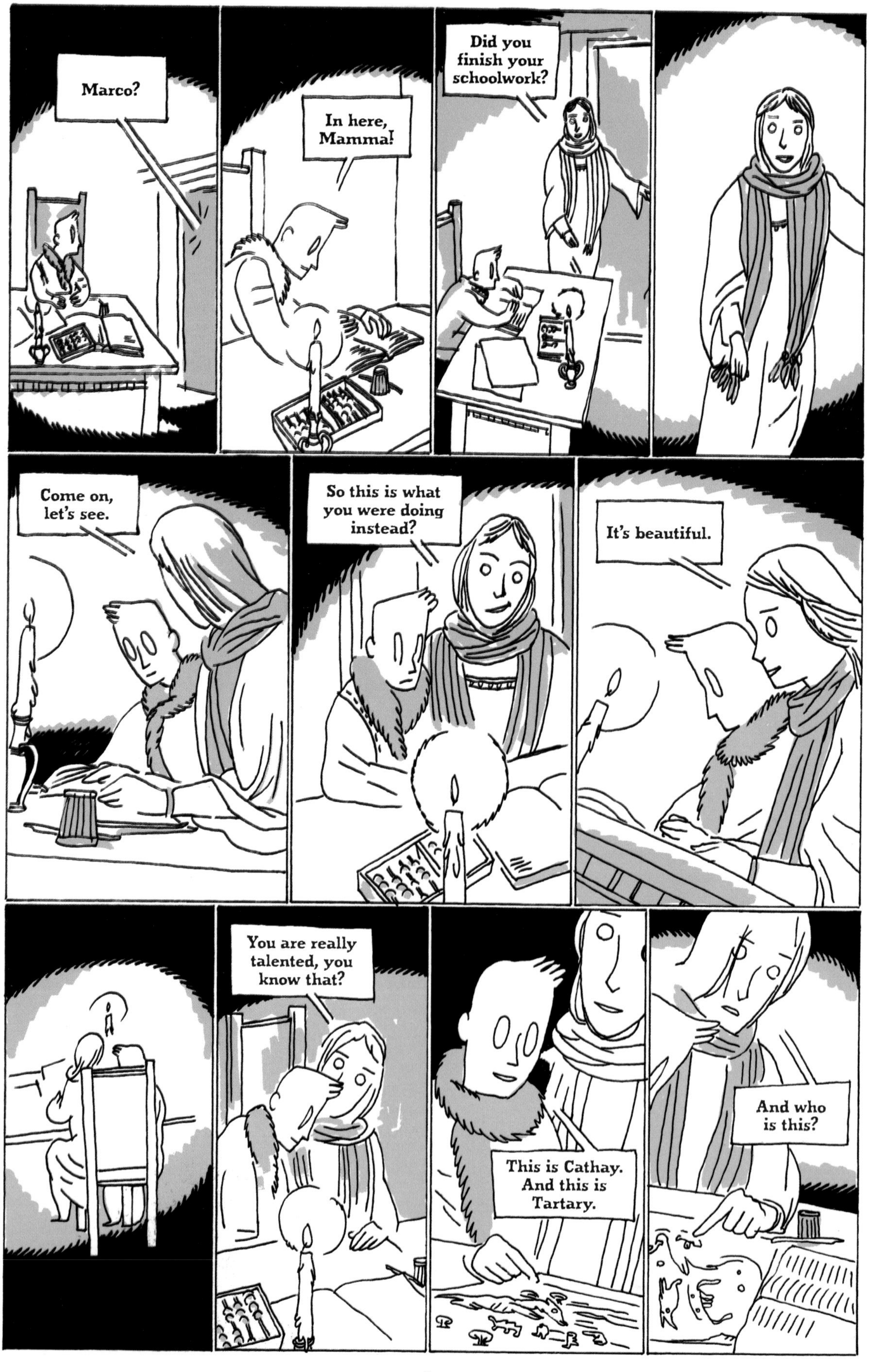

Marco?
In here, Mamma!
Did you finish your schoolwork?
Come on, let's see.
So this is what you were doing instead?
It's beautiful.
You are really talented, you know that?
This is Cathay. And this is Tartary.
And who is this?

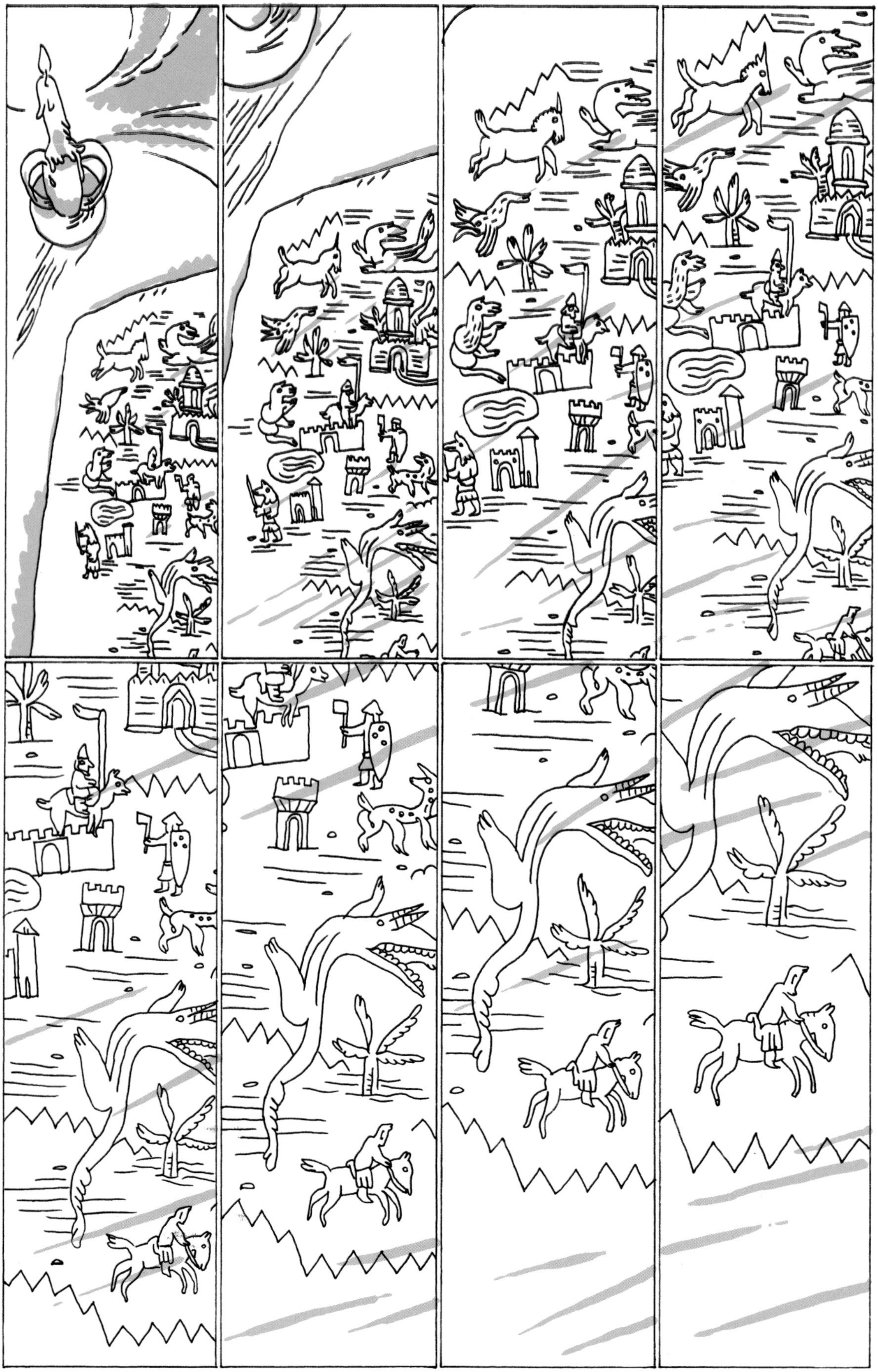

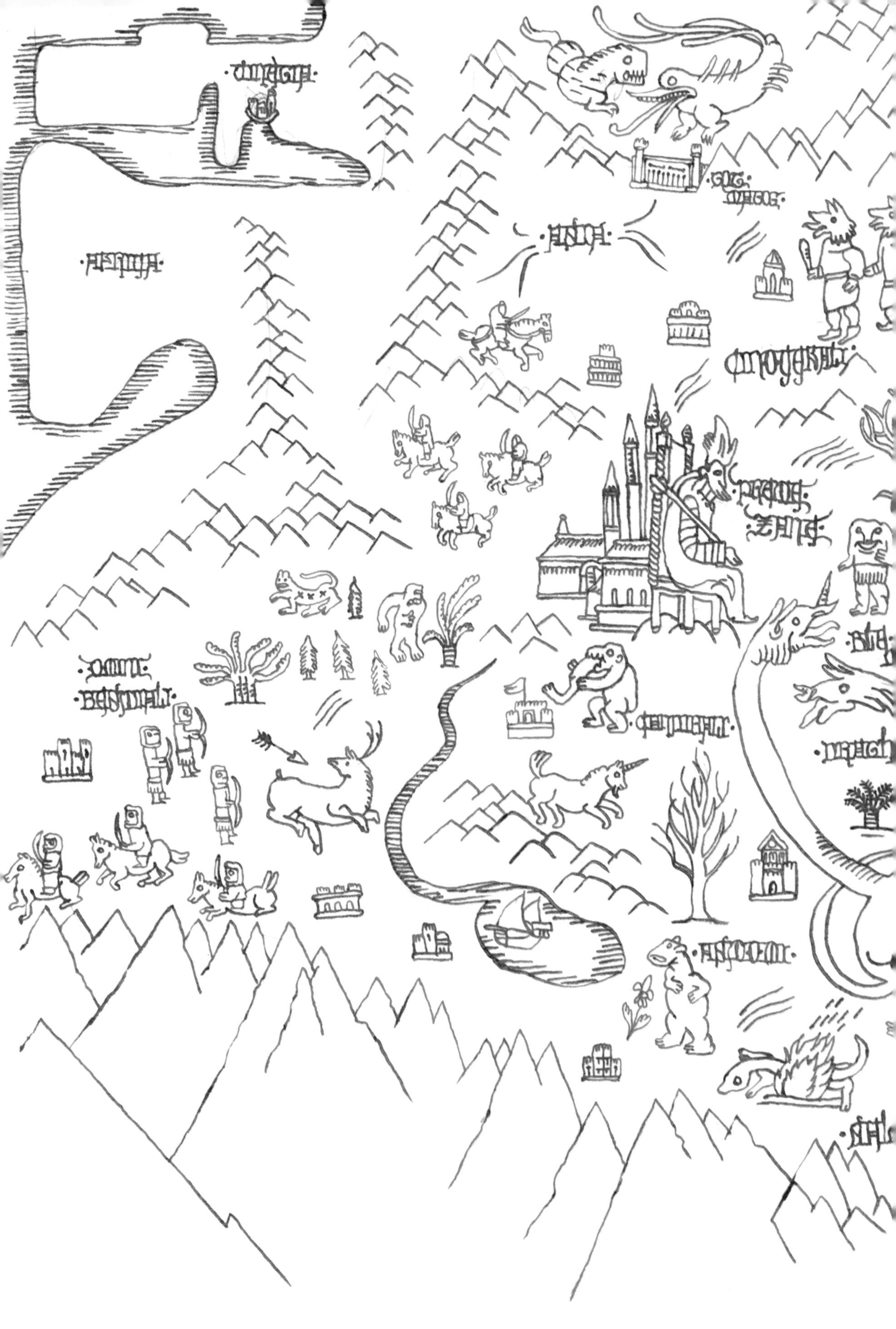
GOG MAGOG

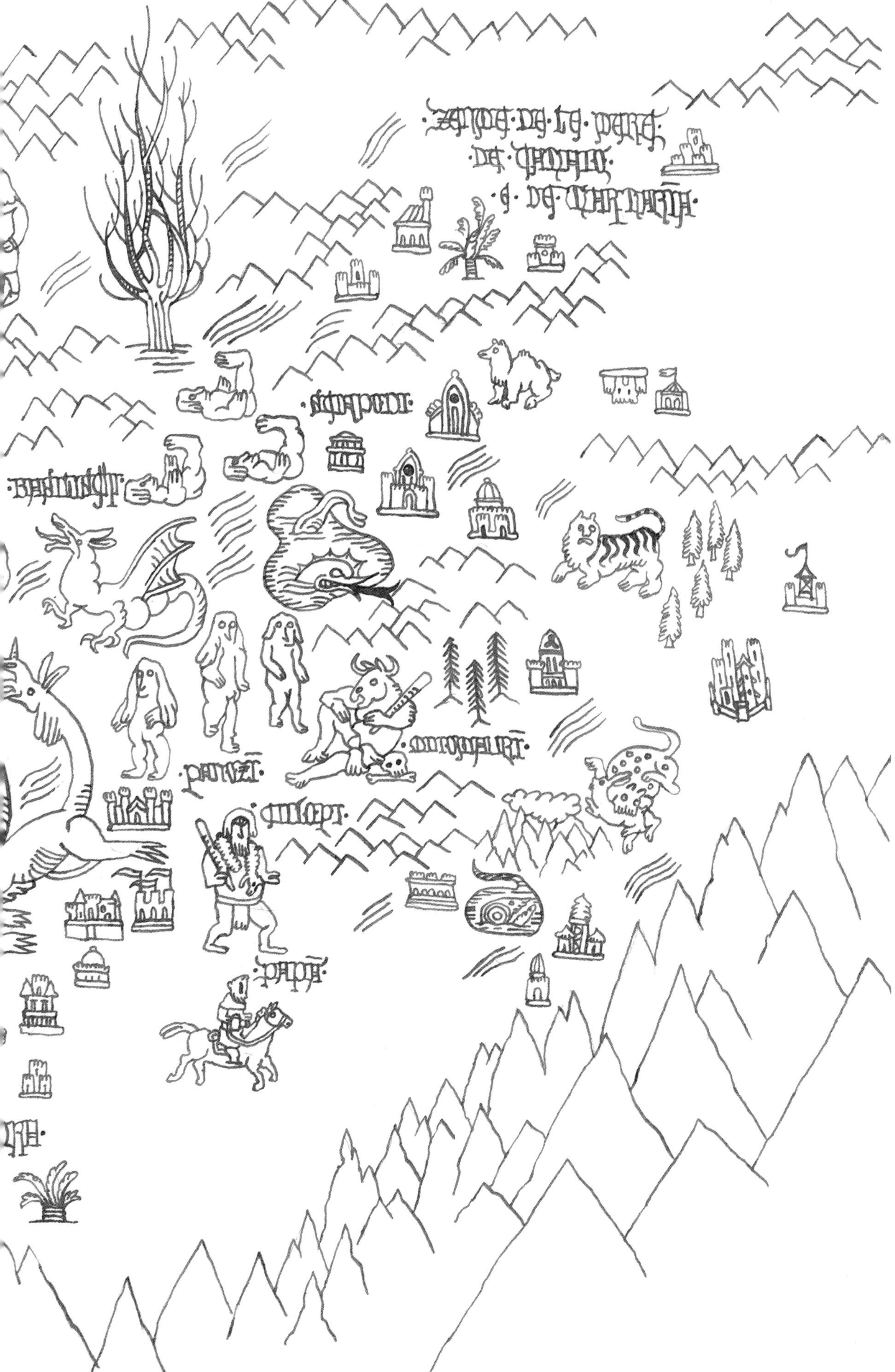

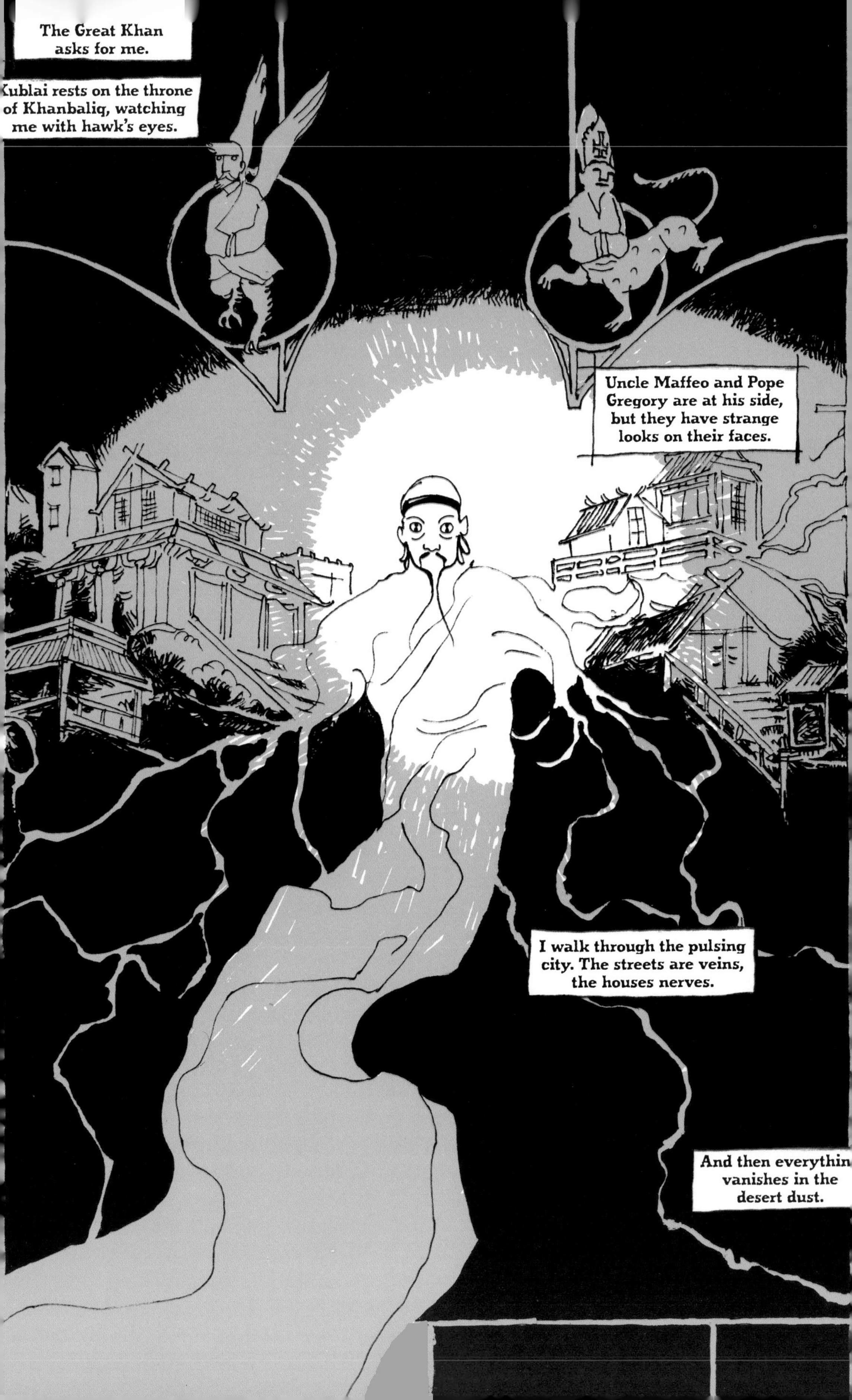
The Great Khan asks for me.
Kublai rests on the throne of Khanbaliq, watching me with hawk's eyes.
Uncle Maffeo and Pope Gregory are at his side, but they have strange looks on their faces.
I walk through the pulsing city. The streets are veins, the houses nerves.
And then everythin vanishes in the desert dust.

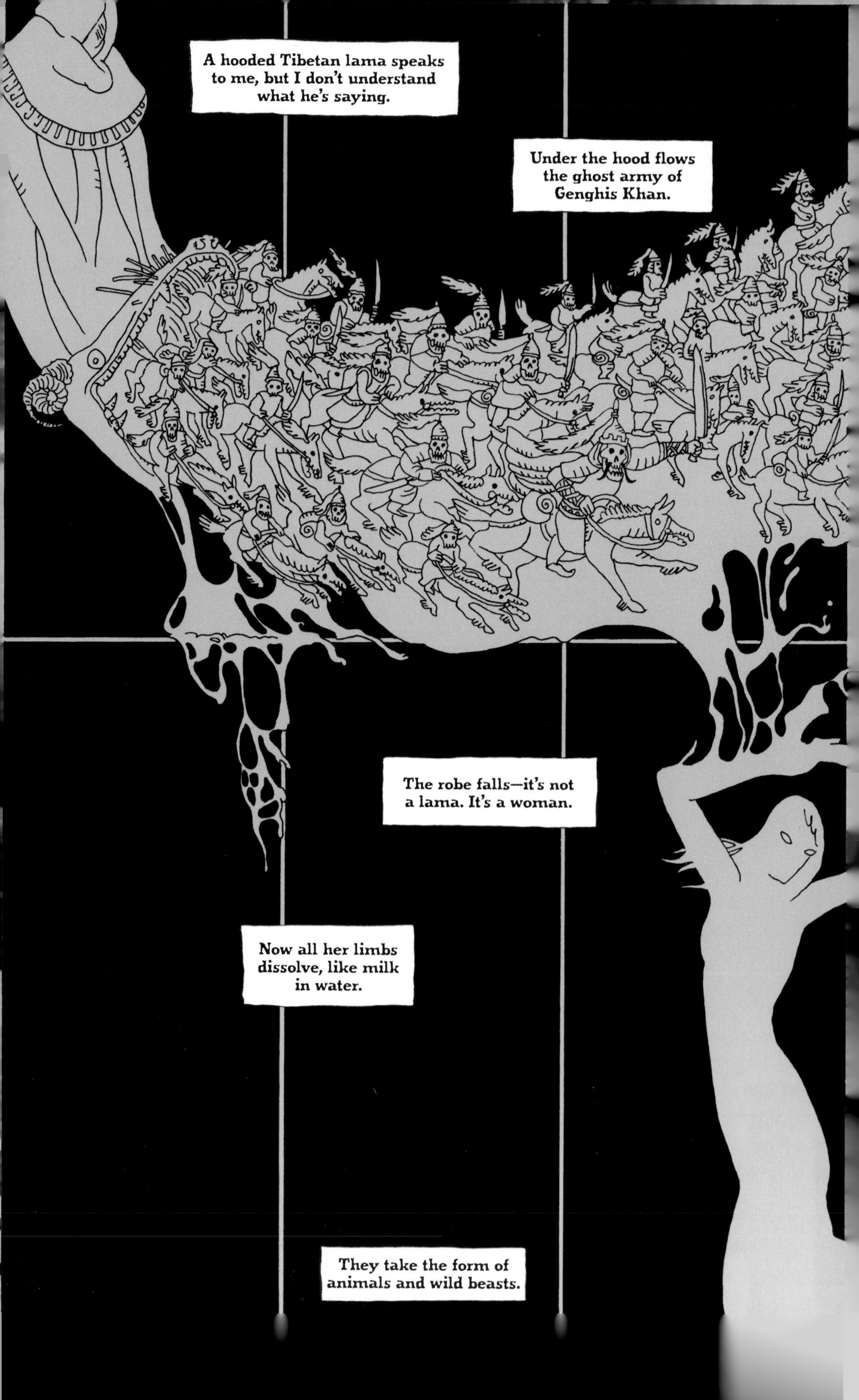
A hooded Tibetan lama speaks to me, but I don't understand what he's saying.
Under the hood flows the ghost army of Genghis Khan.
The robe falls—it's not a lama. It's a woman.
Now all her limbs dissolve, like milk in water.
They take the form of animals and wild beasts.

Genoa, Italy, 1298

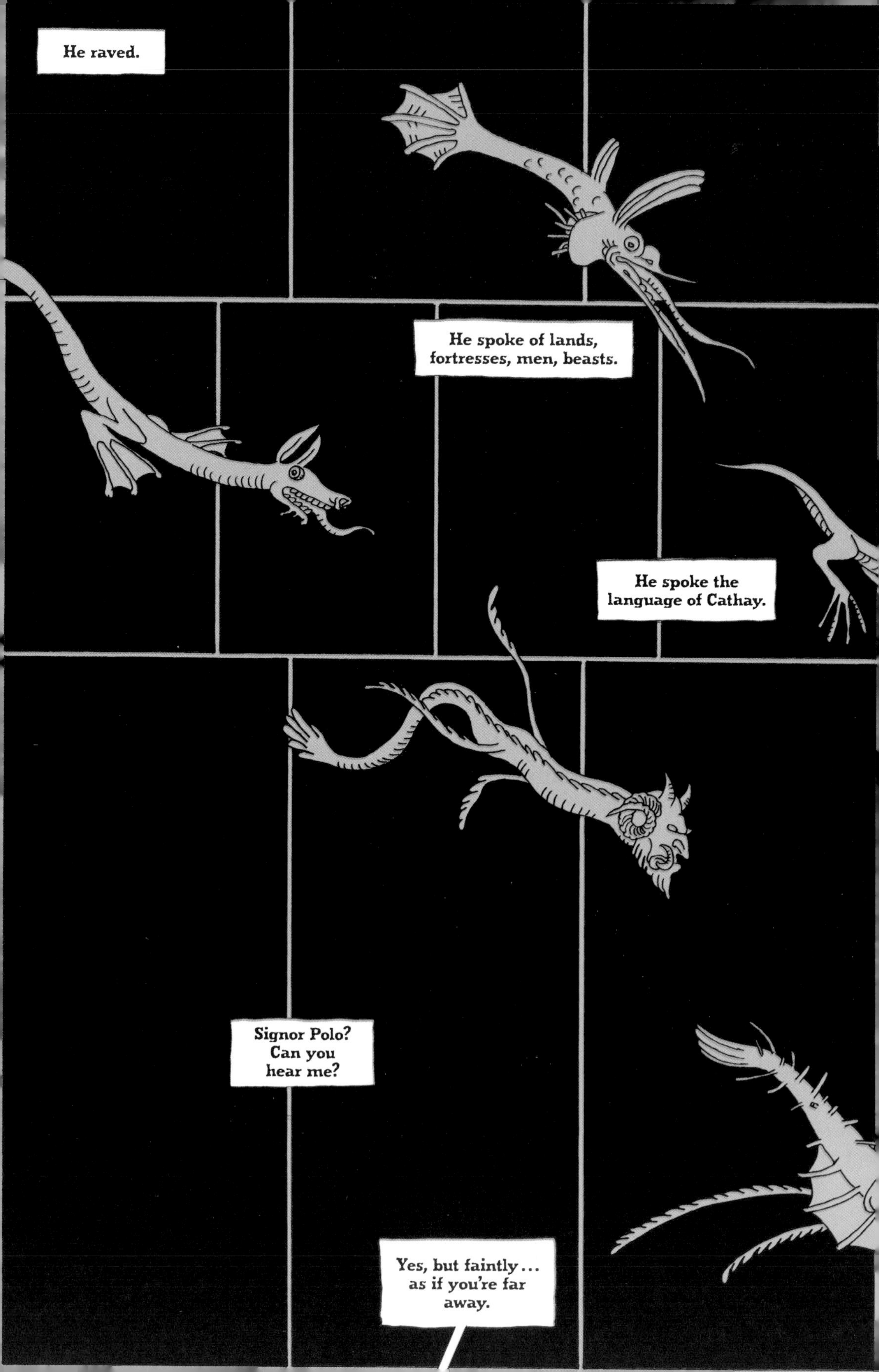
He raved.
He spoke of lands, fortresses, men, beasts.
He spoke the language of Cathay.
Signor Polo? Can you hear me?
Yes, but faintly . . . as if you're far away.

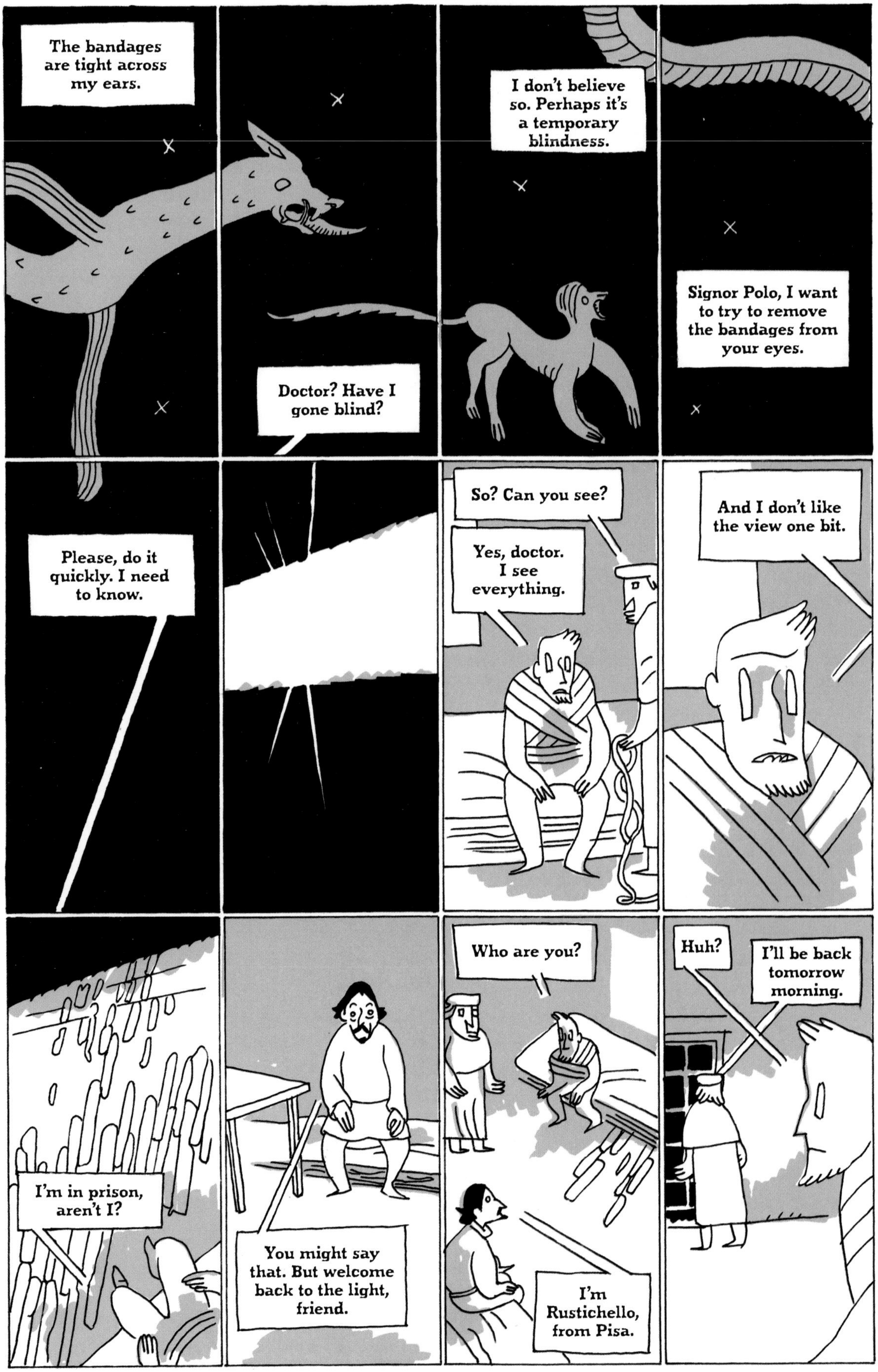
The bandages are tight across my ears.
Doctor? Have I gone blind?
I don't believe so. Perhaps it's a temporary blindness.
Signor Polo, I want to try to remove the bandages from your eyes.
Please, do it quickly. I need to know.
So? Can you see?
Yes, doctor. I see everything.
And I don't like the view one bit.
I'm in prison, aren't I?
You might say that. But welcome back to the light, friend.
Who are you?
I'm Rustichello, from Pisa.
Huh?
I'll be back tomorrow morning.

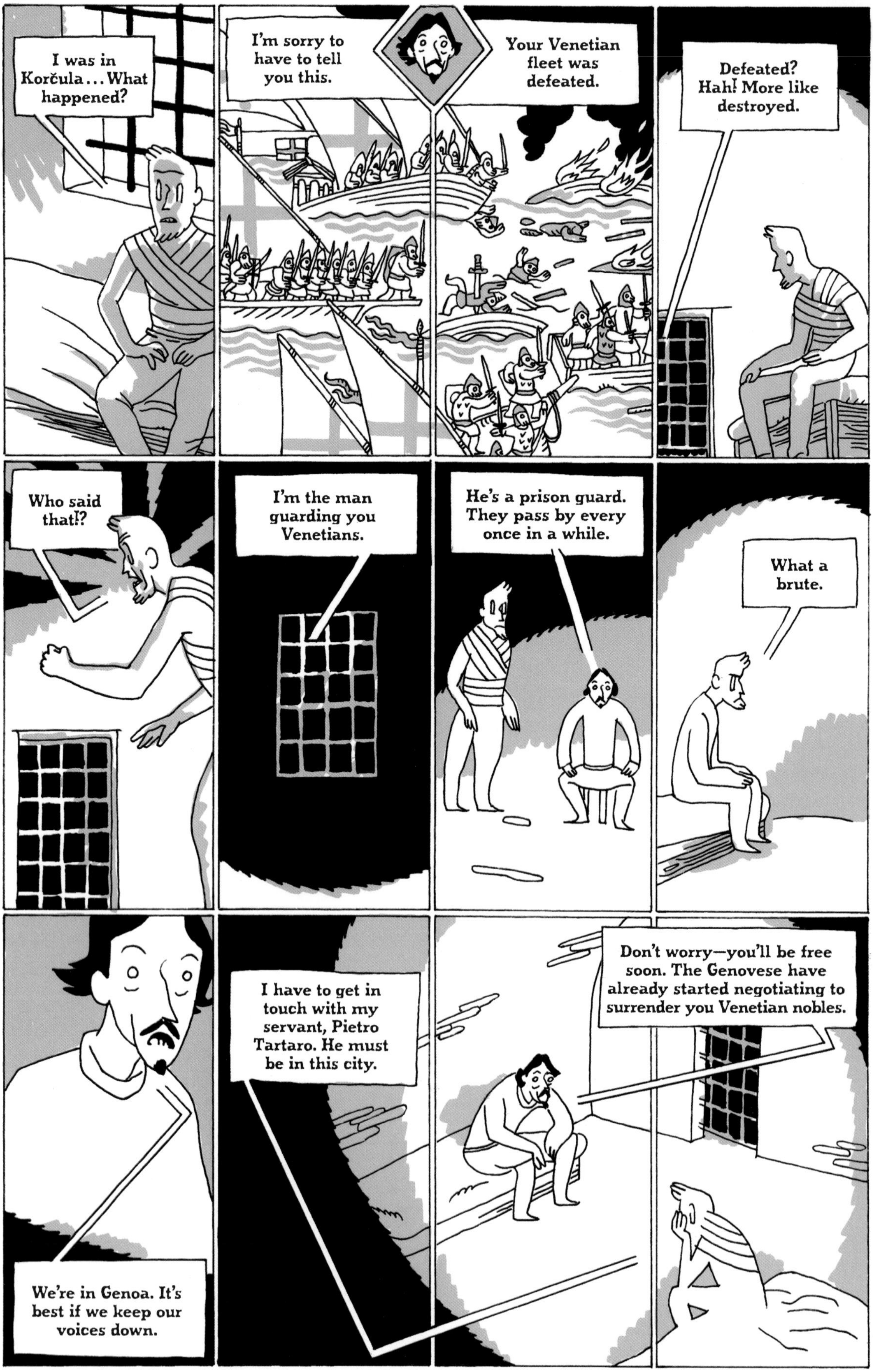
I was in Korčula... What happened?
I'm sorry to have to tell you this.
Your Venetian fleet was defeated.
Defeated? Hah! More like destroyed.
Who said that!?
I'm the man guarding you Venetians.
He's a prison guard. They pass by every once in a while.
What a brute.
We're in Genoa. It's best if we keep our voices down.
I have to get in touch with my servant, Pietro Tartaro. He must be in this city.
Don't worry—you'll be free soon. The Genovese have already started negotiating to surrender you Venetian nobles.

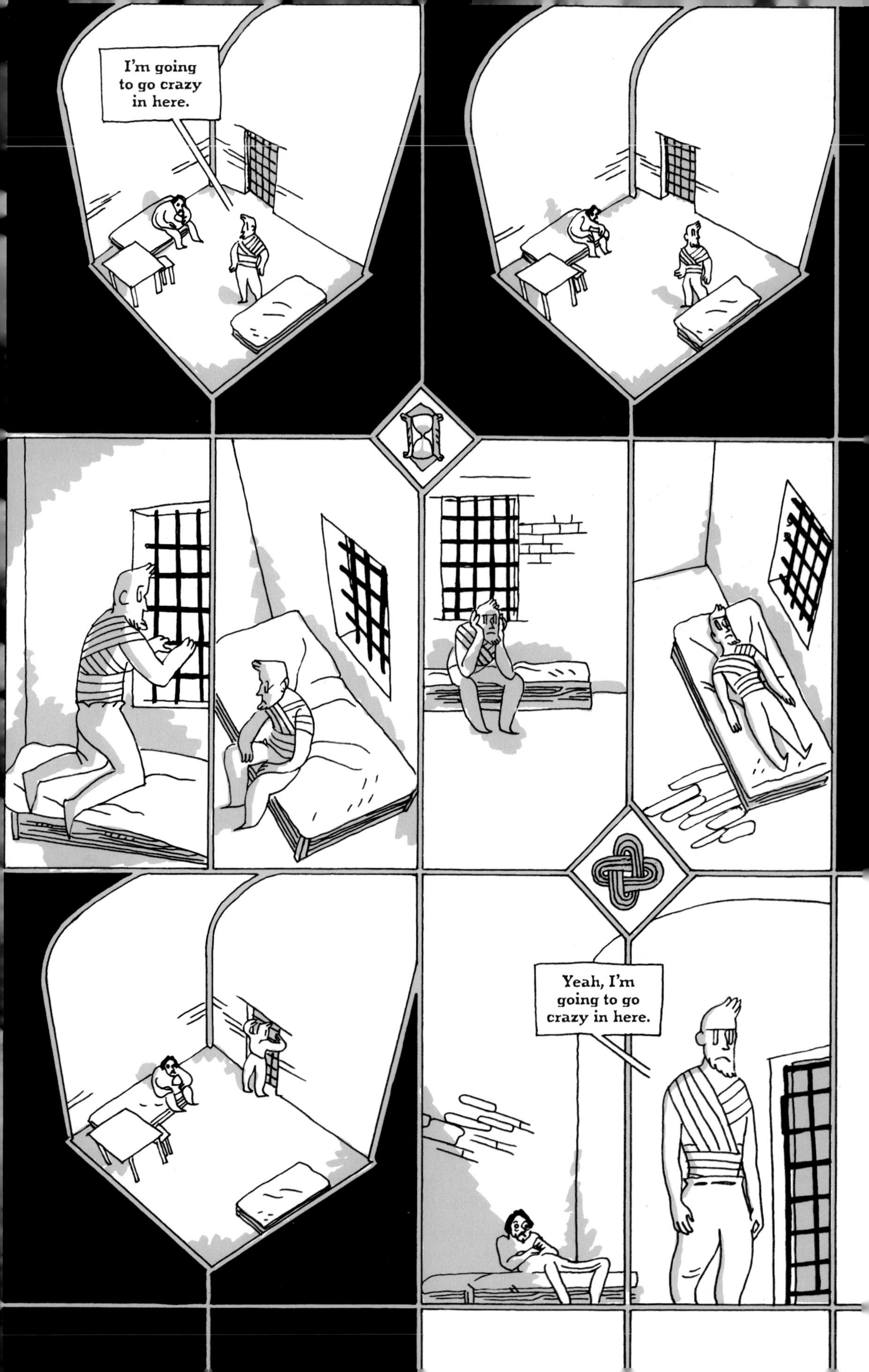
I'm going to go crazy in here.
Yeah, I'm going to go crazy in here.

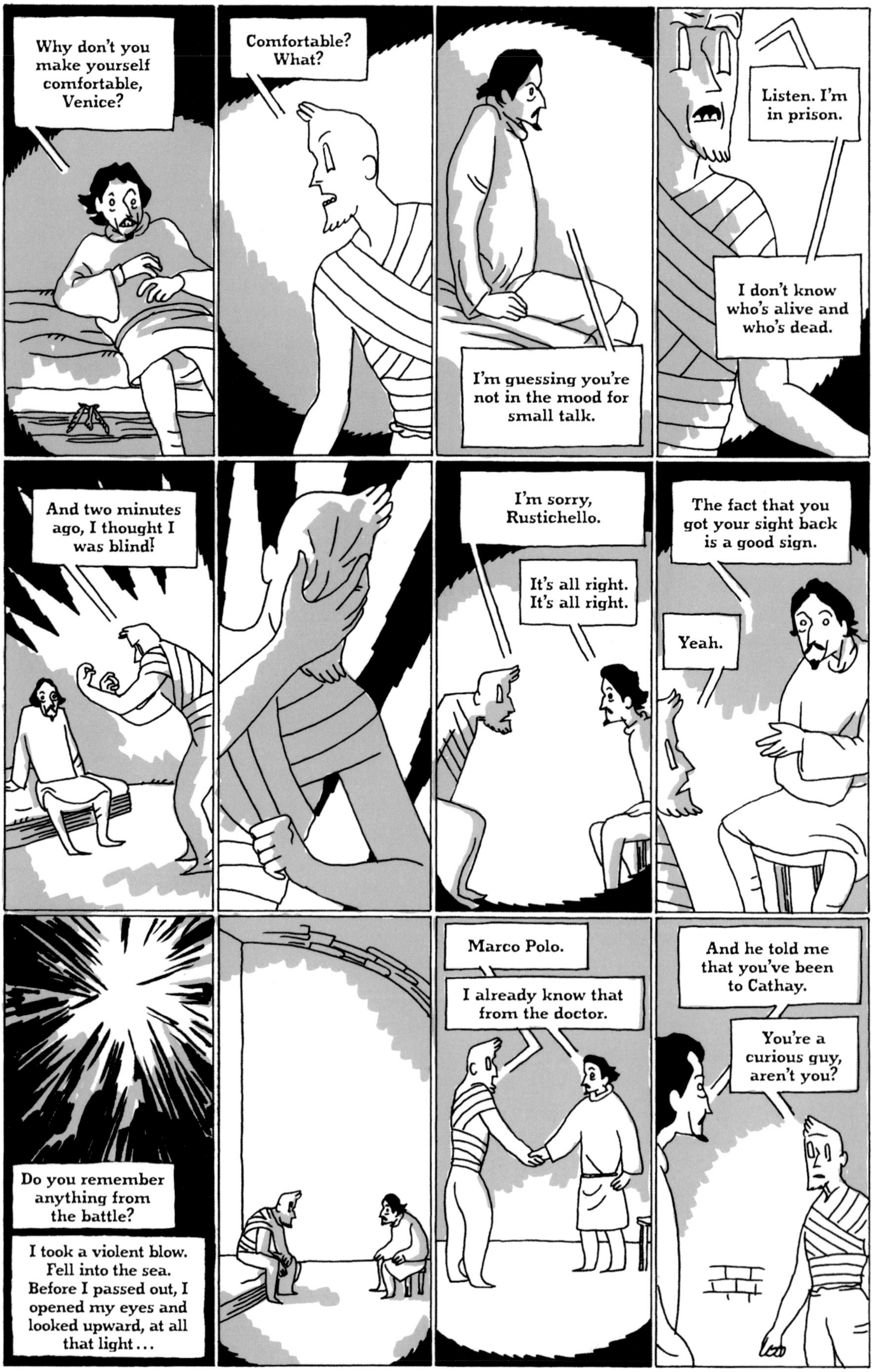

Why don't you make yourself comfortable, Venice?
Comfortable? What?
I'm guessing you're not in the mood for small talk.
Listen. I'm in prison.
I don't know who's alive and who's dead.
And two minutes ago, I thought I was blind!
I'm sorry, Rustichello.
It's all right. It's all right.
The fact that you got your sight back is a good sign.
Yeah.
Do you remember anything from the battle?
I took a violent blow. Fell into the sea. Before I passed out, I opened my eyes and looked upward, at all that light...
Marco Polo.
I already know that from the doctor.
And he told me that you've been to Cathay.
You're a curious guy, aren't you?

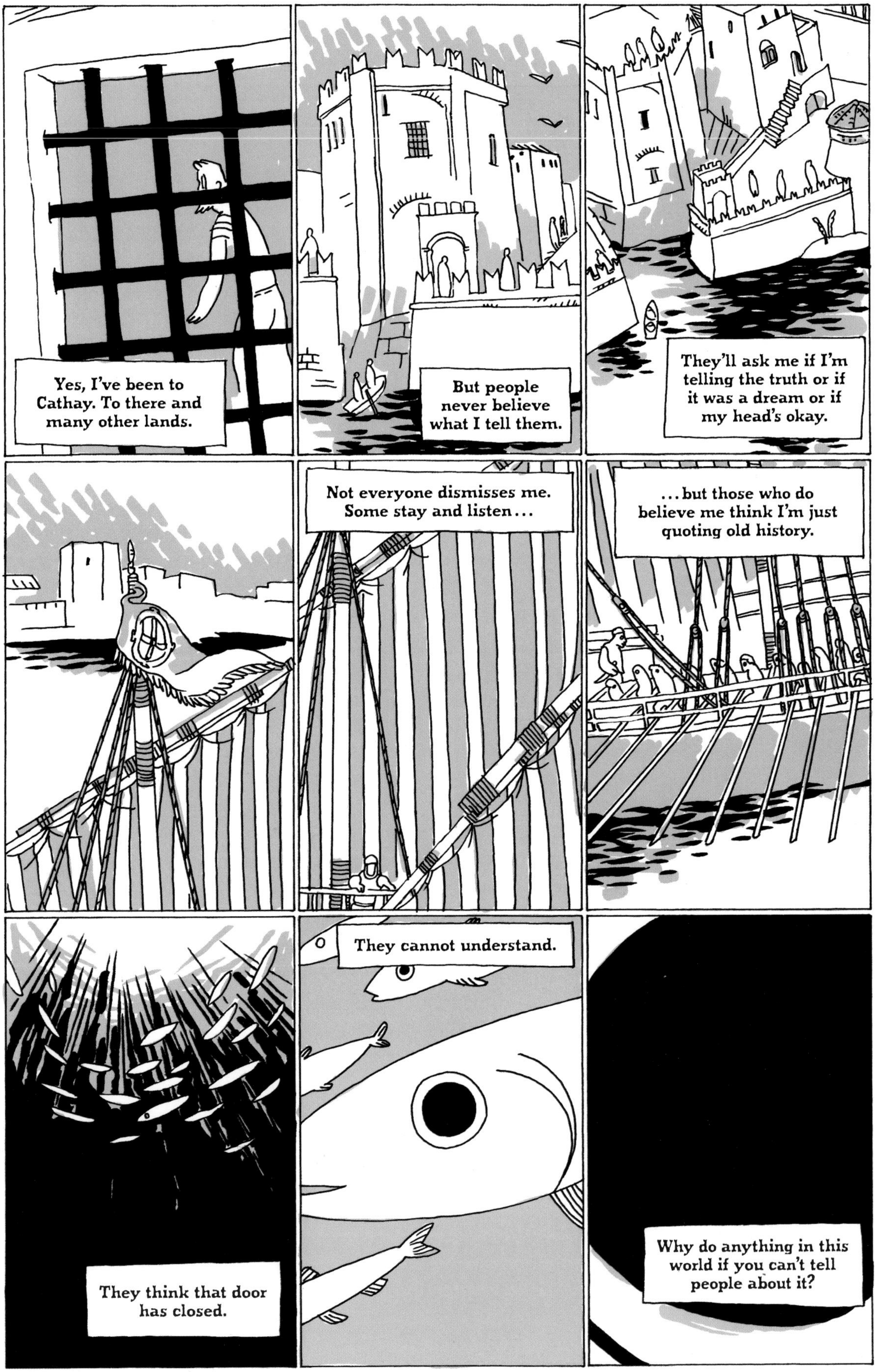
Yes, I've been to Cathay. To there and many other lands.
But people never believe what I tell them.
They'll ask me if I'm telling the truth or if it was a dream or if my head's okay.
Not everyone dismisses me. Some stay and listen...
...but those who do believe me think I'm just quoting old history.
They think that door has closed.
They cannot understand.
Why do anything in this world if you can't tell people about it?

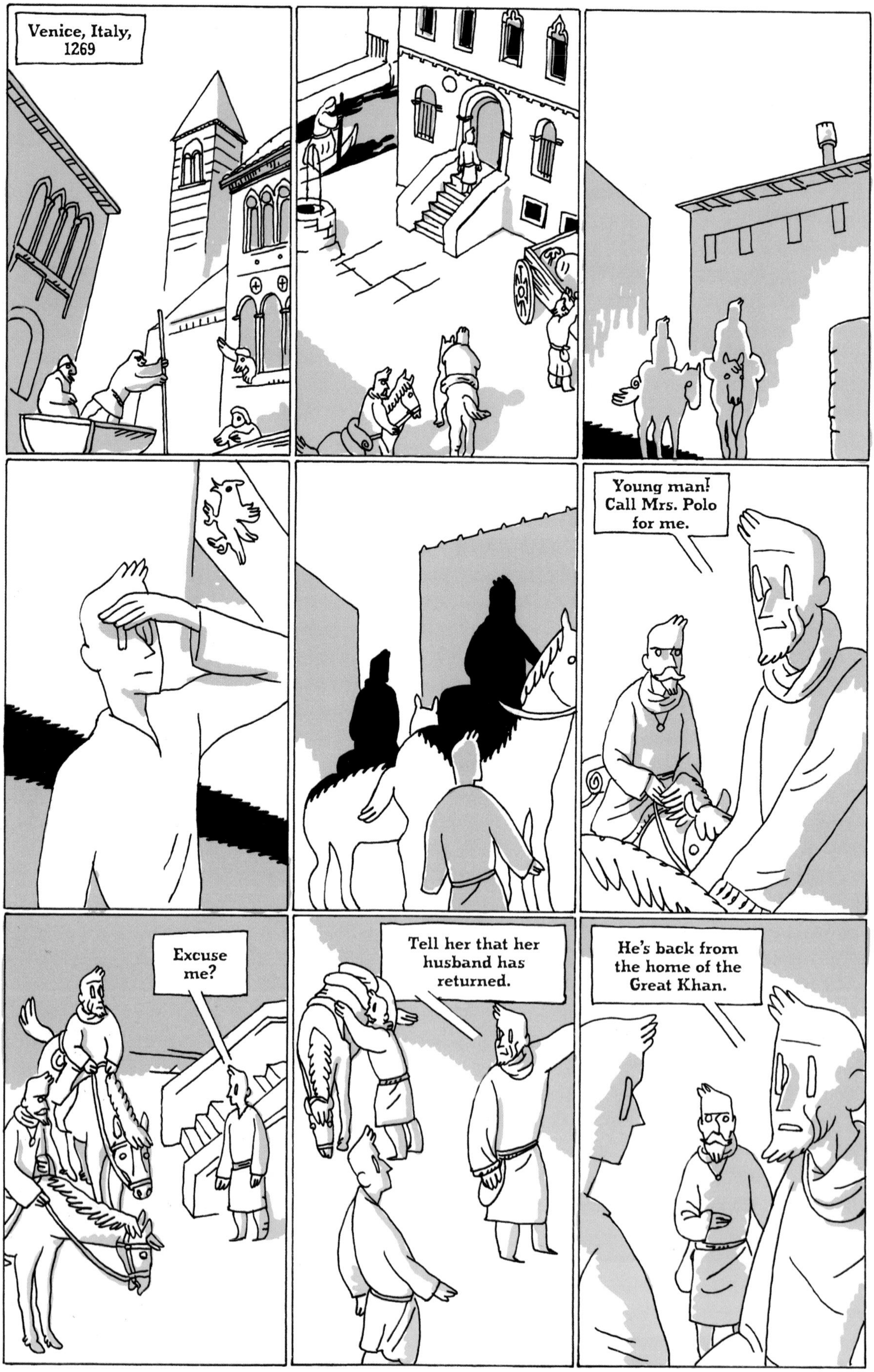
Venice, Italy, 1269
Young man! Call Mrs. Polo for me.
Excuse me?
Tell her that her husband has returned.
He's back from the home of the Great Khan.

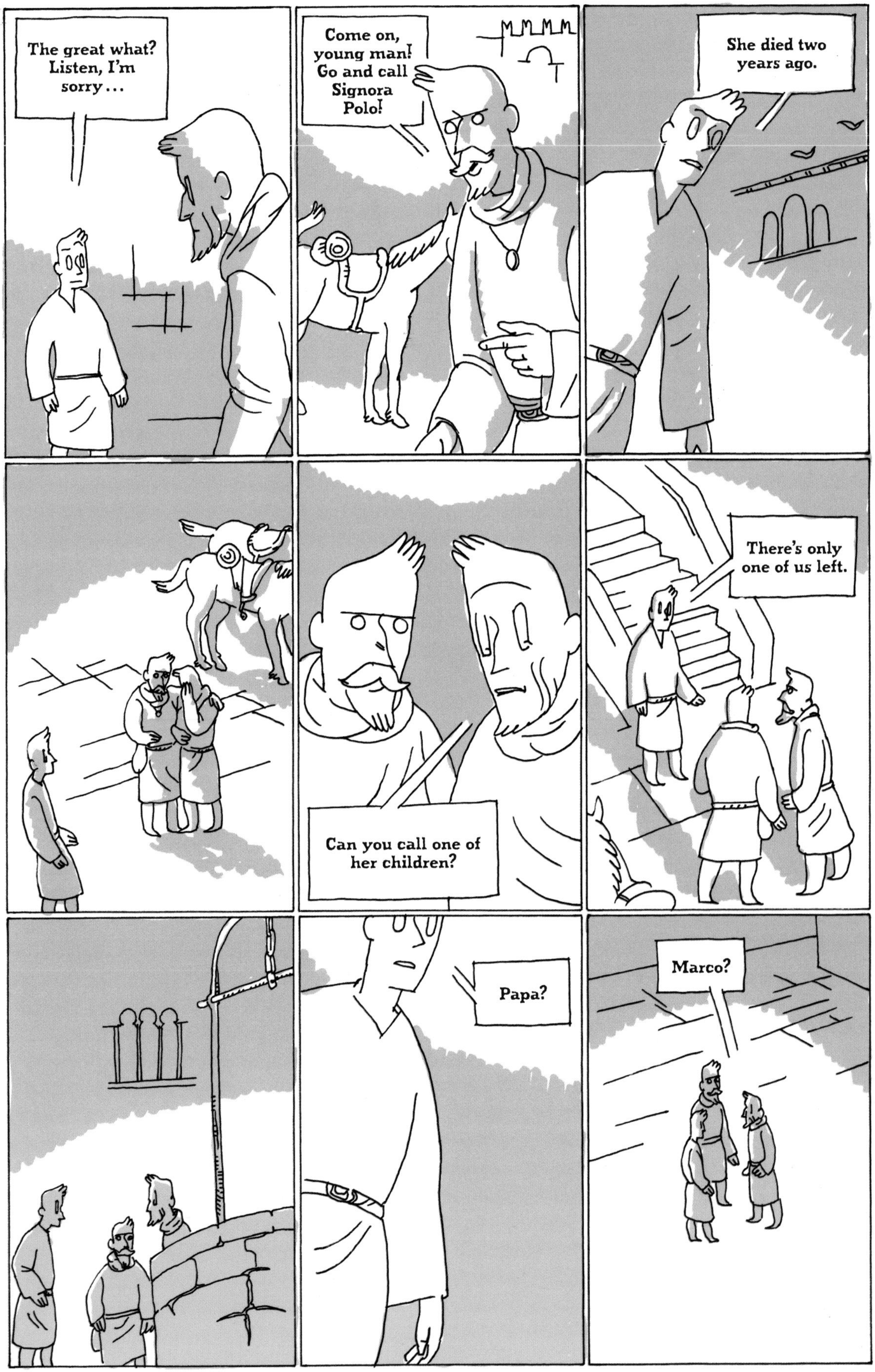
The great what? Listen, I'm sorry . . .
Come on, young man! Go and call Signora Polo!
She died two years ago.
Can you call one of her children?
There's only one of us left.
Papa?
Marco?

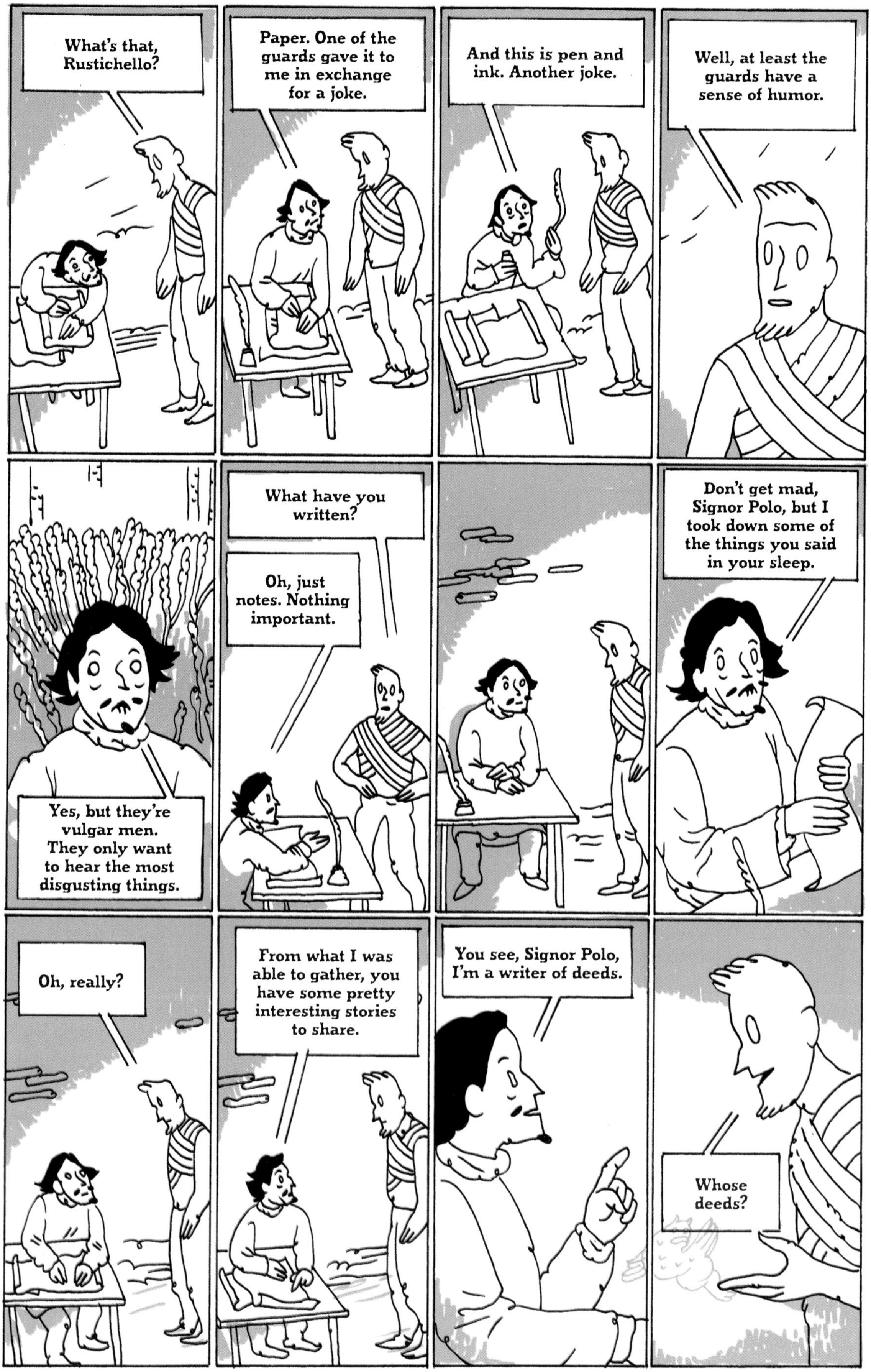
What's that, Rustichello?
Paper. One of the guards gave it to me in exchange for a joke.
And this is pen and ink. Another joke.
Well, at least the guards have a sense of humor.
Yes, but they're vulgar men. They only want to hear the most disgusting things.
What have you written?
Oh, just notes. Nothing important.
Don't get mad, Signor Polo, but I took down some of the things you said in your sleep.
Oh, really?
From what I was able to gather, you have some pretty interesting stories to share.
You see, Signor Polo, I'm a writer of deeds.
Whose deeds?

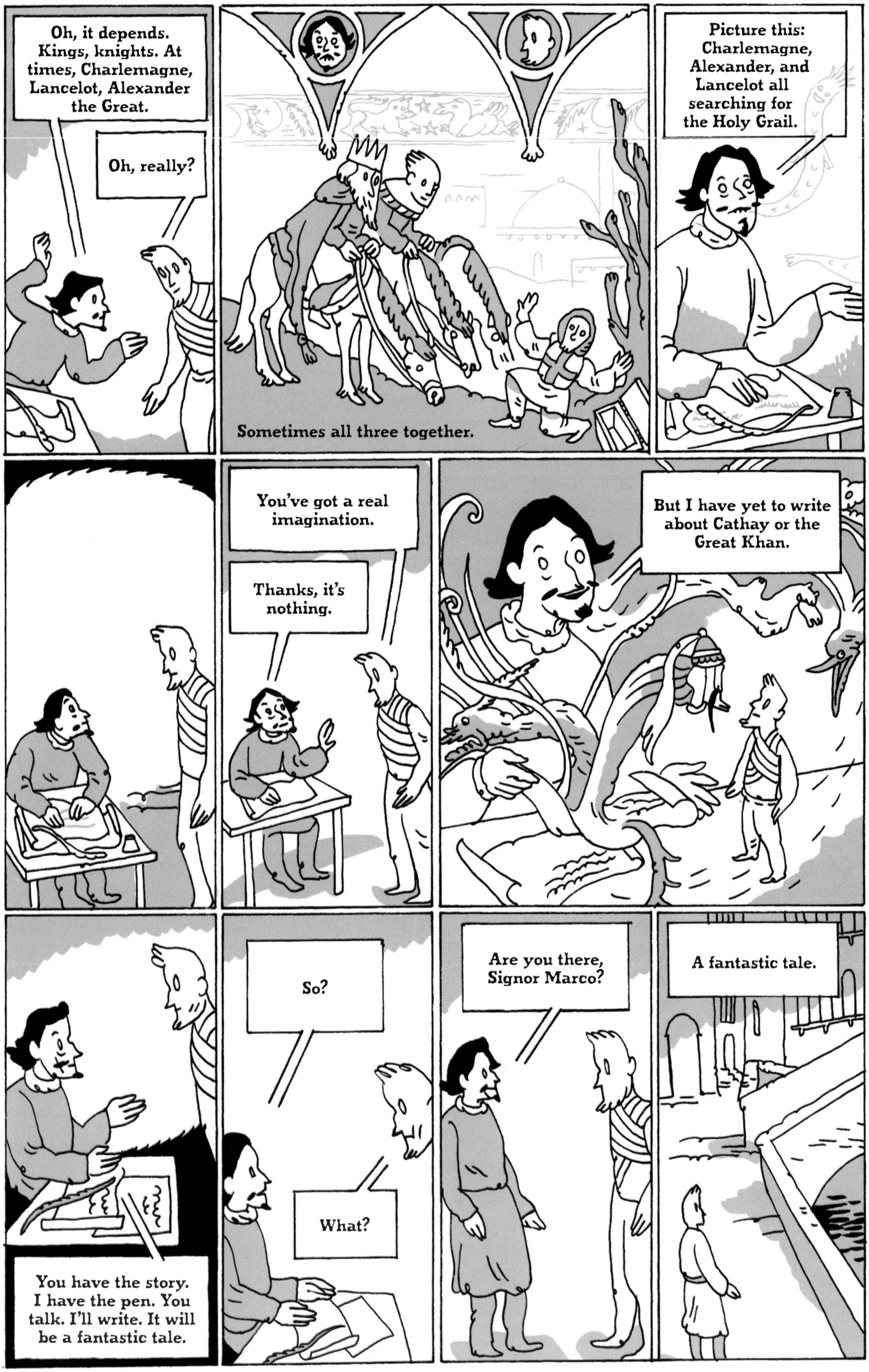

Oh, it depends. Kings, knights. At times, Charlemagne, Lancelot, Alexander the Great.
Oh, really?
Sometimes all three together.
Picture this: Charlemagne, Alexander, and Lancelot all searching for the Holy Grail.
You've got a real imagination.
Thanks, it's nothing.
But I have yet to write about Cathay or the Great Khan.
You have the story. I have the pen. You talk. I'll write. It will be a fantastic tale.
So?
What?
Are you there, Signor Marco?
A fantastic tale.

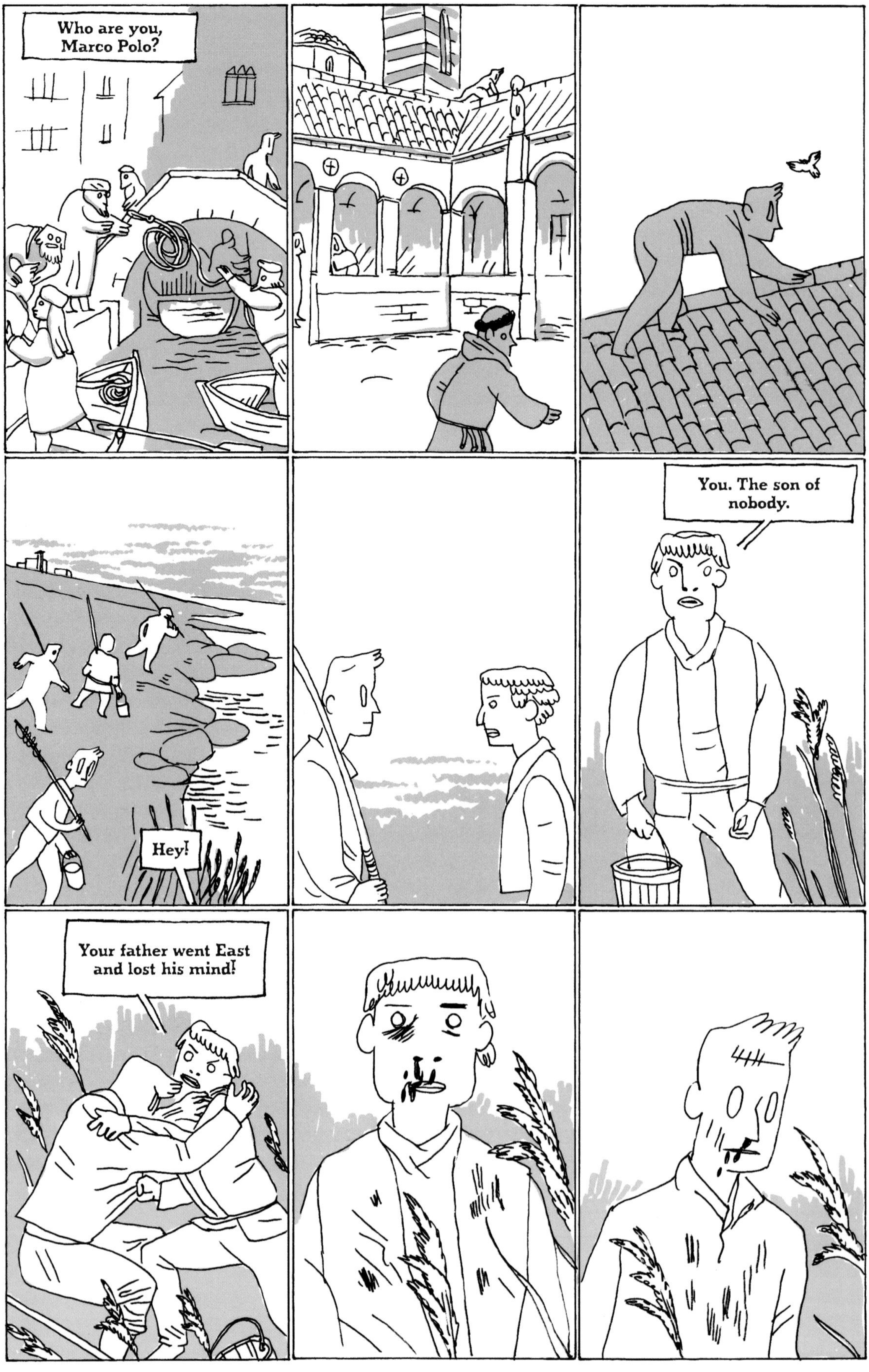

Who are you, Marco Polo?
Hey!
You. The son of nobody.
Your father went East and lost his mind!

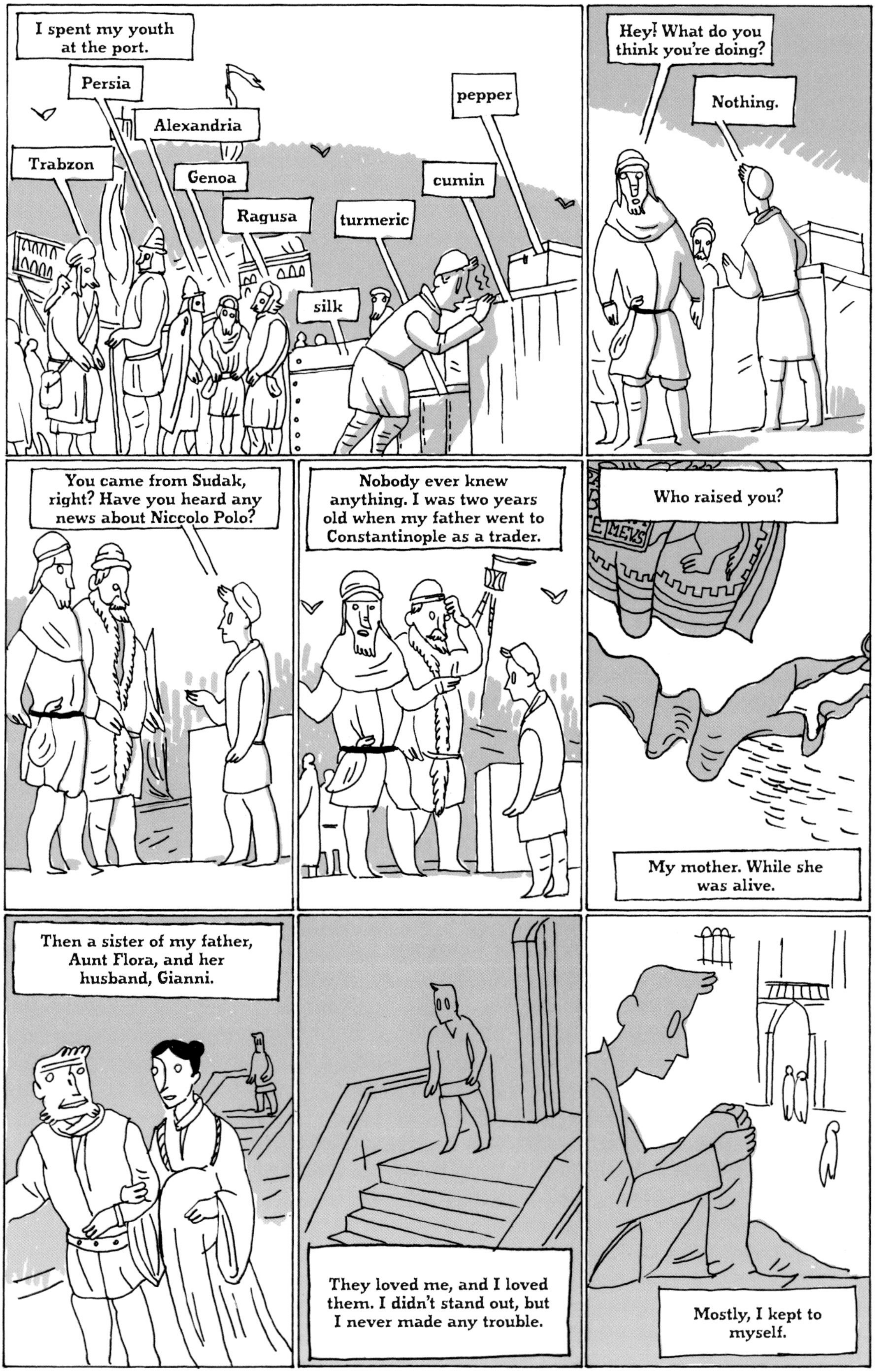
I spent my youth at the port.
Persia
Alexandria
Trabzon
Genoa
Ragusa
turmeric
cumin
pepper
silk
Hey! What do you think you're doing?
Nothing.
You came from Sudak, right? Have you heard any news about Niccolo Polo?
Nobody ever knew anything. I was two years old when my father went to Constantinople as a trader.
Who raised you?
My mother. While she was alive.
Then a sister of my father, Aunt Flora, and her husband, Gianni.
They loved me, and I loved them. I didn't stand out, but I never made any trouble.
Mostly, I kept to myself.

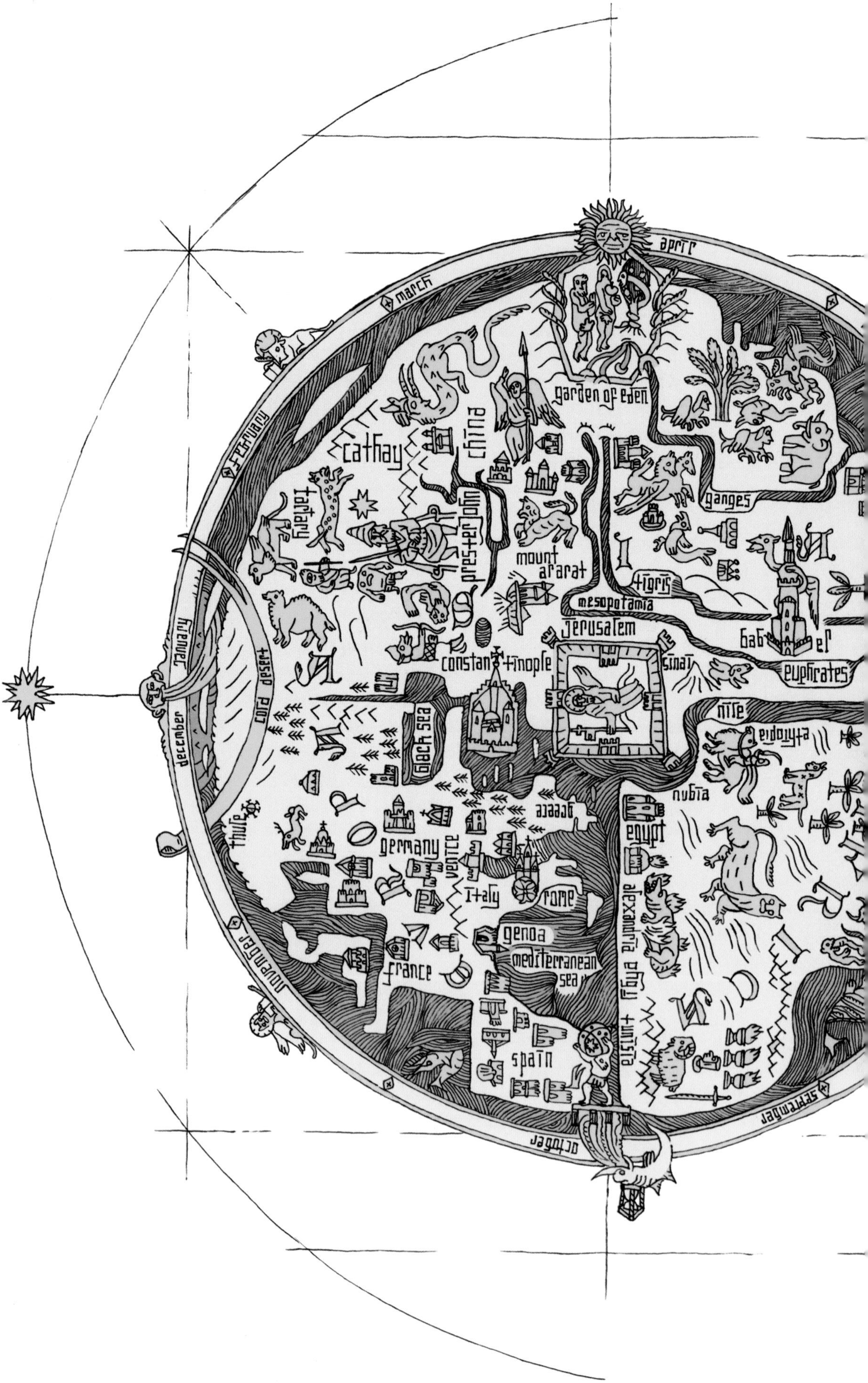

april
march
february
january
december
november
october
september
garden of eden
ganges
cathay
china
tartary
prester john
mount ararat
tigris
mesopotamia
jerusalem
constantinople
sinai
euphrates
nile
cold desert
black sea
ethiopia
nubia
greece
egypt
thule
germany
venice
italy
rome
genoa
mediterranean sea
france
alexandria
spain

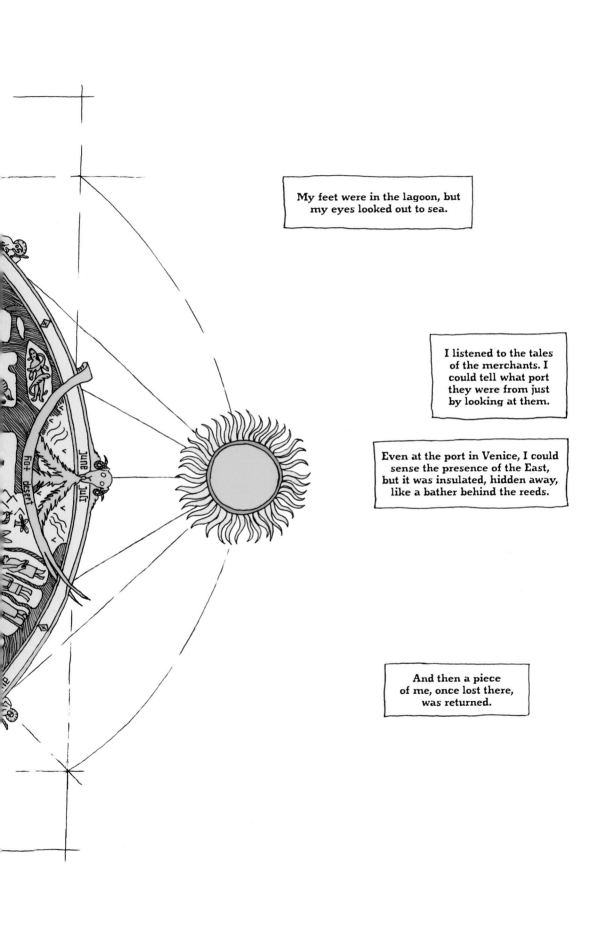

My feet were in the lagoon, but my eyes looked out to sea.

I listened to the tales of the merchants. I could tell what port they were from just by looking at them.

Even at the port in Venice, I could sense the presence of the East, but it was insulated, hidden away, like a bather behind the reeds.

And then a piece of me, once lost there, was returned.

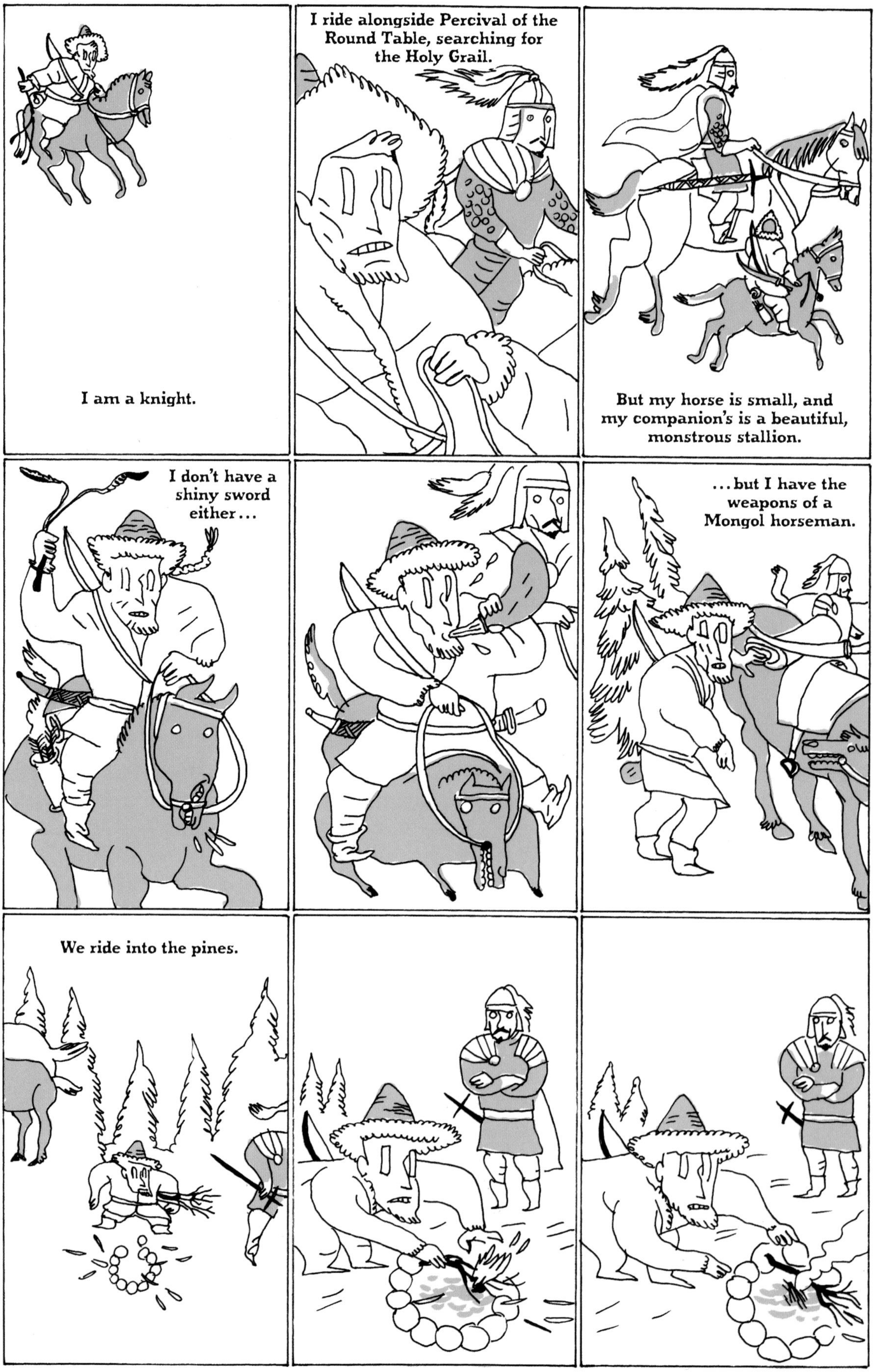
I am a knight.
I ride alongside Percival of the Round Table, searching for the Holy Grail.
But my horse is small, and my companion's is a beautiful, monstrous stallion.
I don't have a shiny sword either...
...but I have the weapons of a Mongol horseman.
We ride into the pines.

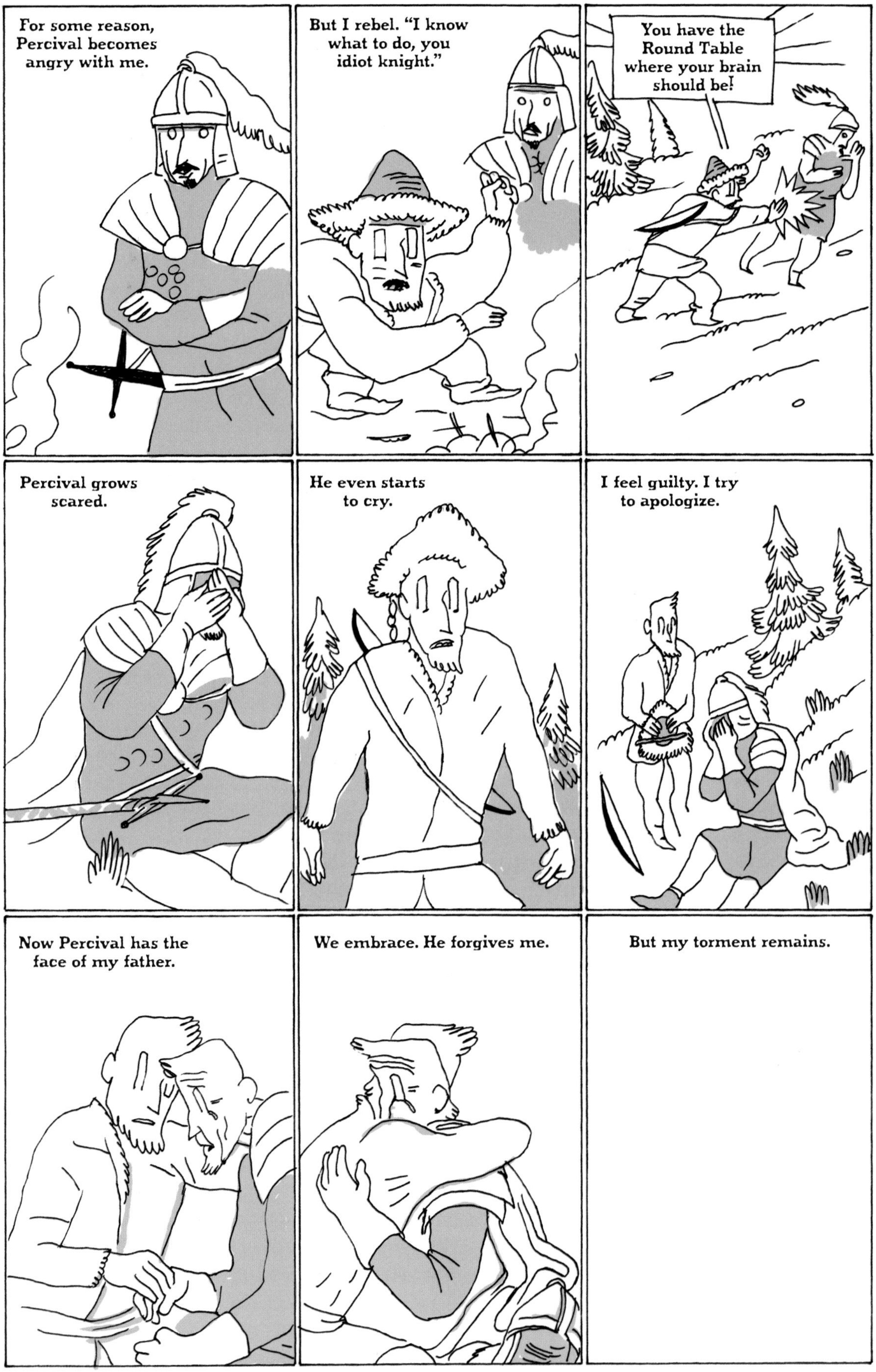
For some reason, Percival becomes angry with me.
But I rebel. "I know what to do, you idiot knight."
You have the Round Table where your brain should be!
Percival grows scared.
He even starts to cry.
I feel guilty. I try to apologize.
Now Percival has the face of my father.
We embrace. He forgives me.
But my torment remains.

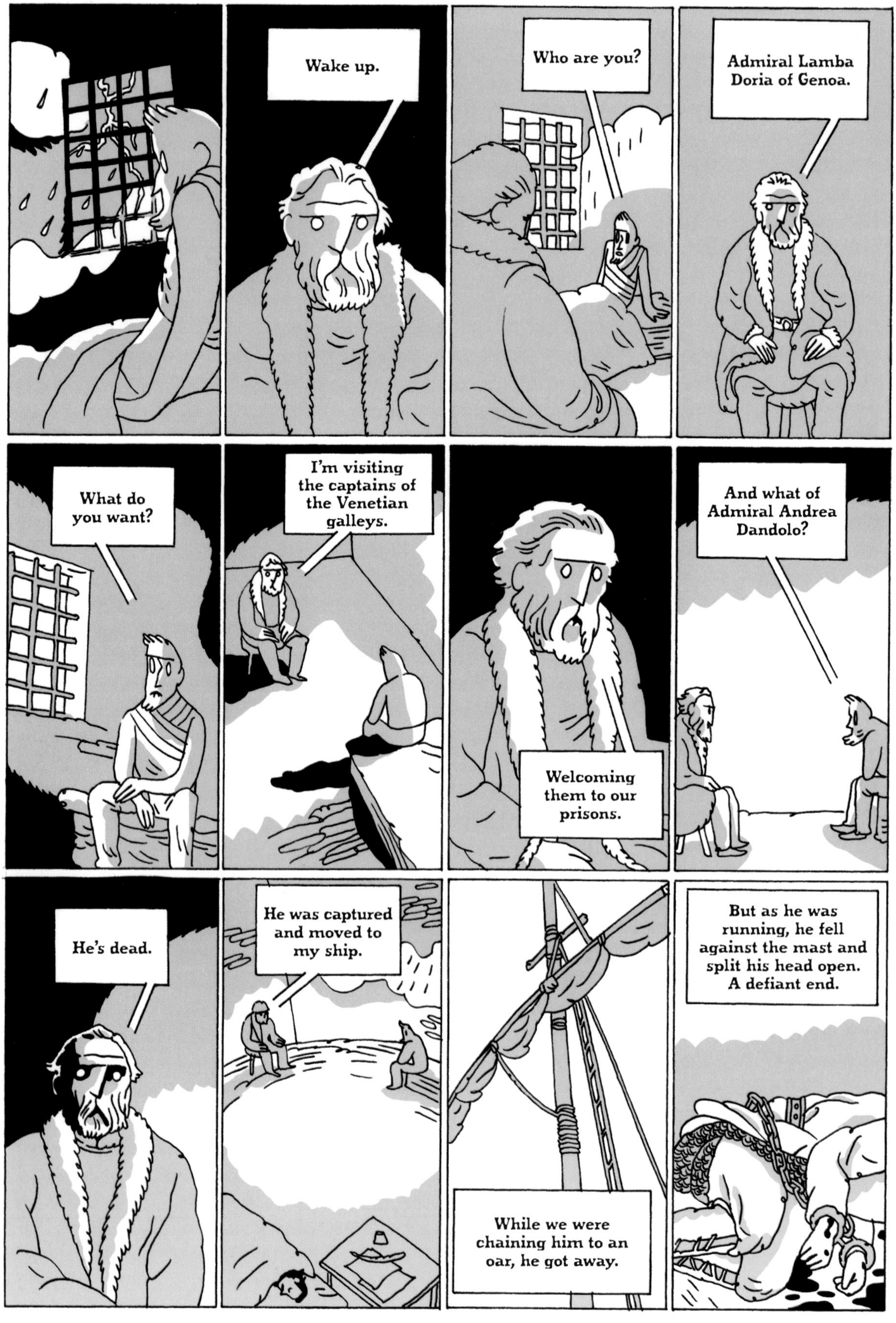

Wake up.
Who are you?
Admiral Lamba Doria of Genoa.
What do you want?
I'm visiting the captains of the Venetian galleys.
Welcoming them to our prisons.
And what of Admiral Andrea Dandolo?
He's dead.
He was captured and moved to my ship.
While we were chaining him to an oar, he got away.
But as he was running, he fell against the mast and split his head open. A defiant end.

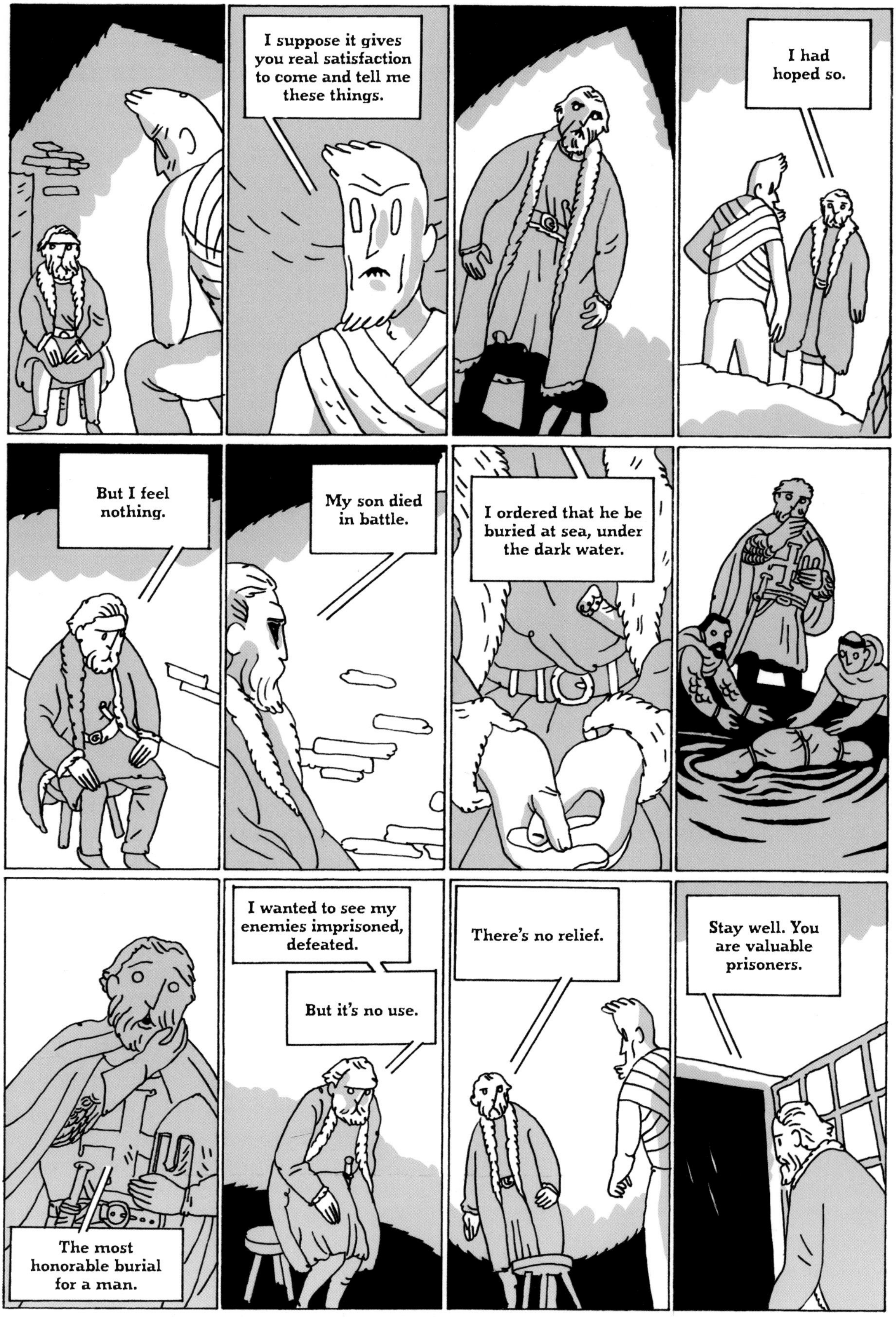
I suppose it gives you real satisfaction to come and tell me these things.
I had hoped so.
But I feel nothing.
My son died in battle.
I ordered that he be buried at sea, under the dark water.
The most honorable burial for a man.
I wanted to see my enemies imprisoned, defeated.
But it's no use.
There's no relief.
Stay well. You are valuable prisoners.

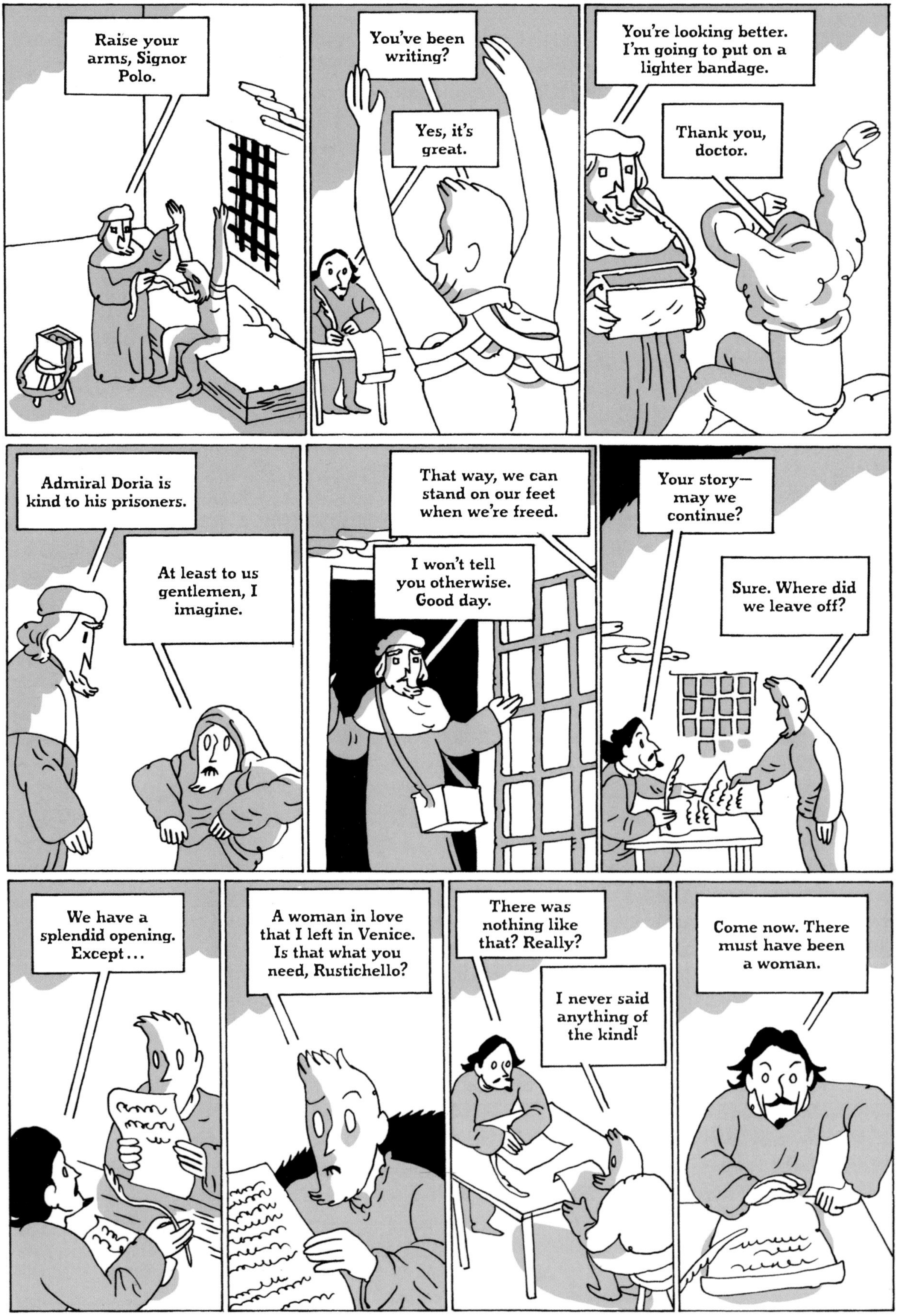
Raise your arms, Signor Polo.
You've been writing?
Yes, it's great.
You're looking better. I'm going to put on a lighter bandage.
Thank you, doctor.
Admiral Doria is kind to his prisoners.
At least to us gentlemen, I imagine.
That way, we can stand on our feet when we're freed.
I won't tell you otherwise. Good day.
Your story— may we continue?
Sure. Where did we leave off?
We have a splendid opening. Except...
A woman in love that I left in Venice. Is that what you need, Rustichello?
There was nothing like that? Really?
I never said anything of the kind!
Come now. There must have been a woman.

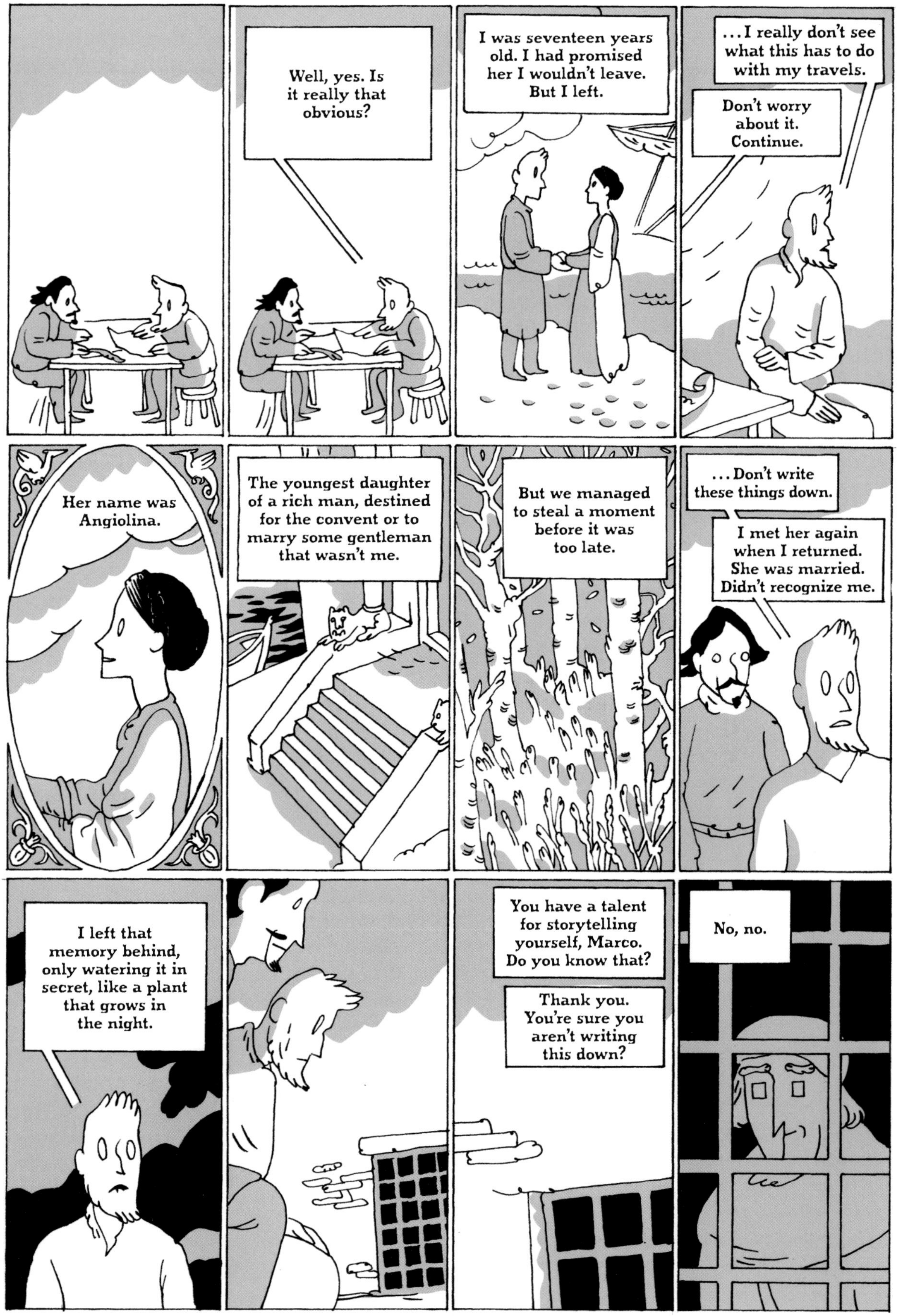
Well, yes. Is it really that obvious?
I was seventeen years old. I had promised her I wouldn't leave. But I left.
...I really don't see what this has to do with my travels.
Don't worry about it. Continue.
Her name was Angiolina.
The youngest daughter of a rich man, destined for the convent or to marry some gentleman that wasn't me.
But we managed to steal a moment before it was too late.
...Don't write these things down.
I met her again when I returned. She was married. Didn't recognize me.
I left that memory behind, only watering it in secret, like a plant that grows in the night.
You have a talent for storytelling yourself, Marco. Do you know that?
Thank you. You're sure you aren't writing this down?
No, no.

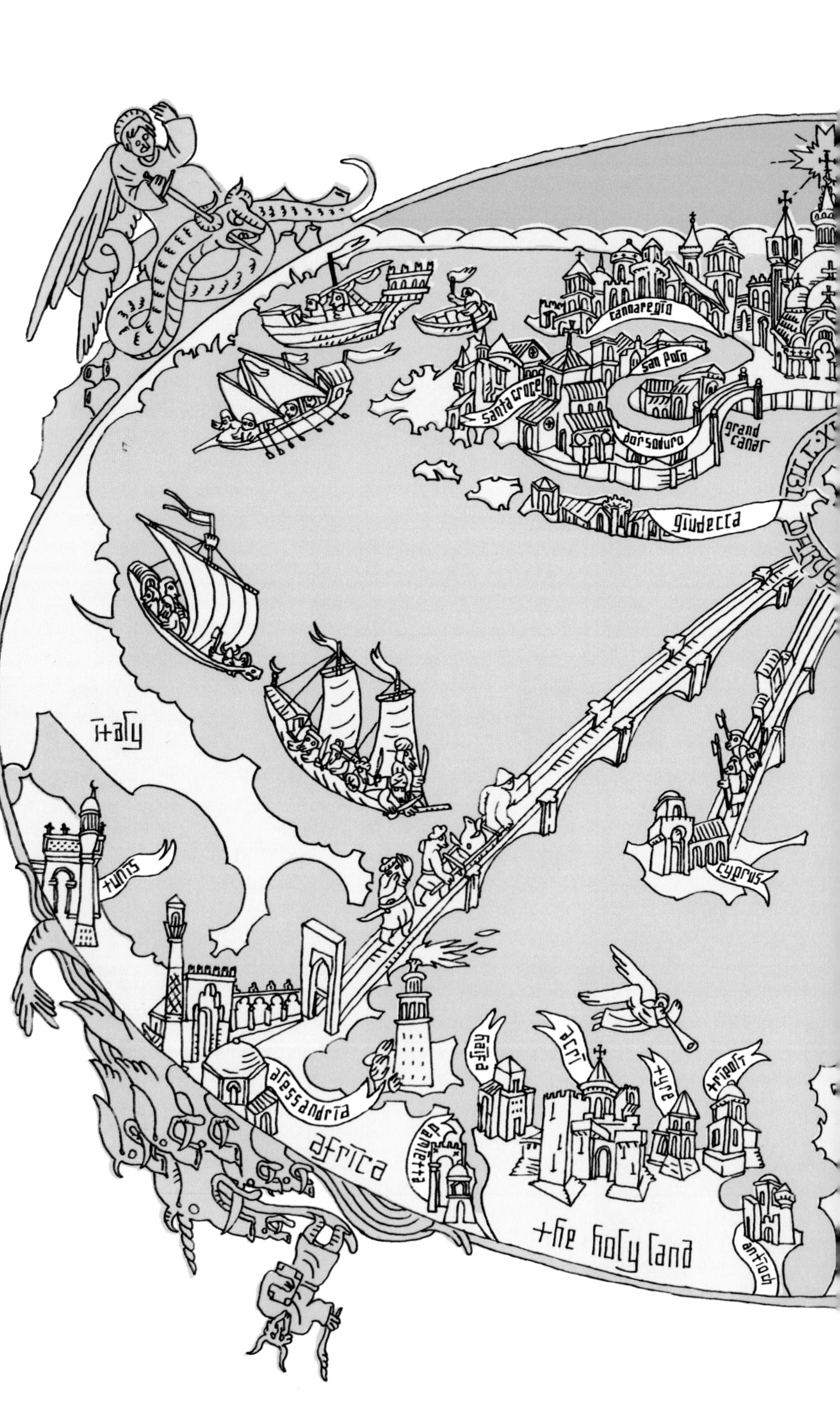
cannaregio
san polo
santa croce
dorsoduro
grand canal
giudecca
italy
tunis
cyprus
alessandria
africa
damietta
haifa
acri
tyre
tripoli
the holy land
antioch

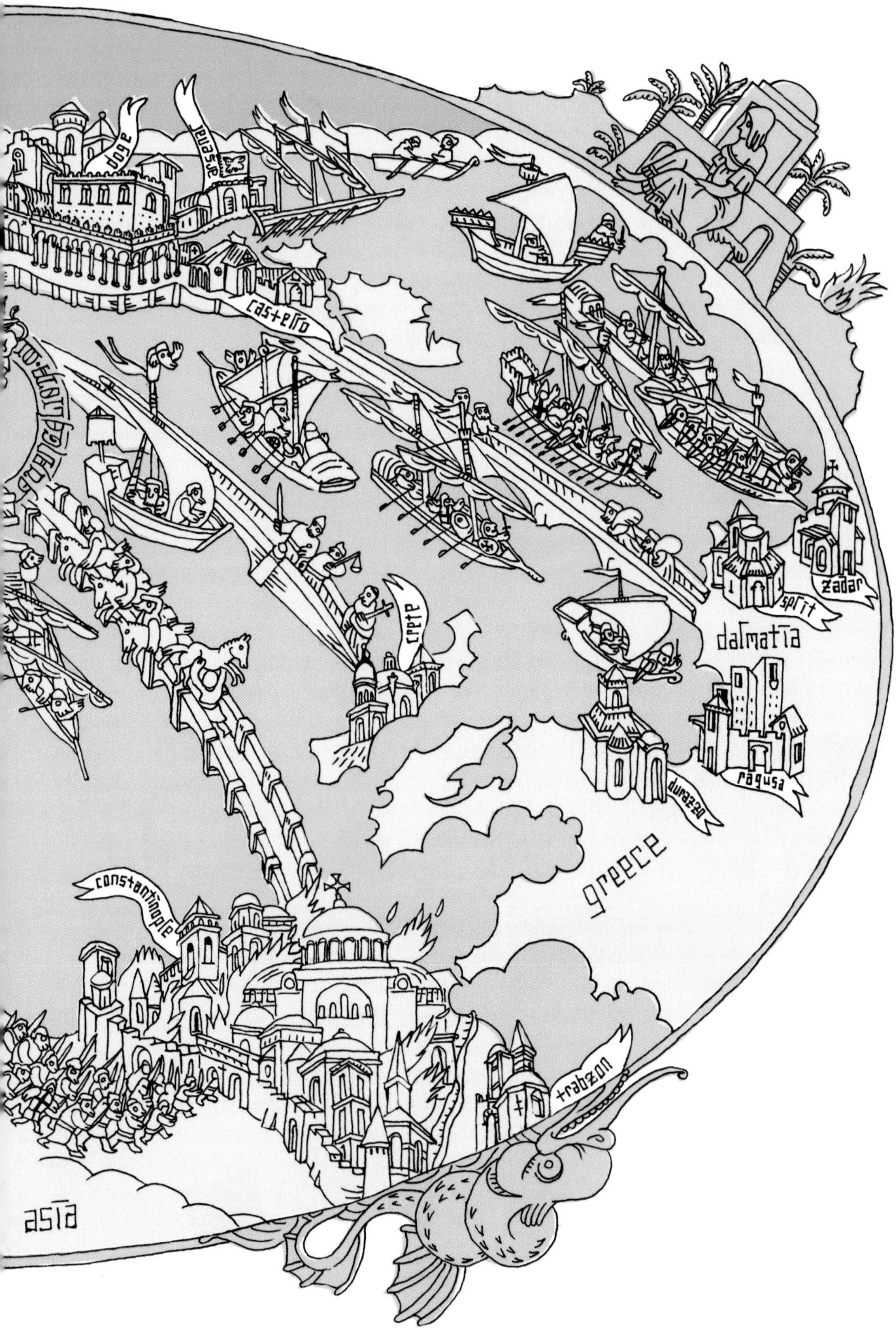

doge
castello
crete
zadar
dalmatia
ragusa
durazzo
greece
constantinople
trabzon
asia

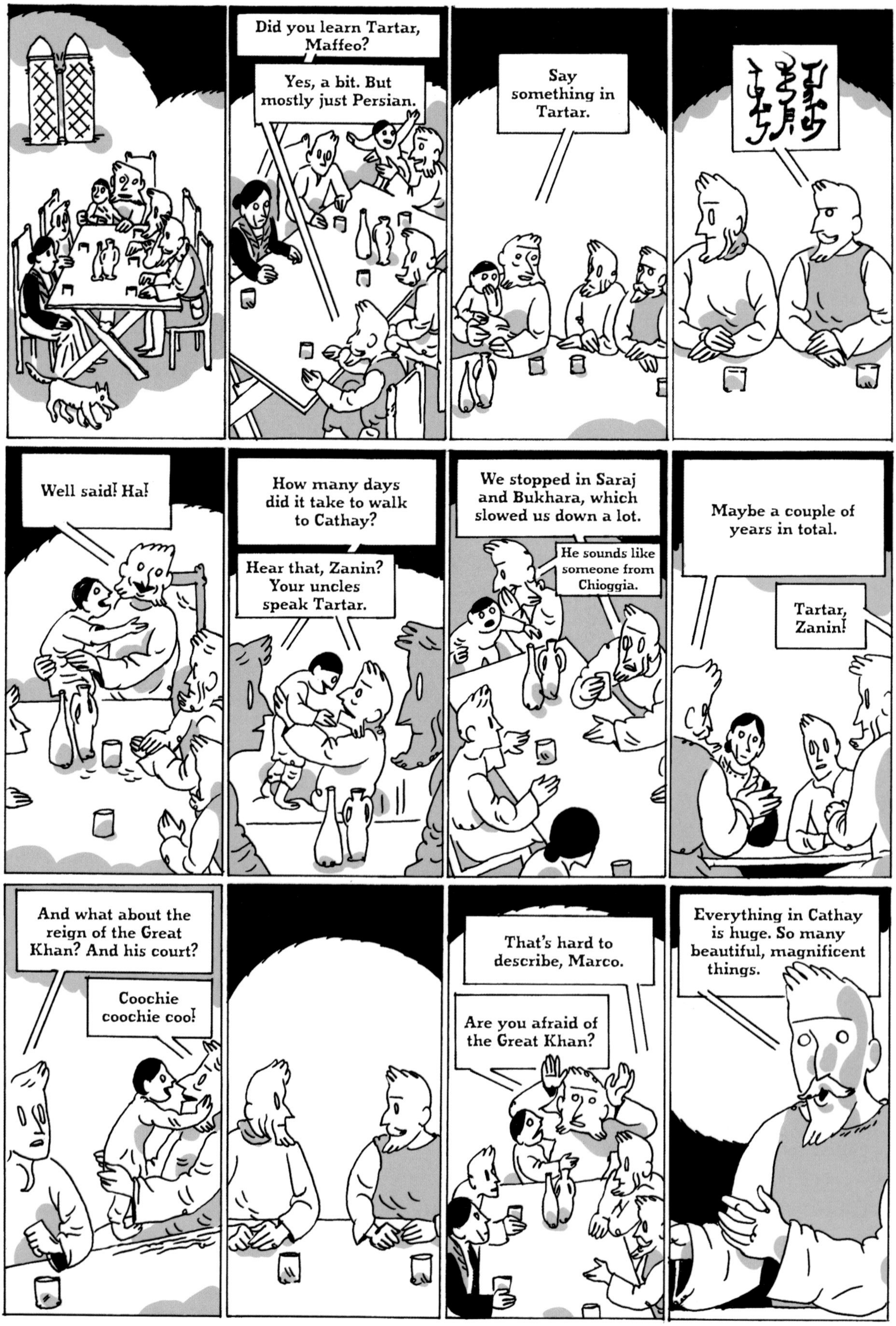
Did you learn Tartar, Maffeo?
Yes, a bit. But mostly just Persian.
Say something in Tartar.
Well said! Ha!
How many days did it take to walk to Cathay?
Hear that, Zanin? Your uncles speak Tartar.
We stopped in Saraj and Bukhara, which slowed us down a lot.
He sounds like someone from Chioggia.
Maybe a couple of years in total.
Tartar, Zanin!
And what about the reign of the Great Khan? And his court?
Coochie coochie coo!
That's hard to describe, Marco.
Are you afraid of the Great Khan?
Everything in Cathay is huge. So many beautiful, magnificent things.

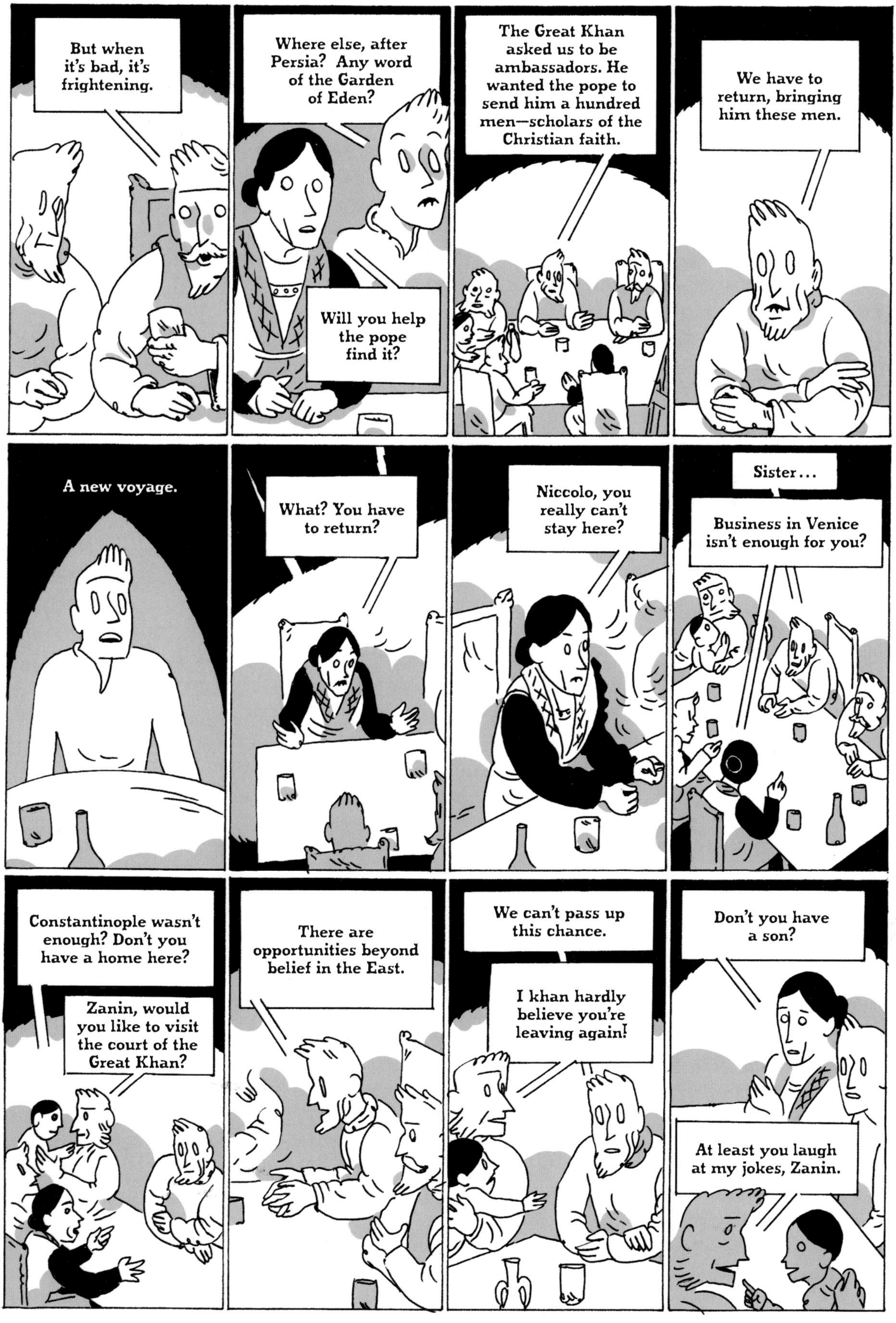

But when it's bad, it's frightening.
Where else, after Persia? Any word of the Garden of Eden?
Will you help the pope find it?
The Great Khan asked us to be ambassadors. He wanted the pope to send him a hundred men—scholars of the Christian faith.
We have to return, bringing him these men.
A new voyage.
What? You have to return?
Niccolo, you really can't stay here?
Sister...
Business in Venice isn't enough for you?
Constantinople wasn't enough? Don't you have a home here?
Zanin, would you like to visit the court of the Great Khan?
There are opportunities beyond belief in the East.
We can't pass up this chance.
I khan hardly believe you're leaving again!
Don't you have a son?
At least you laugh at my jokes, Zanin.

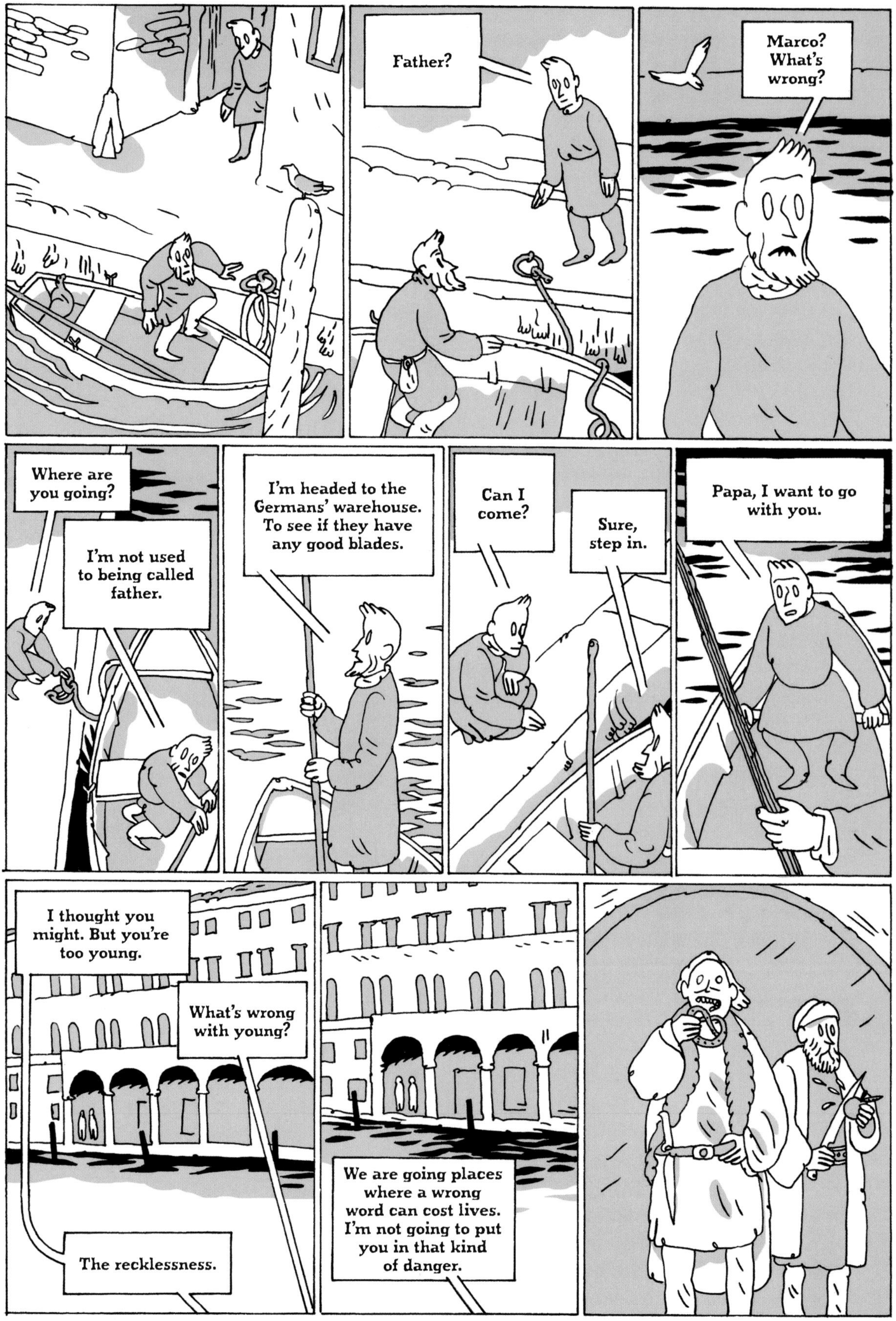
Father?
Marco? What's wrong?
Where are you going?
I'm not used to being called father.
I'm headed to the Germans' warehouse. To see if they have any good blades.
Can I come?
Sure, step in.
Papa, I want to go with you.
I thought you might. But you're too young.
What's wrong with young?
The recklessness.
We are going places where a wrong word can cost lives. I'm not going to put you in that kind of danger.

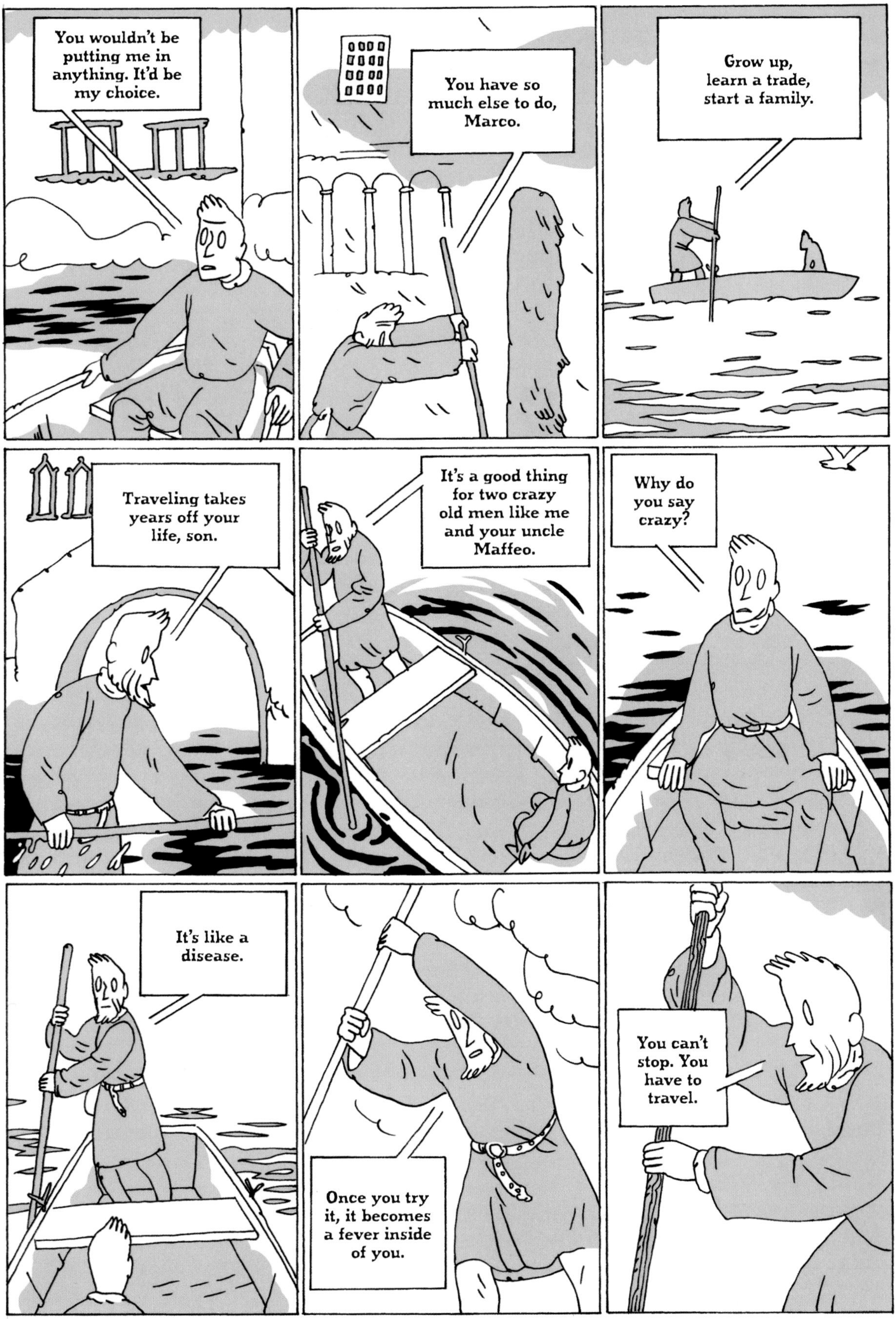

You wouldn't be putting me in anything. It'd be my choice.
You have so much else to do, Marco.
Grow up, learn a trade, start a family.
Traveling takes years off your life, son.
It's a good thing for two crazy old men like me and your uncle Maffeo.
Why do you say crazy?
It's like a disease.
Once you try it, it becomes a fever inside of you.
You can't stop. You have to travel.

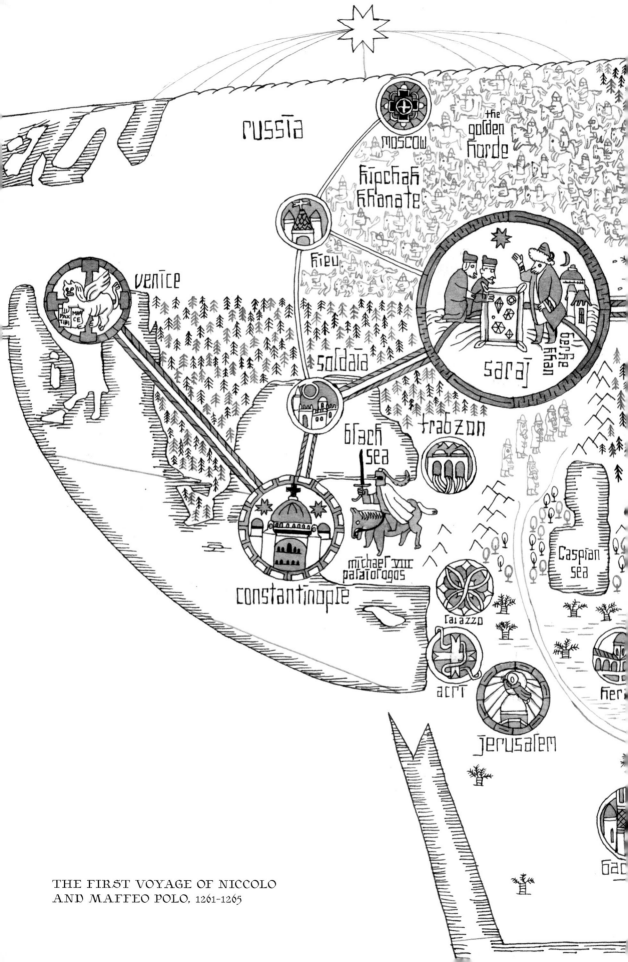

russia

moscow

the golden horde

kipchak khanate

kieu

venice

saldaia

black sea

trabzon

saraj

berke khan

michael viii palaiologos

constantinople

Caspian sea

palazzo

acri

fier

jerusalem

bac

THE FIRST VOYAGE OF NICCOLO
AND MAFFEO POLO, 1261-1265

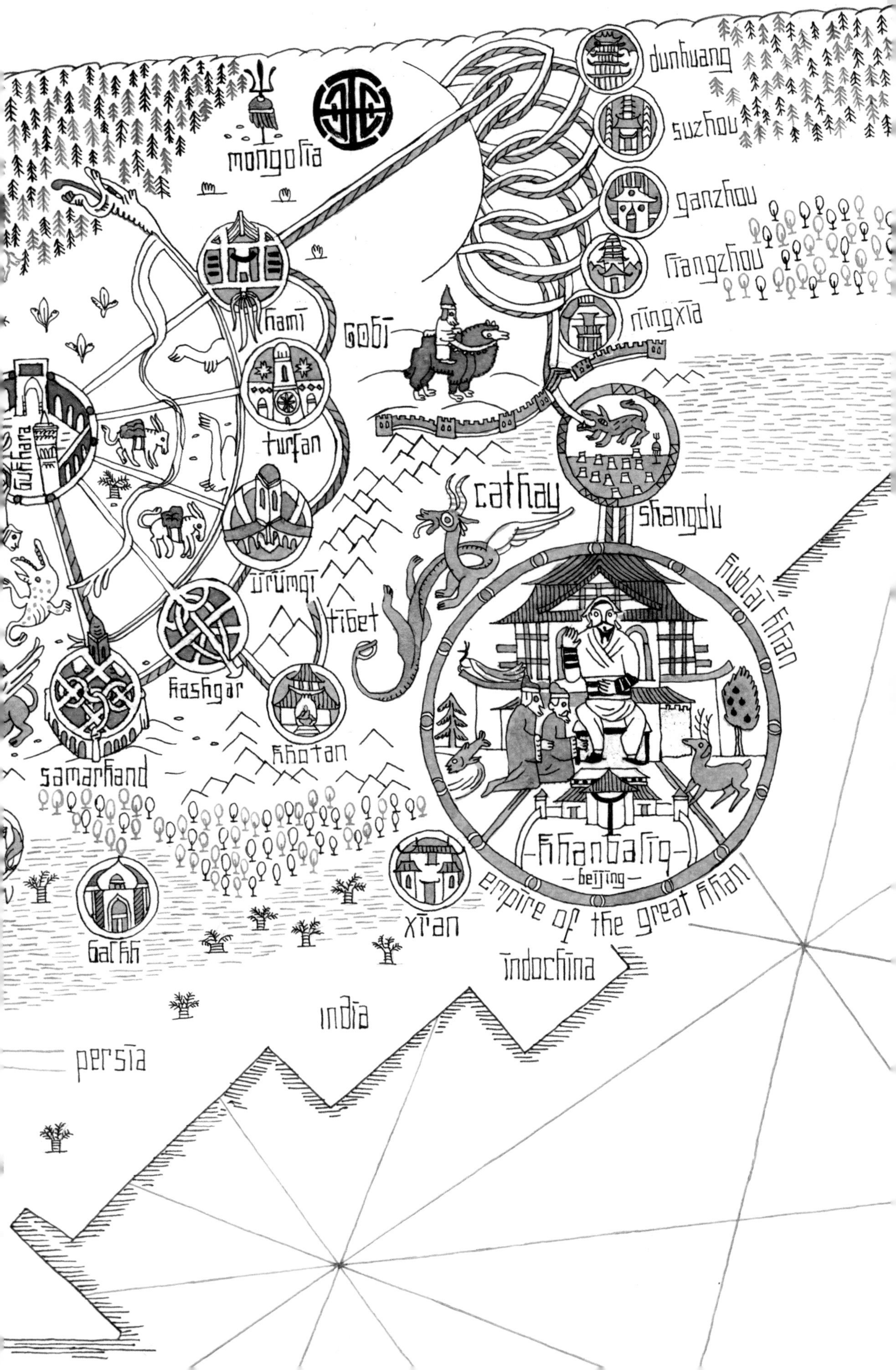
mongolia
dunhuang
suzhou
ganzhou
liangzhou
ningxia
hami
gobi
turfan
cathay
shangdu
bukhara
urumqi
tibet
kashgar
khotan
samarkand
kublai khan
khanbaliq
beijing
empire of the great khan
xian
balkh
indochina
india
persia

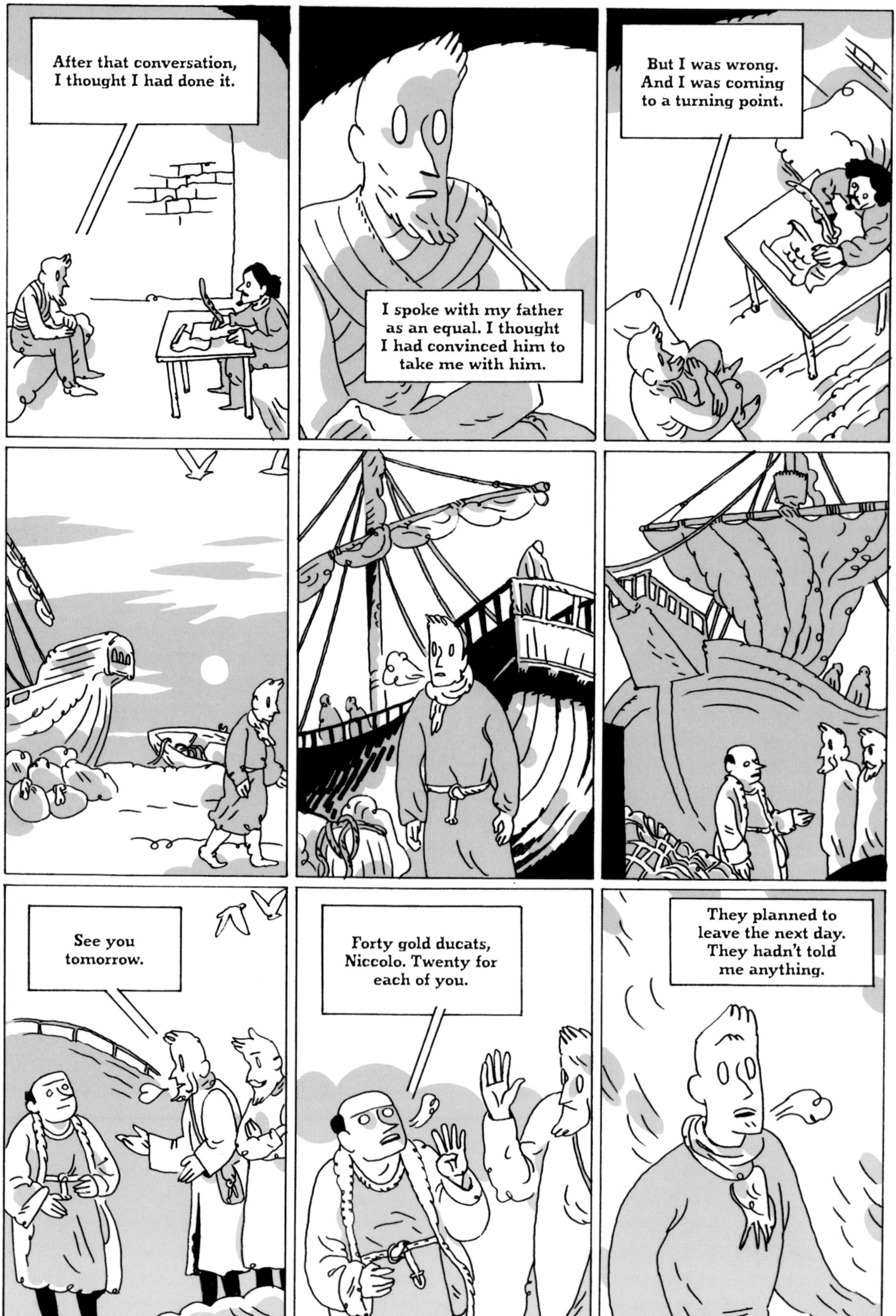

After that conversation, I thought I had done it.
I spoke with my father as an equal. I thought I had convinced him to take me with him.
But I was wrong. And I was coming to a turning point.
See you tomorrow.
Forty gold ducats, Niccolo. Twenty for each of you.
They planned to leave the next day. They hadn't told me anything.

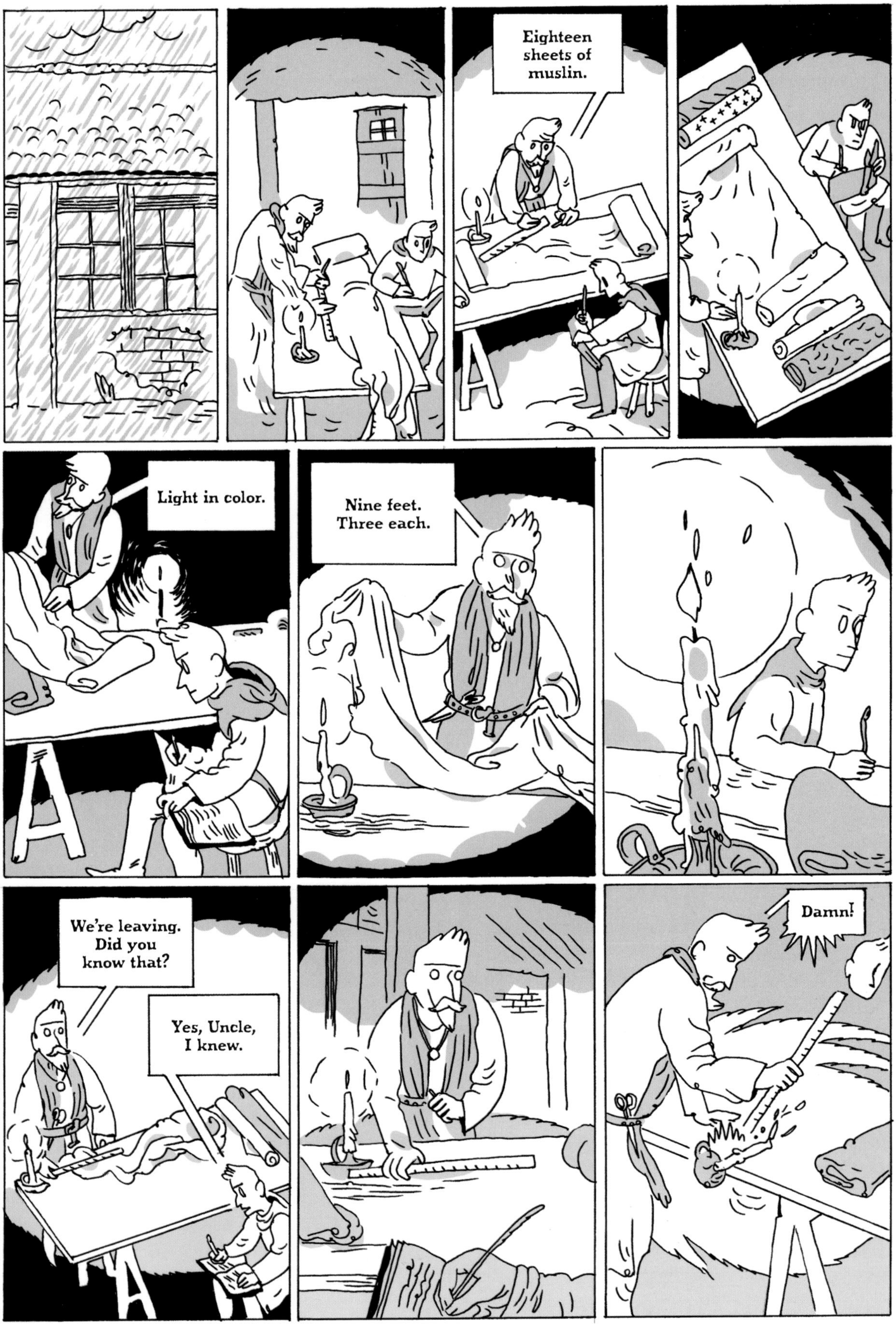
Eighteen sheets of muslin.
Light in color.
Nine feet. Three each.
We're leaving. Did you know that?
Yes, Uncle, I knew.
Damn!

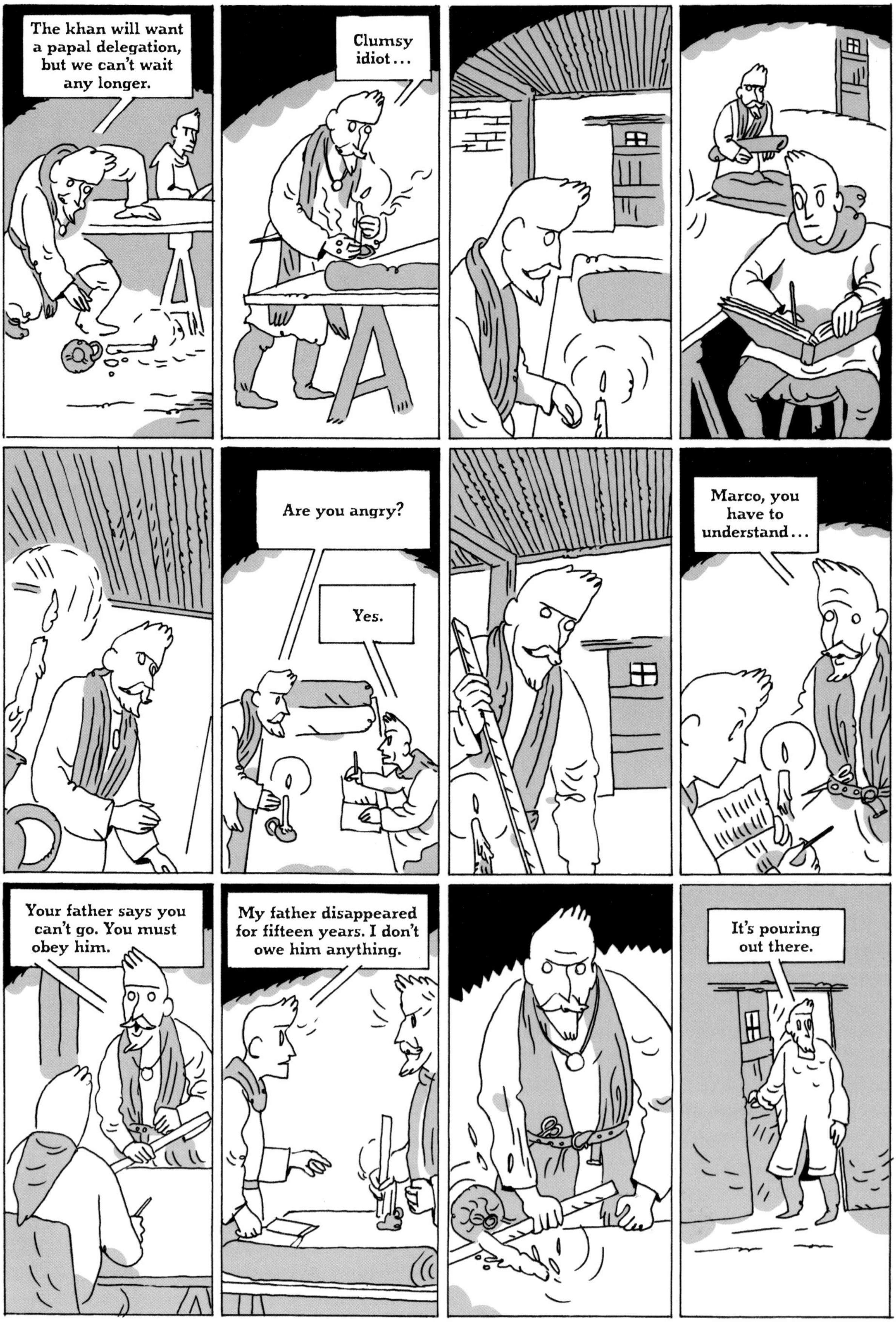
The khan will want a papal delegation, but we can't wait any longer.
Clumsy idiot...
Are you angry?
Yes.
Marco, you have to understand...
Your father says you can't go. You must obey him.
My father disappeared for fifteen years. I don't owe him anything.
It's pouring out there.

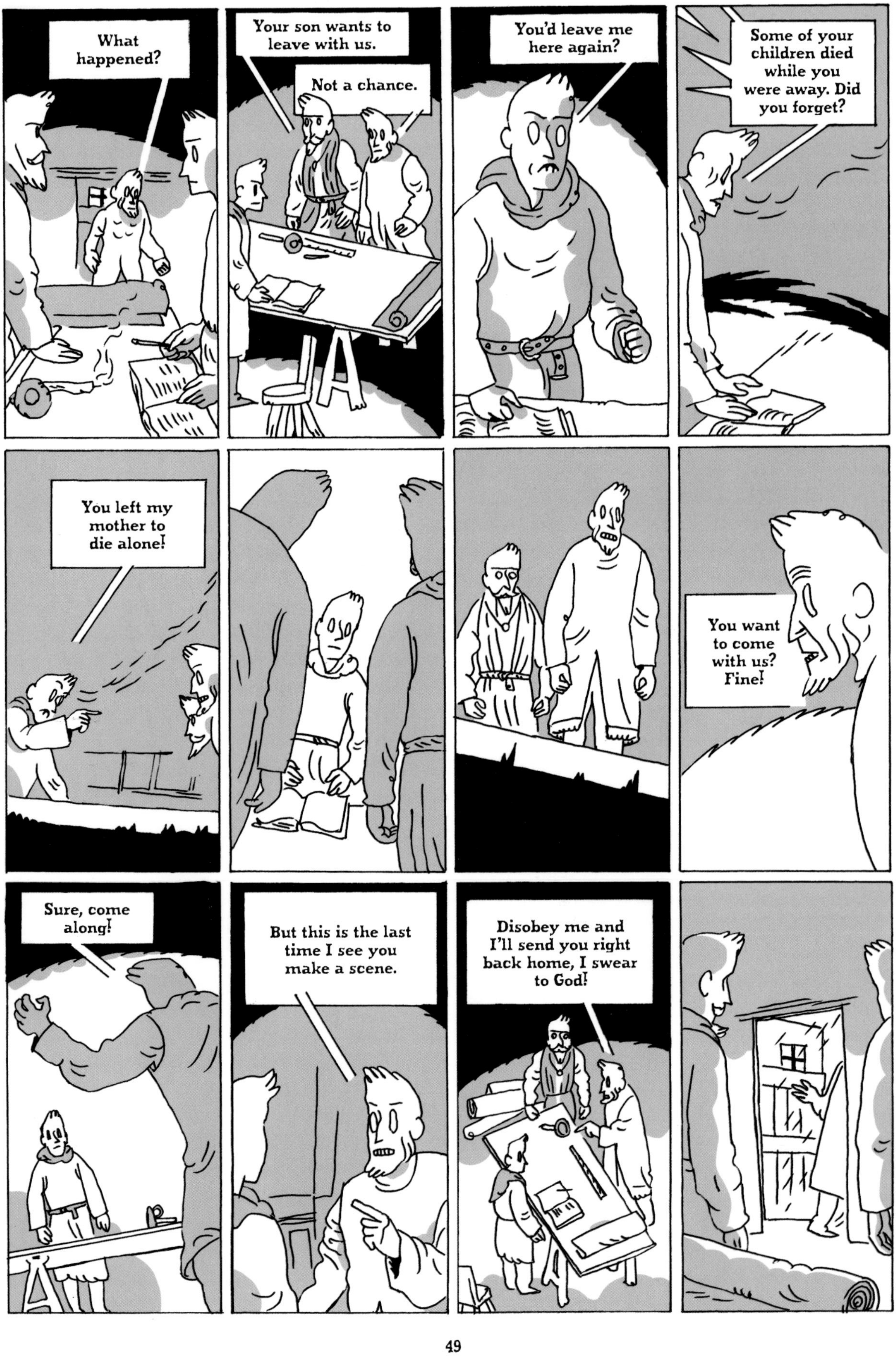
What happened?
Your son wants to leave with us.
Not a chance.
You'd leave me here again?
Some of your children died while you were away. Did you forget?
You left my mother to die alone!
You want to come with us? Fine!
Sure, come along!
But this is the last time I see you make a scene.
Disobey me and I'll send you right back home, I swear to God!

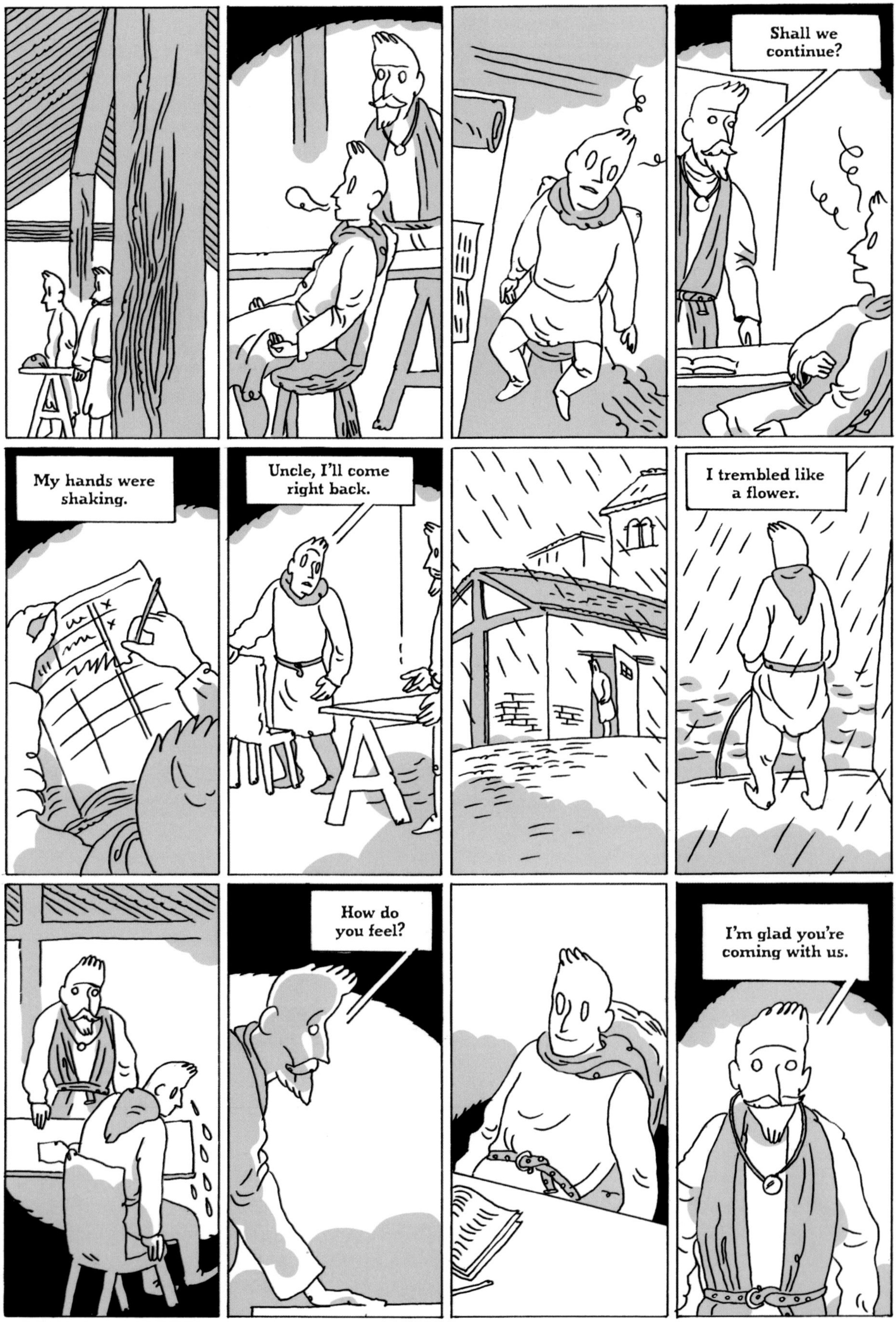
Shall we continue?
My hands were shaking.
Uncle, I'll come right back.
I trembled like a flower.
How do you feel?
I'm glad you're coming with us.

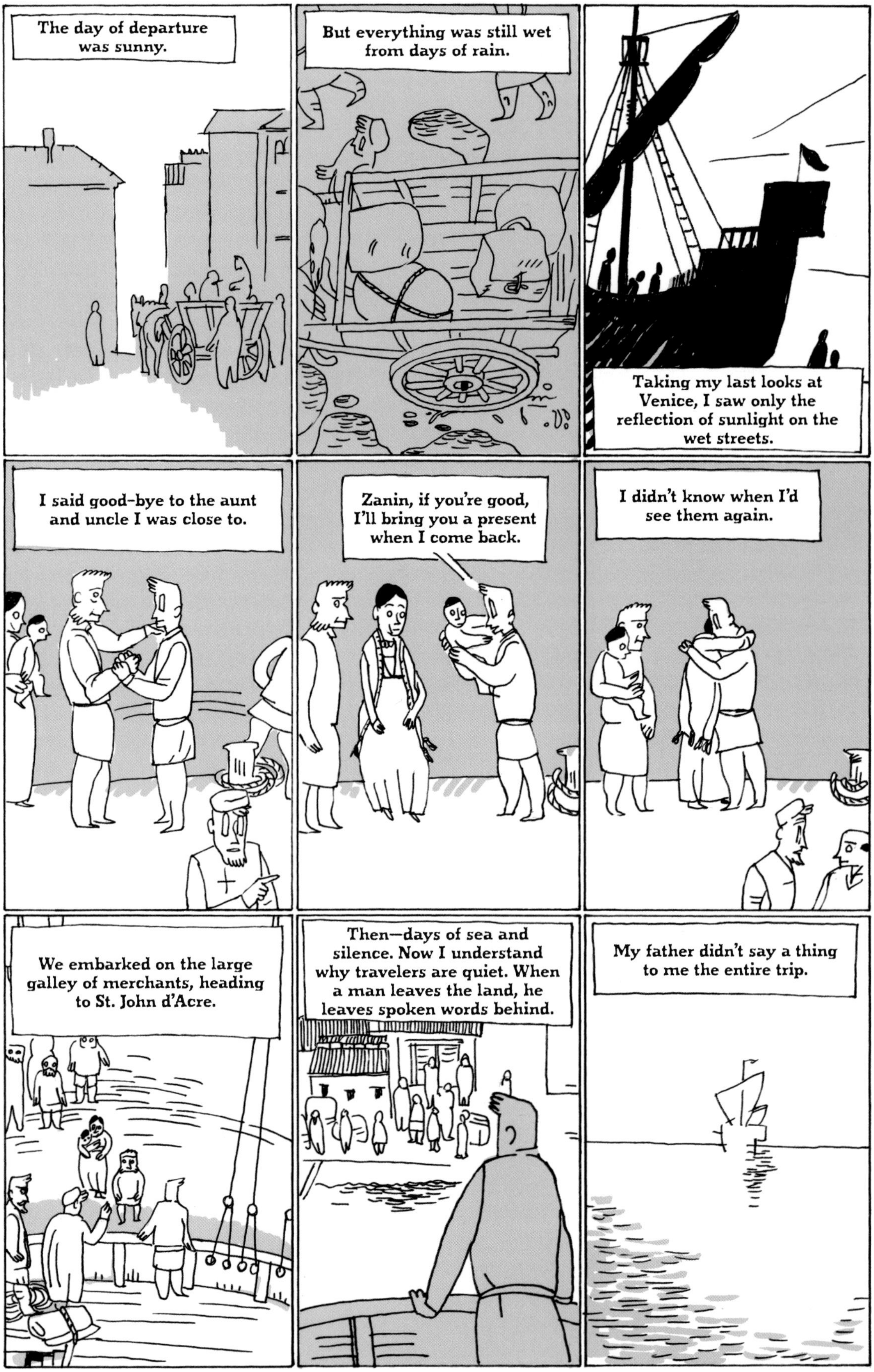
The day of departure was sunny.
But everything was still wet from days of rain.
Taking my last looks at Venice, I saw only the reflection of sunlight on the wet streets.
I said good-bye to the aunt and uncle I was close to.
Zanin, if you're good, I'll bring you a present when I come back.
I didn't know when I'd see them again.
We embarked on the large galley of merchants, heading to St. John d'Acre.
Then—days of sea and silence. Now I understand why travelers are quiet. When a man leaves the land, he leaves spoken words behind.
My father didn't say a thing to me the entire trip.

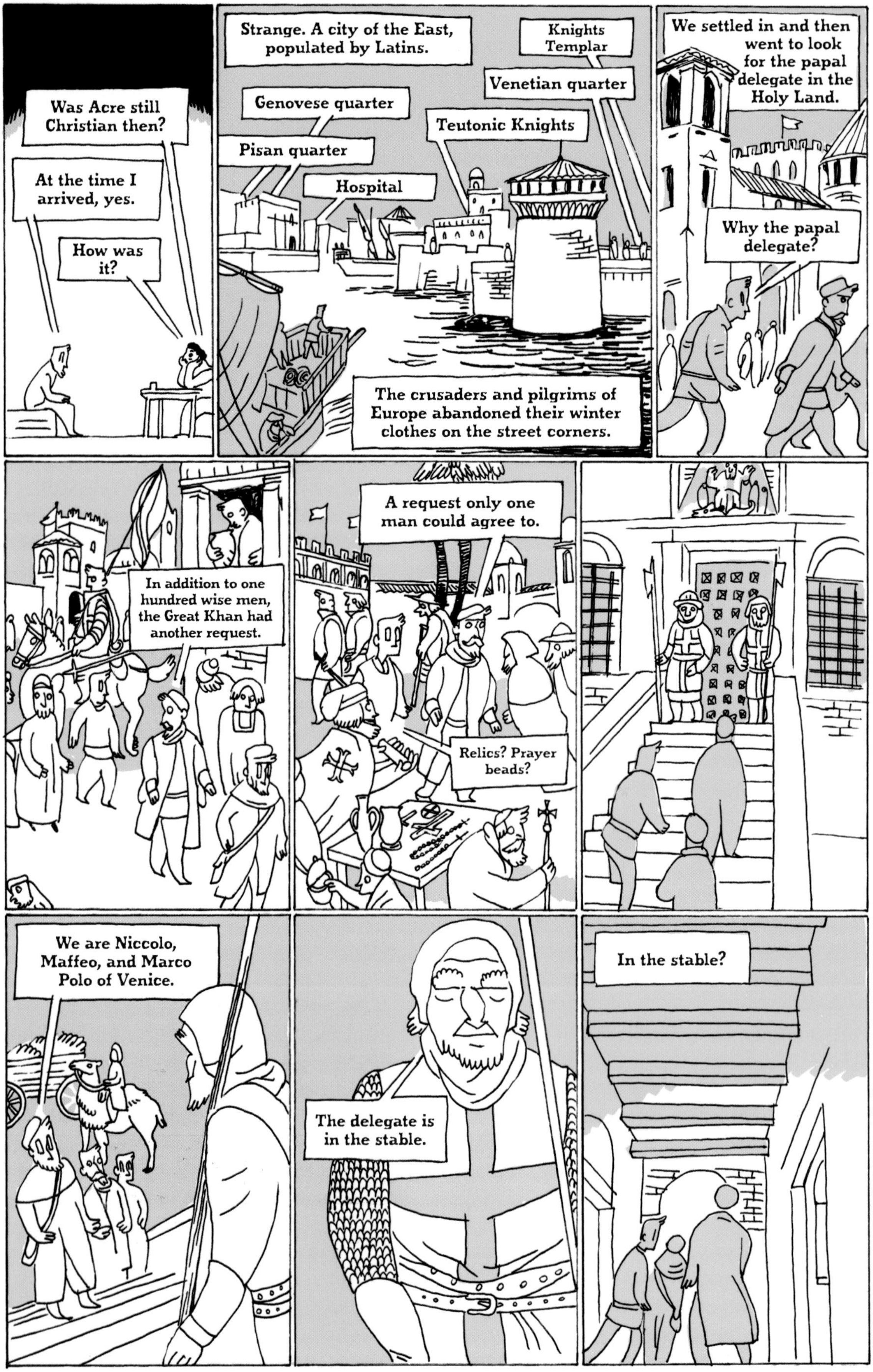

Was Acre still Christian then?
At the time I arrived, yes.
How was it?
Strange. A city of the East, populated by Latins.
Knights Templar
Venetian quarter
Genovese quarter
Teutonic Knights
Pisan quarter
Hospital
The crusaders and pilgrims of Europe abandoned their winter clothes on the street corners.
We settled in and then went to look for the papal delegate in the Holy Land.
Why the papal delegate?
In addition to one hundred wise men, the Great Khan had another request.
A request only one man could agree to.
Relics? Prayer beads?
We are Niccolo, Maffeo, and Marco Polo of Venice.
The delegate is in the stable.
In the stable?

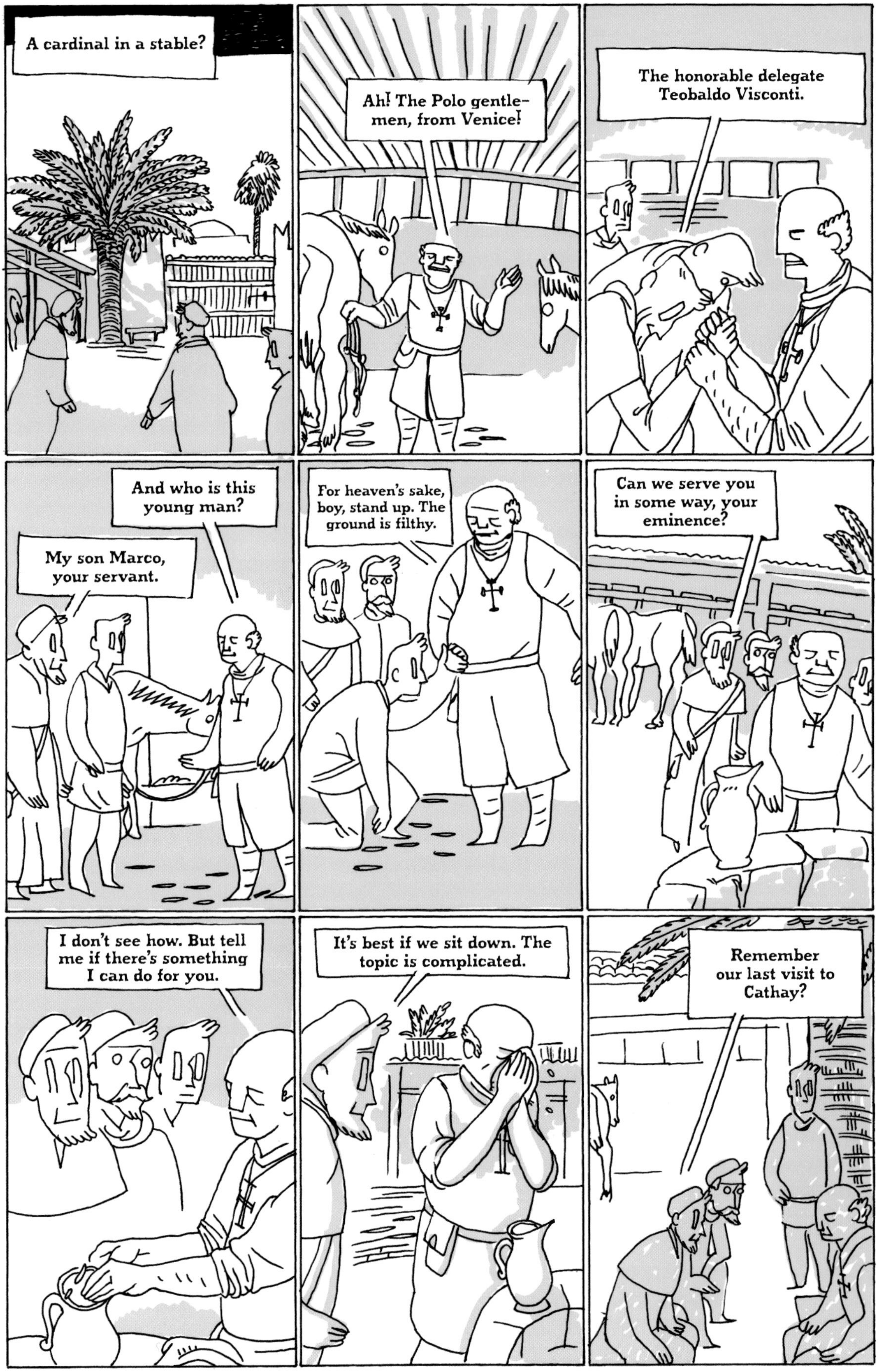
A cardinal in a stable?
Ah! The Polo gentlemen, from Venice!
The honorable delegate Teobaldo Visconti.
And who is this young man?
My son Marco, your servant.
For heaven's sake, boy, stand up. The ground is filthy.
Can we serve you in some way, your eminence?
I don't see how. But tell me if there's something I can do for you.
It's best if we sit down. The topic is complicated.
Remember our last visit to Cathay?

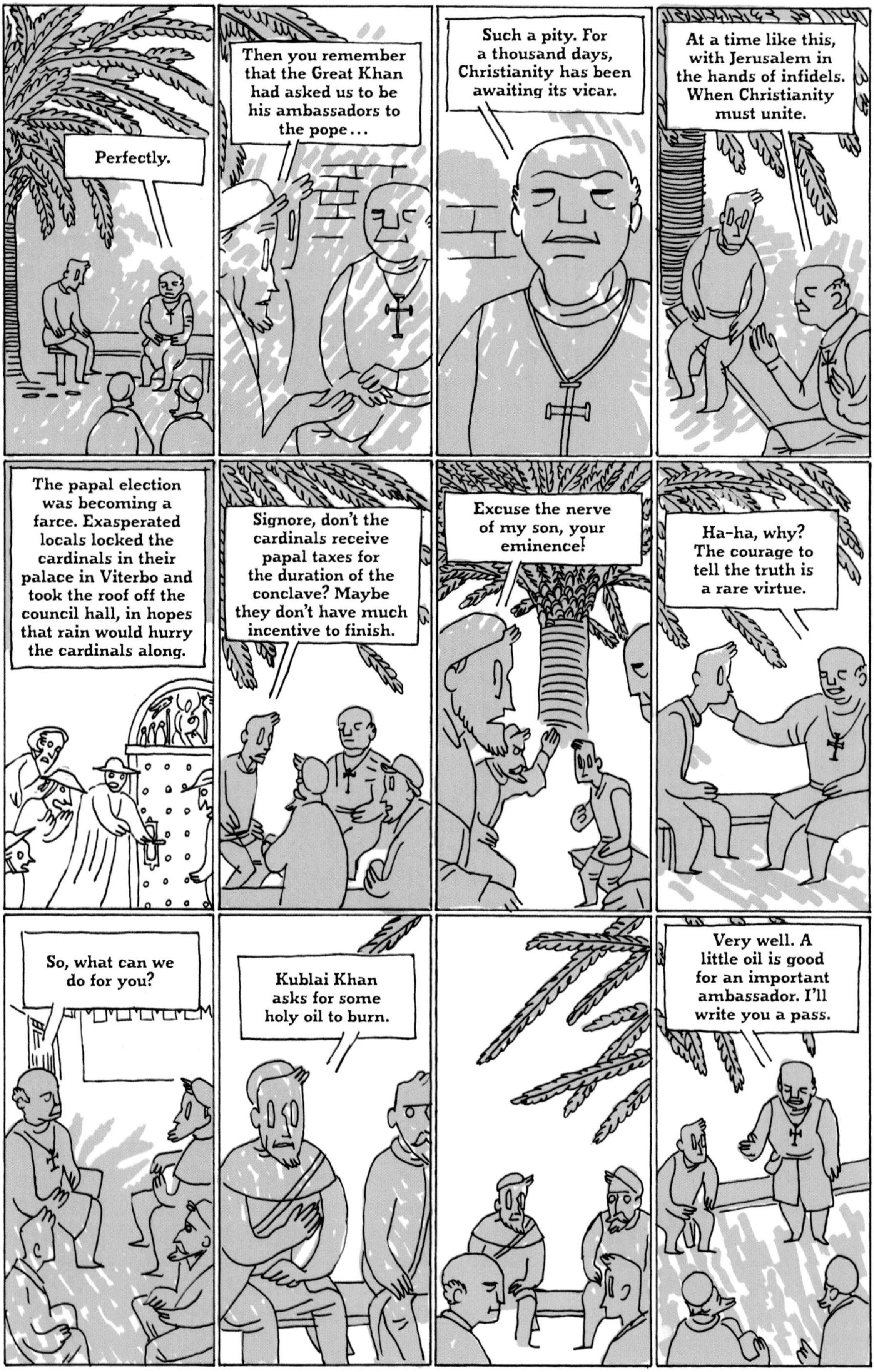
Perfectly.
Then you remember that the Great Khan had asked us to be his ambassadors to the pope...
Such a pity. For a thousand days, Christianity has been awaiting its vicar.
At a time like this, with Jerusalem in the hands of infidels. When Christianity must unite.
The papal election was becoming a farce. Exasperated locals locked the cardinals in their palace in Viterbo and took the roof off the council hall, in hopes that rain would hurry the cardinals along.
Signore, don't the cardinals receive papal taxes for the duration of the conclave? Maybe they don't have much incentive to finish.
Excuse the nerve of my son, your eminence!
Ha-ha, why? The courage to tell the truth is a rare virtue.
So, what can we do for you?
Kublai Khan asks for some holy oil to burn.
Very well. A little oil is good for an important ambassador. I'll write you a pass.

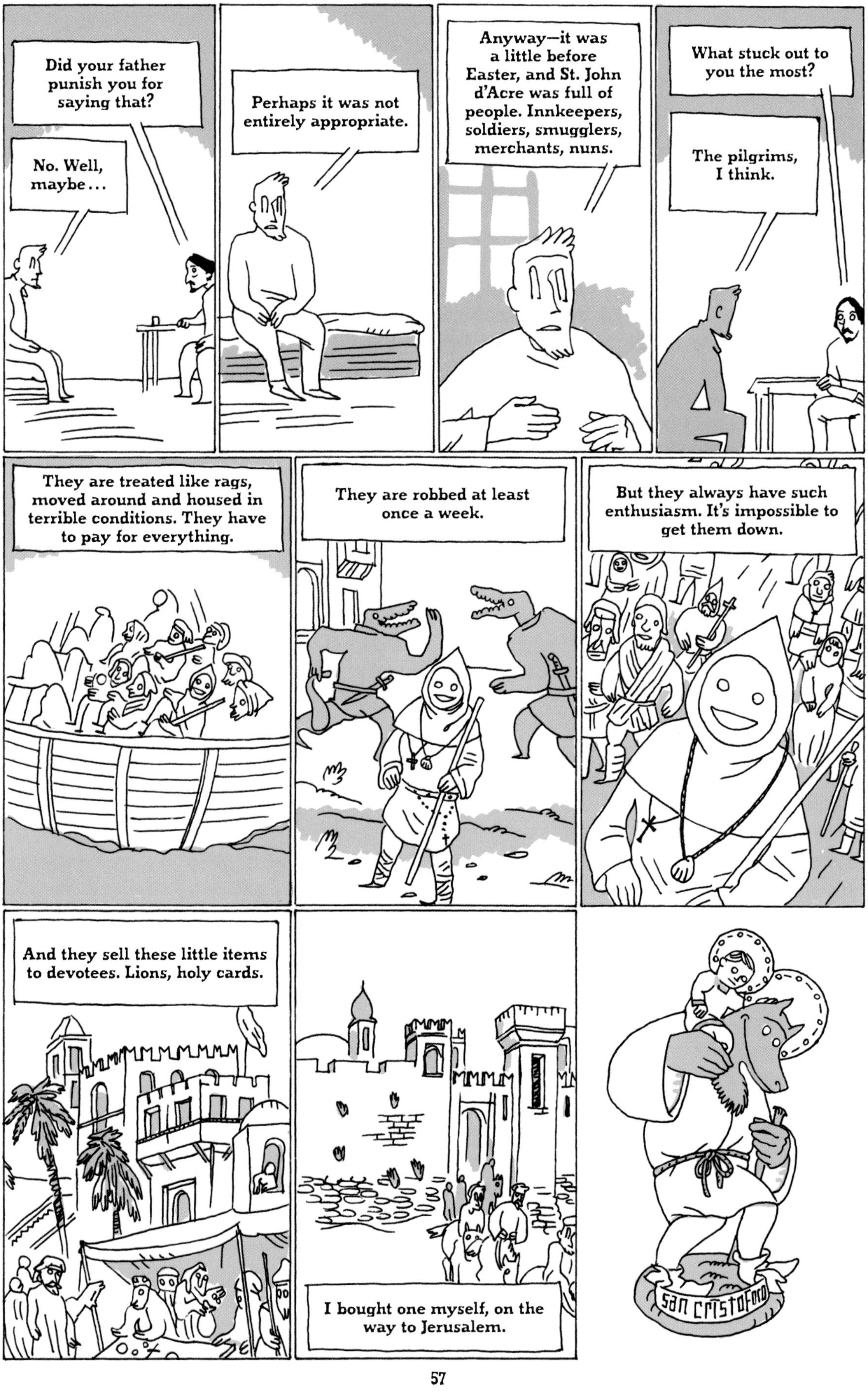

Did your father punish you for saying that?
No. Well, maybe...
Perhaps it was not entirely appropriate.
Anyway—it was a little before Easter, and St. John d'Acre was full of people. Innkeepers, soldiers, smugglers, merchants, nuns.
What stuck out to you the most?
The pilgrims, I think.
They are treated like rags, moved around and housed in terrible conditions. They have to pay for everything.
They are robbed at least once a week.
But they always have such enthusiasm. It's impossible to get them down.
And they sell these little items to devotees. Lions, holy cards.
I bought one myself, on the way to Jerusalem.
SAN CRISTOFORO

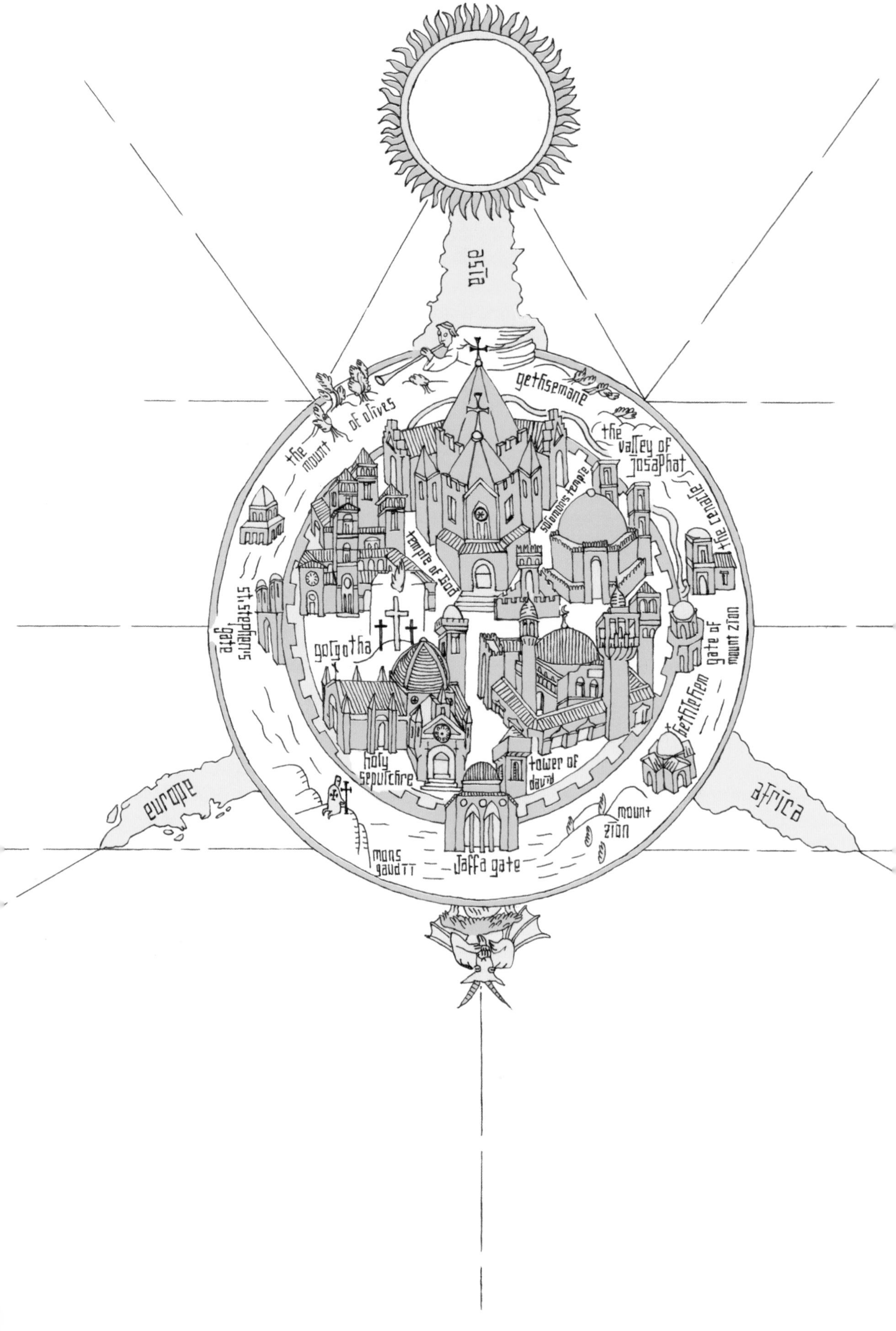
asia
the mount of olives
gethsemane
the valley of josaphat
solomon's temple
temple of God
the cenacle
st. stephen's gate
golgotha
gate of mount zion
bethlehem
holy sepulchre
tower of david
europe
africa
mount zion
mons gaudii
jaffa gate

Now, Jerusalem—what can I tell you about the city that you don't already know?

The garden of olive trees, the tomb, the crucifixion site?

The Temple of Solomon and the magnificent mosques of stone and gold?

The old walls and the intermingling of chants, bells, and prayer calls?

Jerusalem etches itself in your body for a lifetime.

And the city is exactly how you imagine it. Street by street, tower by tower.

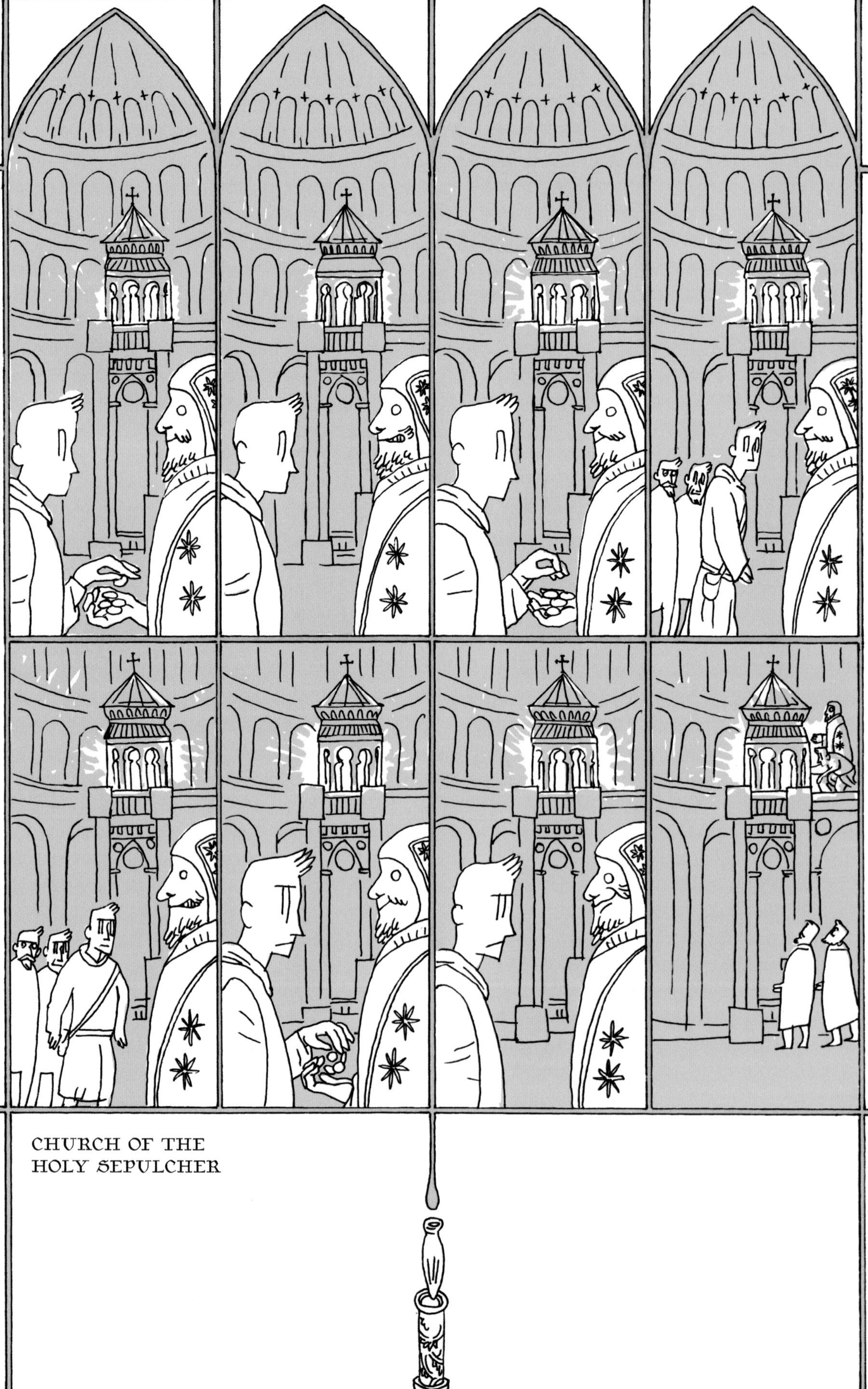

CHURCH OF THE
HOLY SEPULCHER

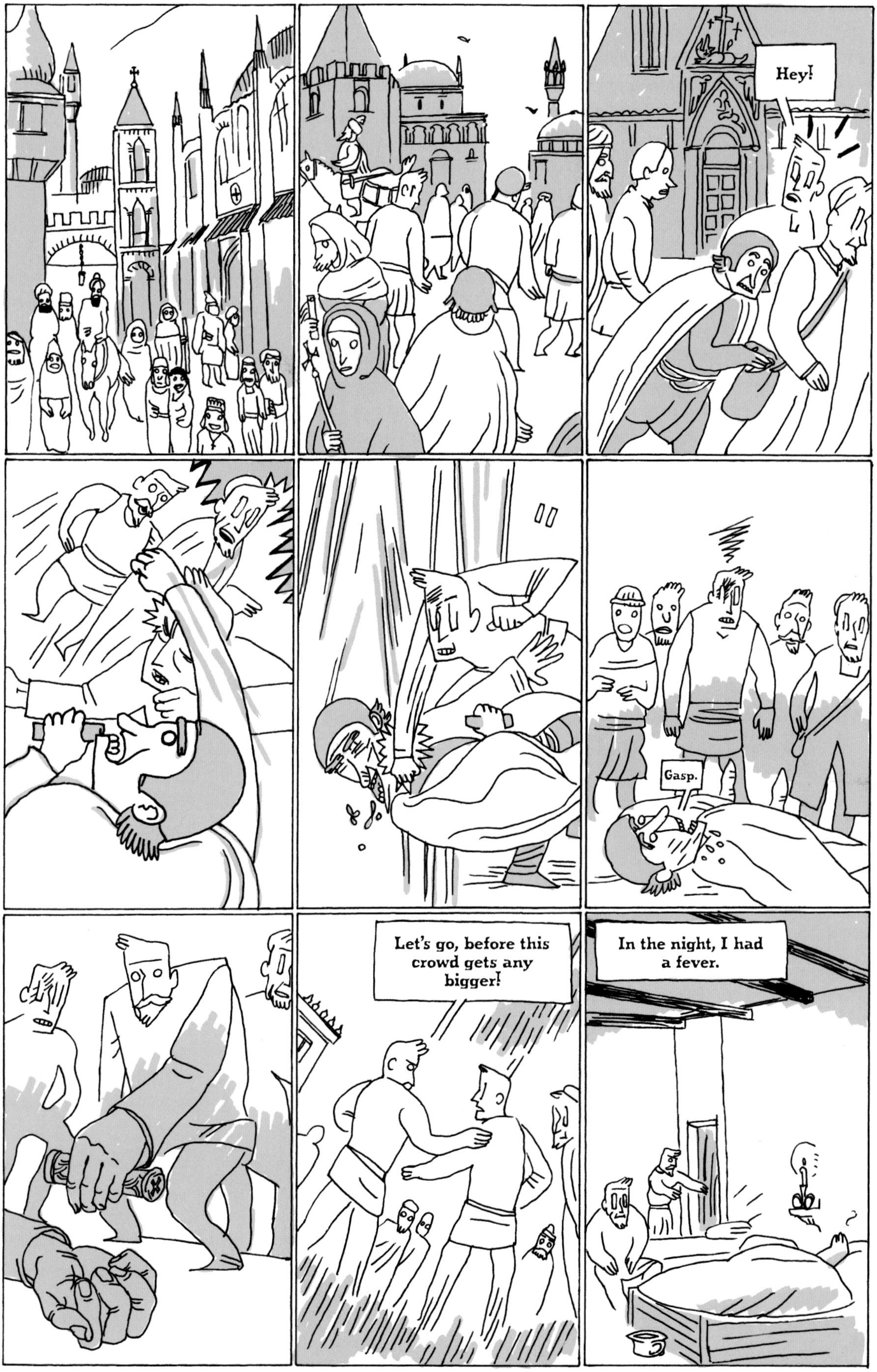

Hey!
Gasp.
Let's go, before this crowd gets any bigger!
In the night, I had a fever.

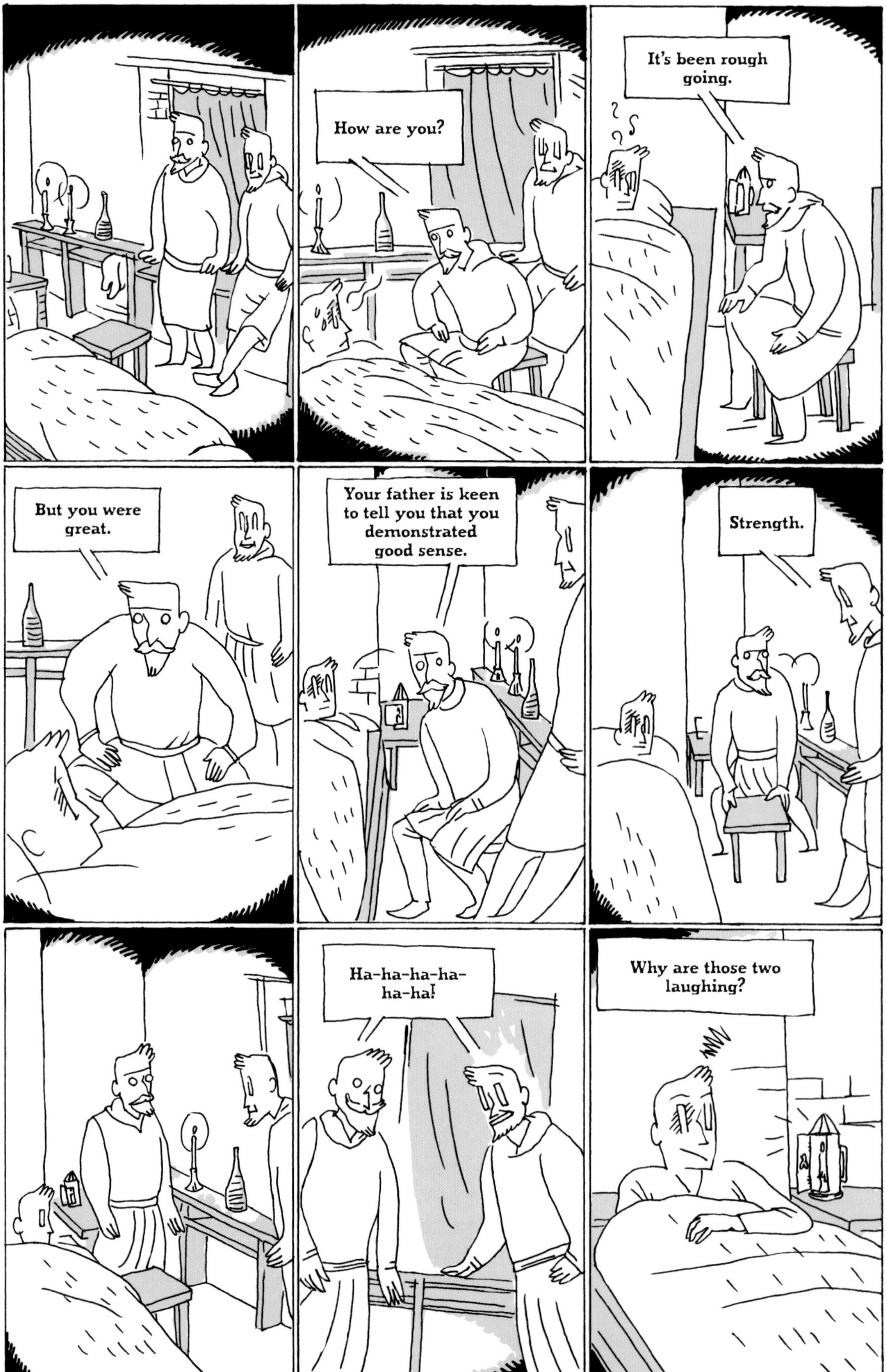
How are you?
It's been rough going.
But you were great.
Your father is keen to tell you that you demonstrated good sense.
Strength.
Ha-ha-ha-ha-ha-ha!
Why are those two laughing?

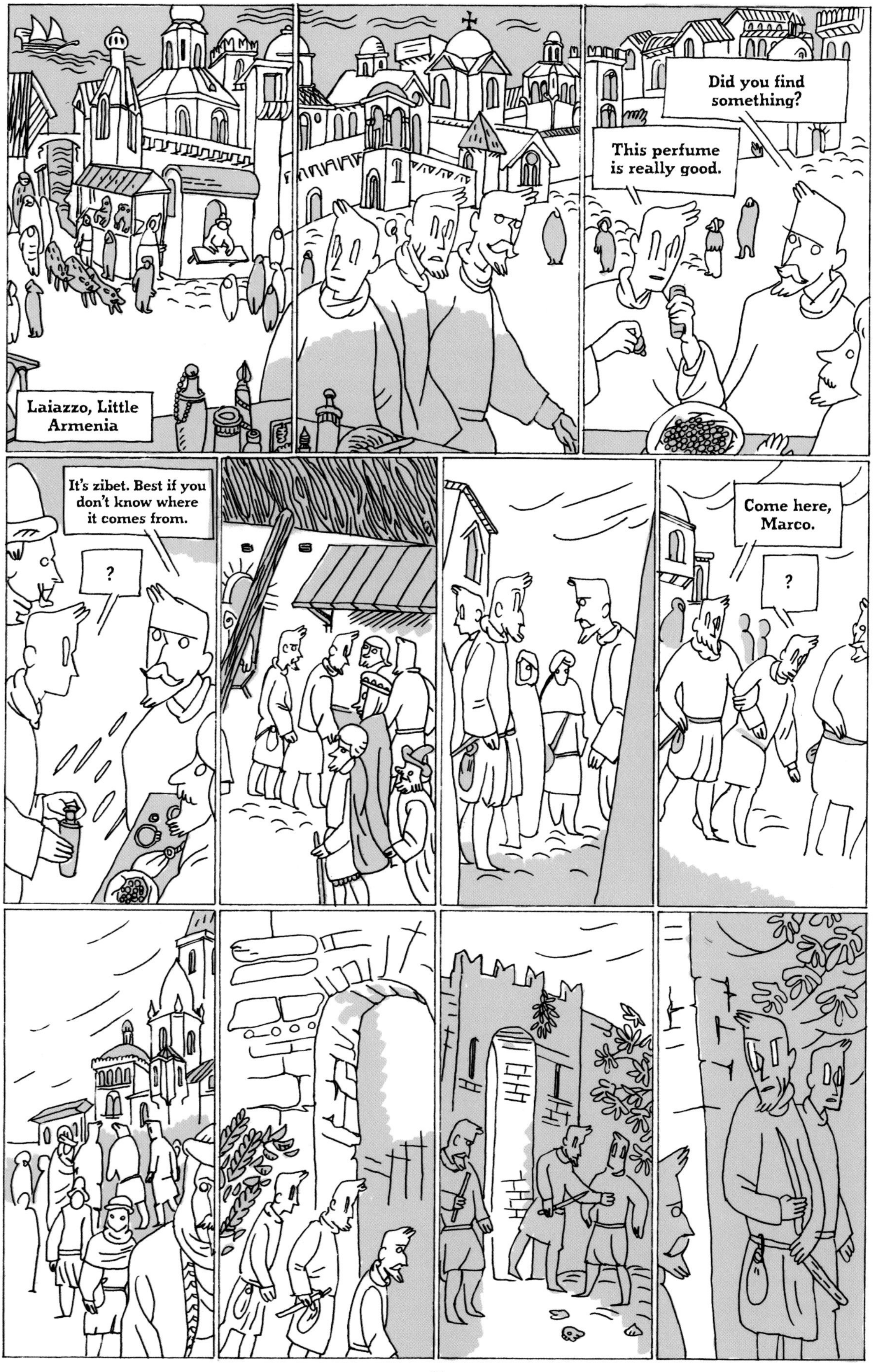
Laiazzo, Little Armenia
Did you find something?
This perfume is really good.
It's zibet. Best if you don't know where it comes from.
?
Come here, Marco.
?

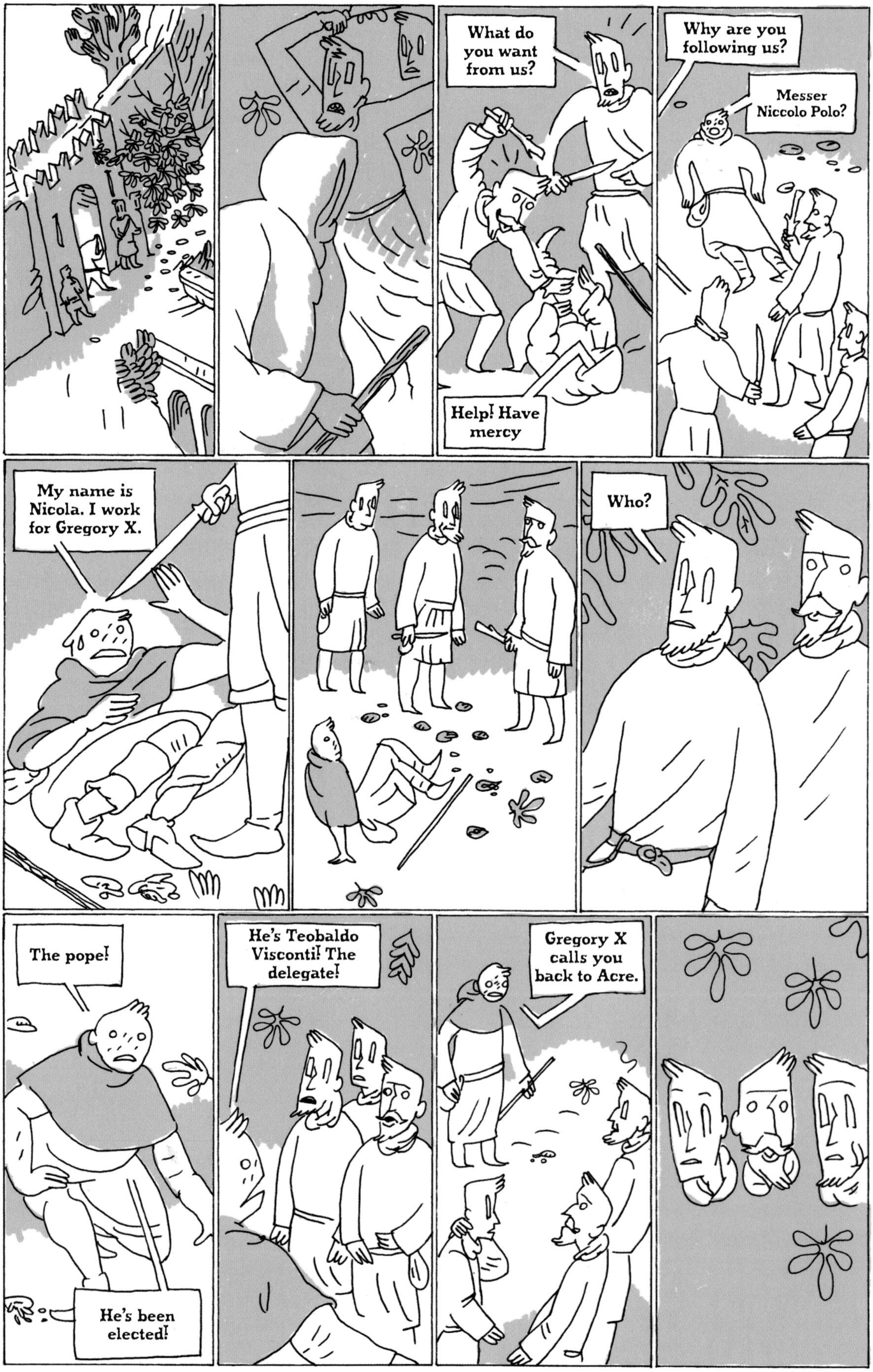
What do you want from us?
Help! Have mercy
Why are you following us?
Messer Niccolo Polo?
My name is Nicola. I work for Gregory X.
Who?
The pope!
He's been elected!
He's Teobaldo Visconti! The delegate!
Gregory X calls you back to Acre.

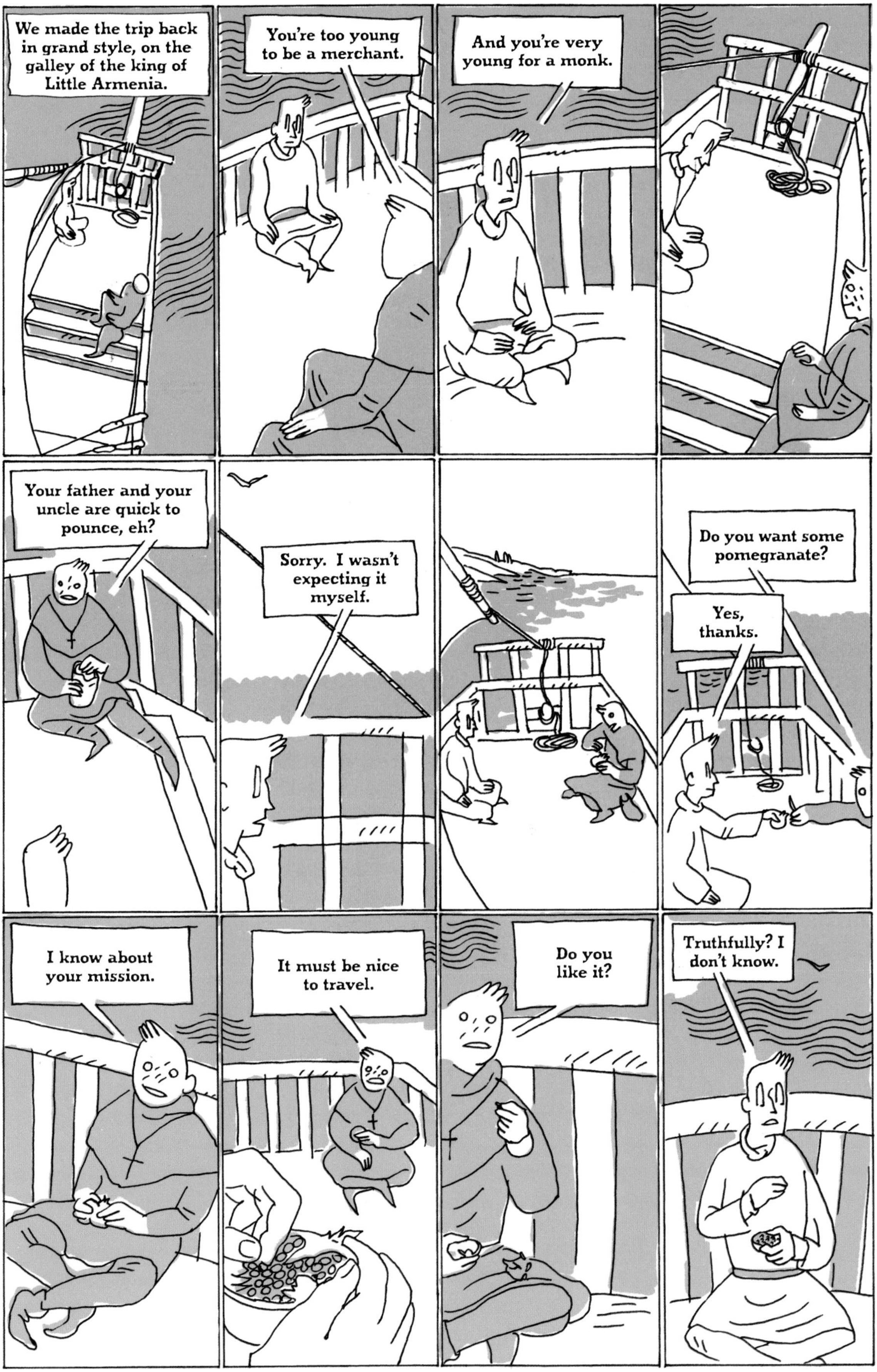
We made the trip back in grand style, on the galley of the king of Little Armenia.
You're too young to be a merchant.
And you're very young for a monk.
Your father and your uncle are quick to pounce, eh?
Sorry. I wasn't expecting it myself.
Do you want some pomegranate?
Yes, thanks.
I know about your mission.
It must be nice to travel.
Do you like it?
Truthfully? I don't know.

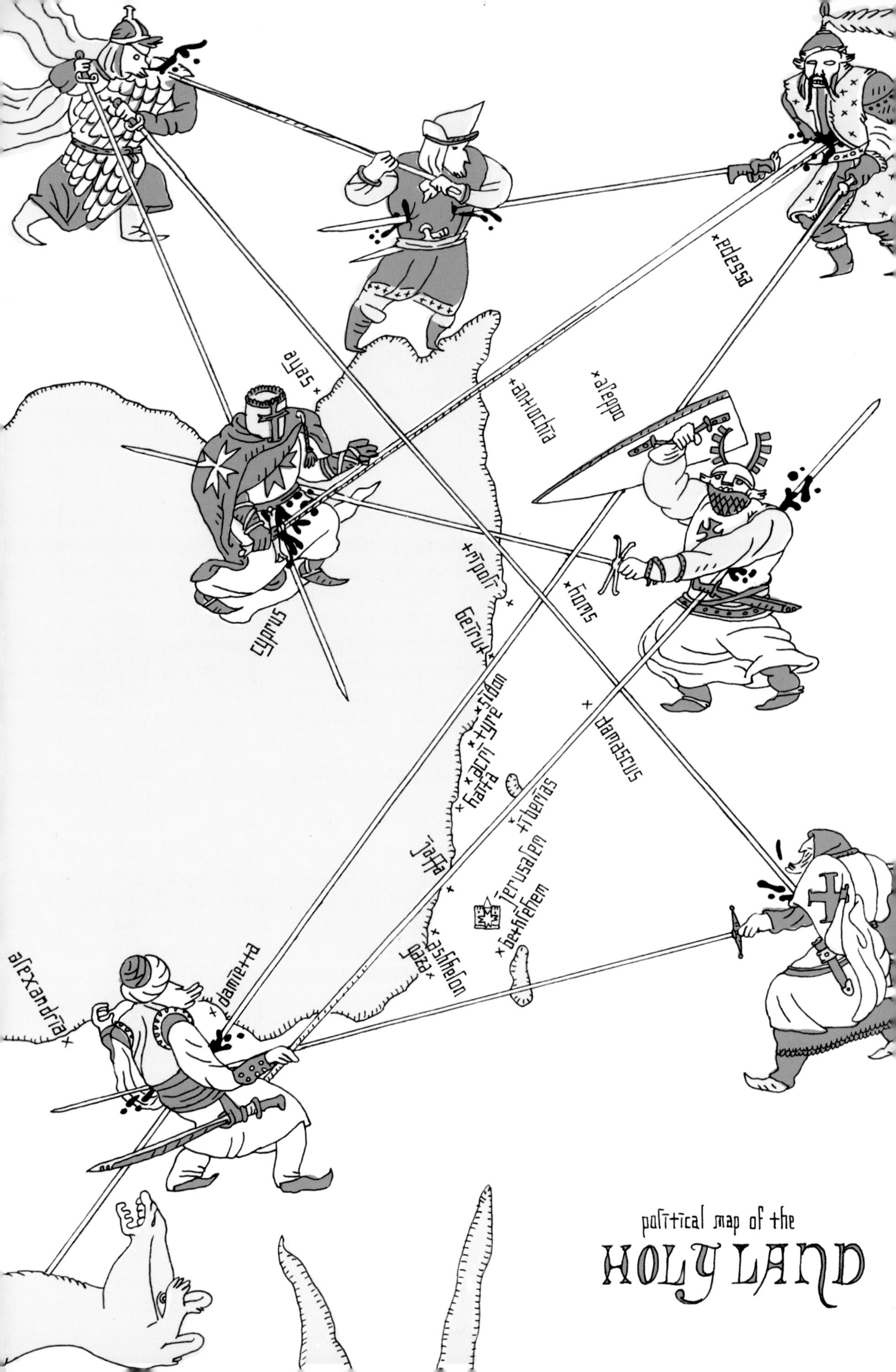
edessa
ayas
antiochia
aleppo
tripoli
homs
beirut
cyprus
sidon
tyre
acri
haifa
damascus
tiberias
jaffa
jerusalem
bethlehem
ashkelon
gaza
alexandria
dametta
political map of the
HOLY LAND

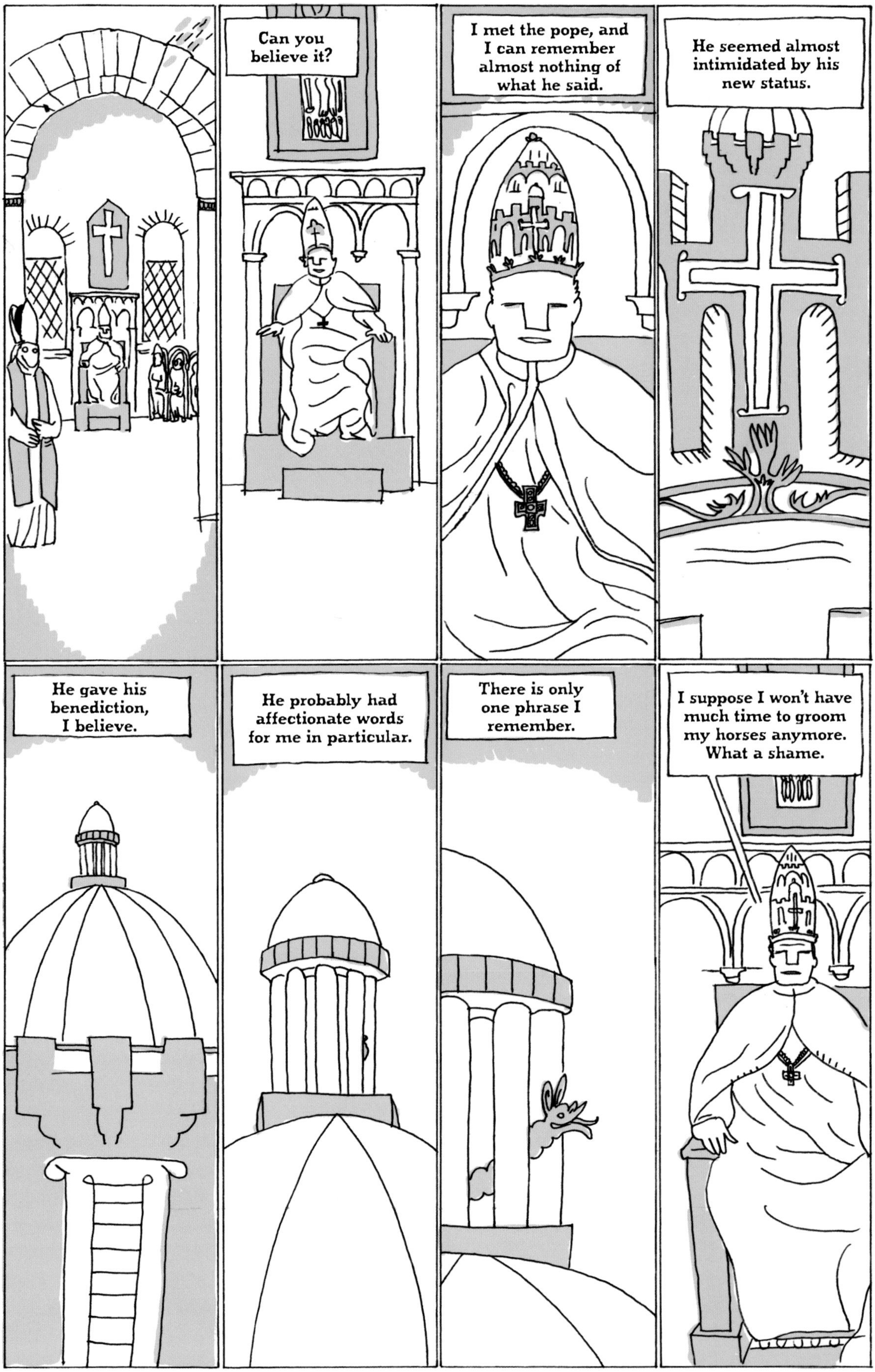
Can you believe it?
I met the pope, and I can remember almost nothing of what he said.
He seemed almost intimidated by his new status.
He gave his benediction, I believe.
He probably had affectionate words for me in particular.
There is only one phrase I remember.
I suppose I won't have much time to groom my horses anymore. What a shame.

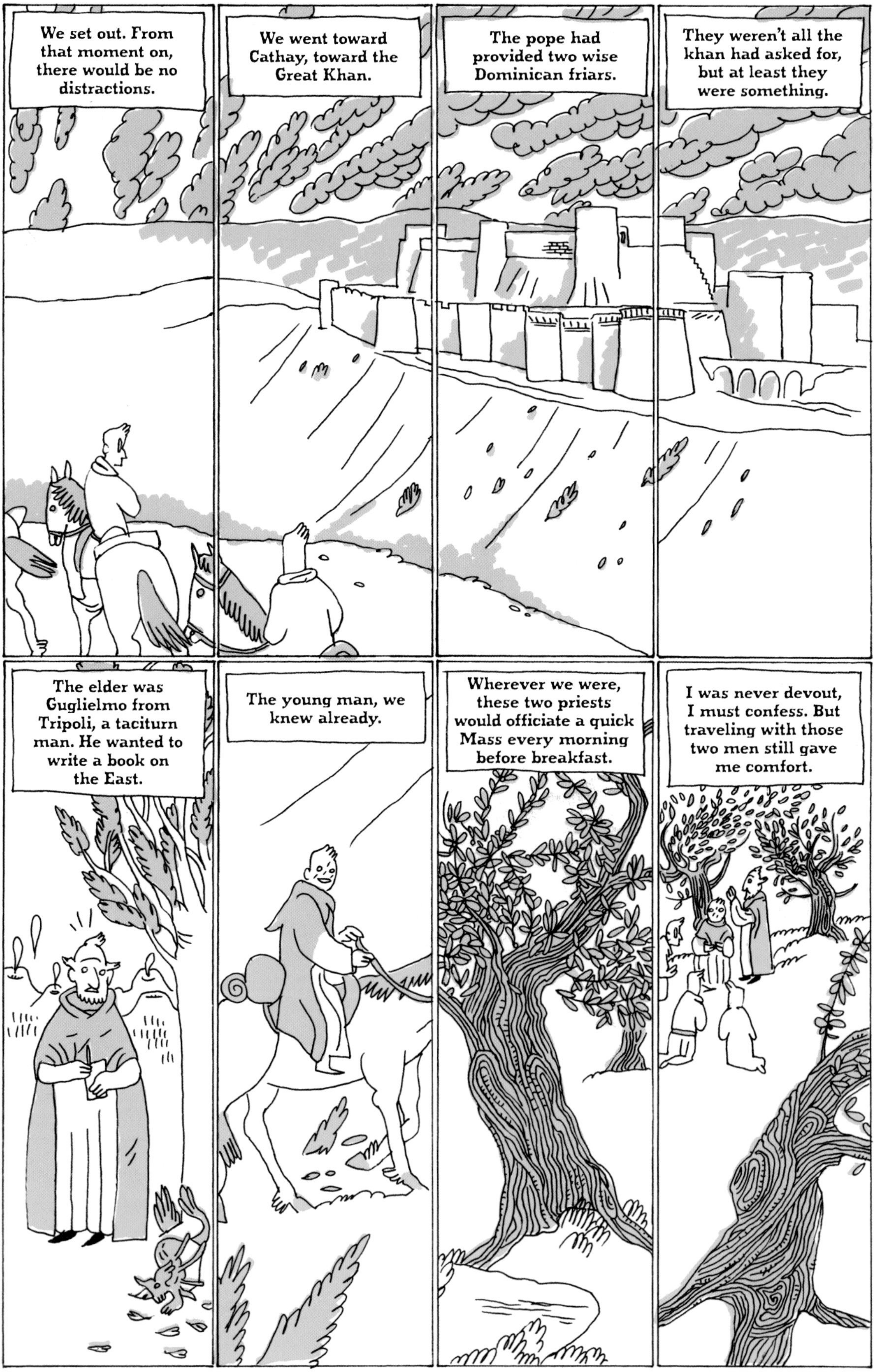
We set out. From that moment on, there would be no distractions.
We went toward Cathay, toward the Great Khan.
The pope had provided two wise Dominican friars.
They weren't all the khan had asked for, but at least they were something.
The elder was Guglielmo from Tripoli, a taciturn man. He wanted to write a book on the East.
The young man, we knew already.
Wherever we were, these two priests would officiate a quick Mass every morning before breakfast.
I was never devout, I must confess. But traveling with those two men still gave me comfort.

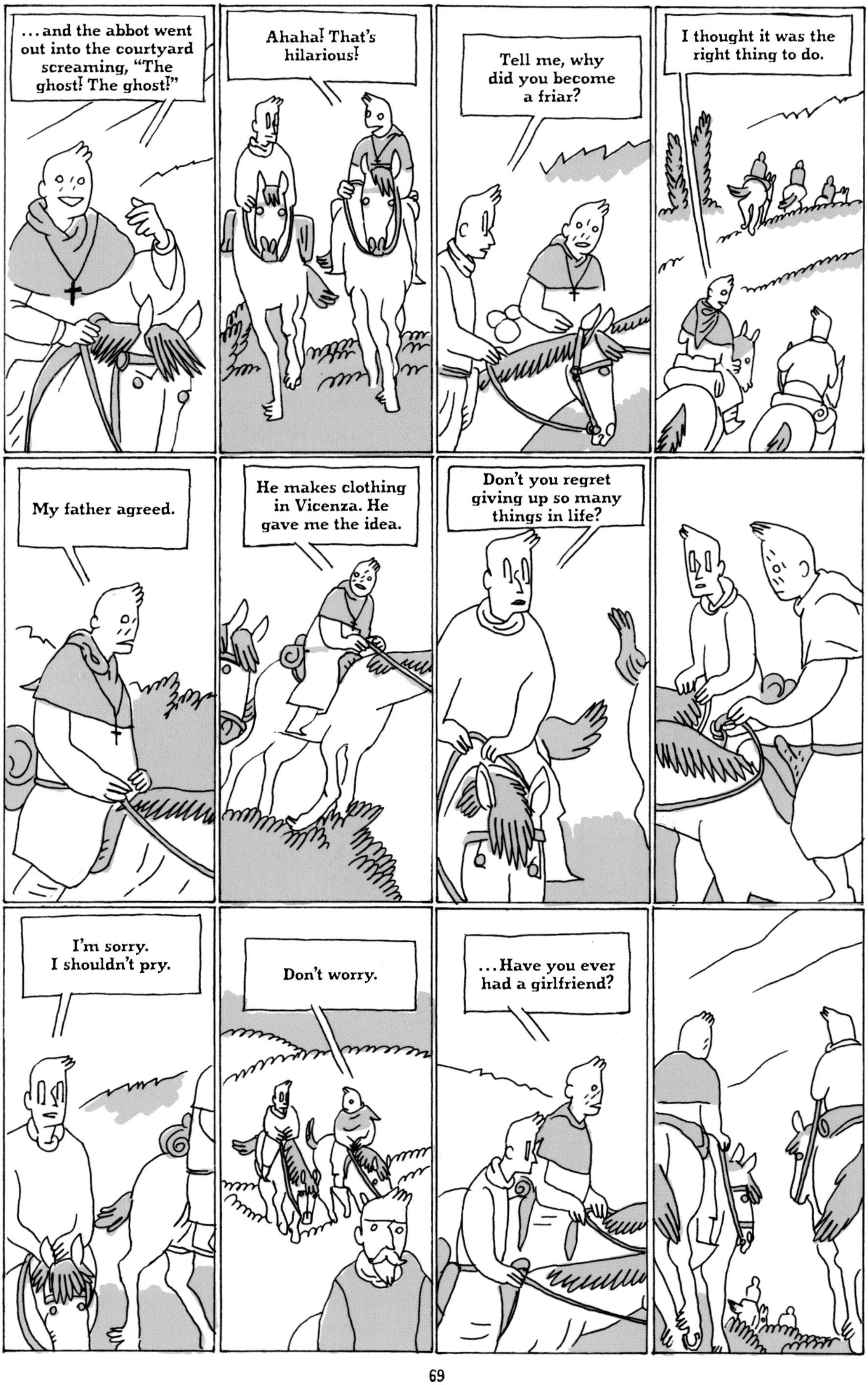
...and the abbot went out into the courtyard screaming, "The ghost! The ghost!"
Ahaha! That's hilarious!
Tell me, why did you become a friar?
I thought it was the right thing to do.
My father agreed.
He makes clothing in Vicenza. He gave me the idea.
Don't you regret giving up so many things in life?
I'm sorry. I shouldn't pry.
Don't worry.
...Have you ever had a girlfriend?

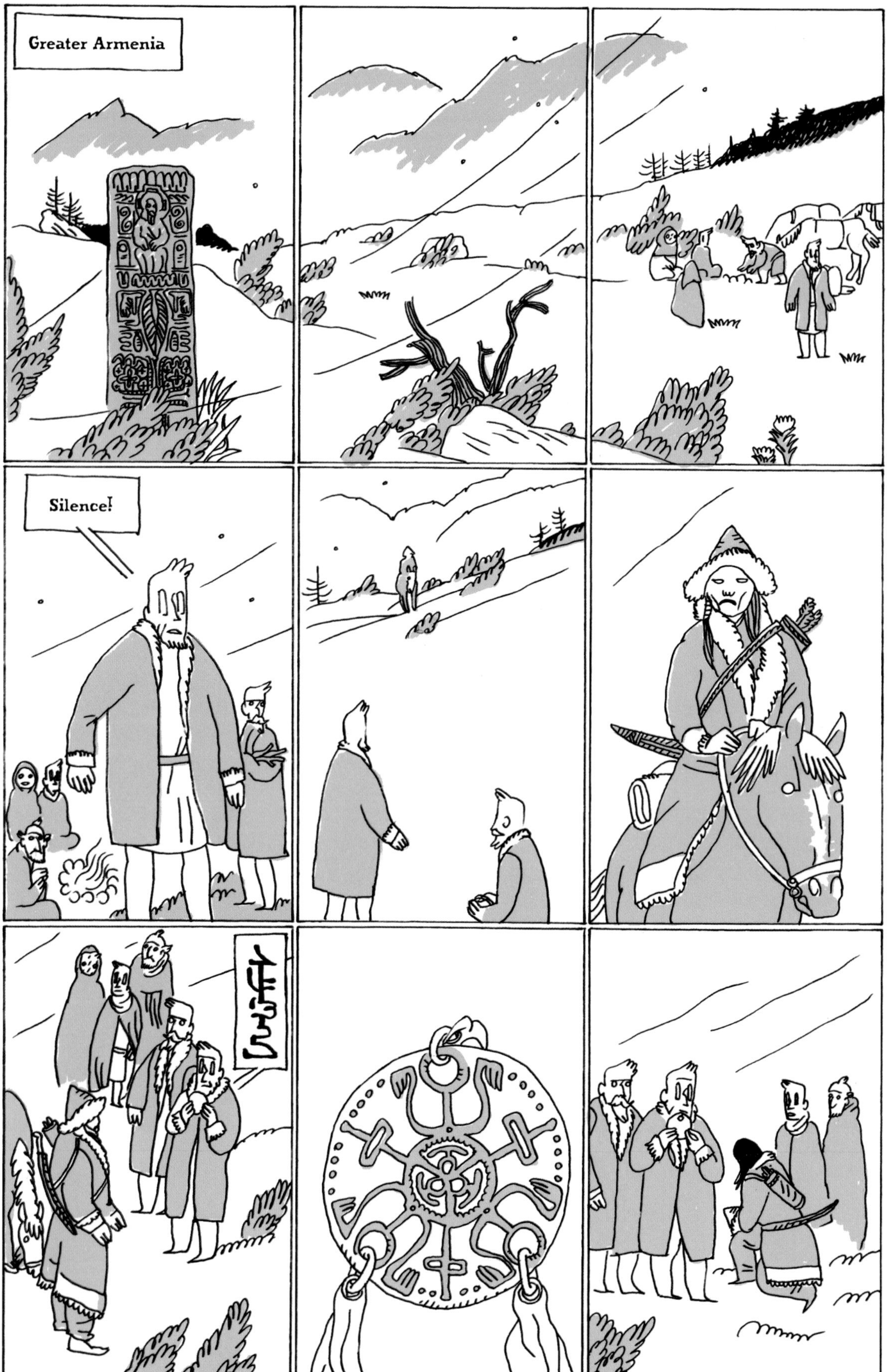

Greater Armenia
Silence!

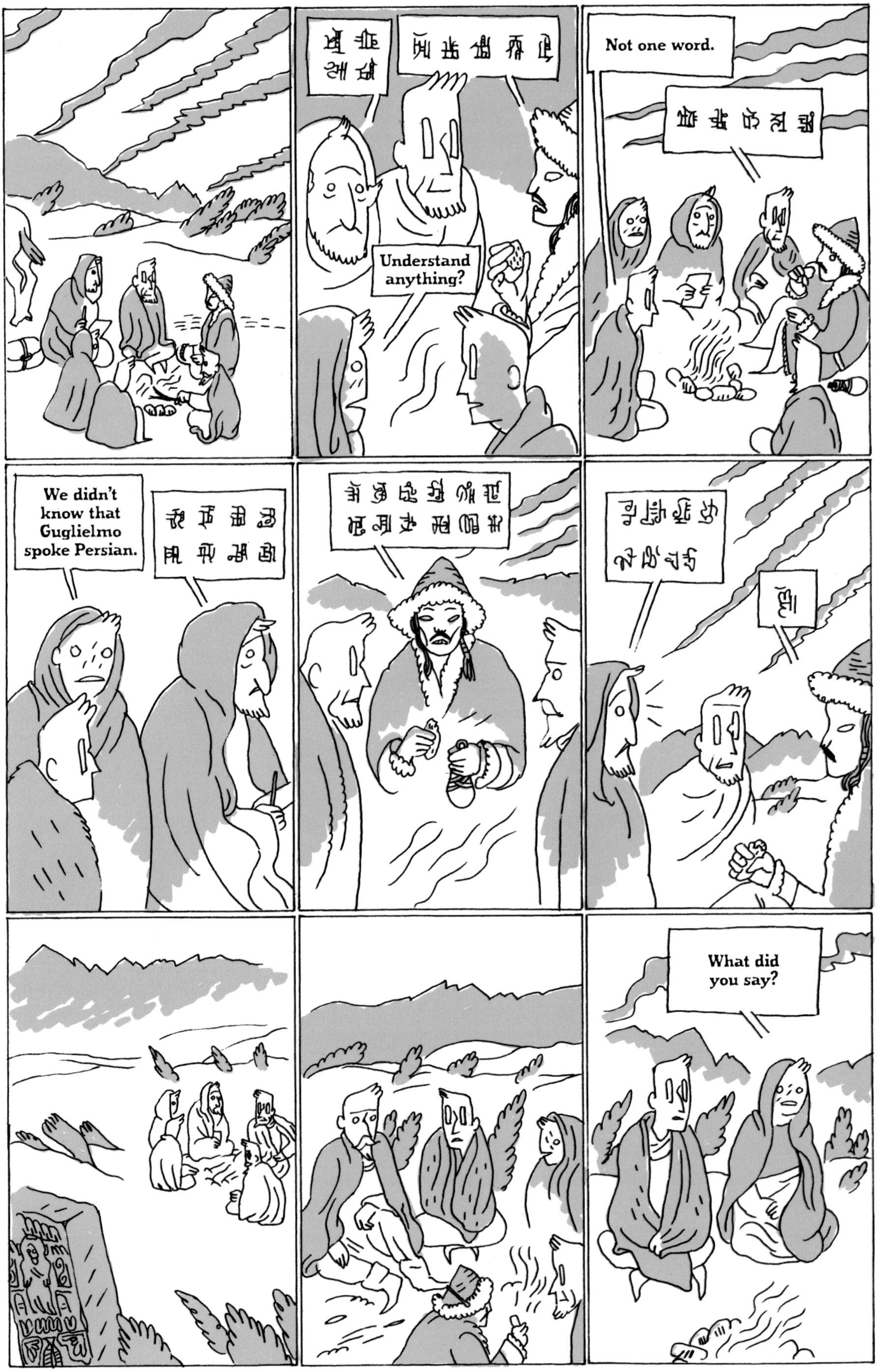
Understand anything?
Not one word.
We didn't know that Guglielmo spoke Persian.
What did you say?

THE TWENTIETH* NIGHT VISION** OF FRIAR GUGLIELMO FROM TRIPOLI

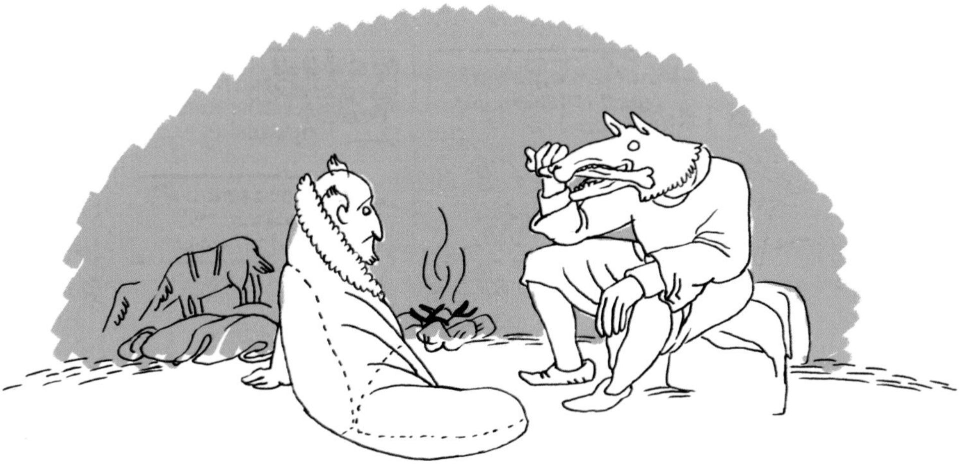

*It's not that he keeps track, but the fact is that this is not the first time Guglielmo has seen things that don't exist. This worries the Dominican from Tripoli.

**Guglielmo has never mentioned his visions to anybody. In fact, only a few years ago, he publicly mocked an old sexton, claiming the elder man was not quite right in the head.

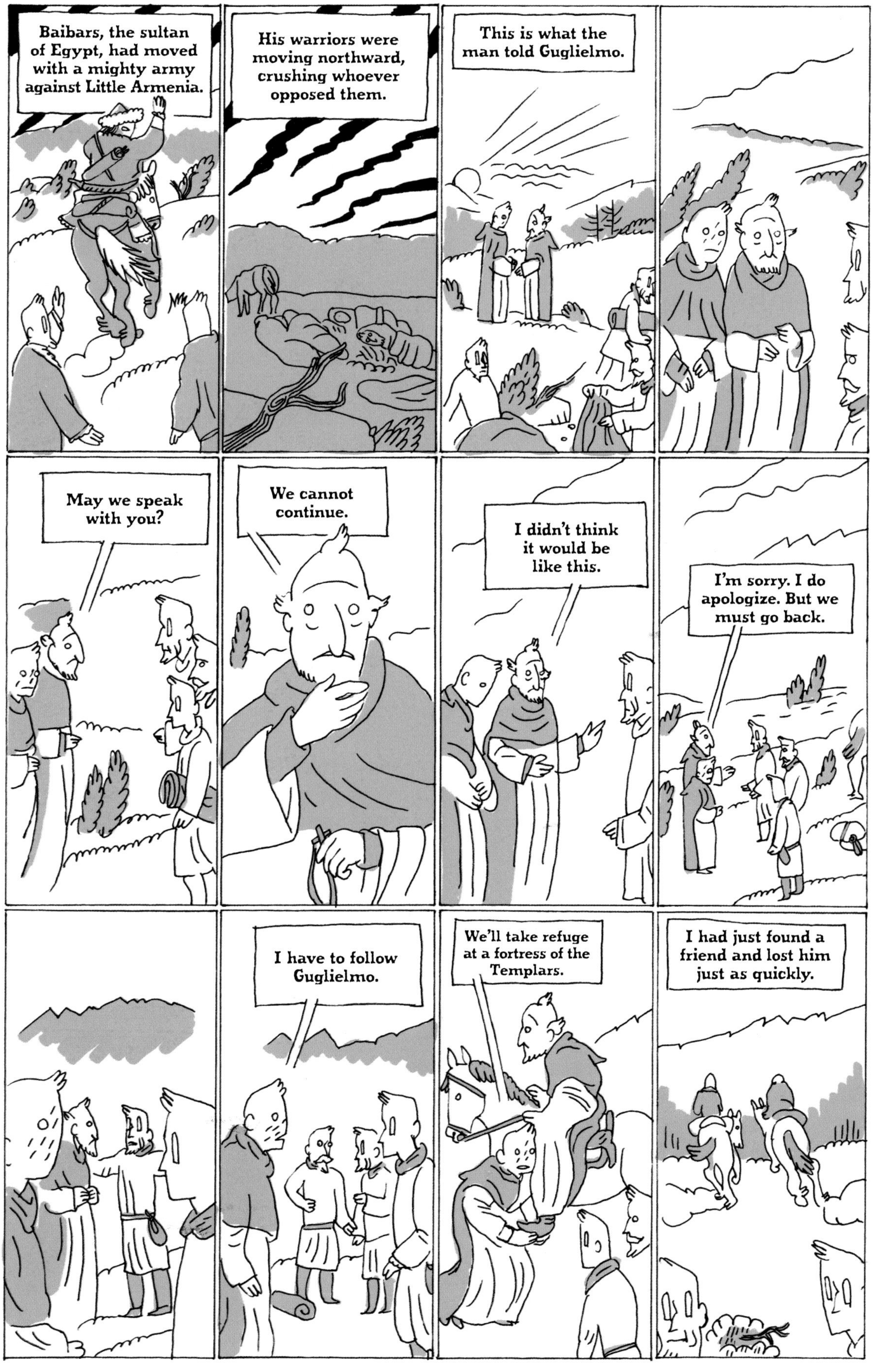
Baibars, the sultan of Egypt, had moved with a mighty army against Little Armenia.
His warriors were moving northward, crushing whoever opposed them.
This is what the man told Guglielmo.
May we speak with you?
We cannot continue.
I didn't think it would be like this.
I'm sorry. I do apologize. But we must go back.
I have to follow Guglielmo.
We'll take refuge at a fortress of the Templars.
I had just found a friend and lost him just as quickly.

Men at the ports would say that the Mongols learn to ride before walking.

They are deadly warriors. They do not fight covered in iron, like our soldiers. They bring with them only bows, arrows, and light swords.

Nothing can wear them down.

Riding days without stopping, through the wastelands and hot deserts, they get almost no sleep.

They eat little. Just meat and fermented milk from the horses.

When there is nothing to eat, a warrior opens the vein of his horse and drinks the blood.

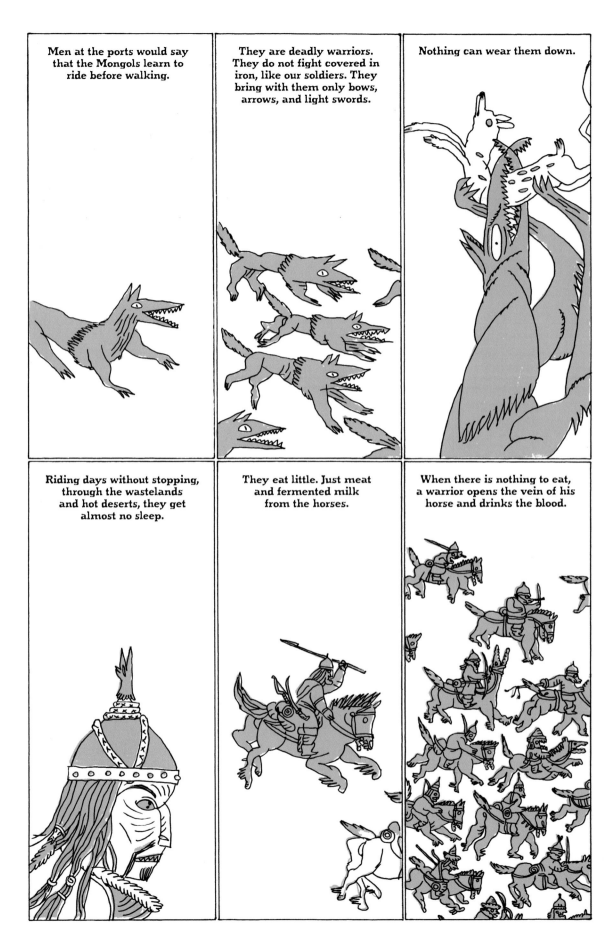

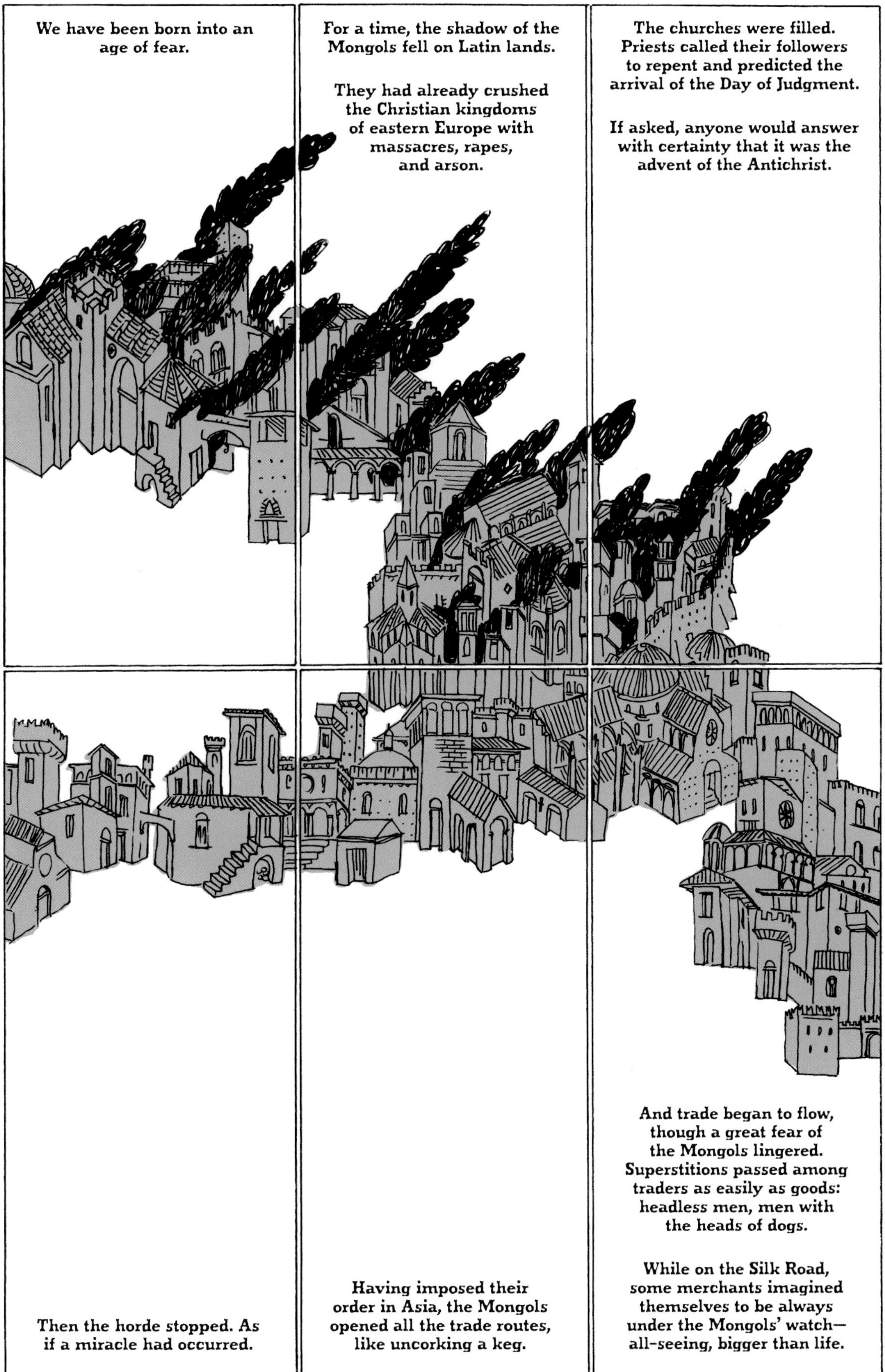
We have been born into an age of fear.
For a time, the shadow of the Mongols fell on Latin lands.
They had already crushed the Christian kingdoms of eastern Europe with massacres, rapes, and arson.
The churches were filled. Priests called their followers to repent and predicted the arrival of the Day of Judgment.
If asked, anyone would answer with certainty that it was the advent of the Antichrist.
Then the horde stopped. As if a miracle had occurred.
Having imposed their order in Asia, the Mongols opened all the trade routes, like uncorking a keg.
And trade began to flow, though a great fear of the Mongols lingered. Superstitions passed among traders as easily as goods: headless men, men with the heads of dogs.
While on the Silk Road, some merchants imagined themselves to be always under the Mongols' watch—all-seeing, bigger than life.

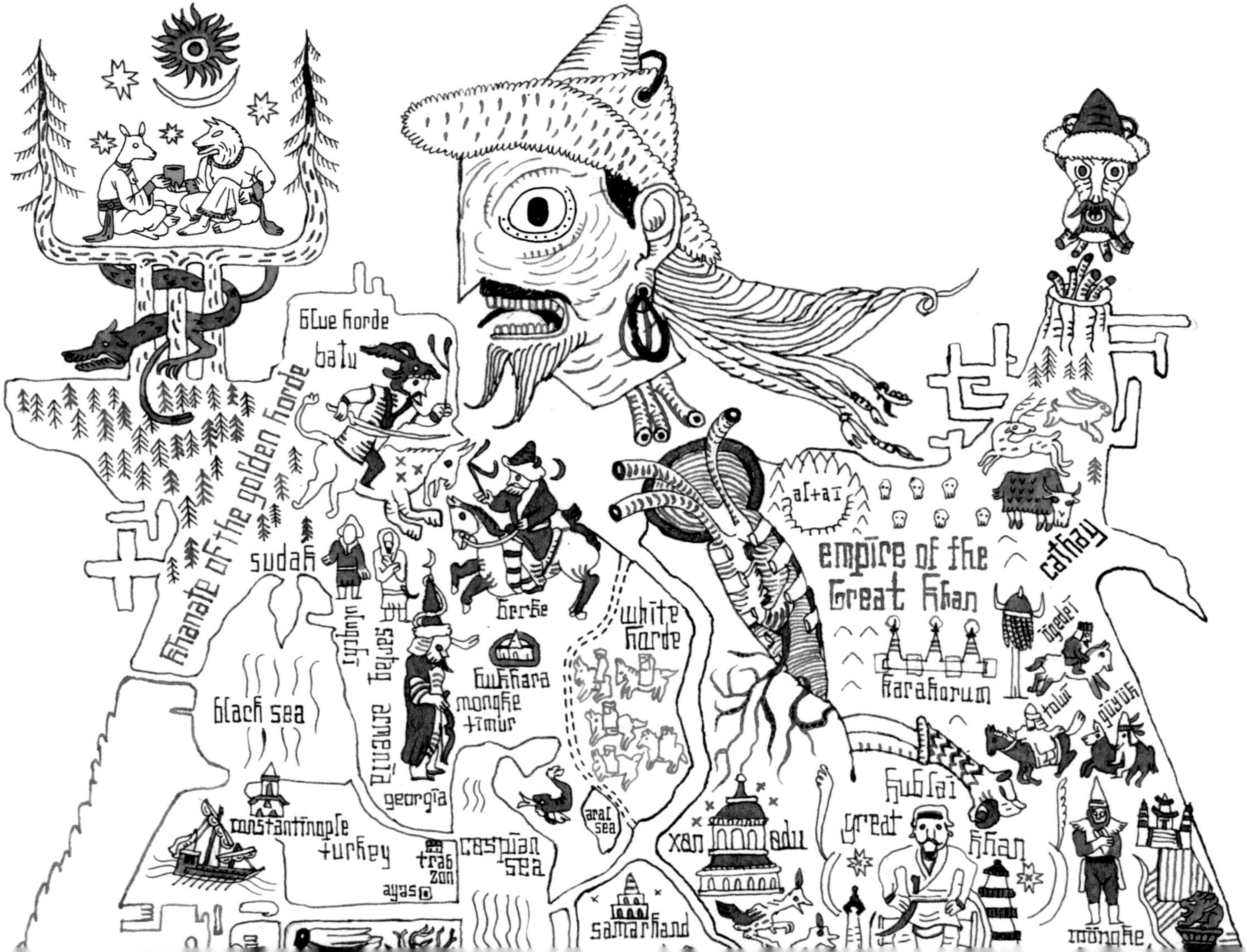
blue horde
batu
khanate of the golden horde
sudak
ulughchi
sartaq
berke
white horde
bukhara
monghe timur
black sea
armenia
georgia
constantinople
turkey
trab zon
ayas
caspian sea
aral sea
samarkand
altai
empire of the Great Khan
cathay
ögedei
karakorum
tolui
güyük
kublai
great khan
xan adu
mönghe

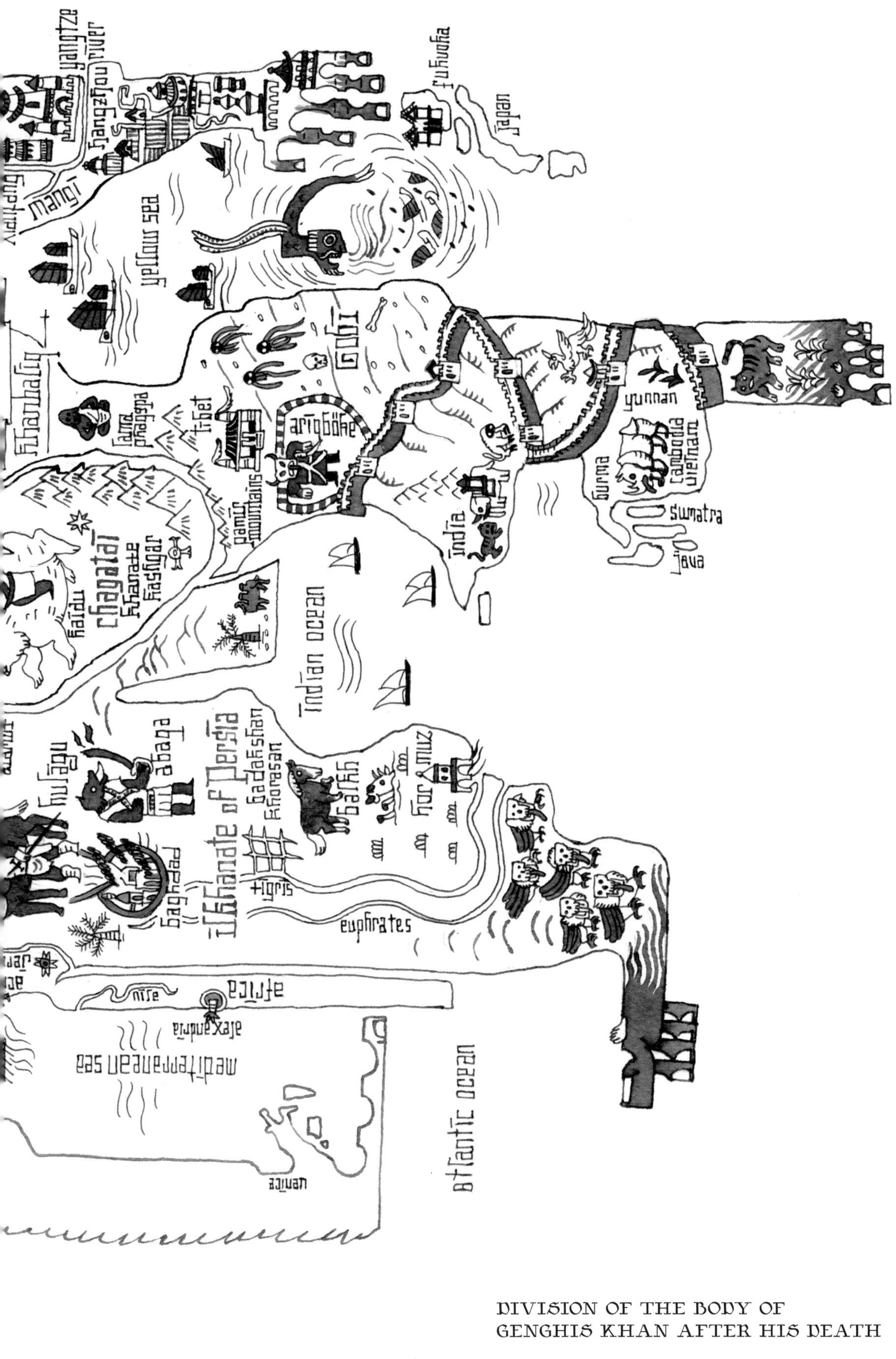
yangtze river
hangzhou
mangi
yellow sea
fukuoka
japan
khanbaliq
gobi
arigböke
tibet
lama phagspa
pamir mountains
india
yunnan
burma
cambodia
vietnam
sumatra
java
chagatai khanate
kashgar
kaidu
indian ocean
ilkhanate of persia
badakshan
khorasan
balkh
hormuz
hulagu
abaqa
baghdad
tigris
euphrates
africa
nile
alexandria
mediterranean sea
venice
atlantic ocean

DIVISION OF THE BODY OF
GENGHIS KHAN AFTER HIS DEATH

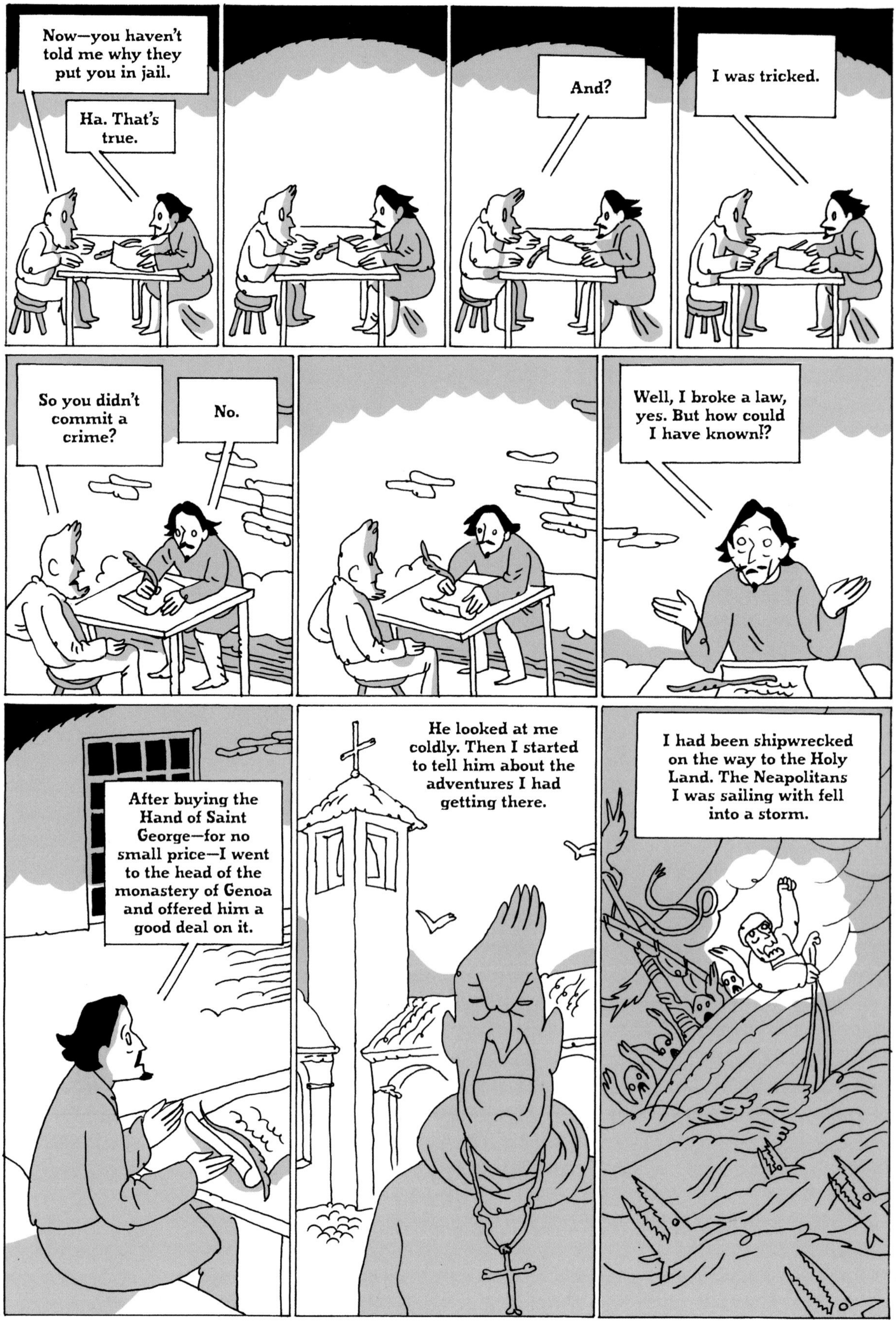

Now—you haven't told me why they put you in jail.
Ha. That's true.
And?
I was tricked.
So you didn't commit a crime?
No.
Well, I broke a law, yes. But how could I have known!?
After buying the Hand of Saint George—for no small price—I went to the head of the monastery of Genoa and offered him a good deal on it.
He looked at me coldly. Then I started to tell him about the adventures I had getting there.
I had been shipwrecked on the way to the Holy Land. The Neapolitans I was sailing with fell into a storm.

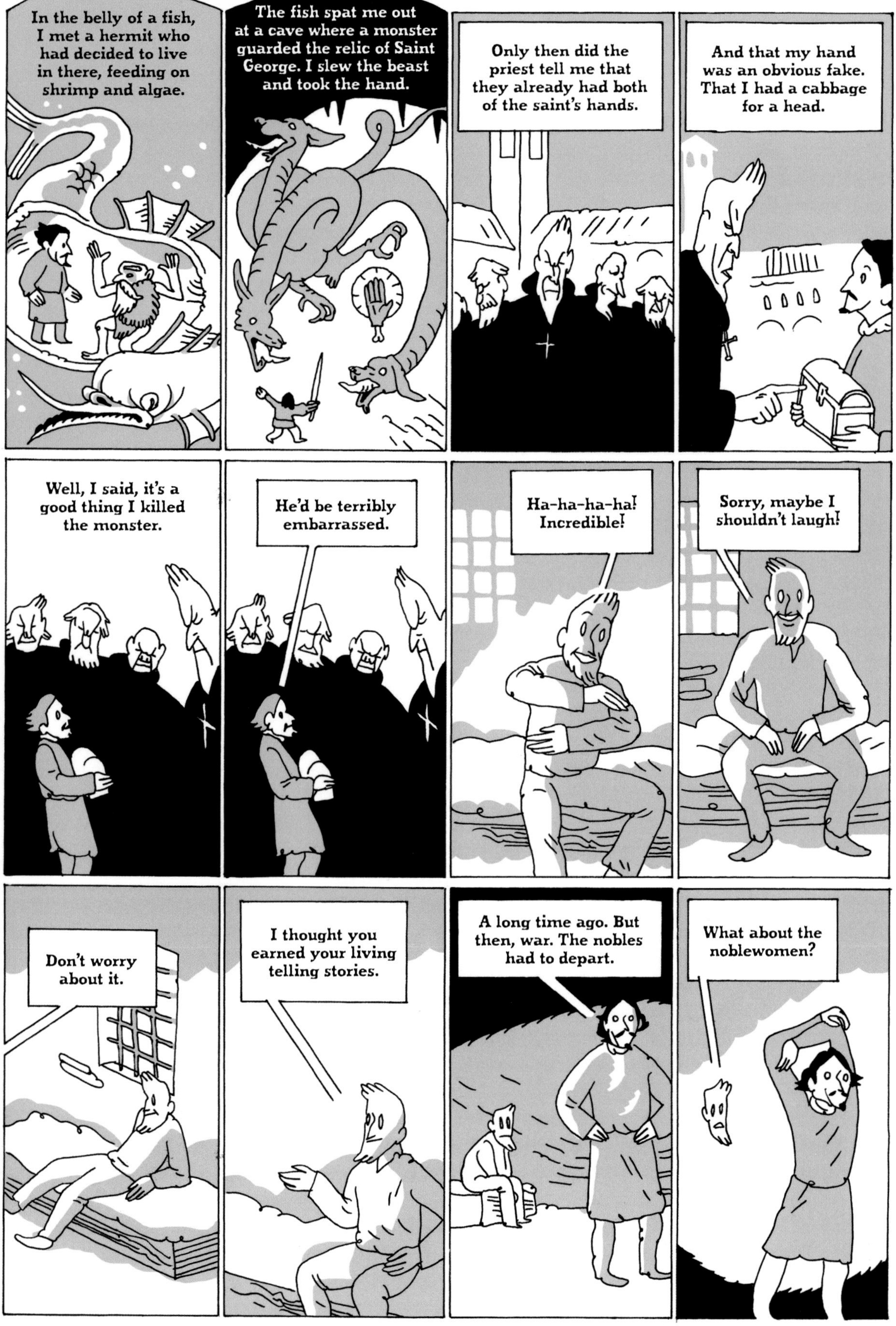
In the belly of a fish, I met a hermit who had decided to live in there, feeding on shrimp and algae.
The fish spat me out at a cave where a monster guarded the relic of Saint George. I slew the beast and took the hand.
Only then did the priest tell me that they already had both of the saint's hands.
And that my hand was an obvious fake. That I had a cabbage for a head.
Well, I said, it's a good thing I killed the monster.
He'd be terribly embarrassed.
Ha-ha-ha-ha! Incredible!
Sorry, maybe I shouldn't laugh!
Don't worry about it.
I thought you earned your living telling stories.
A long time ago. But then, war. The nobles had to depart.
What about the noblewomen?

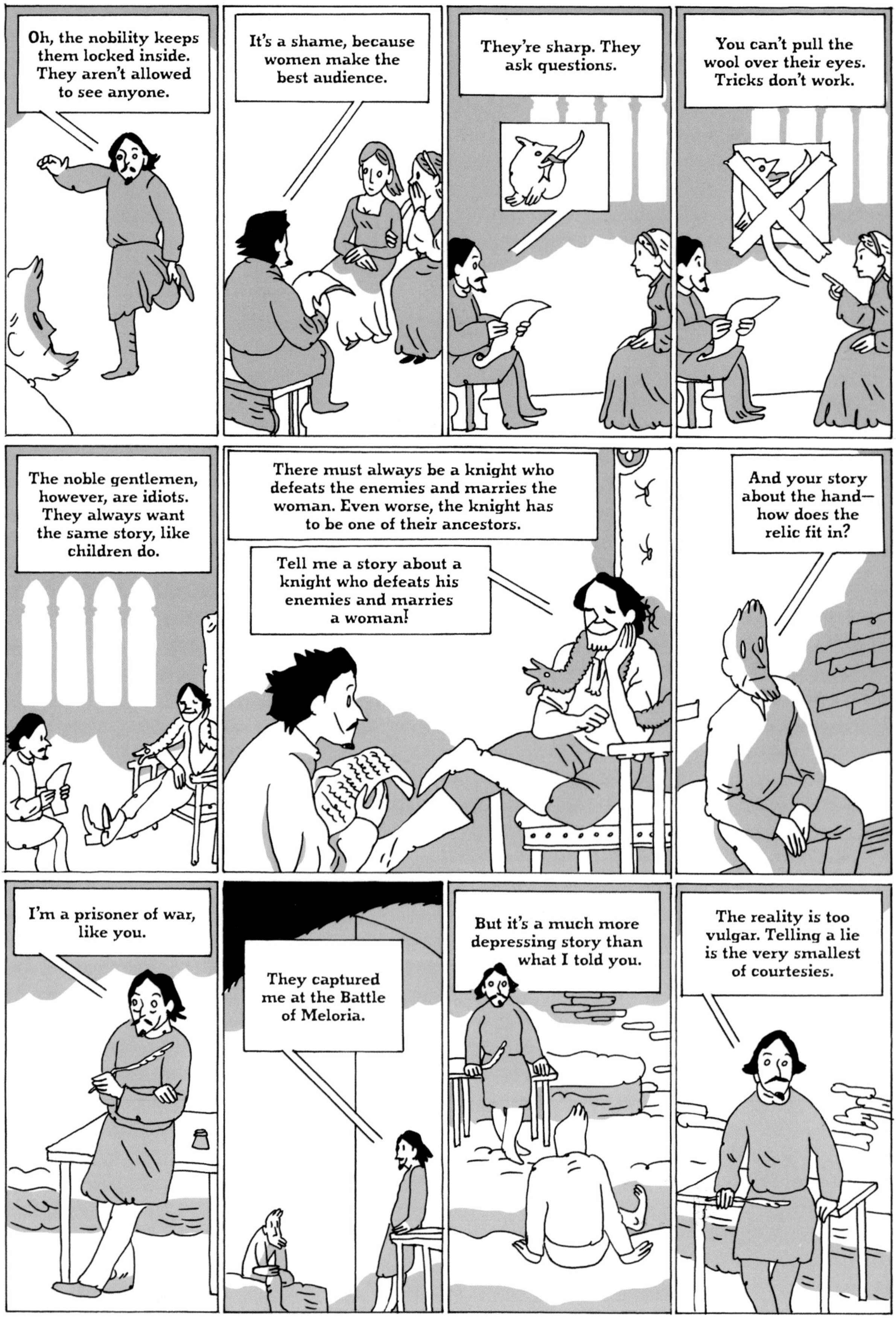
Oh, the nobility keeps them locked inside. They aren't allowed to see anyone.
It's a shame, because women make the best audience.
They're sharp. They ask questions.
You can't pull the wool over their eyes. Tricks don't work.
The noble gentlemen, however, are idiots. They always want the same story, like children do.
There must always be a knight who defeats the enemies and marries the woman. Even worse, the knight has to be one of their ancestors.
Tell me a story about a knight who defeats his enemies and marries a woman!
And your story about the hand—how does the relic fit in?
I'm a prisoner of war, like you.
They captured me at the Battle of Meloria.
But it's a much more depressing story than what I told you.
The reality is too vulgar. Telling a lie is the very smallest of courtesies.

ARMENIA

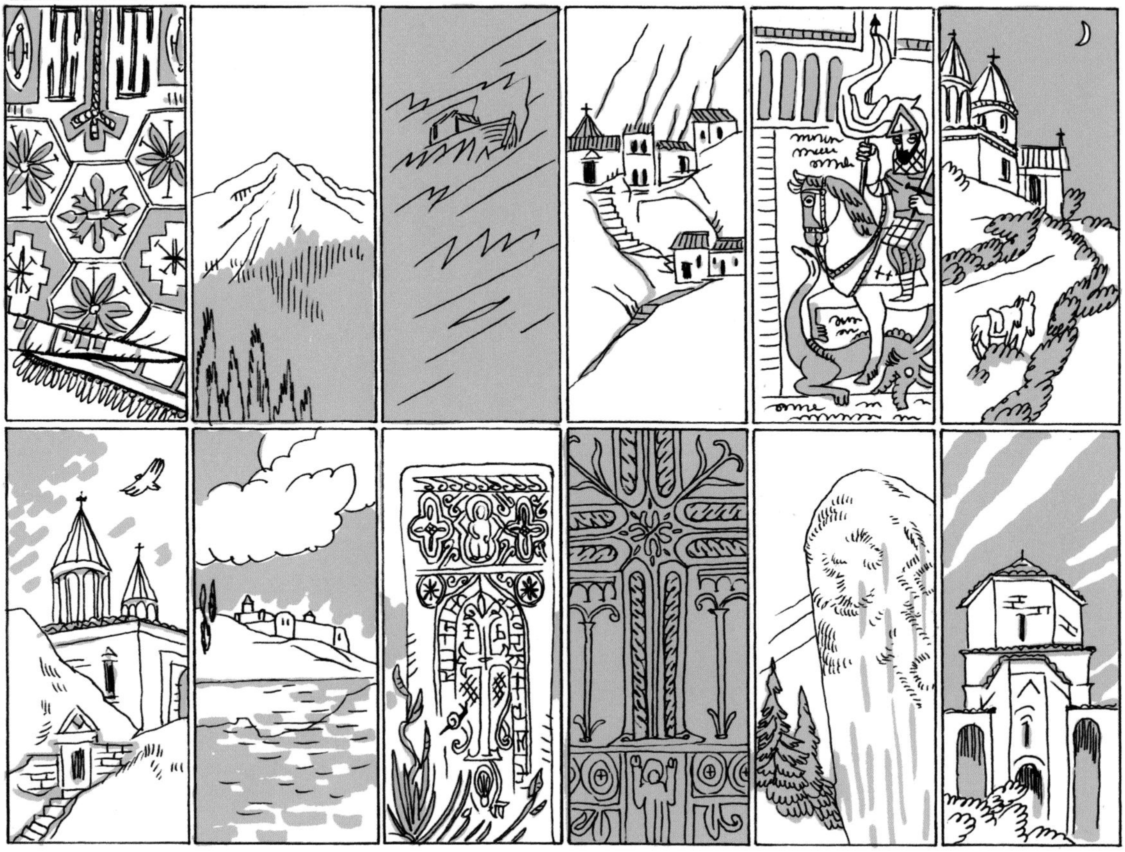

GEORGIA MOSUL

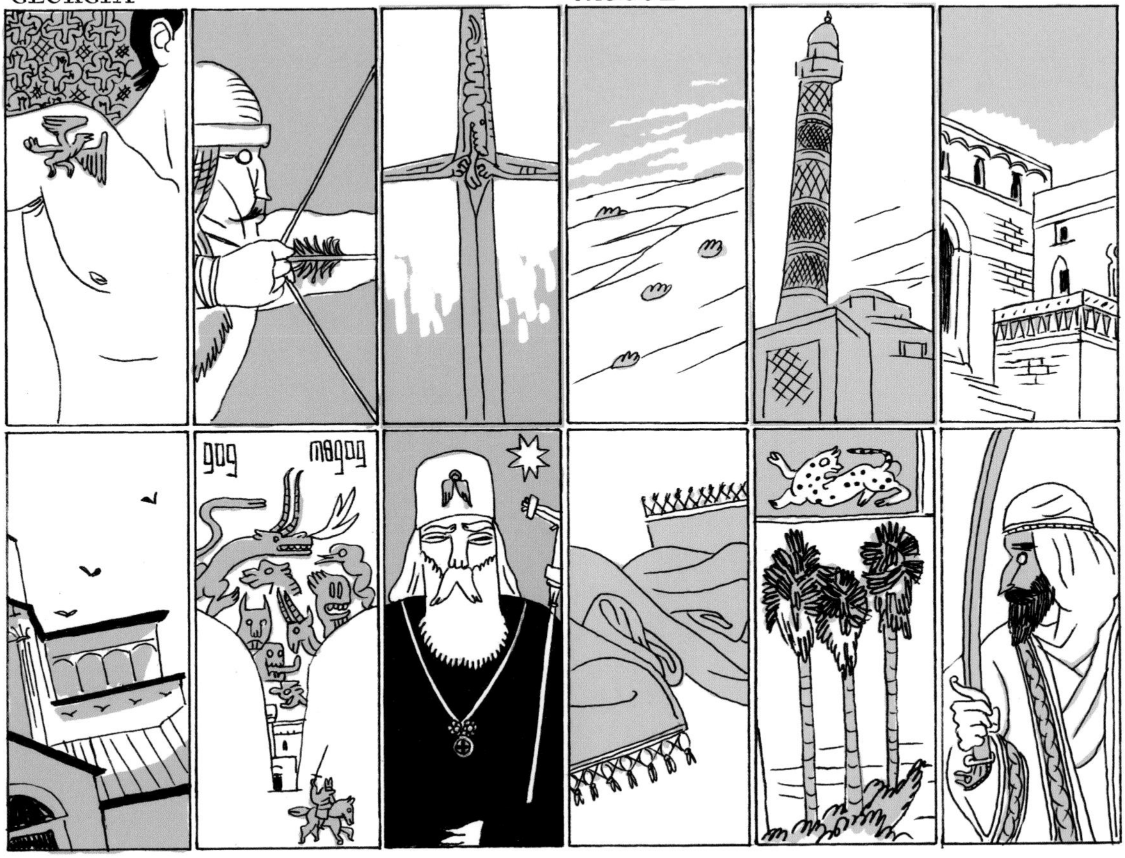
gog
magog

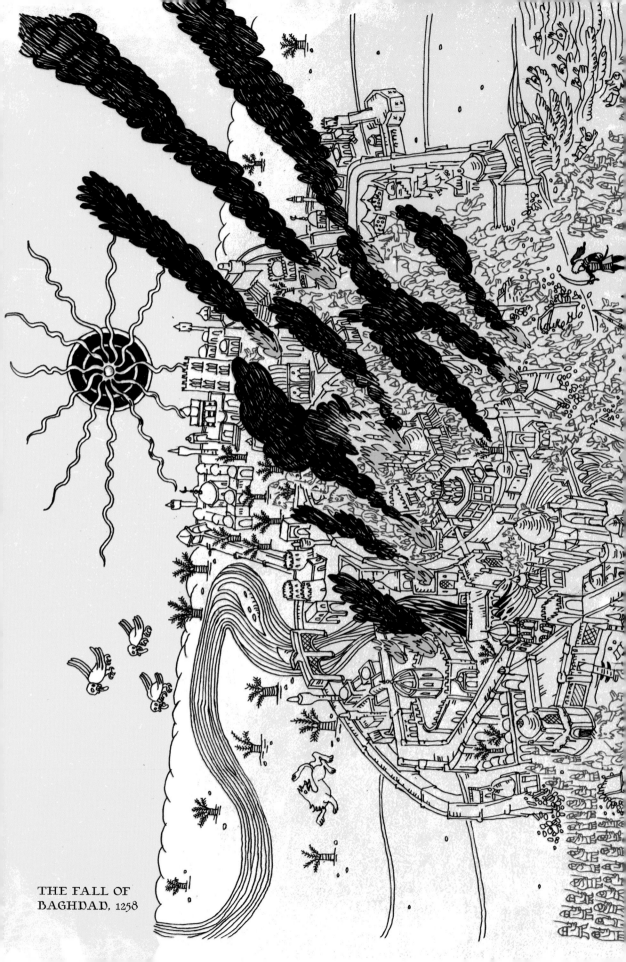

THE FALL OF
BAGHDAD, 1258

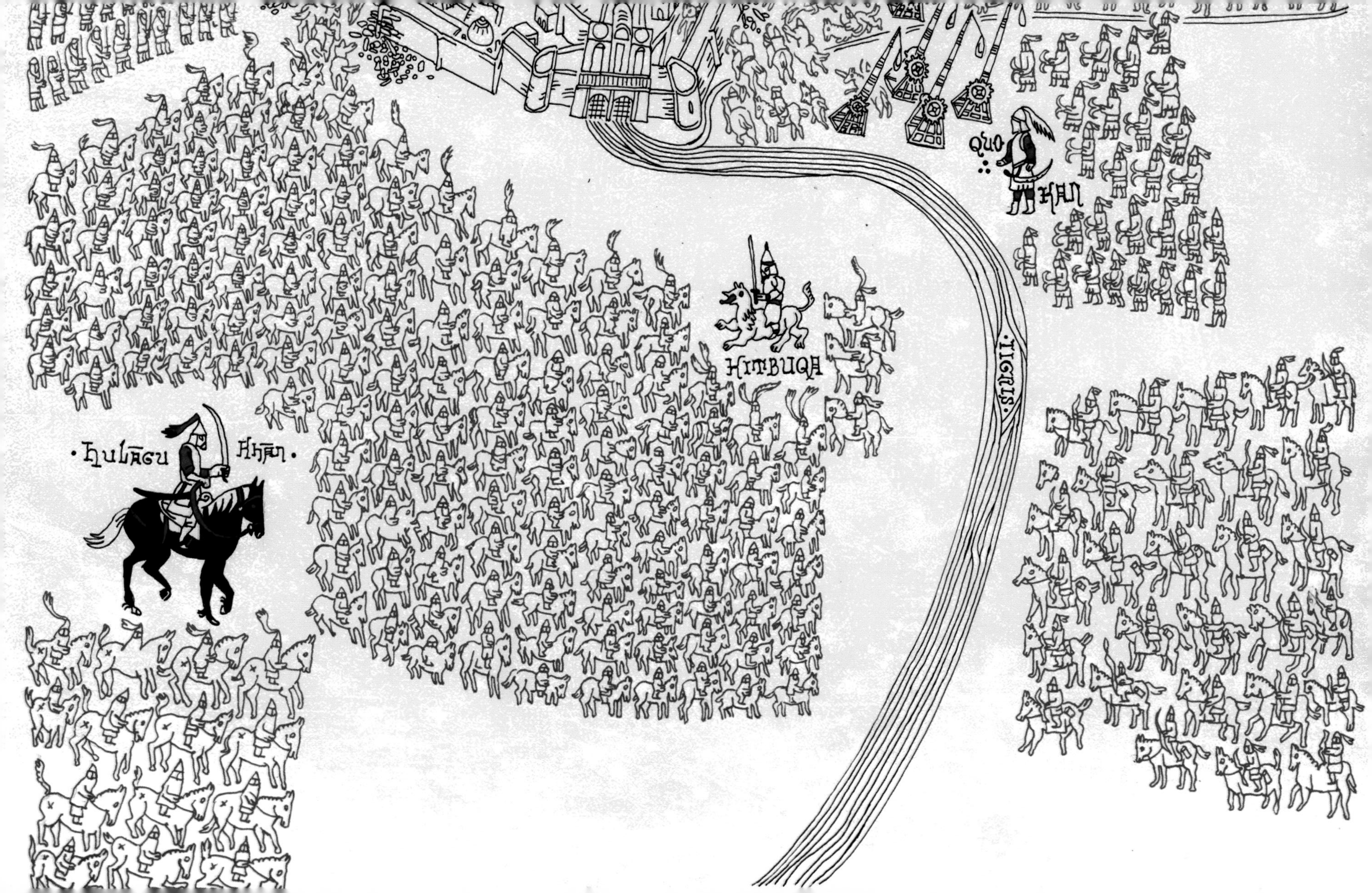
QUO: KAN
·TIGRIS·
KITBUQA
·HULAGU KHAN·

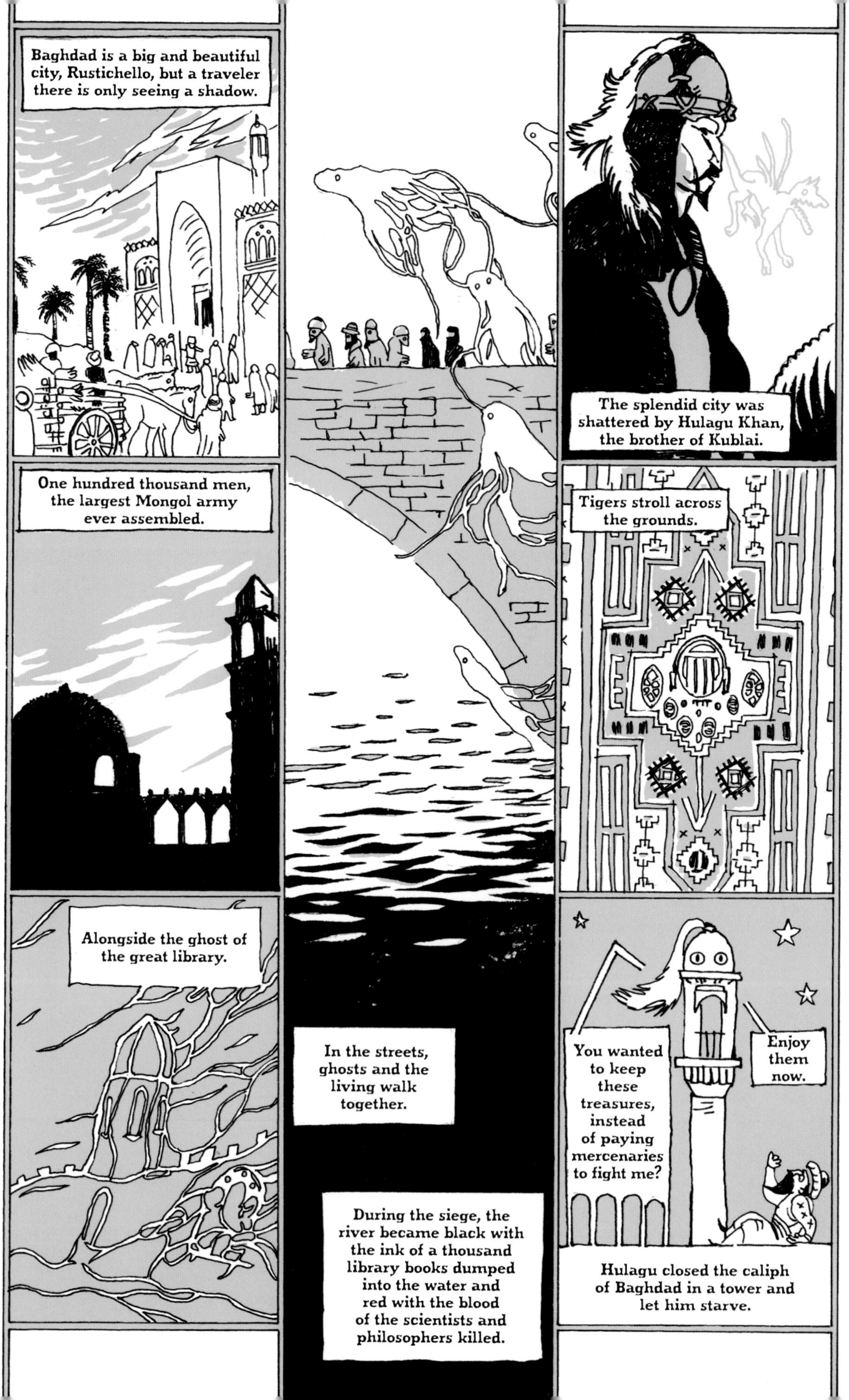
Baghdad is a big and beautiful city, Rustichello, but a traveler there is only seeing a shadow.
One hundred thousand men, the largest Mongol army ever assembled.
Alongside the ghost of the great library.
In the streets, ghosts and the living walk together.
During the siege, the river became black with the ink of a thousand library books dumped into the water and red with the blood of the scientists and philosophers killed.
The splendid city was shattered by Hulagu Khan, the brother of Kublai.
Tigers stroll across the grounds.
You wanted to keep these treasures, instead of paying mercenaries to fight me?
Enjoy them now.
Hulagu closed the caliph of Baghdad in a tower and let him starve.

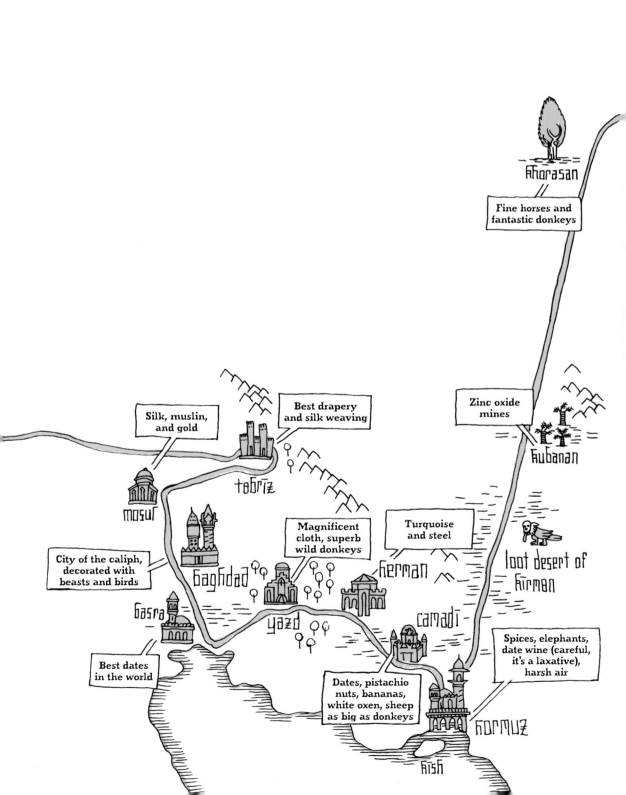

Ahorasan

Fine horses and
fantastic donkeys

Zinc oxide
mines

Silk, muslin,
and gold

Best drapery
and silk weaving

Kubanan

tebriz

Magnificent
cloth, superb
wild donkeys

Turquoise
and steel

loot desert of
Kirman

mosul

City of the caliph,
decorated with
beasts and birds

Baghdad

Kerman

basra

yazd

camadi

Spices, elephants,
date wine (careful,
it's a laxative),
harsh air

Best dates
in the world

Dates, pistachio
nuts, bananas,
white oxen, sheep
as big as donkeys

hormuz

kish

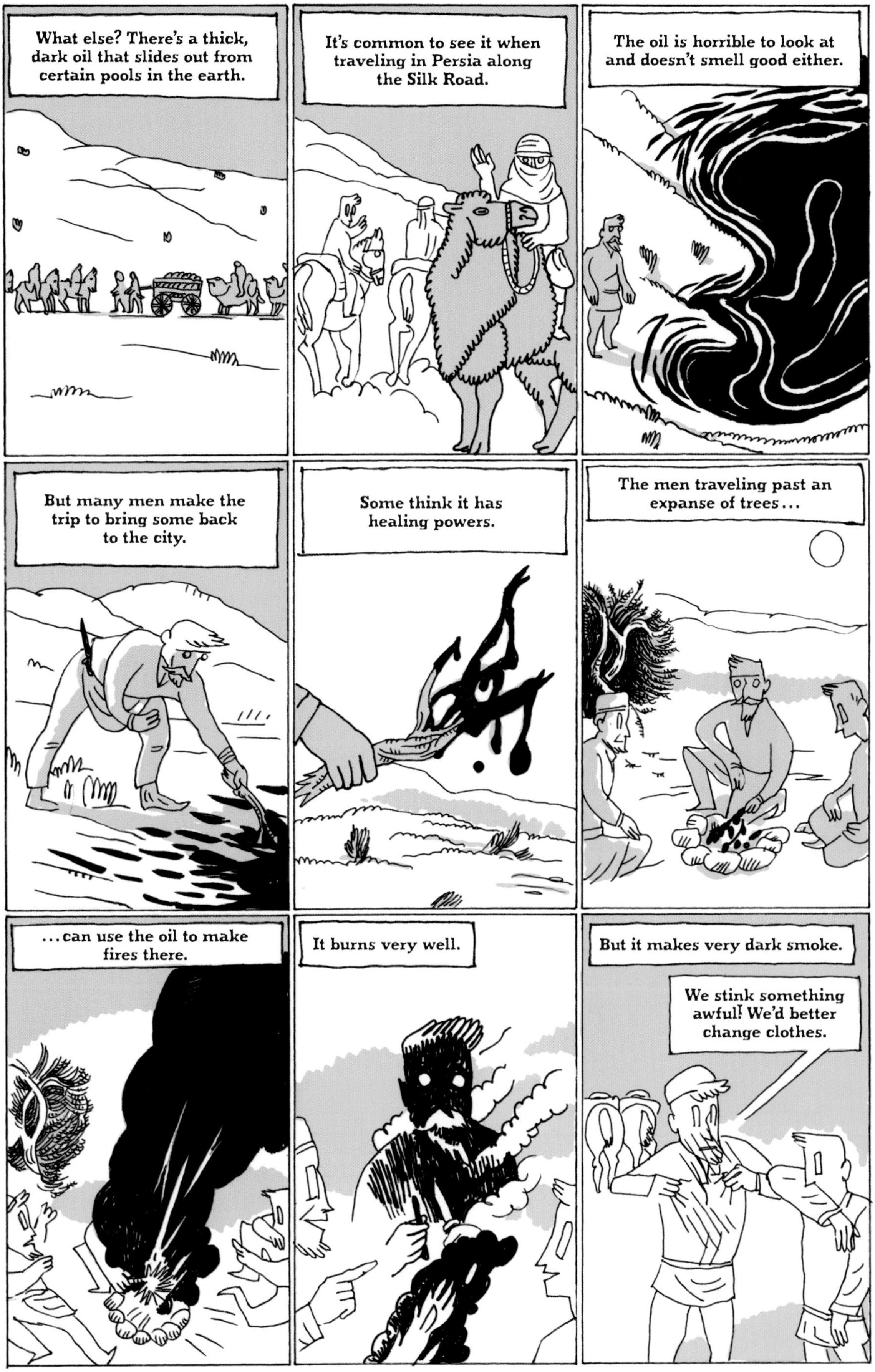
What else? There's a thick, dark oil that slides out from certain pools in the earth.
It's common to see it when traveling in Persia along the Silk Road.
The oil is horrible to look at and doesn't smell good either.
But many men make the trip to bring some back to the city.
Some think it has healing powers.
The men traveling past an expanse of trees...
...can use the oil to make fires there.
It burns very well.
But it makes very dark smoke.
We stink something awful! We'd better change clothes.

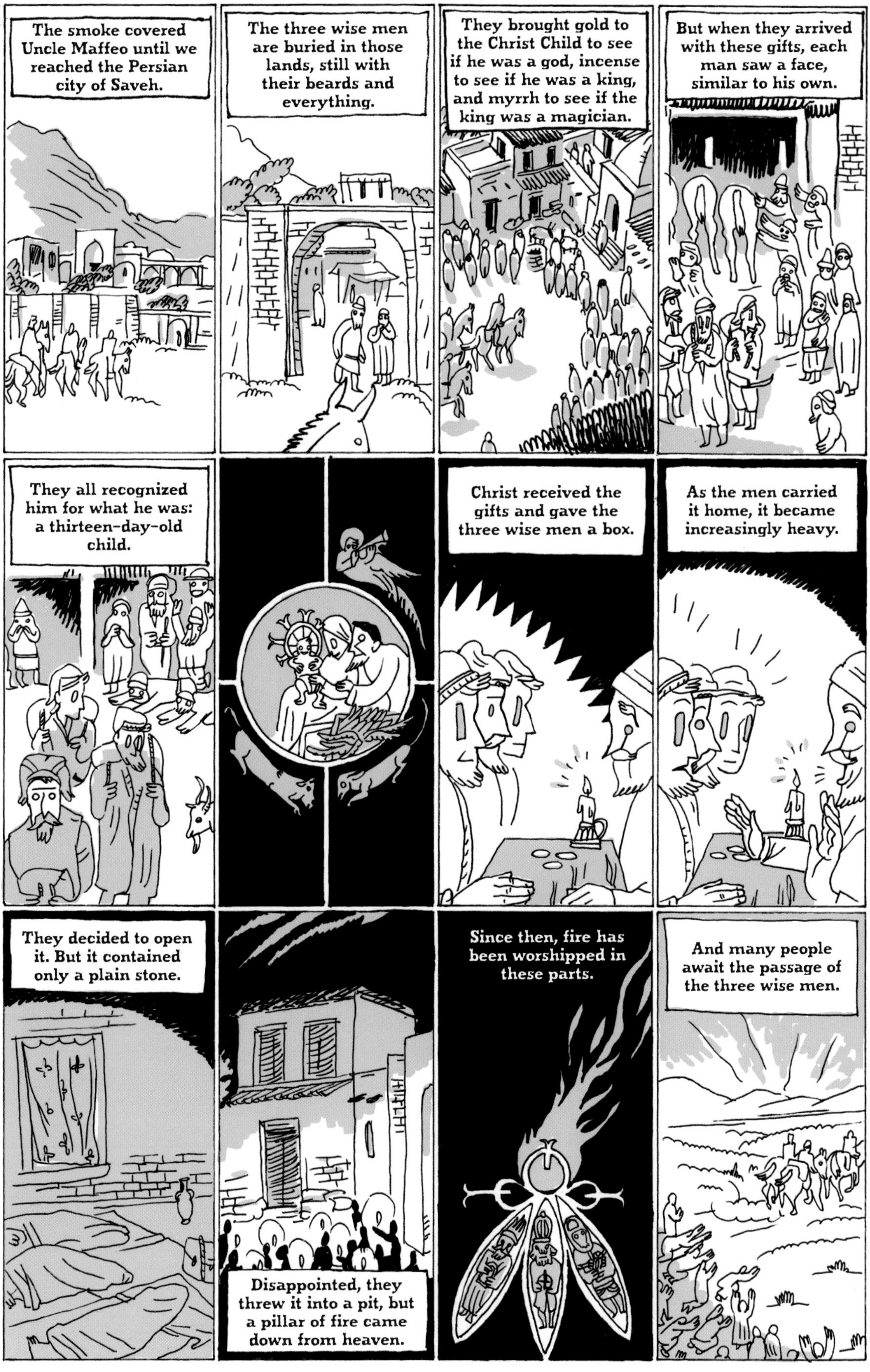
The smoke covered Uncle Maffeo until we reached the Persian city of Saveh.
The three wise men are buried in those lands, still with their beards and everything.
They brought gold to the Christ Child to see if he was a god, incense to see if he was a king, and myrrh to see if the king was a magician.
But when they arrived with these gifts, each man saw a face, similar to his own.
They all recognized him for what he was: a thirteen-day-old child.
Christ received the gifts and gave the three wise men a box.
As the men carried it home, it became increasingly heavy.
They decided to open it. But it contained only a plain stone.
Disappointed, they threw it into a pit, but a pillar of fire came down from heaven.
Since then, fire has been worshipped in these parts.
And many people await the passage of the three wise men.

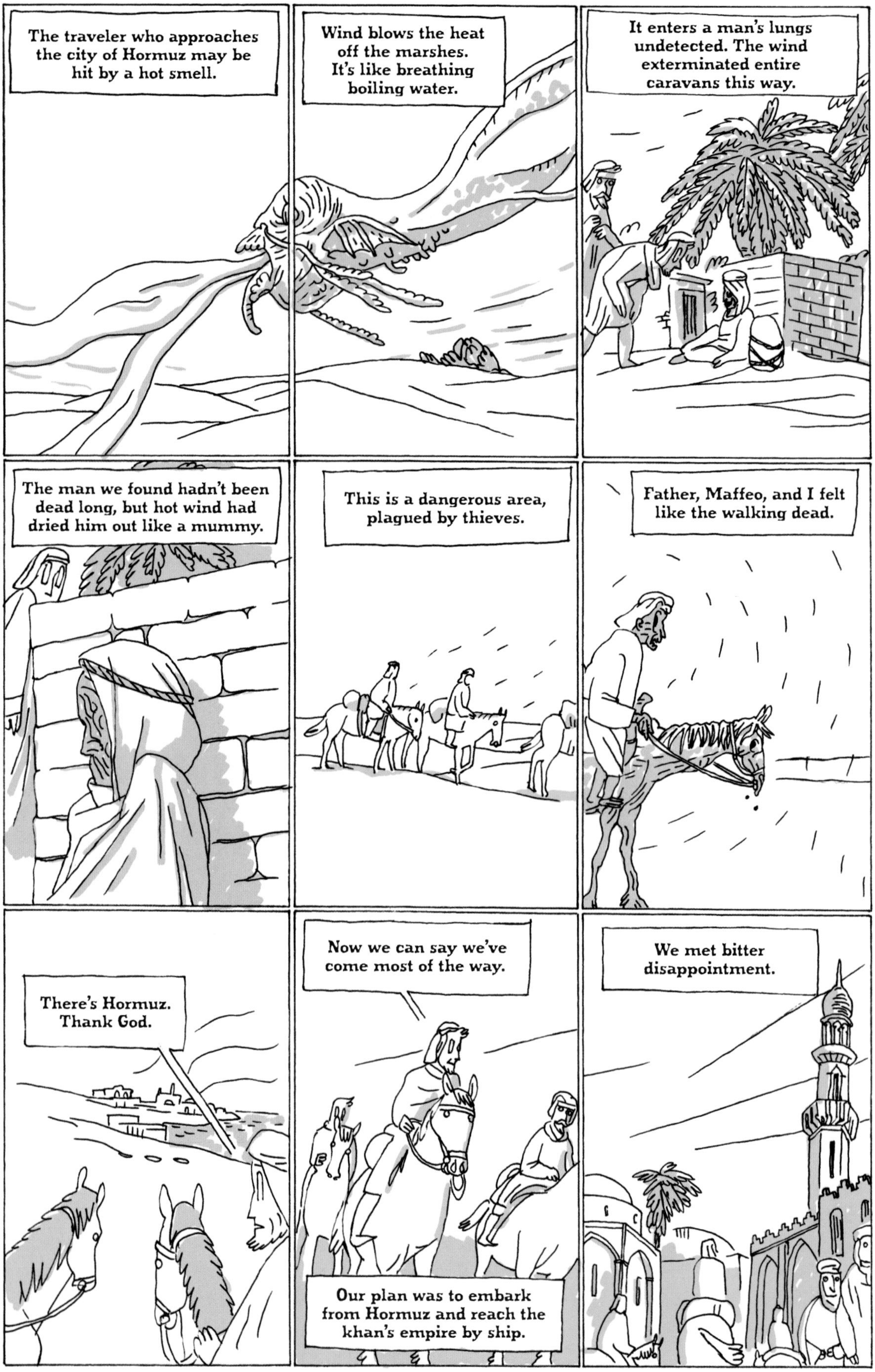
The traveler who approaches the city of Hormuz may be hit by a hot smell.
Wind blows the heat off the marshes. It's like breathing boiling water.
It enters a man's lungs undetected. The wind exterminated entire caravans this way.
The man we found hadn't been dead long, but hot wind had dried him out like a mummy.
This is a dangerous area, plagued by thieves.
Father, Maffeo, and I felt like the walking dead.
There's Hormuz. Thank God.
Now we can say we've come most of the way.
Our plan was to embark from Hormuz and reach the khan's empire by ship.
We met bitter disappointment.

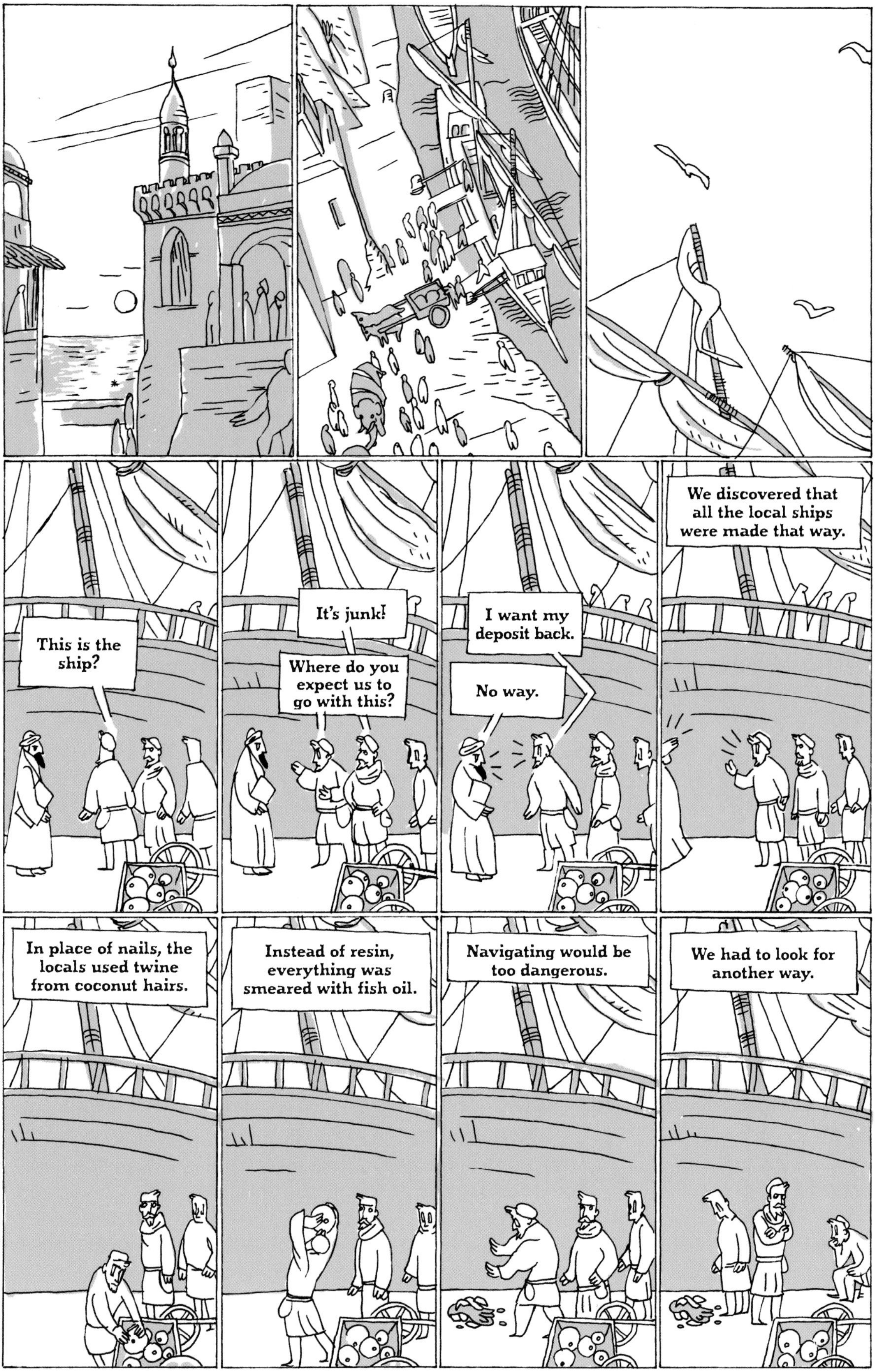
This is the ship?
It's junk!
Where do you expect us to go with this?
I want my deposit back.
No way.
We discovered that all the local ships were made that way.
In place of nails, the locals used twine from coconut hairs.
Instead of resin, everything was smeared with fish oil.
Navigating would be too dangerous.
We had to look for another way.

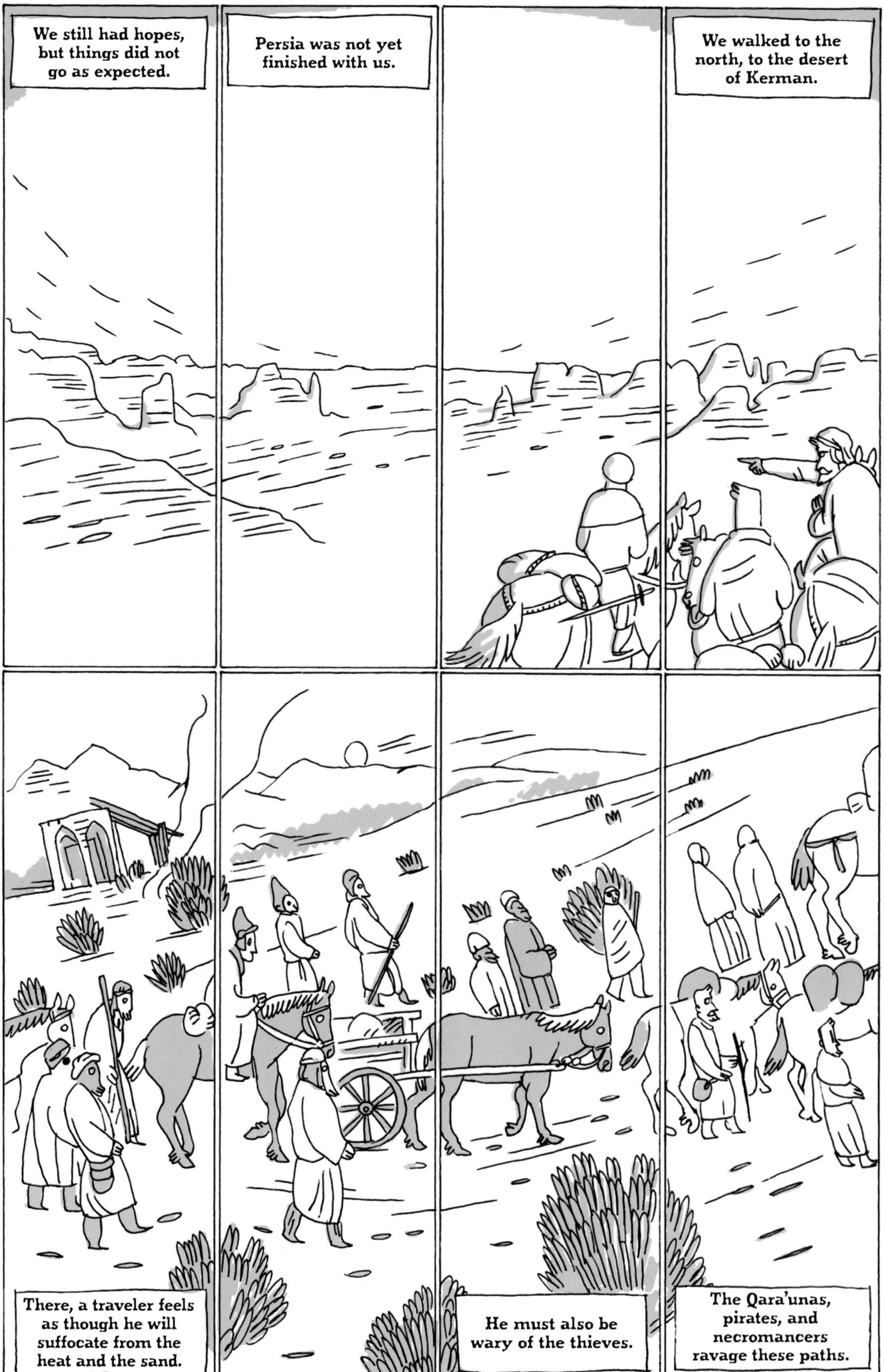
We still had hopes, but things did not go as expected.
Persia was not yet finished with us.
We walked to the north, to the desert of Kerman.
There, a traveler feels as though he will suffocate from the heat and the sand.
He must also be wary of the thieves.
The Qara'unas, pirates, and necromancers ravage these paths.

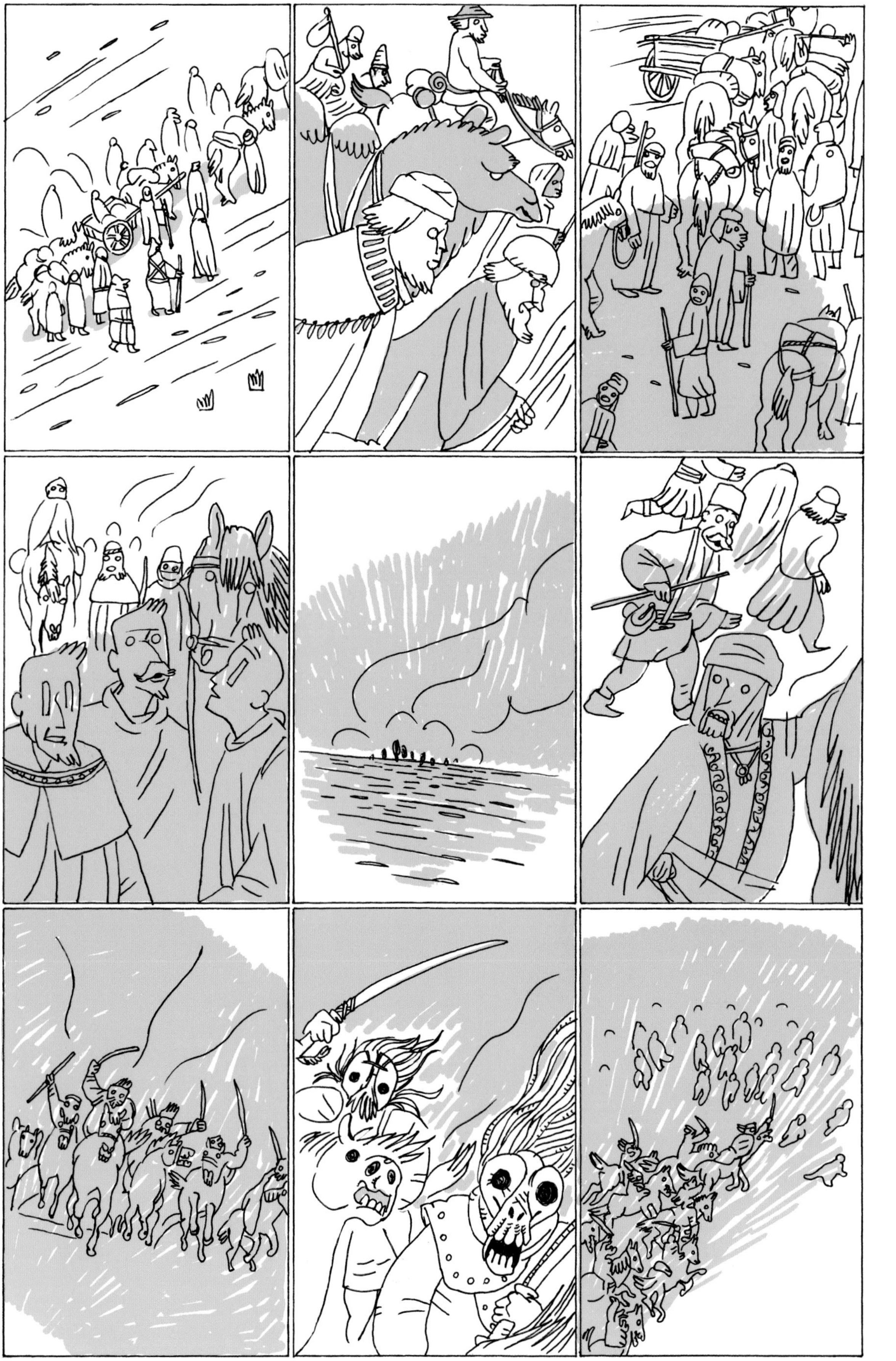

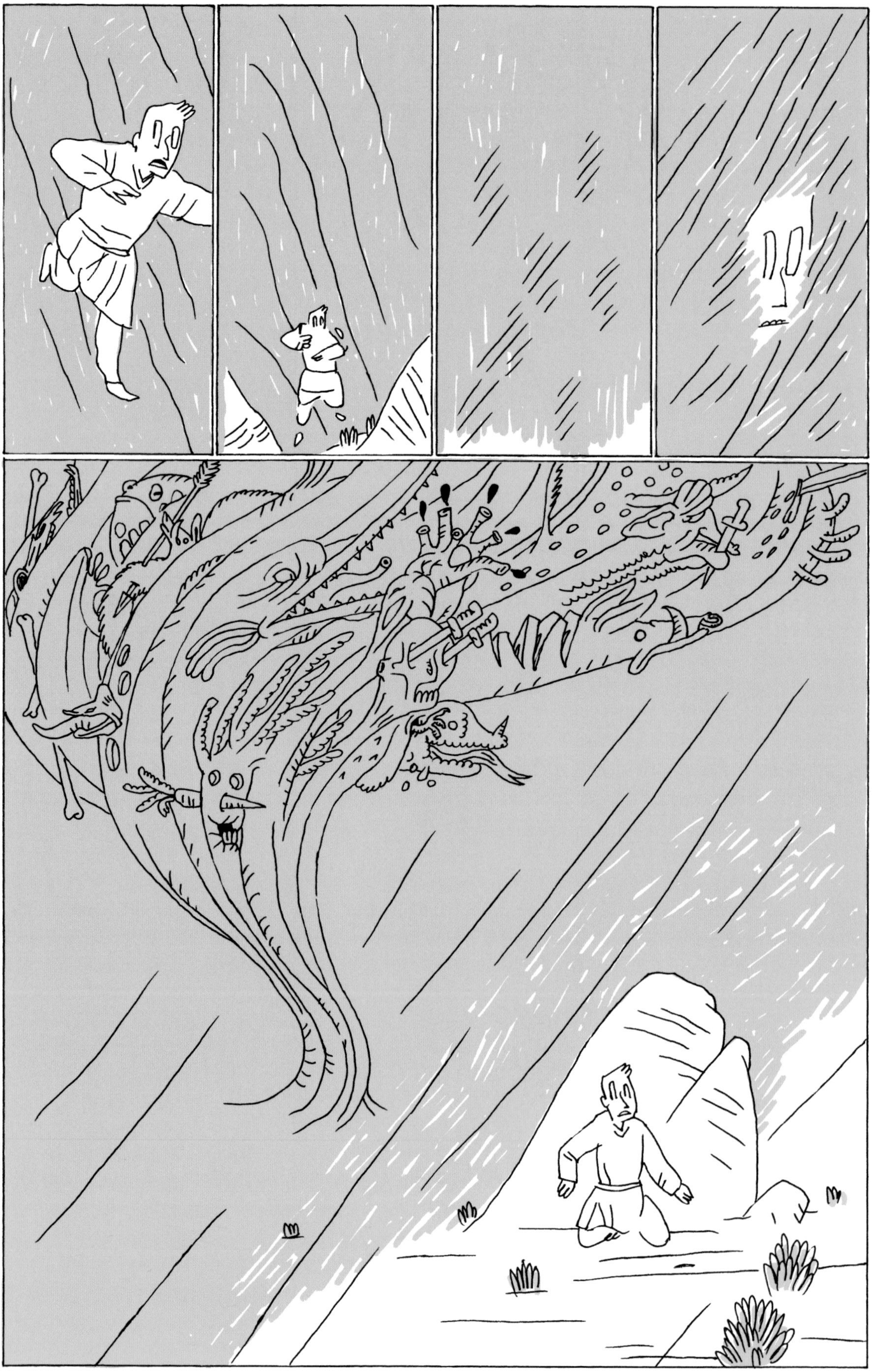

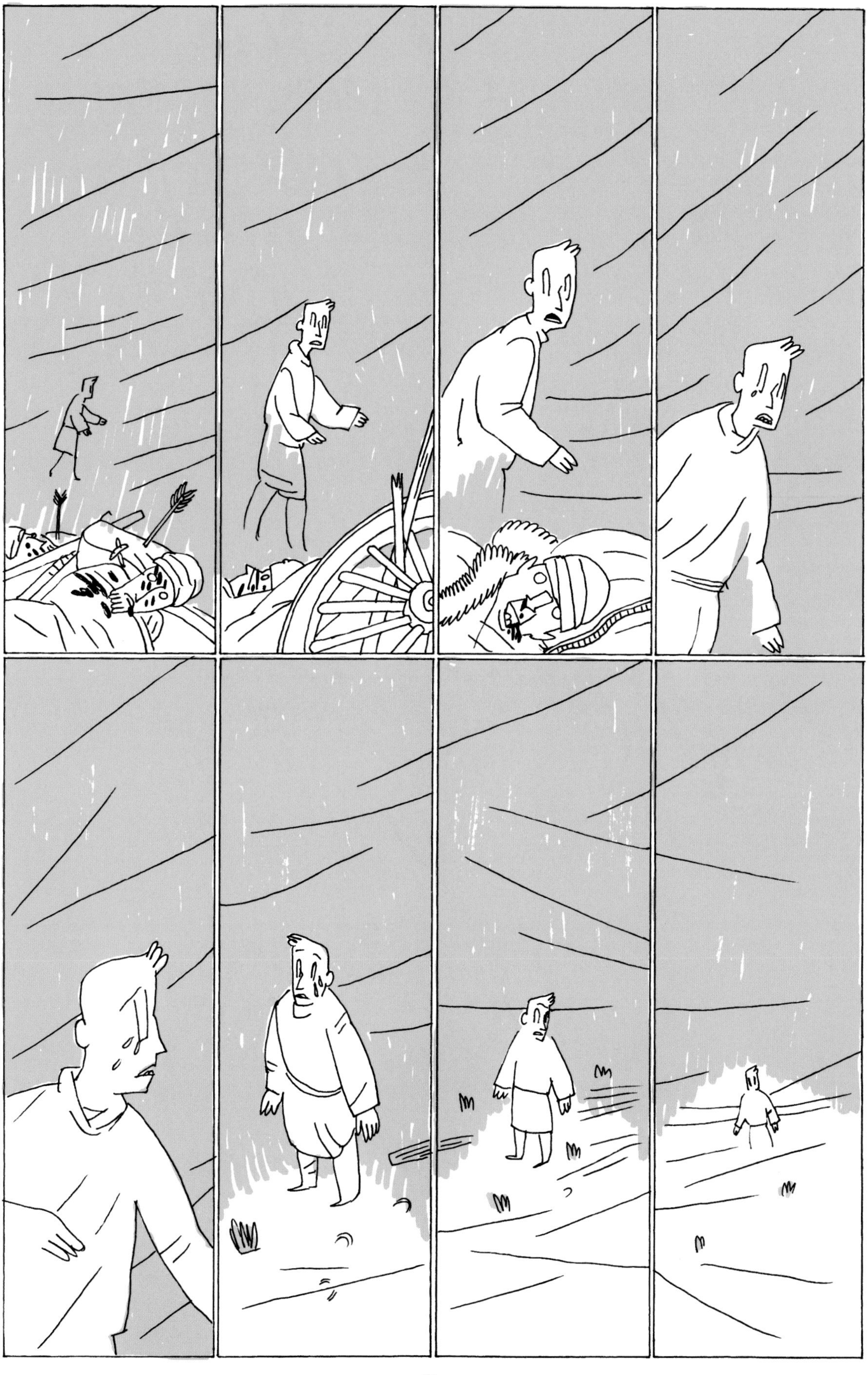

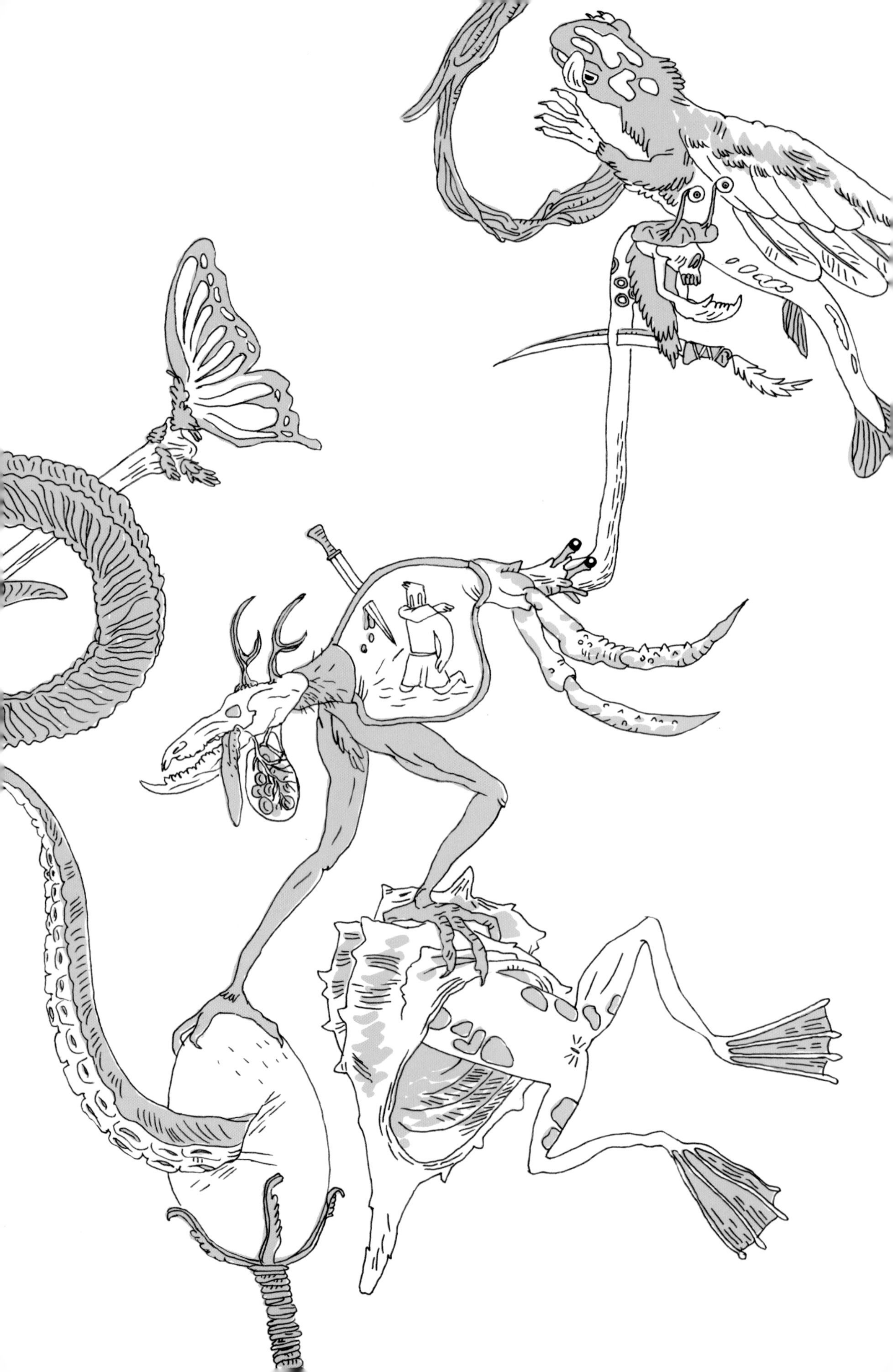

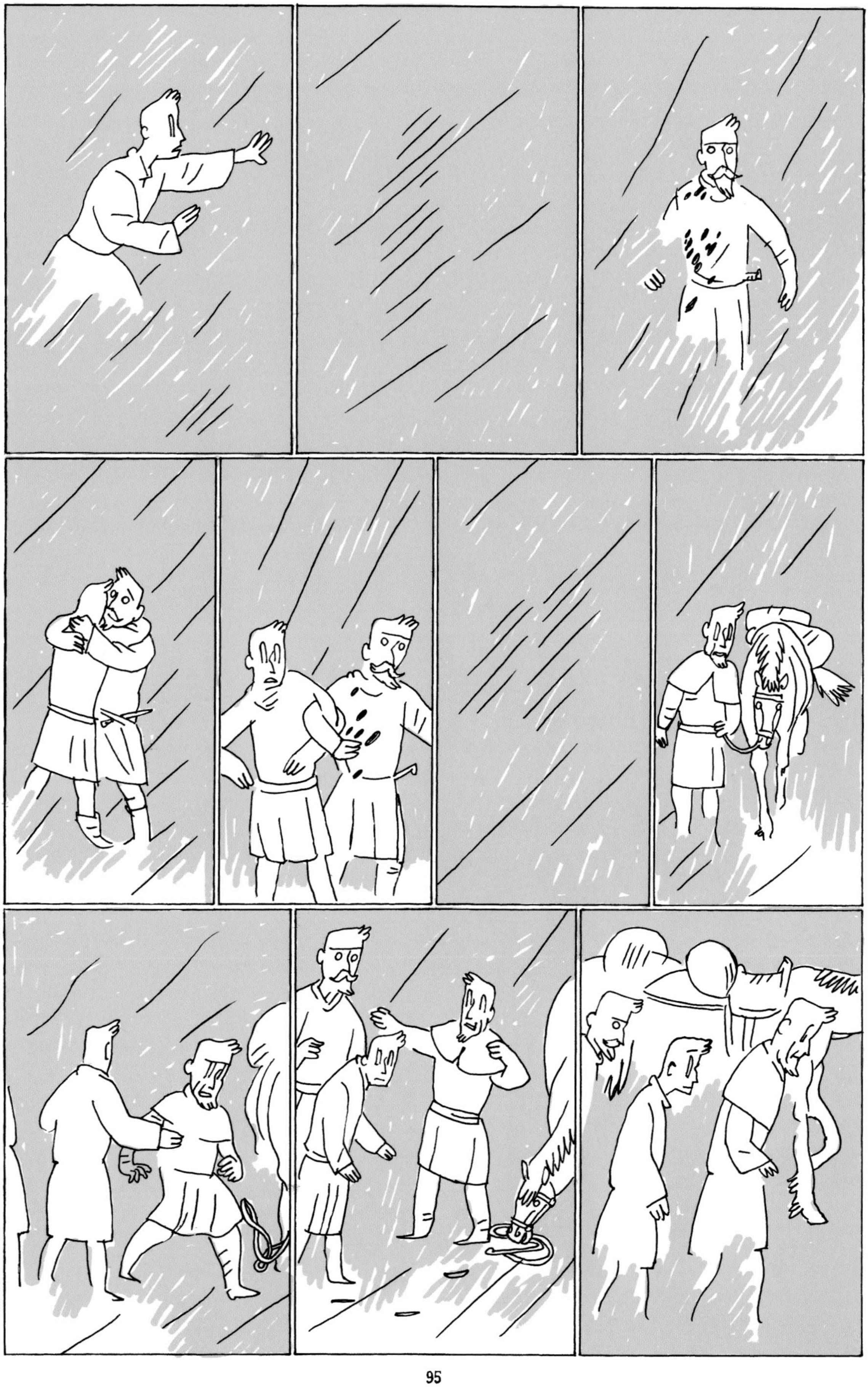

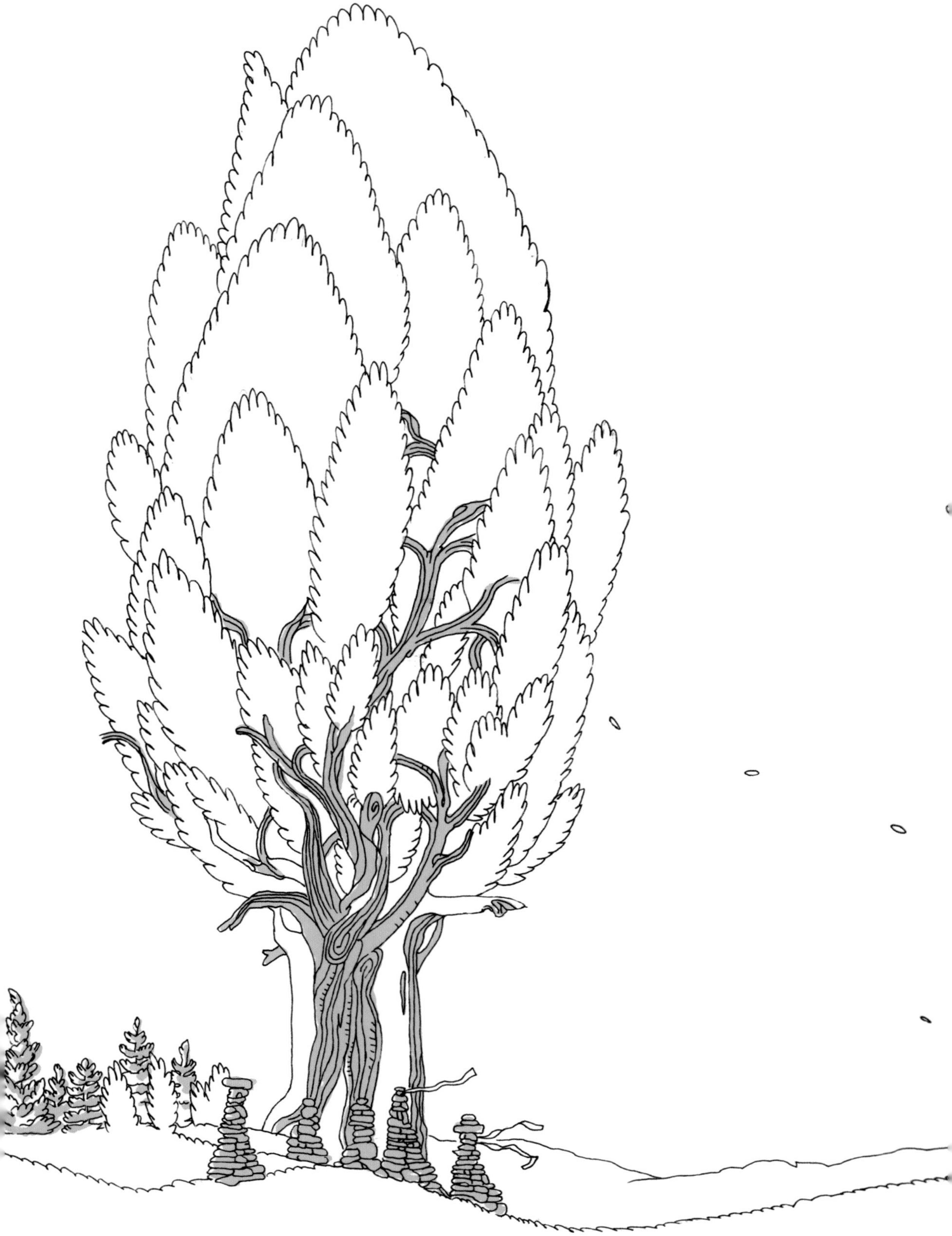

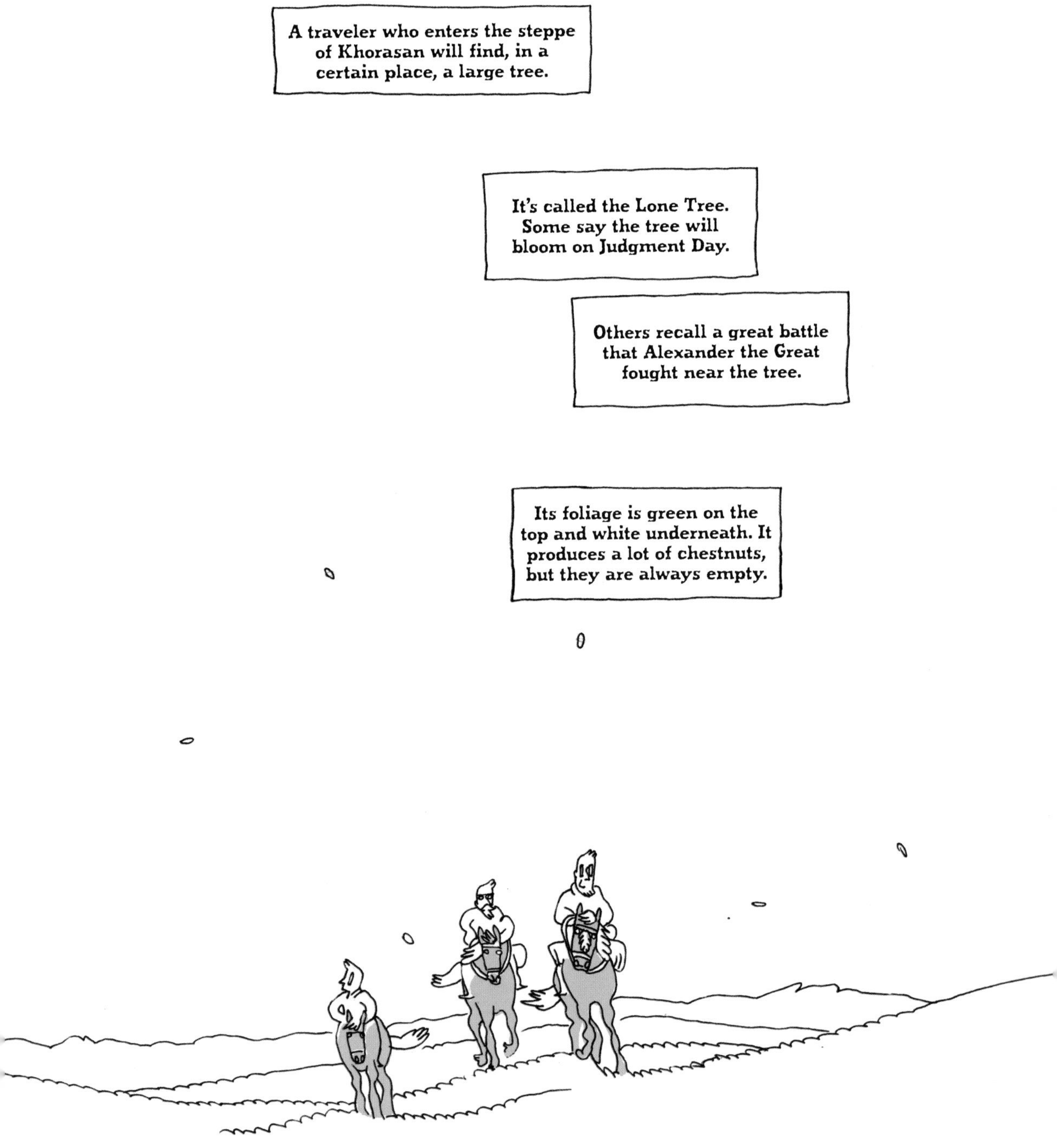
A traveler who enters the steppe of Khorasan will find, in a certain place, a large tree.
It's called the Lone Tree. Some say the tree will bloom on Judgment Day.
Others recall a great battle that Alexander the Great fought near the tree.
Its foliage is green on the top and white underneath. It produces a lot of chestnuts, but they are always empty.

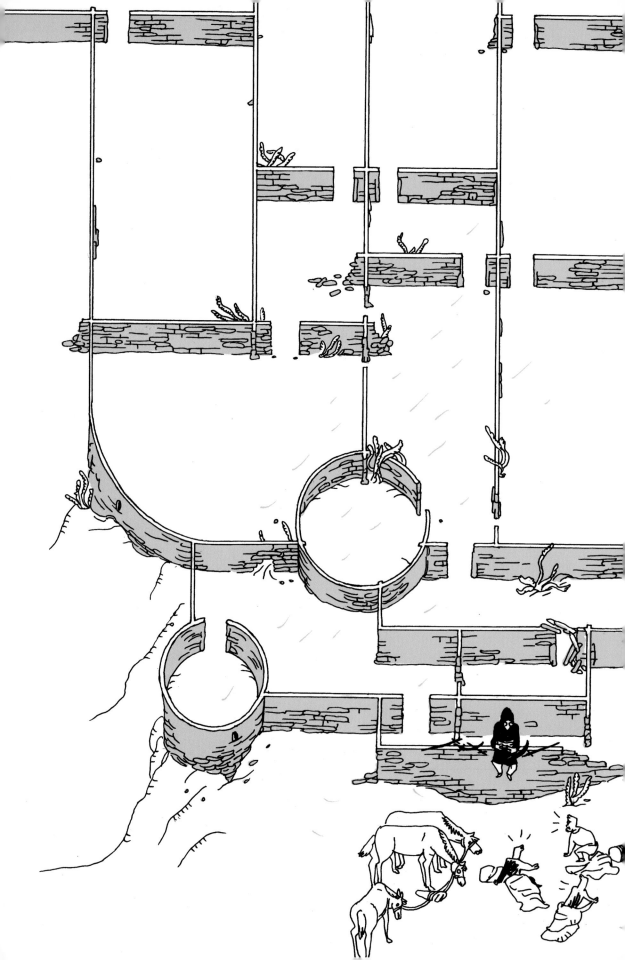

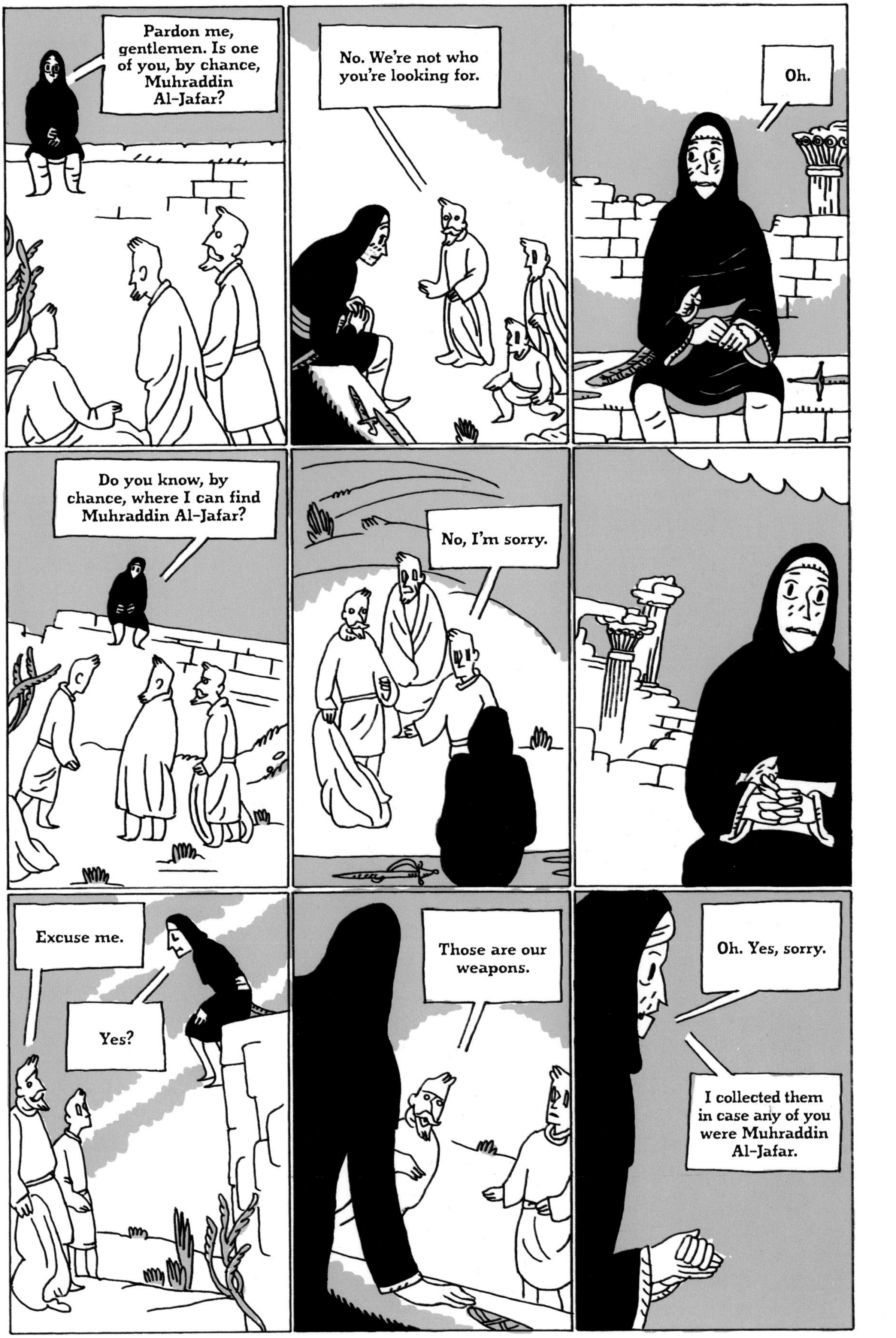
Pardon me, gentlemen. Is one of you, by chance, Muhraddin Al-Jafar?
No. We're not who you're looking for.
Oh.
Do you know, by chance, where I can find Muhraddin Al-Jafar?
No, I'm sorry.
Excuse me.
Yes?
Those are our weapons.
Oh. Yes, sorry.
I collected them in case any of you were Muhraddin Al-Jafar.

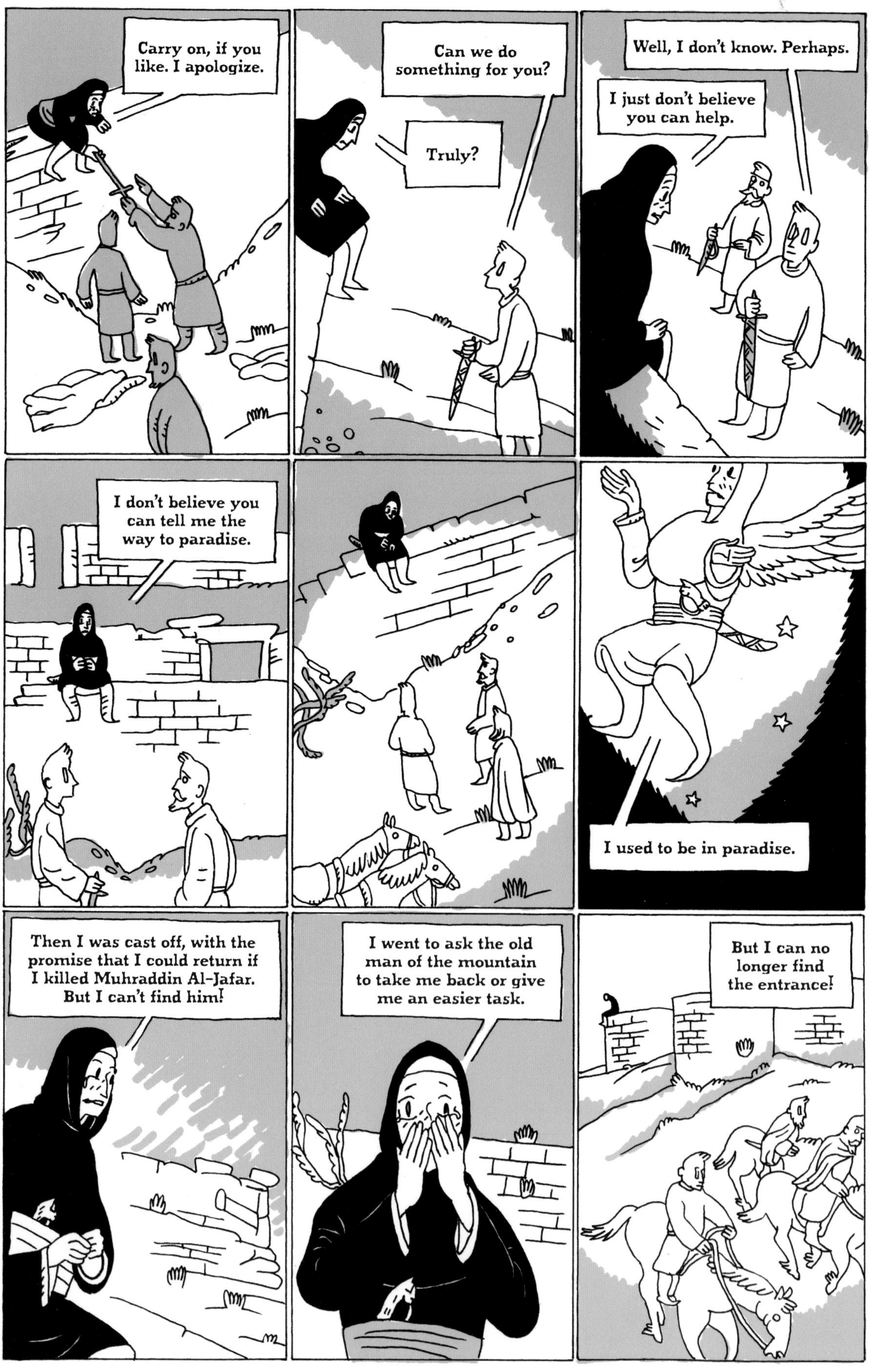

Carry on, if you like. I apologize.
Can we do something for you?
Truly?
Well, I don't know. Perhaps.
I just don't believe you can help.
I don't believe you can tell me the way to paradise.
I used to be in paradise.
Then I was cast off, with the promise that I could return if I killed Muhraddin Al-Jafar. But I can't find him!
I went to ask the old man of the mountain to take me back or give me an easier task.
But I can no longer find the entrance!

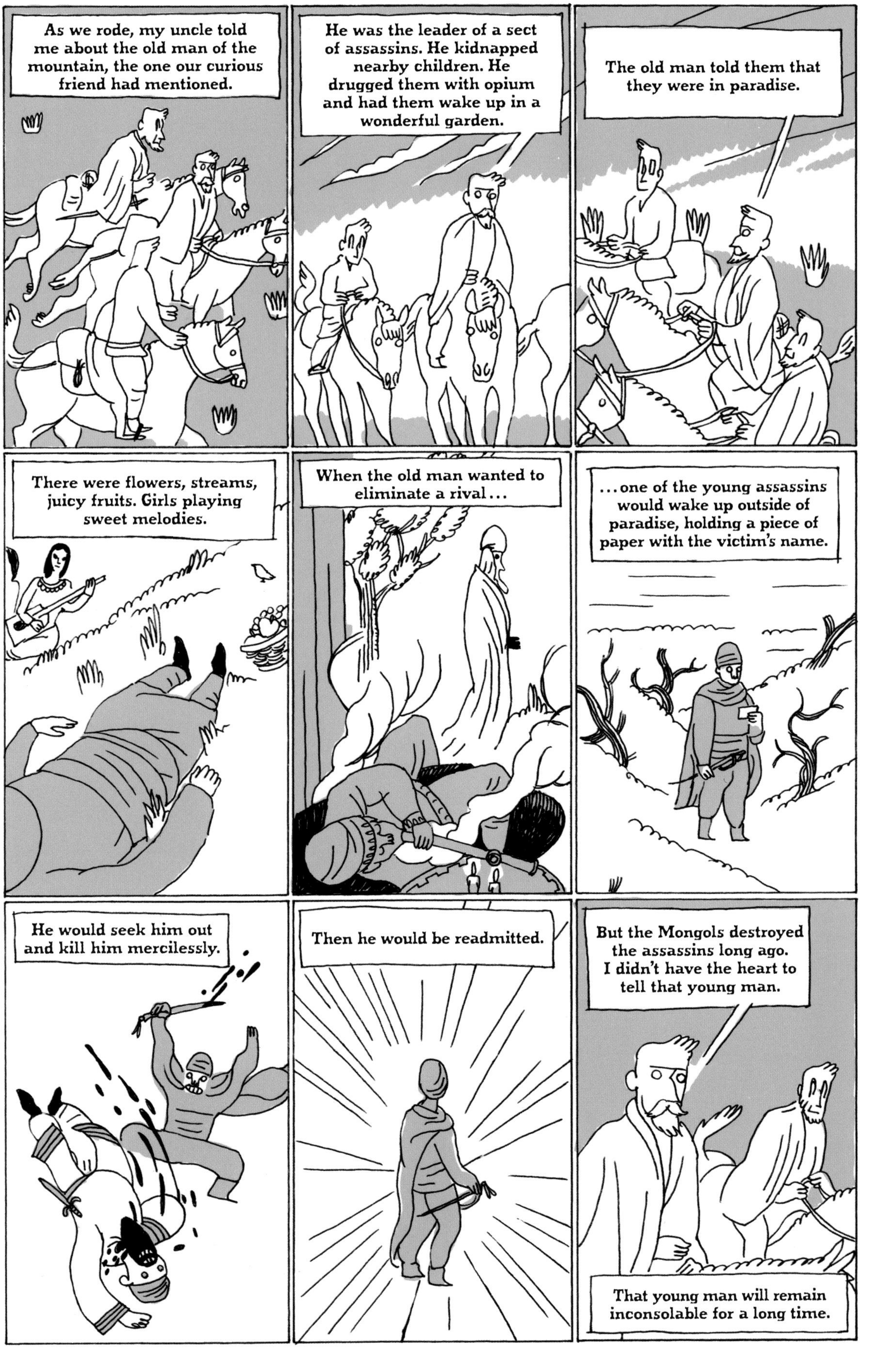
As we rode, my uncle told me about the old man of the mountain, the one our curious friend had mentioned.
He was the leader of a sect of assassins. He kidnapped nearby children. He drugged them with opium and had them wake up in a wonderful garden.
The old man told them that they were in paradise.
There were flowers, streams, juicy fruits. Girls playing sweet melodies.
When the old man wanted to eliminate a rival...
...one of the young assassins would wake up outside of paradise, holding a piece of paper with the victim's name.
He would seek him out and kill him mercilessly.
Then he would be readmitted.
But the Mongols destroyed the assassins long ago. I didn't have the heart to tell that young man.
That young man will remain inconsolable for a long time.

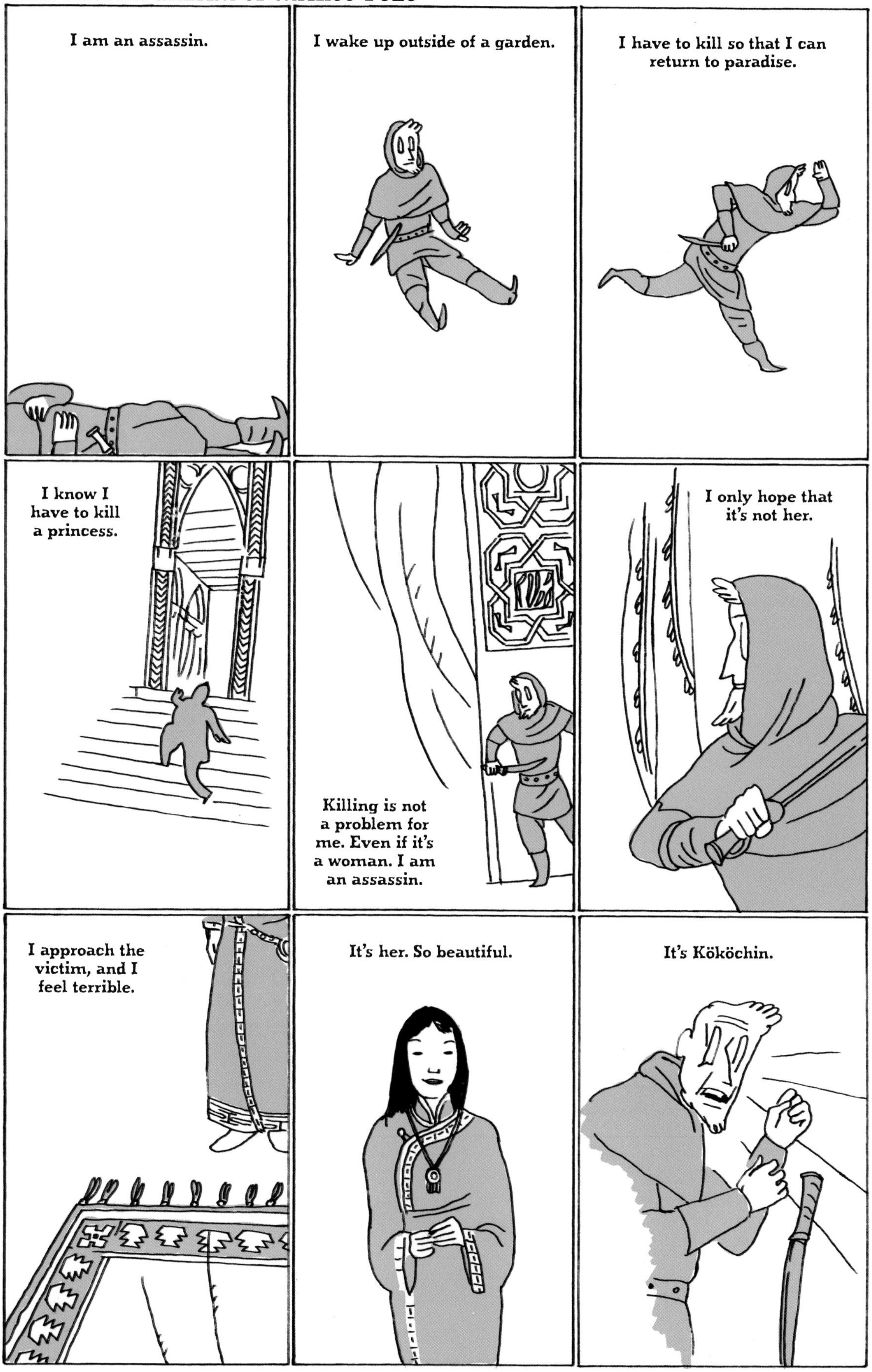
I am an assassin.
I wake up outside of a garden.
I have to kill so that I can return to paradise.
I know I have to kill a princess.
Killing is not a problem for me. Even if it's a woman. I am an assassin.
I only hope that it's not her.
I approach the victim, and I feel terrible.
It's her. So beautiful.
It's Kököchin.

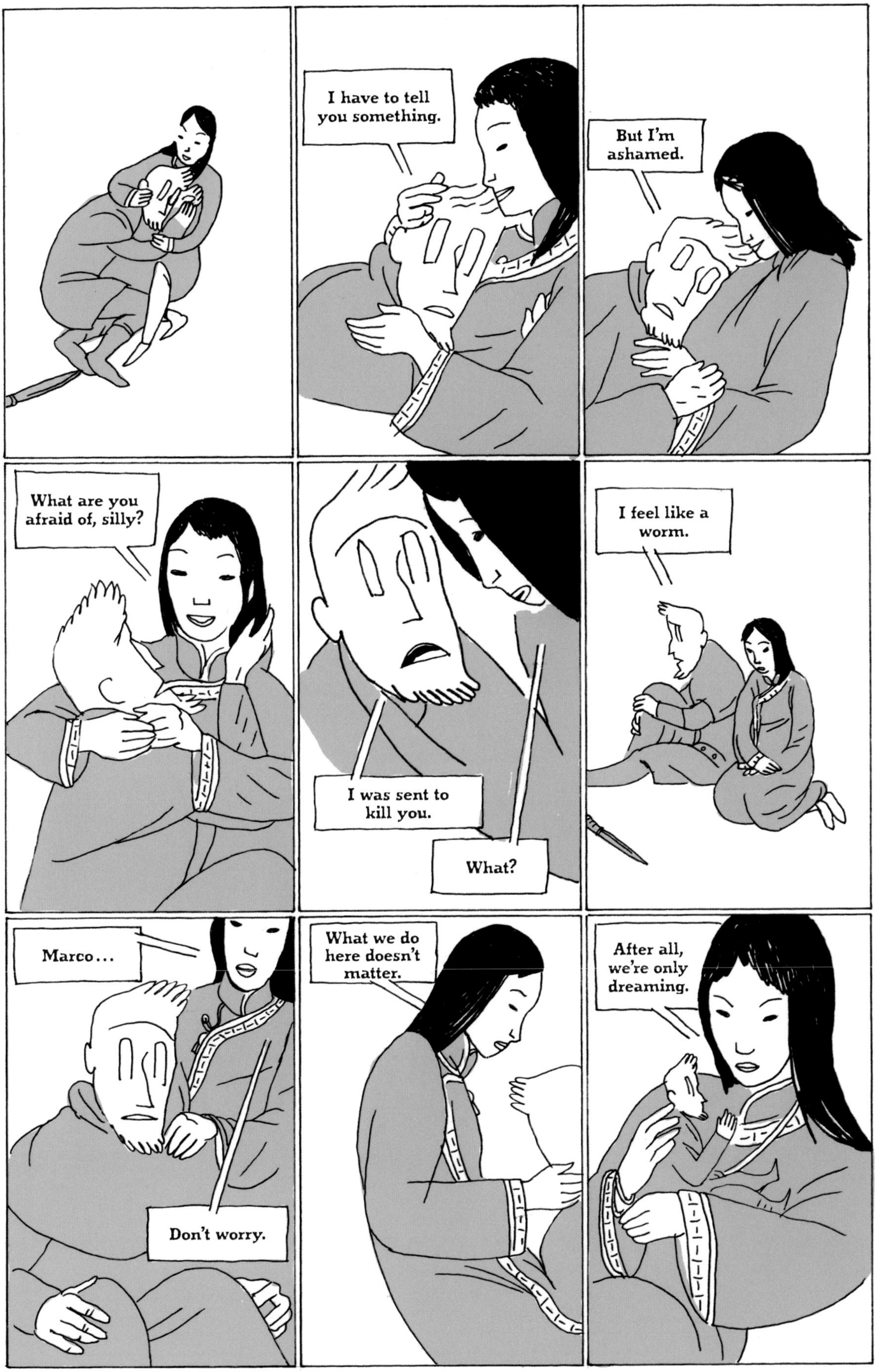

I have to tell you something.
But I'm ashamed.
What are you afraid of, silly?
I was sent to kill you.
What?
I feel like a worm.
Marco...
Don't worry.
What we do here doesn't matter.
After all, we're only dreaming.

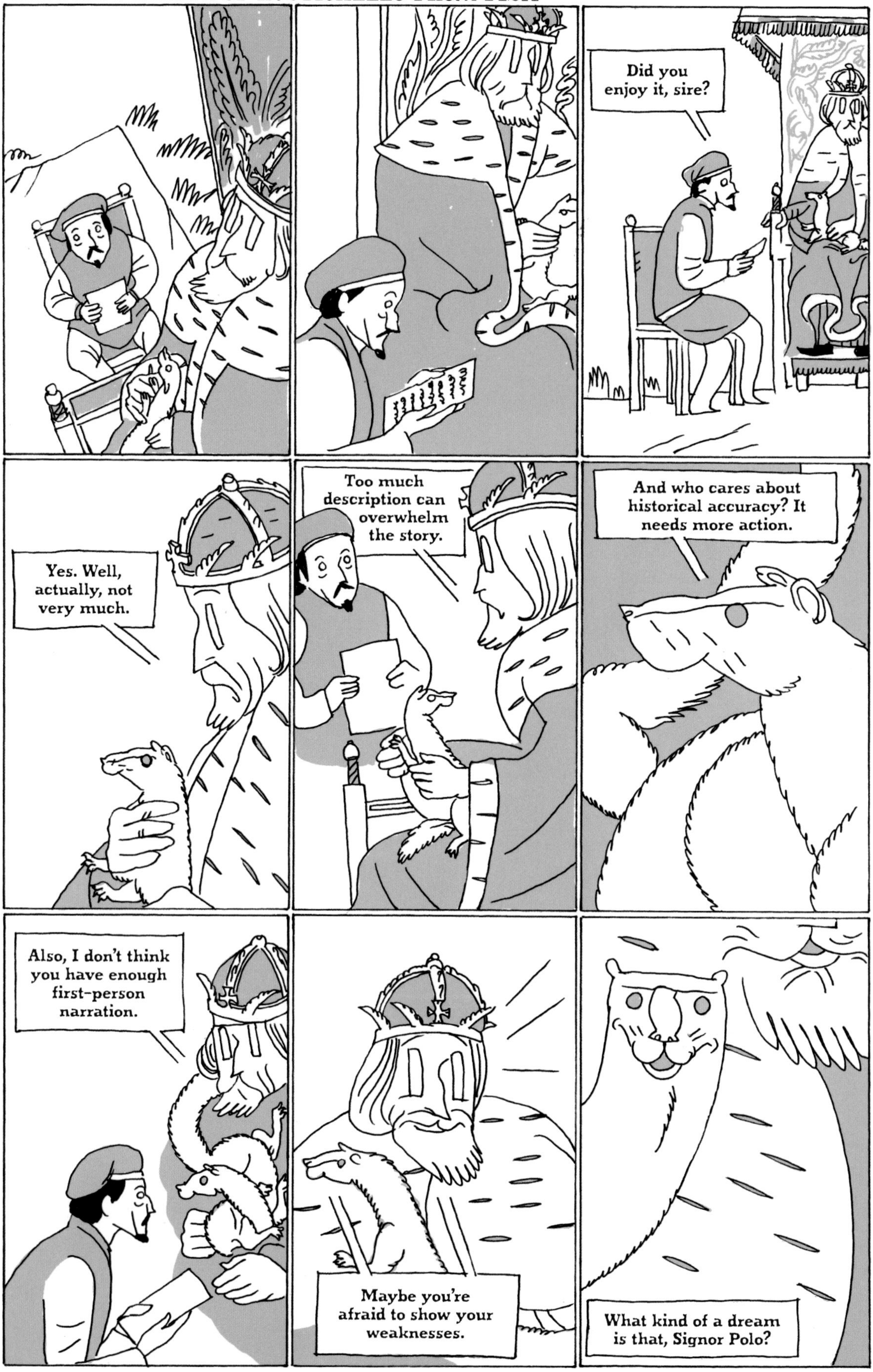
Did you enjoy it, sire?
Yes. Well, actually, not very much.
Too much description can overwhelm the story.
And who cares about historical accuracy? It needs more action.
Also, I don't think you have enough first-person narration.
Maybe you're afraid to show your weaknesses.
What kind of a dream is that, Signor Polo?

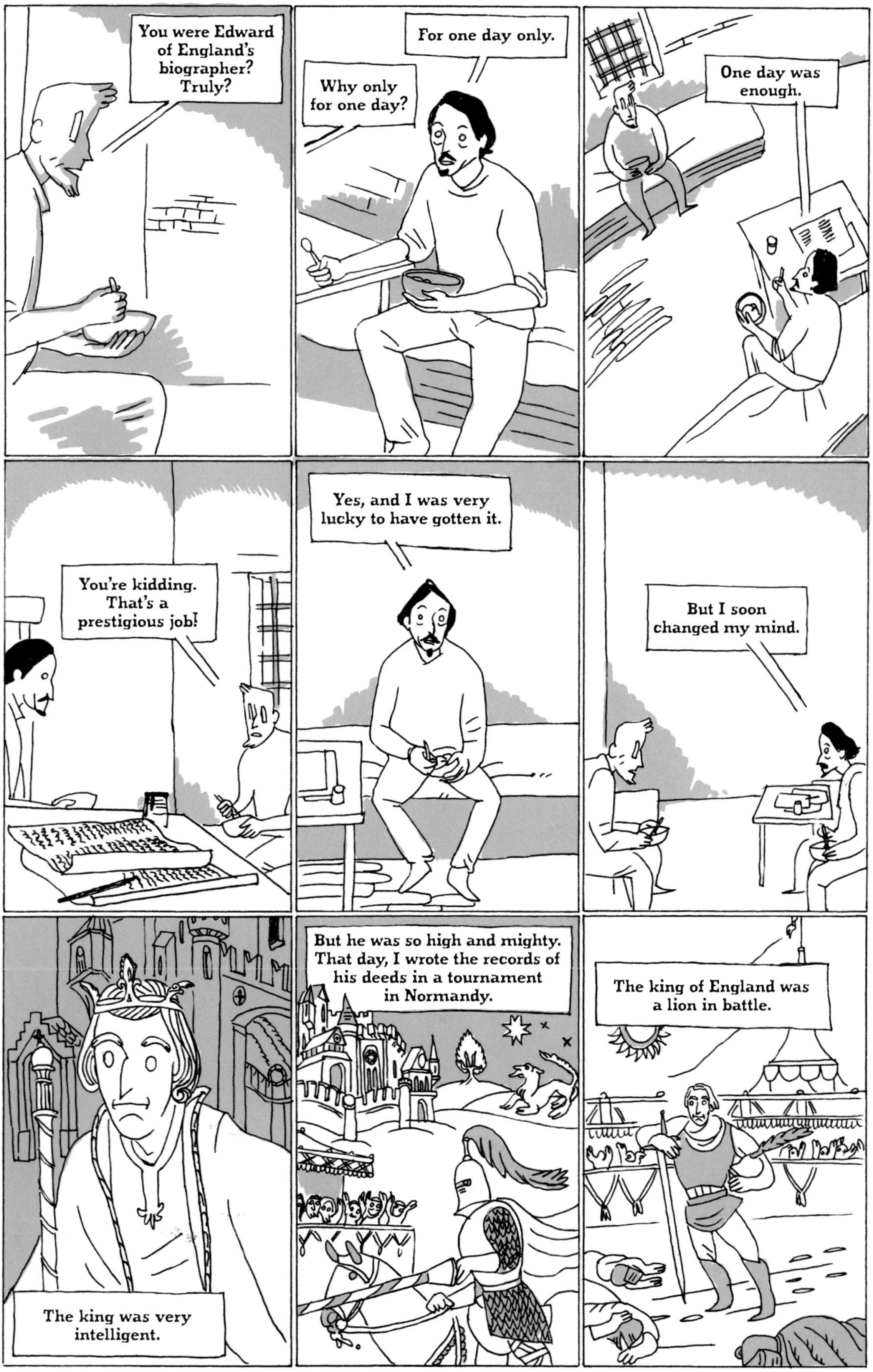
You were Edward of England's biographer? Truly?
For one day only.
Why only for one day?
One day was enough.
You're kidding. That's a prestigious job!
Yes, and I was very lucky to have gotten it.
But I soon changed my mind.
The king was very intelligent.
But he was so high and mighty. That day, I wrote the records of his deeds in a tournament in Normandy.
The king of England was a lion in battle.

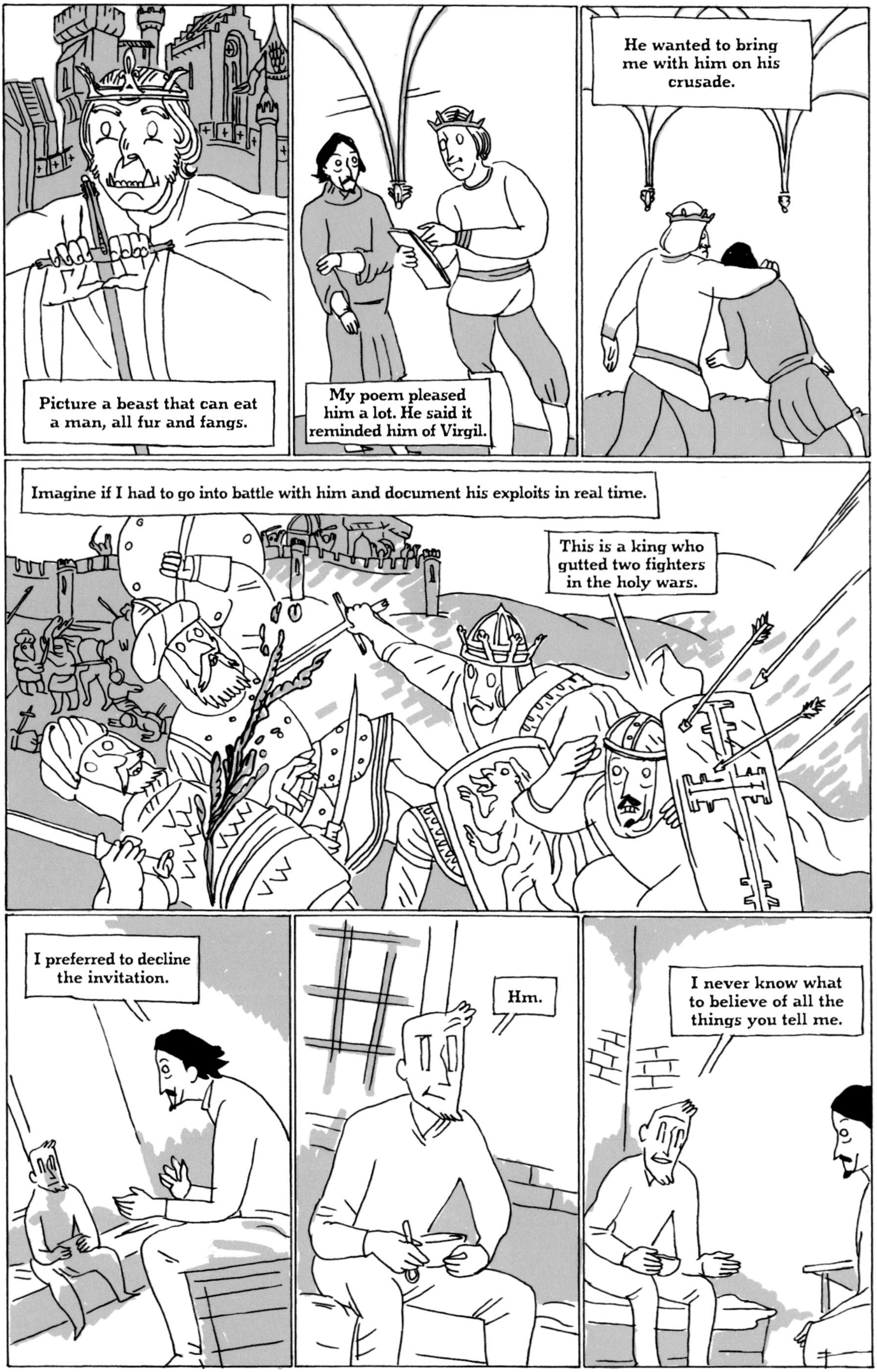

Picture a beast that can eat a man, all fur and fangs.
My poem pleased him a lot. He said it reminded him of Virgil.
He wanted to bring me with him on his crusade.
Imagine if I had to go into battle with him and document his exploits in real time.
This is a king who gutted two fighters in the holy wars.
I preferred to decline the invitation.
Hm.
I never know what to believe of all the things you tell me.

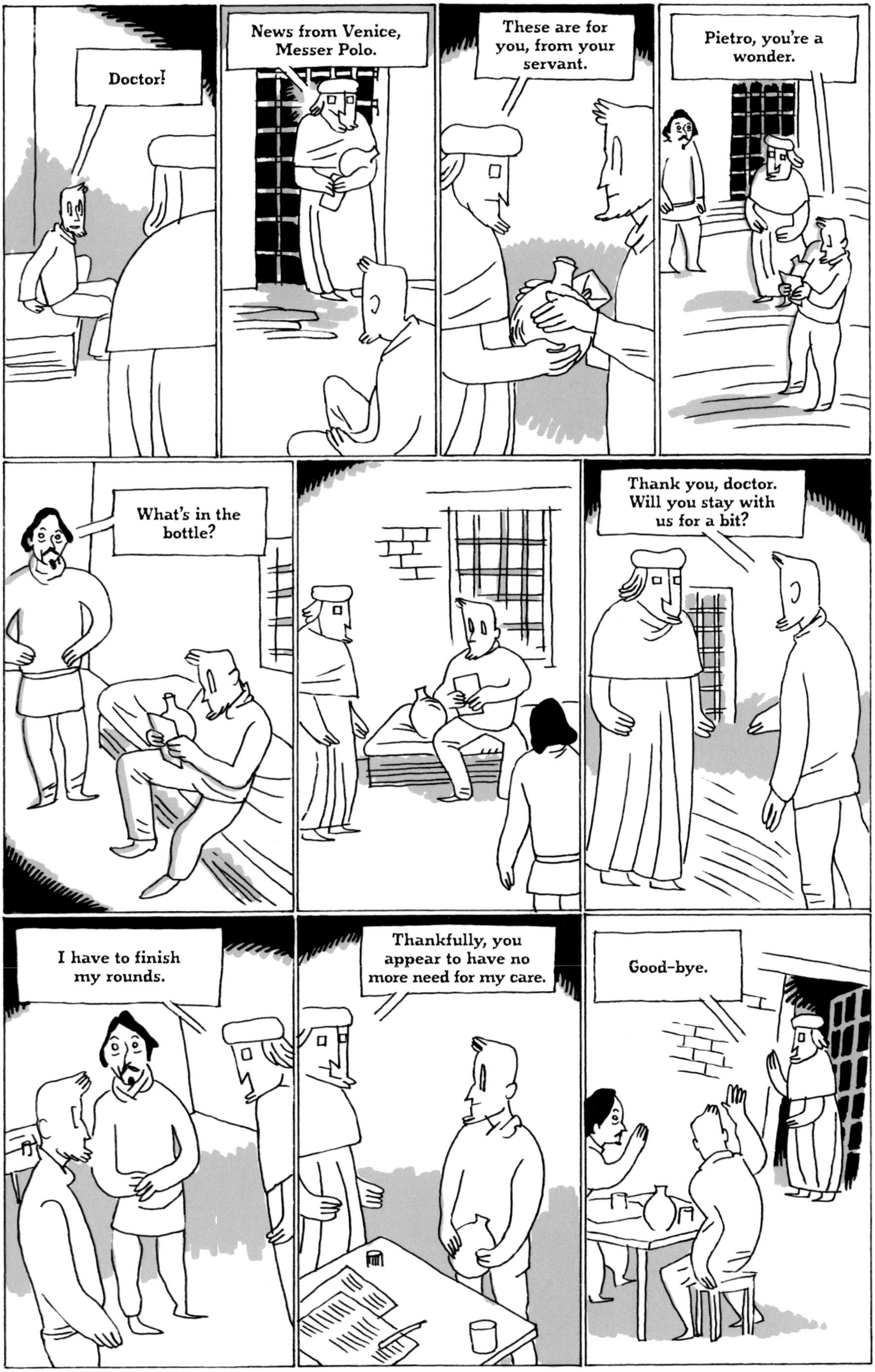
Doctor!
News from Venice, Messer Polo.
These are for you, from your servant.
Pietro, you're a wonder.
What's in the bottle?
Thank you, doctor. Will you stay with us for a bit?
I have to finish my rounds.
Thankfully, you appear to have no more need for my care.
Good-bye.

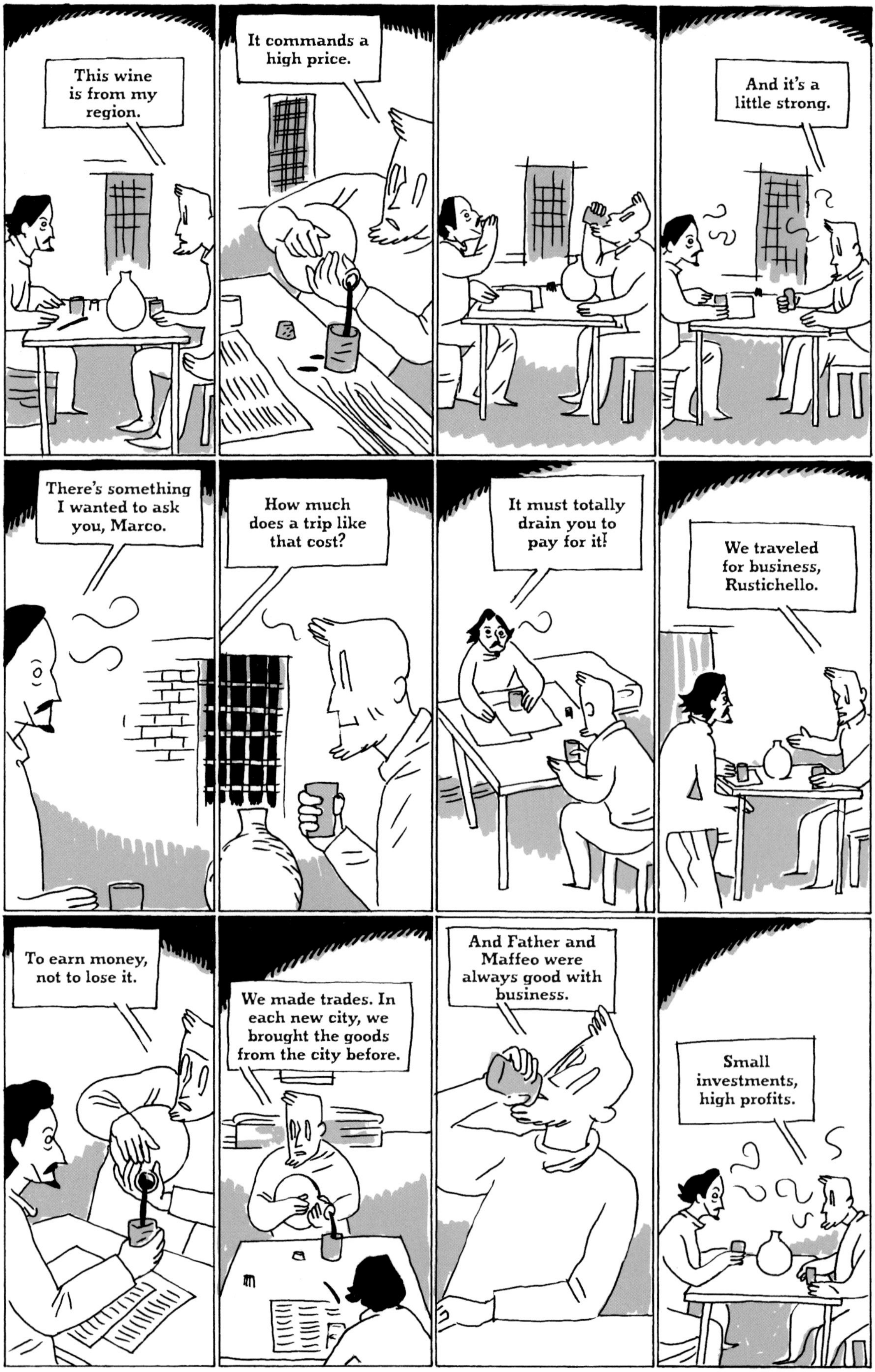
This wine is from my region.
It commands a high price.
And it's a little strong.
There's something I wanted to ask you, Marco.
How much does a trip like that cost?
It must totally drain you to pay for it!
We traveled for business, Rustichello.
To earn money, not to lose it.
We made trades. In each new city, we brought the goods from the city before.
And Father and Maffeo were always good with business.
Small investments, high profits.

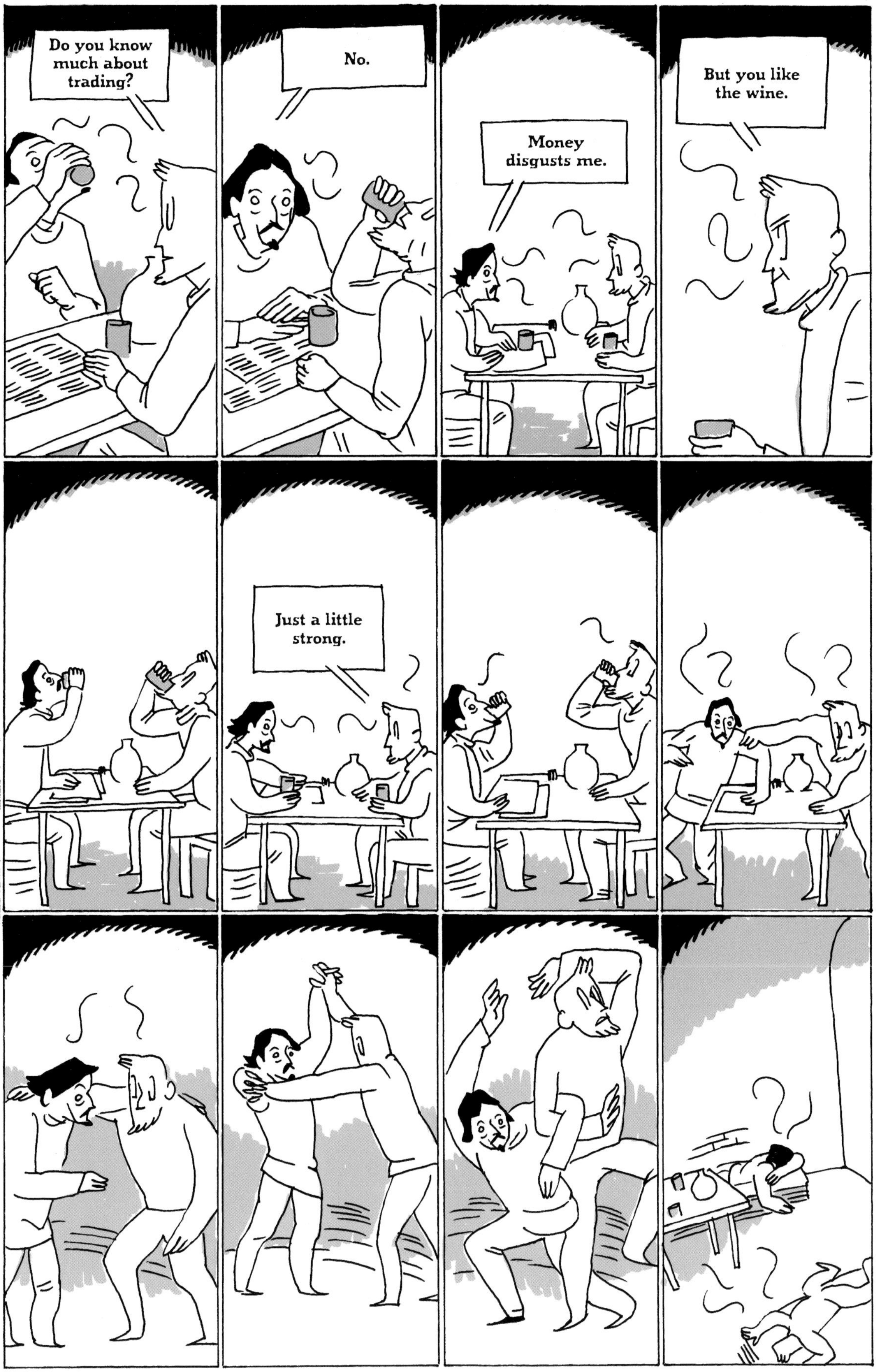
Do you know much about trading?
No.
Money disgusts me.
But you like the wine.
Just a little strong.

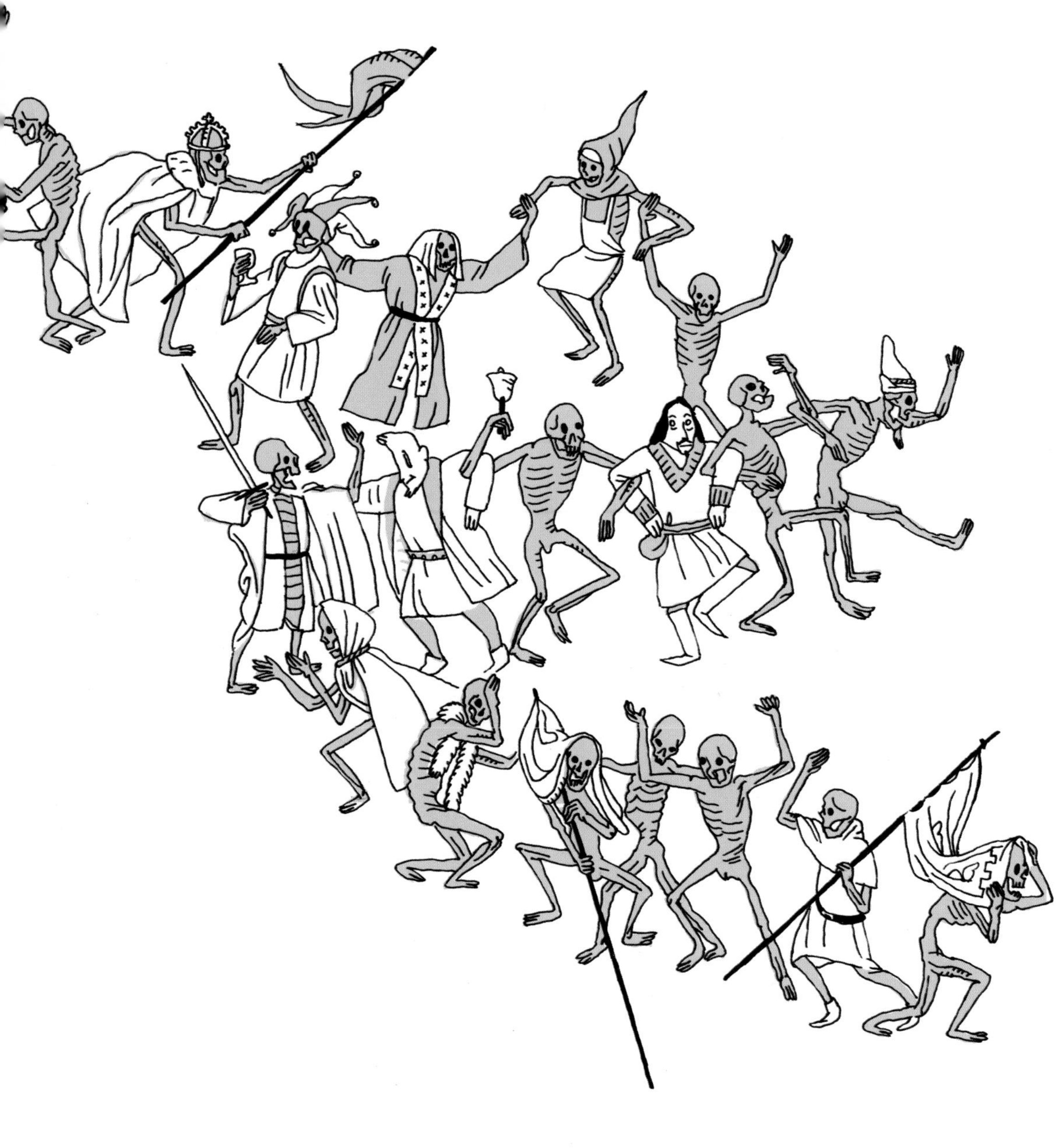

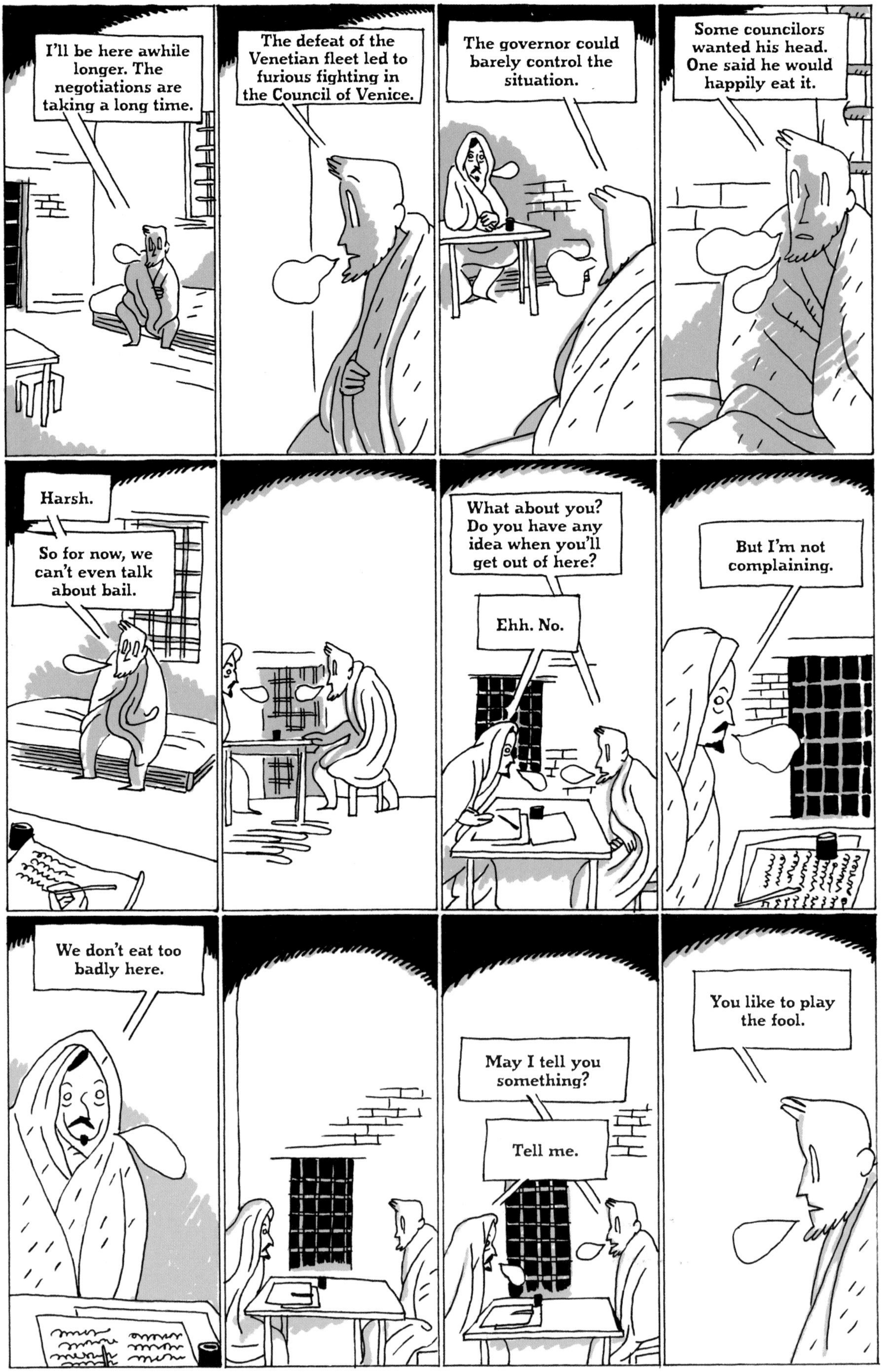
I'll be here awhile longer. The negotiations are taking a long time.
The defeat of the Venetian fleet led to furious fighting in the Council of Venice.
The governor could barely control the situation.
Some councilors wanted his head. One said he would happily eat it.
Harsh.
So for now, we can't even talk about bail.
What about you? Do you have any idea when you'll get out of here?
Ehh. No.
But I'm not complaining.
We don't eat too badly here.
May I tell you something?
Tell me.
You like to play the fool.

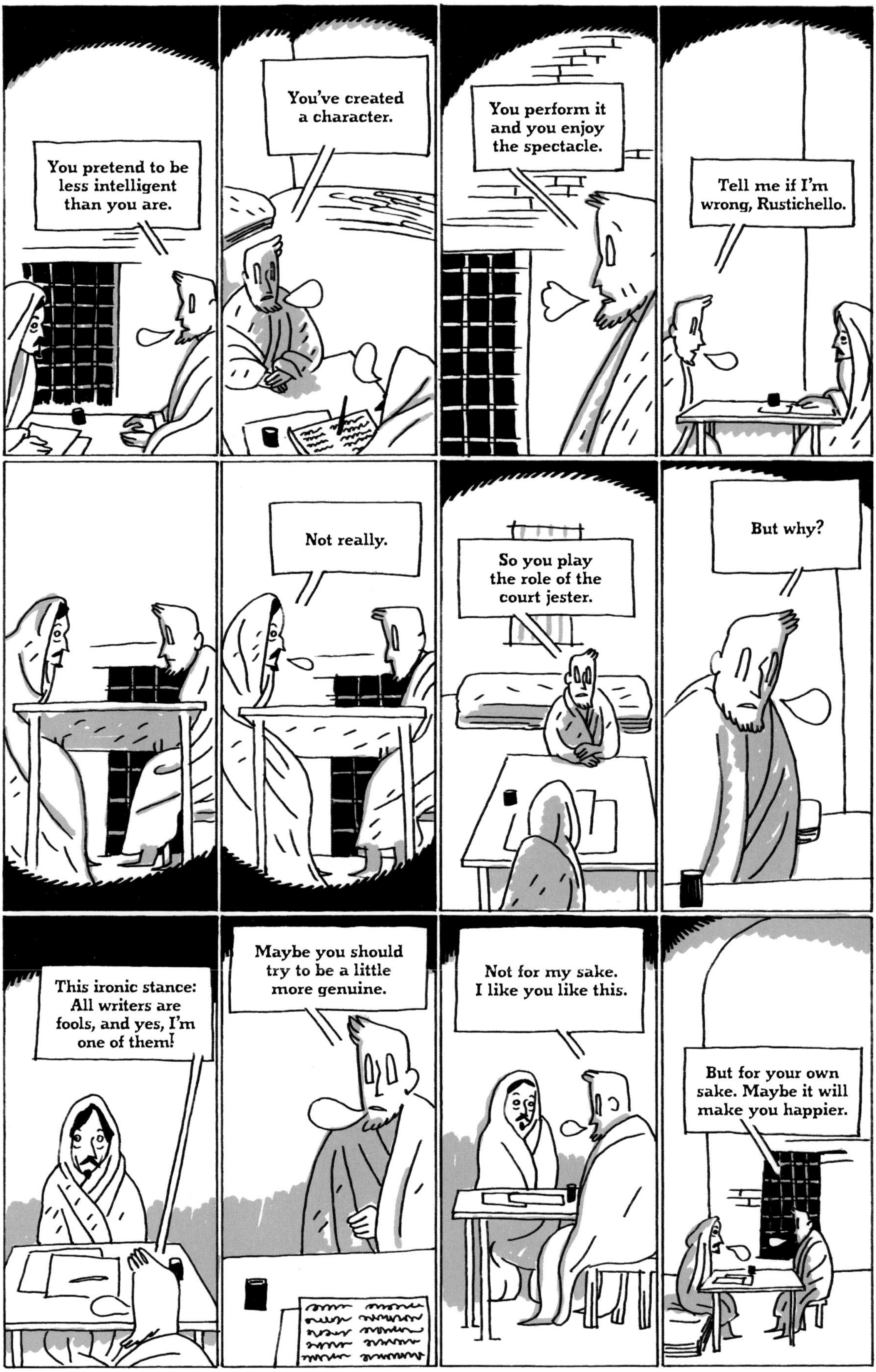
You pretend to be less intelligent than you are.
You've created a character.
You perform it and you enjoy the spectacle.
Tell me if I'm wrong, Rustichello.
Not really.
So you play the role of the court jester.
But why?
This ironic stance: All writers are fools, and yes, I'm one of them!
Maybe you should try to be a little more genuine.
Not for my sake. I like you like this.
But for your own sake. Maybe it will make you happier.

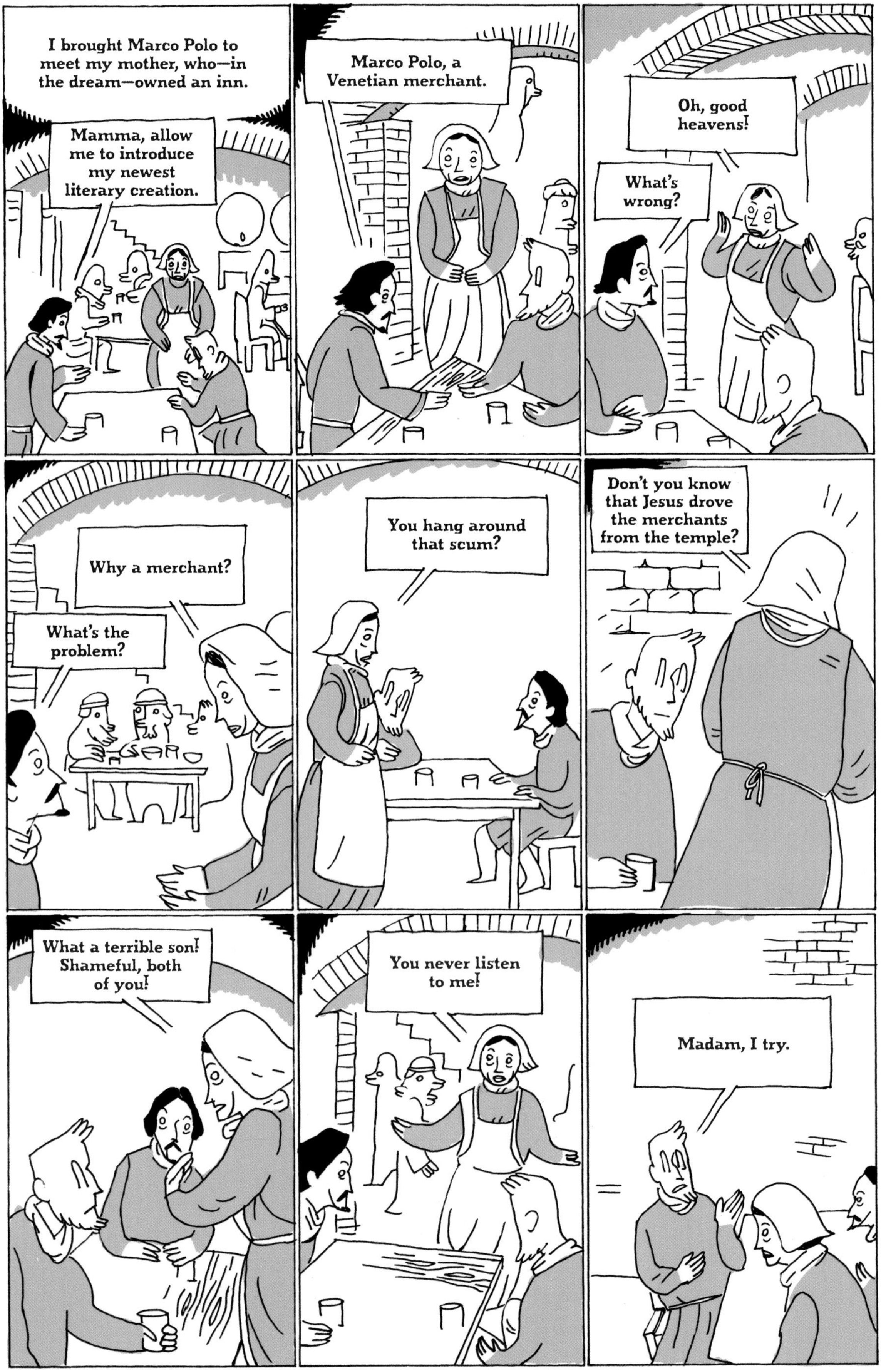
I brought Marco Polo to meet my mother, who—in the dream—owned an inn.
Mamma, allow me to introduce my newest literary creation.
Marco Polo, a Venetian merchant.
Oh, good heavens!
What's wrong?
Why a merchant?
What's the problem?
You hang around that scum?
Don't you know that Jesus drove the merchants from the temple?
What a terrible son! Shameful, both of you!
You never listen to me!
Madam, I try.

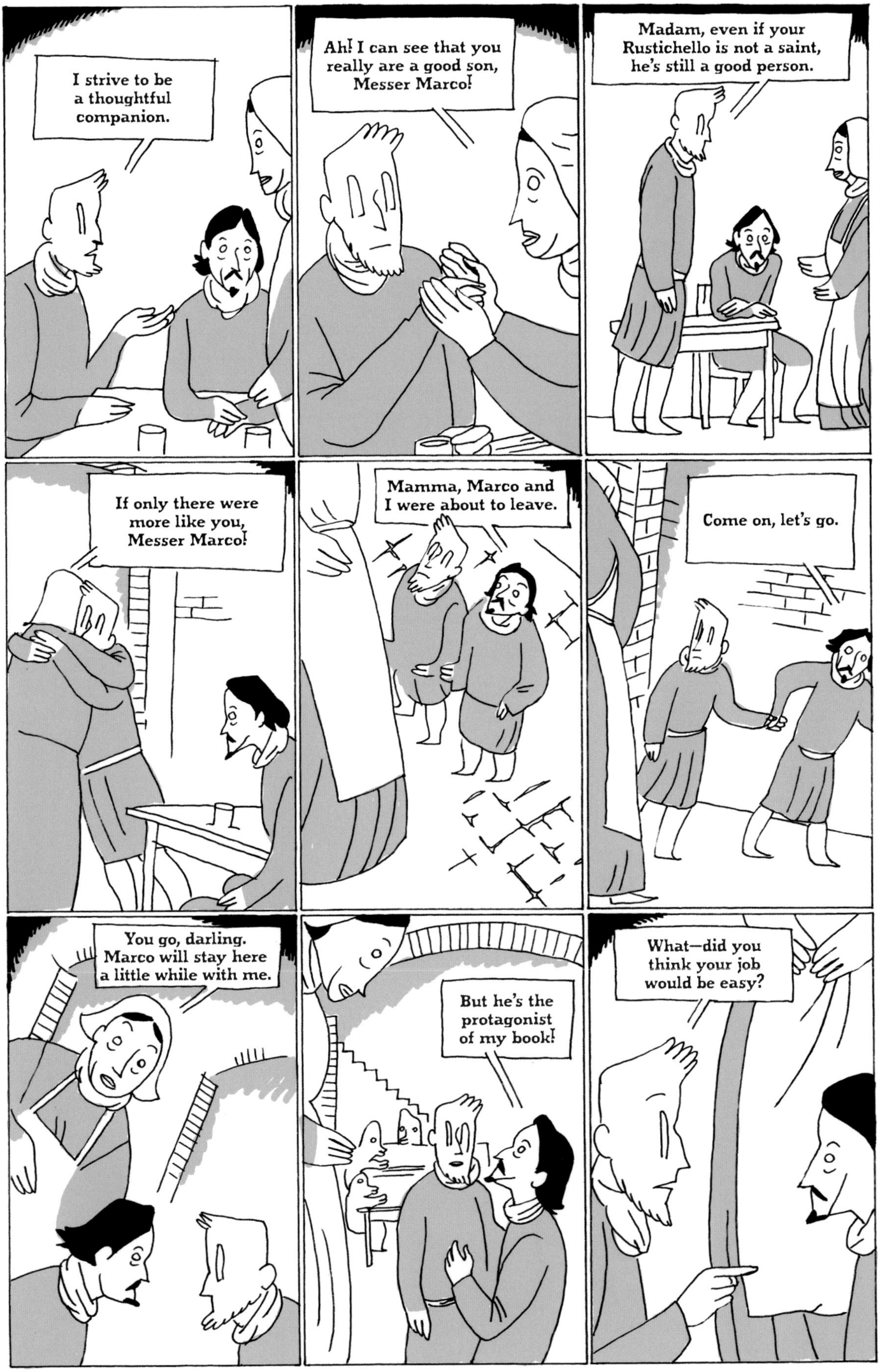
I strive to be a thoughtful companion.
Ah! I can see that you really are a good son, Messer Marco!
Madam, even if your Rustichello is not a saint, he's still a good person.
If only there were more like you, Messer Marco!
Mamma, Marco and I were about to leave.
Come on, let's go.
You go, darling. Marco will stay here a little while with me.
But he's the protagonist of my book!
What—did you think your job would be easy?

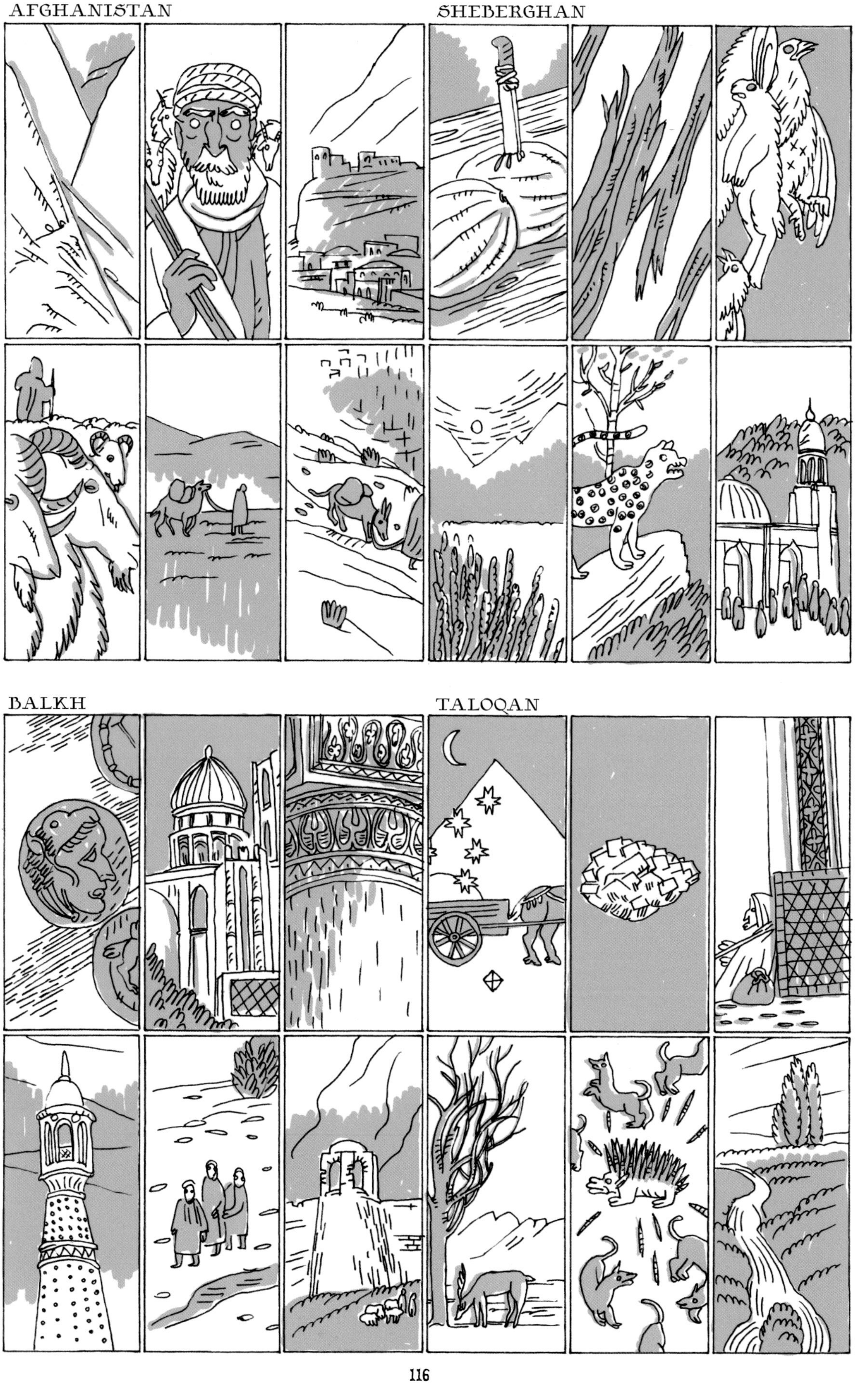
AFGHANISTAN
SHEBERGHAN
BALKH
TALOQAN

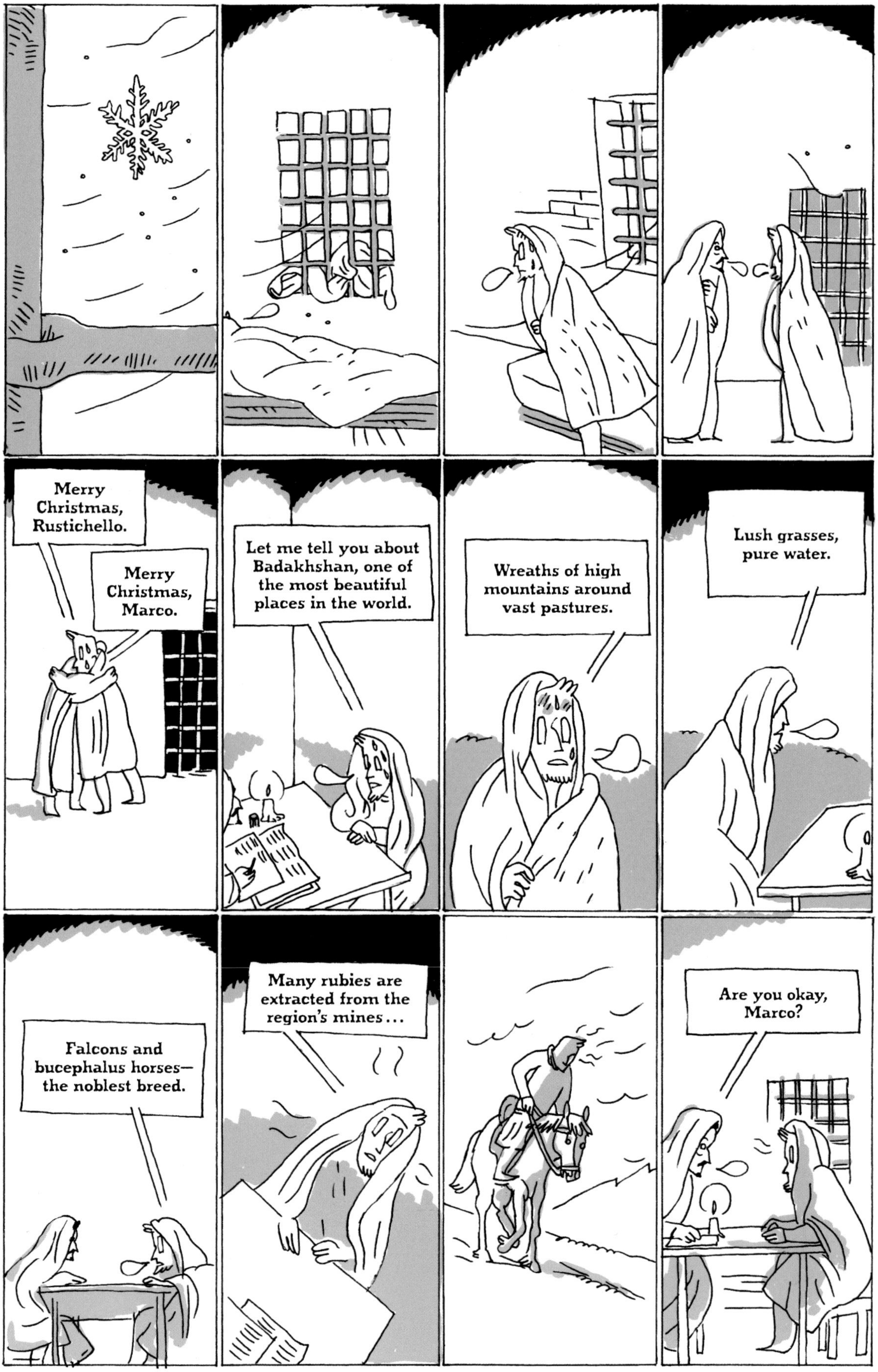
Merry Christmas, Rustichello.
Merry Christmas, Marco.
Let me tell you about Badakhshan, one of the most beautiful places in the world.
Wreaths of high mountains around vast pastures.
Lush grasses, pure water.
Falcons and bucephalus horses—the noblest breed.
Many rubies are extracted from the region's mines . . .
Are you okay, Marco?

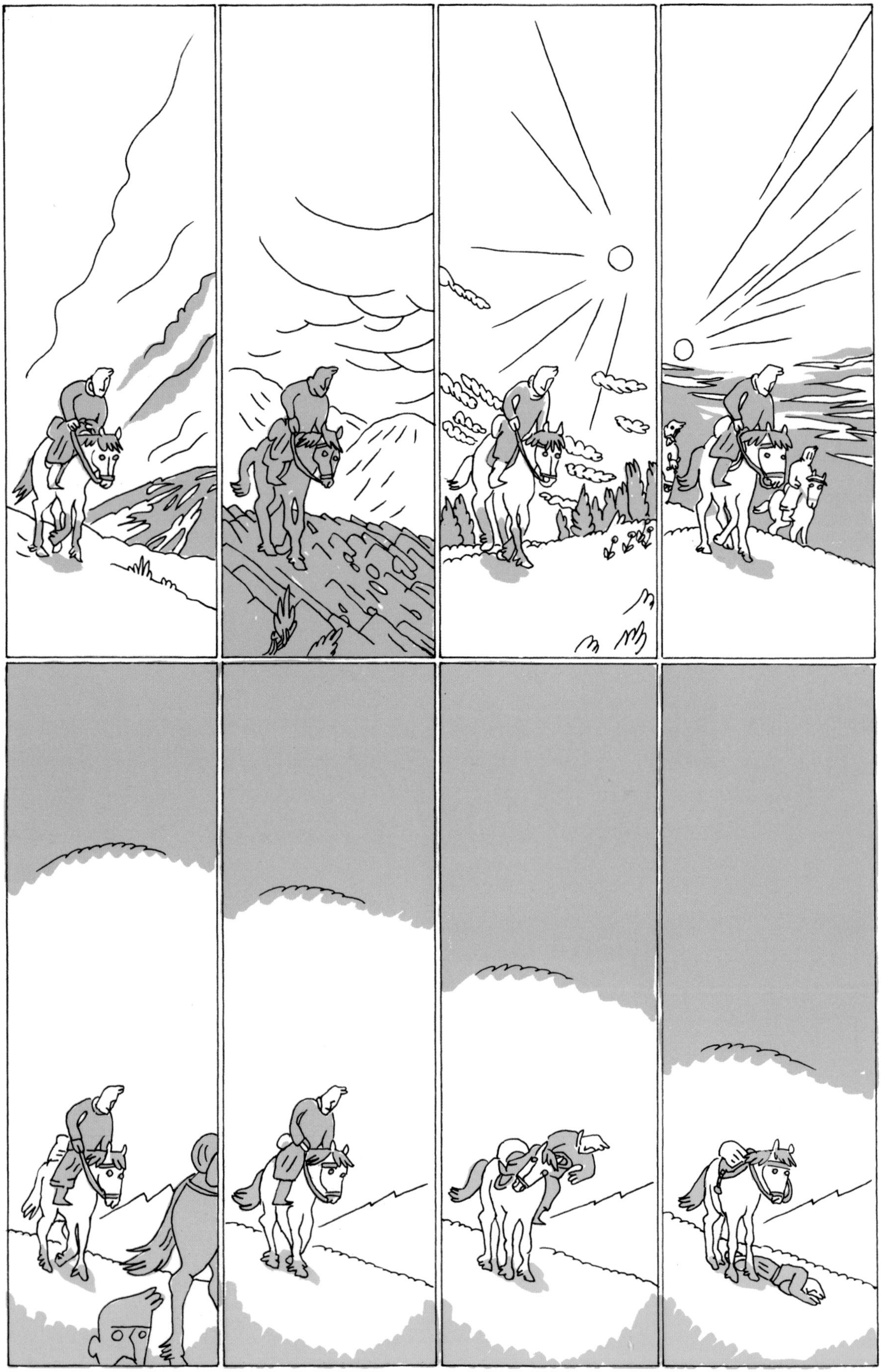

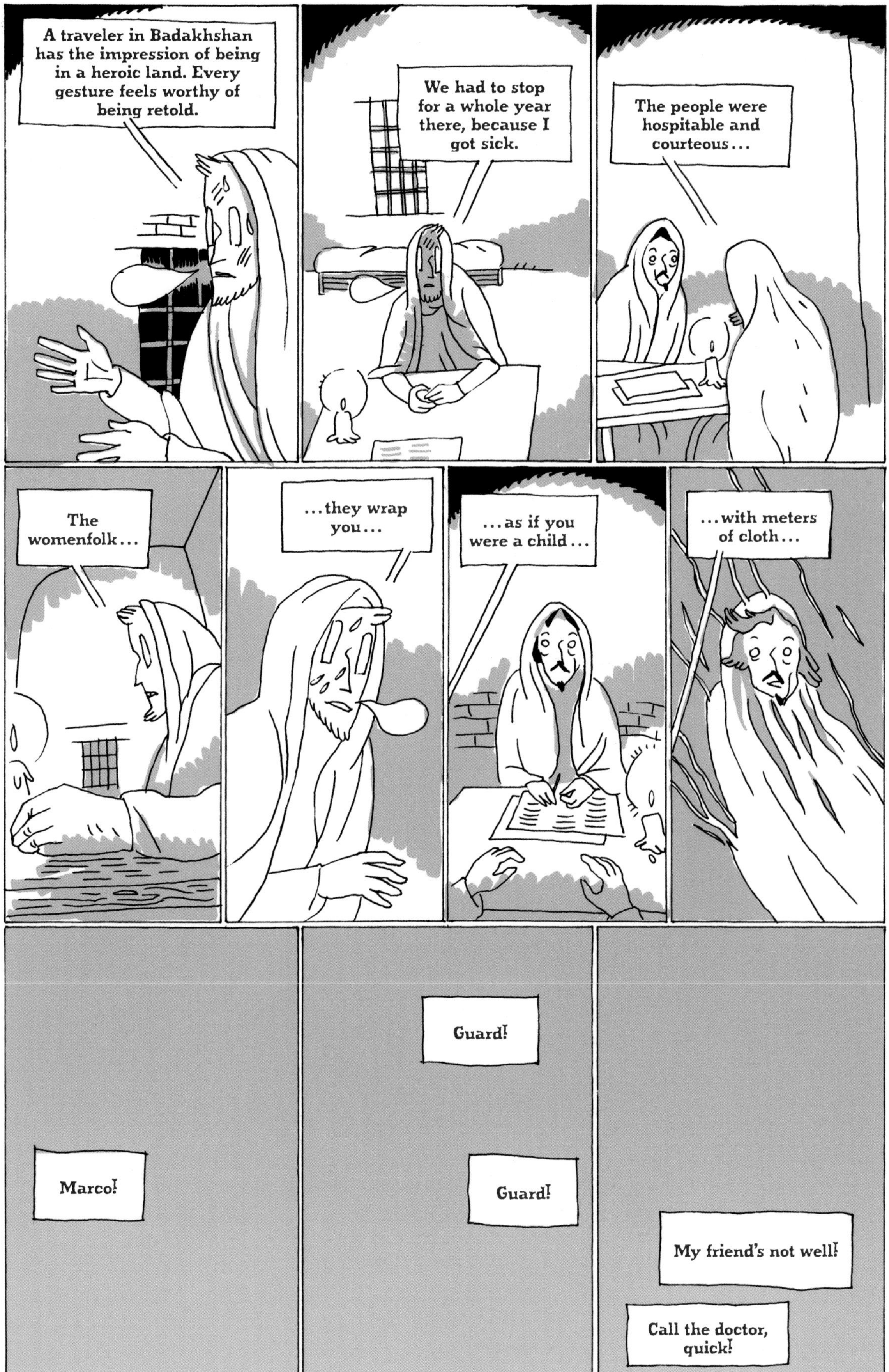
A traveler in Badakhshan has the impression of being in a heroic land. Every gesture feels worthy of being retold.
We had to stop for a whole year there, because I got sick.
The people were hospitable and courteous...
The womenfolk...
...they wrap you...
...as if you were a child...
...with meters of cloth...
Marco!
Guard!
Guard!
My friend's not well!
Call the doctor, quick!

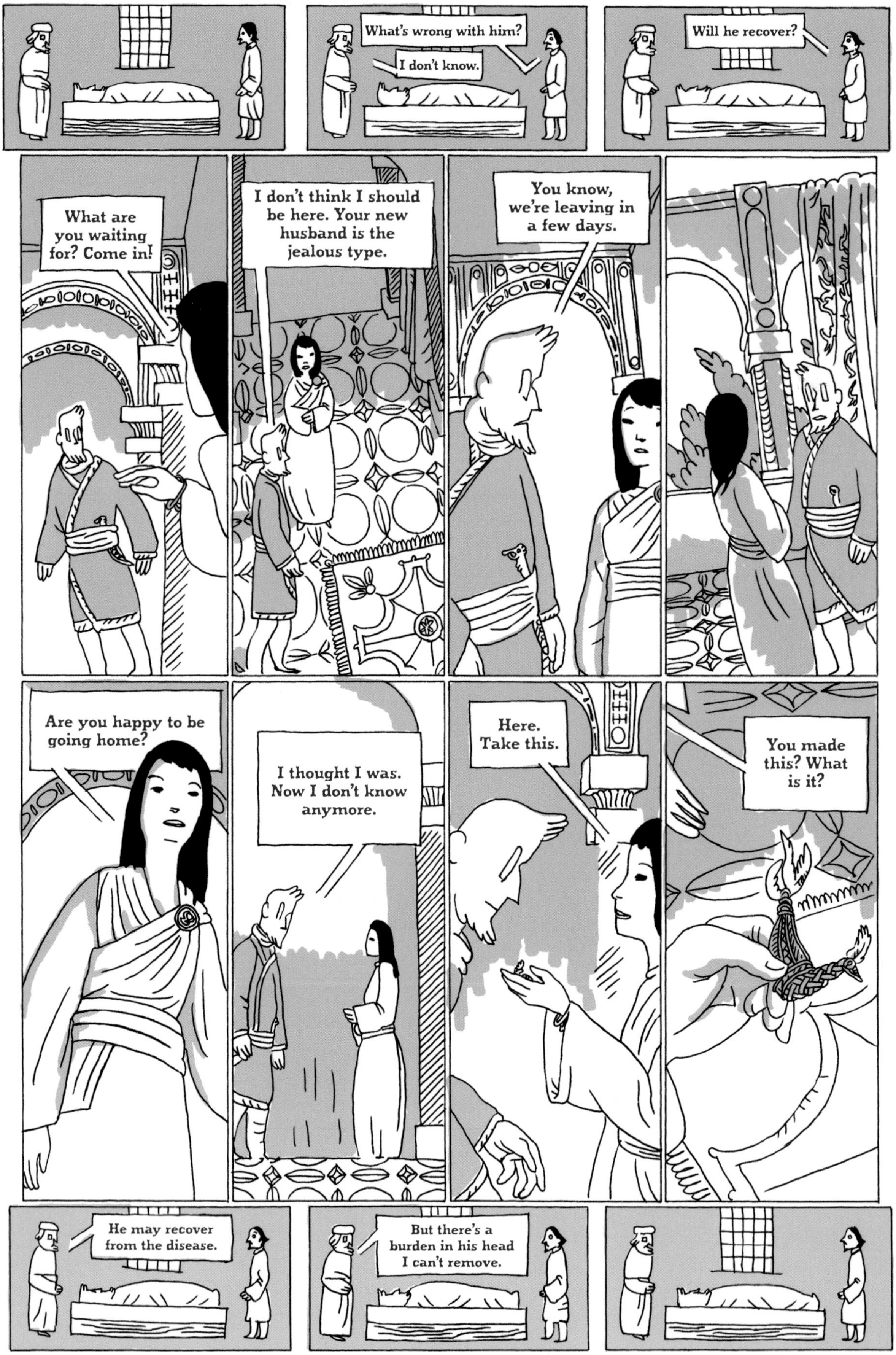
What's wrong with him?
I don't know.
Will he recover?
What are you waiting for? Come in!
I don't think I should be here. Your new husband is the jealous type.
You know, we're leaving in a few days.
Are you happy to be going home?
I thought I was. Now I don't know anymore.
Here. Take this.
You made this? What is it?
He may recover from the disease.
But there's a burden in his head I can't remove.

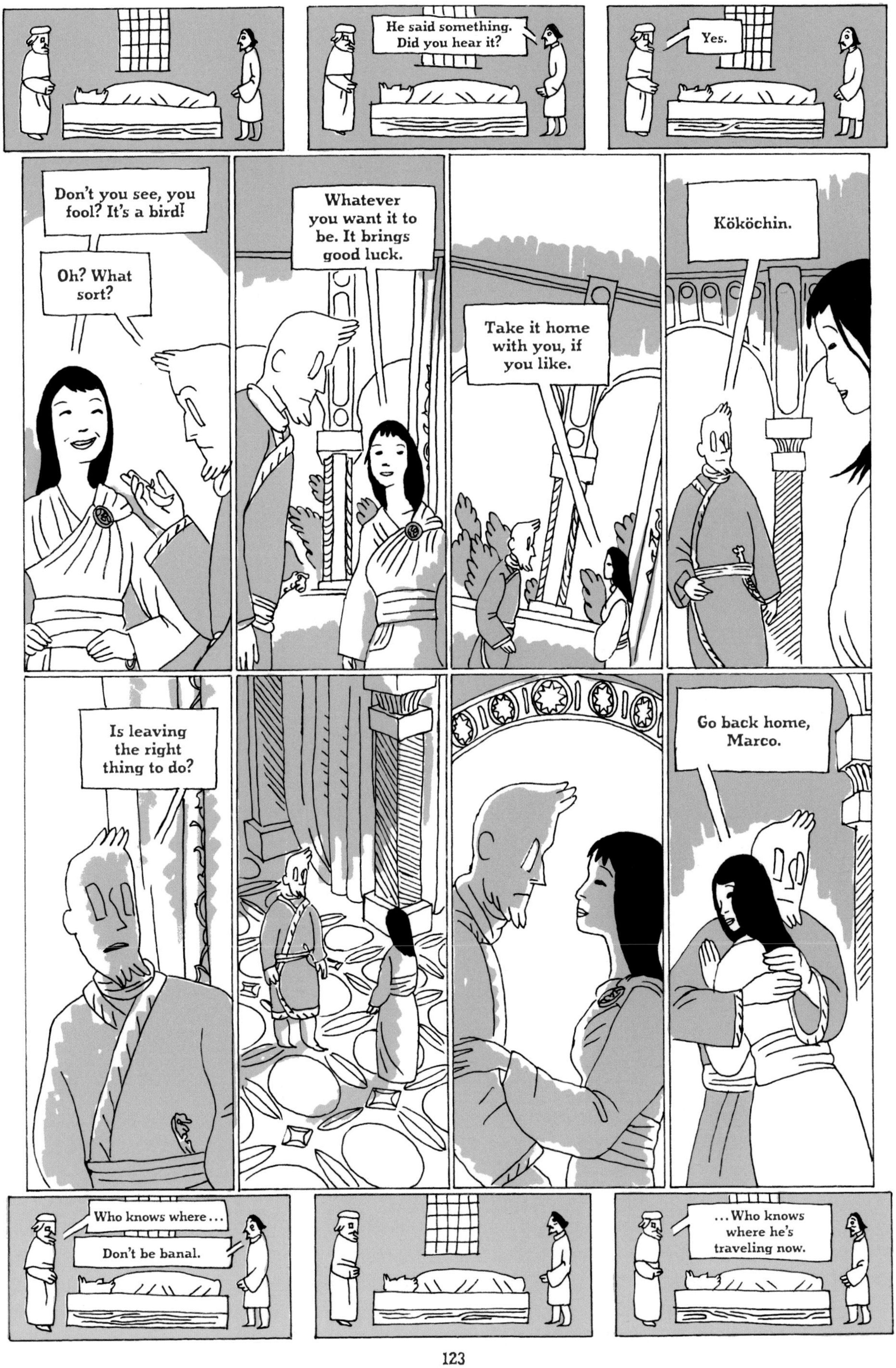
He said something.
Did you hear it?
Yes.
Don't you see, you fool? It's a bird!
Oh? What sort?
Whatever you want it to be. It brings good luck.
Take it home with you, if you like.
Kököchin.
Is leaving the right thing to do?
Go back home, Marco.
Who knows where...
Don't be banal.
...Who knows where he's traveling now.

The Wakhan is the name of a land squeezed between high mountains.

The nomads who live there call it the Roof of the World.

The mountain chains of Karakorum, the Pamir, and the Hindu Kush dominate a traveler's view, like a constant thought.

We went to the
rock walls, where
monk healers live in
hermitages above the
emptiness.

We climbed the
Pamir Mountains.

Flocks of sheep and
wolves roamed the area.

Bones and horns were piled up
in the drifts of snow.

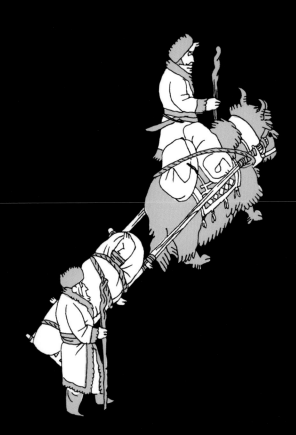

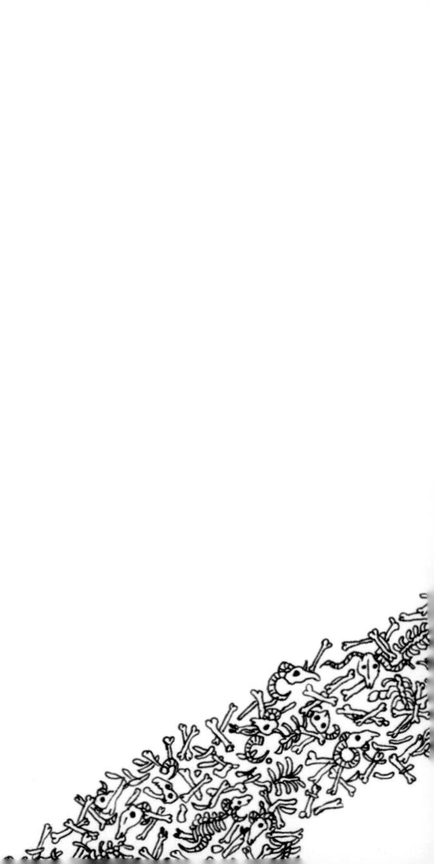

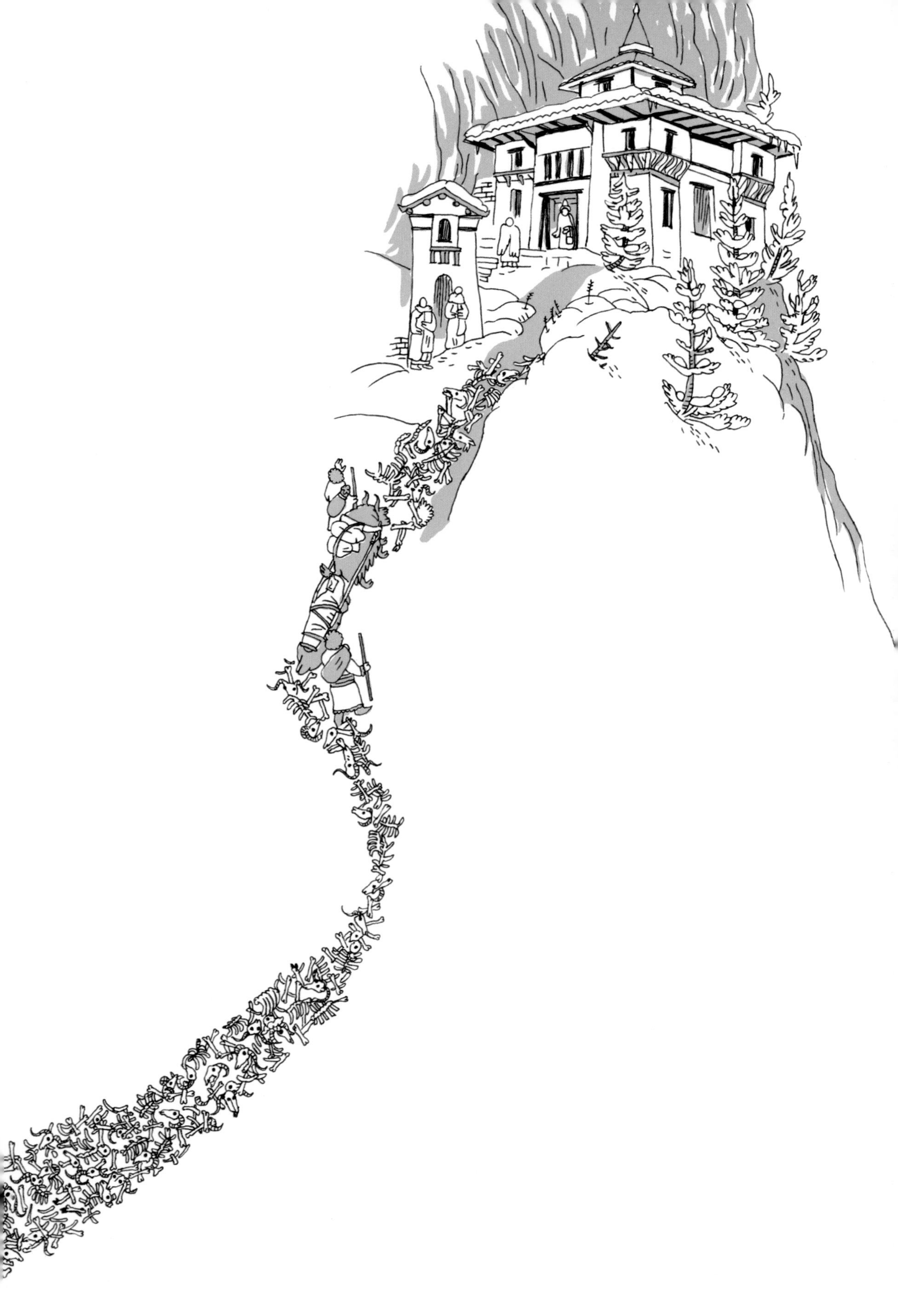

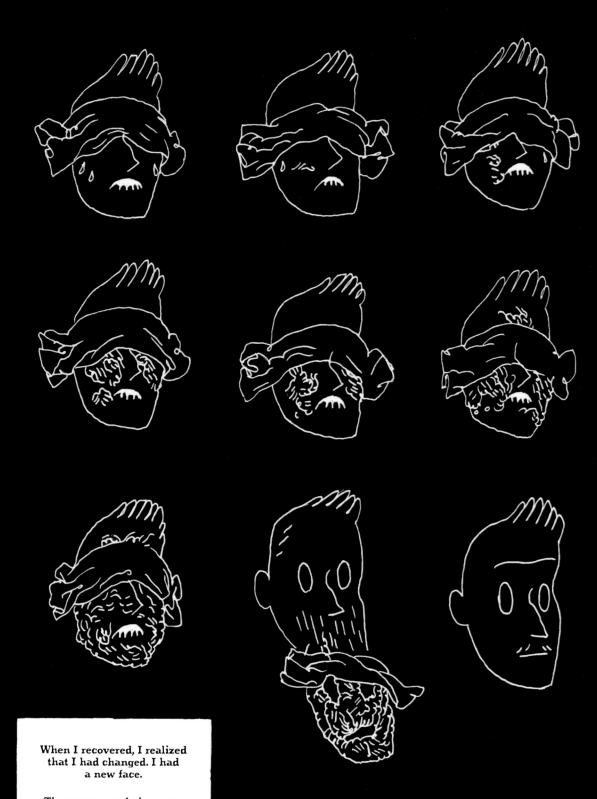

When I recovered, I realized that I had changed. I had a new face.

There was new hair on my head. And I was taller by a foot.

I tried out my new body on the way down from the mountains.

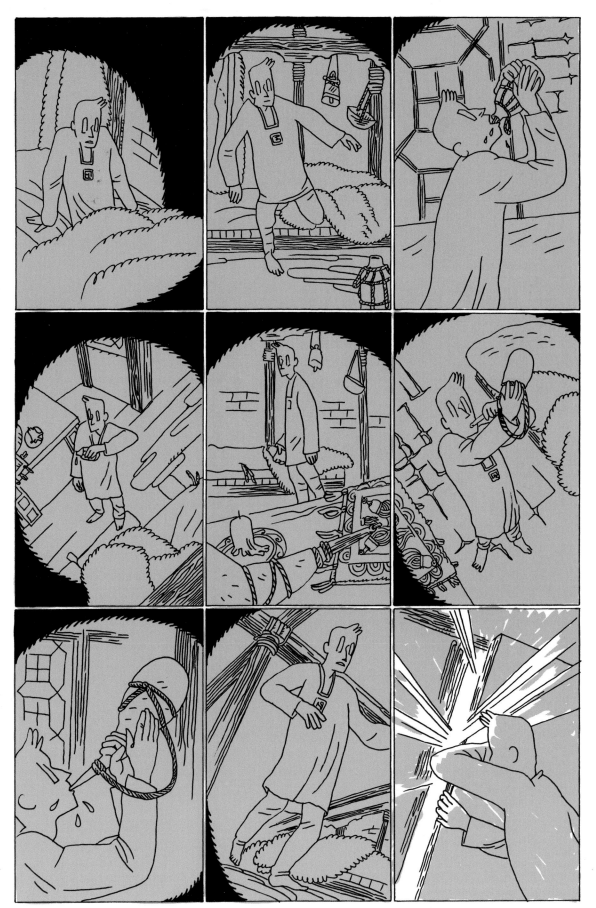

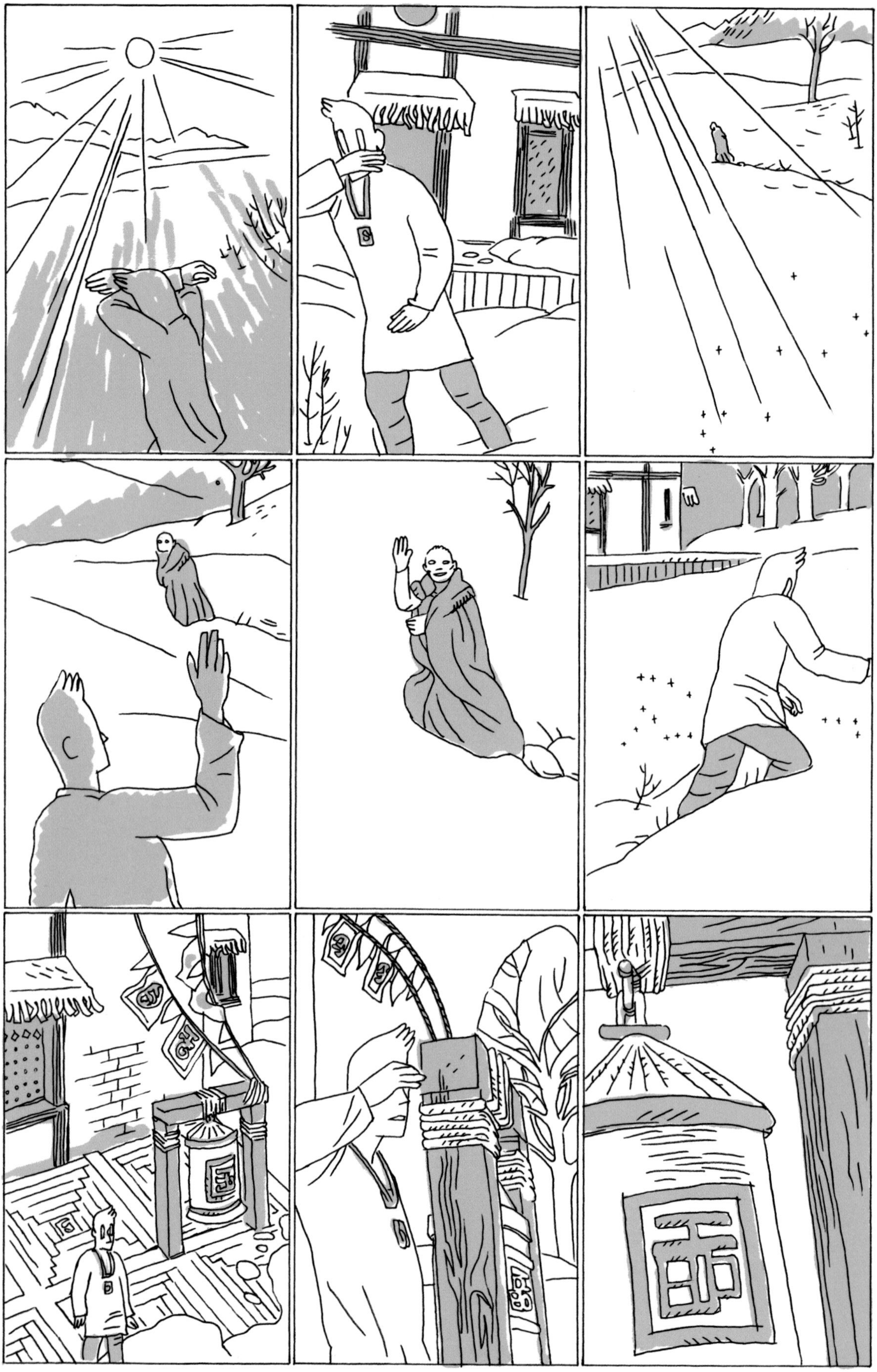

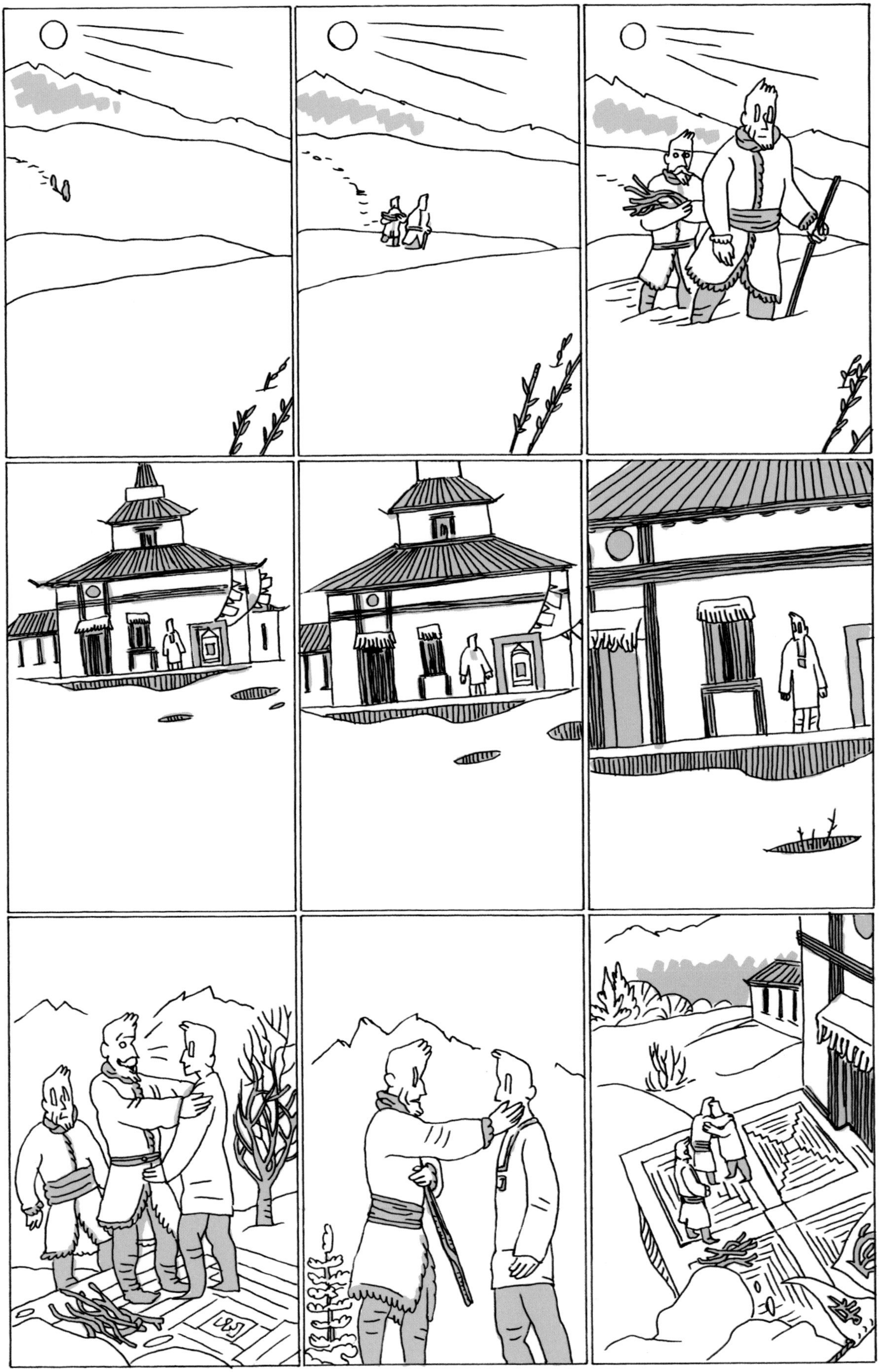

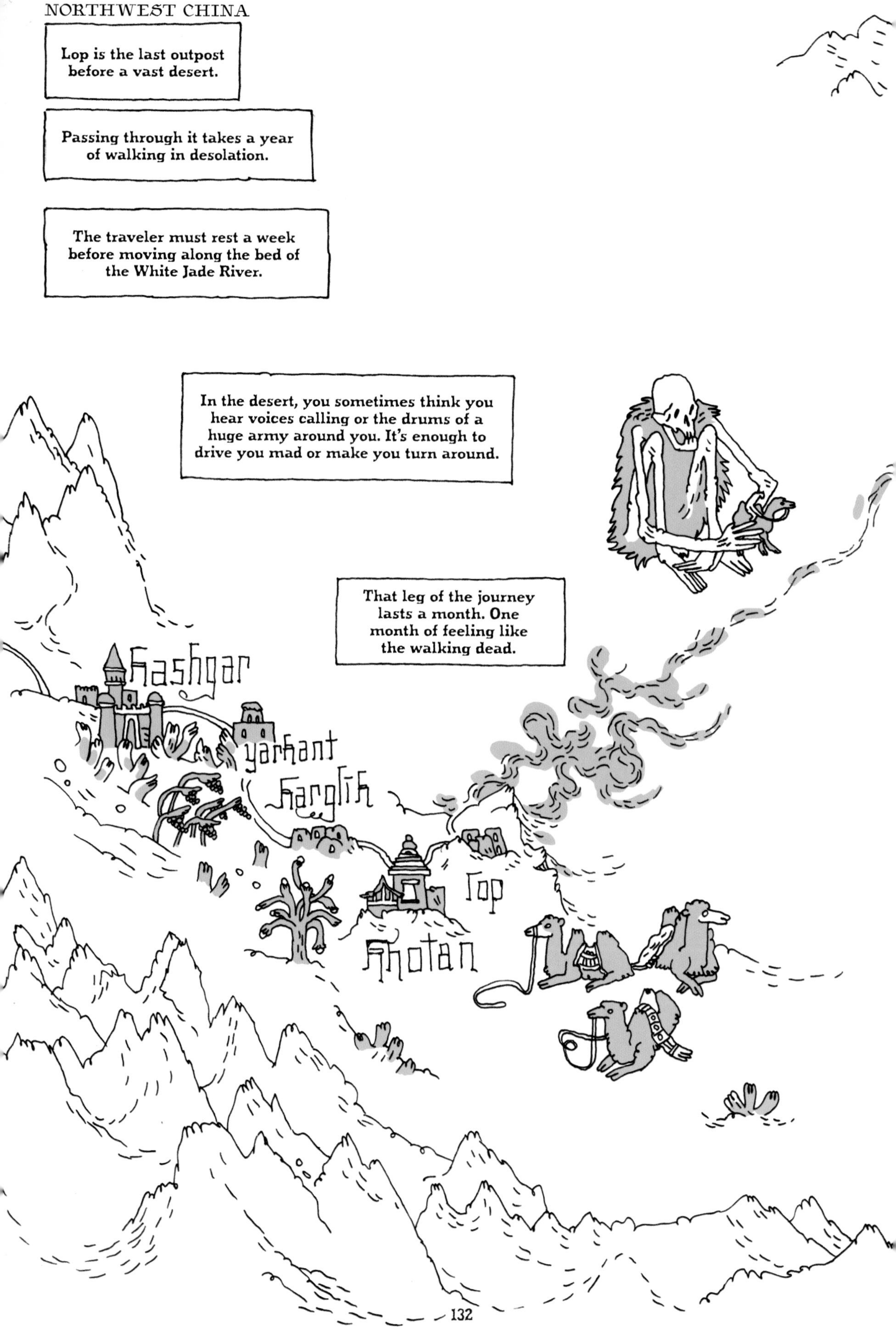
NORTHWEST CHINA
Lop is the last outpost before a vast desert.
Passing through it takes a year of walking in desolation.
The traveler must rest a week before moving along the bed of the White Jade River.
In the desert, you sometimes think you hear voices calling or the drums of a huge army around you. It's enough to drive you mad or make you turn around.
That leg of the journey lasts a month. One month of feeling like the walking dead.
Kashgar
yarkant
Karglik
Lop
Khotan

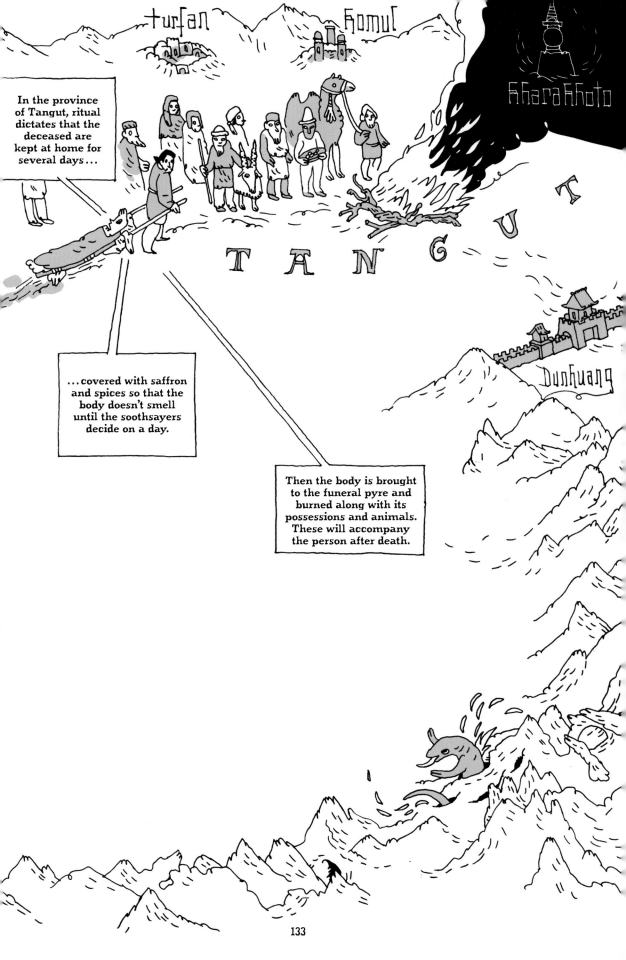

turfan

Ћomul

Ћara Ћoto

In the province of Tangut, ritual dictates that the deceased are kept at home for several days...

TANGUT

Dunhuang

...covered with saffron and spices so that the body doesn't smell until the soothsayers decide on a day.

Then the body is brought to the funeral pyre and burned along with its possessions and animals. These will accompany the person after death.

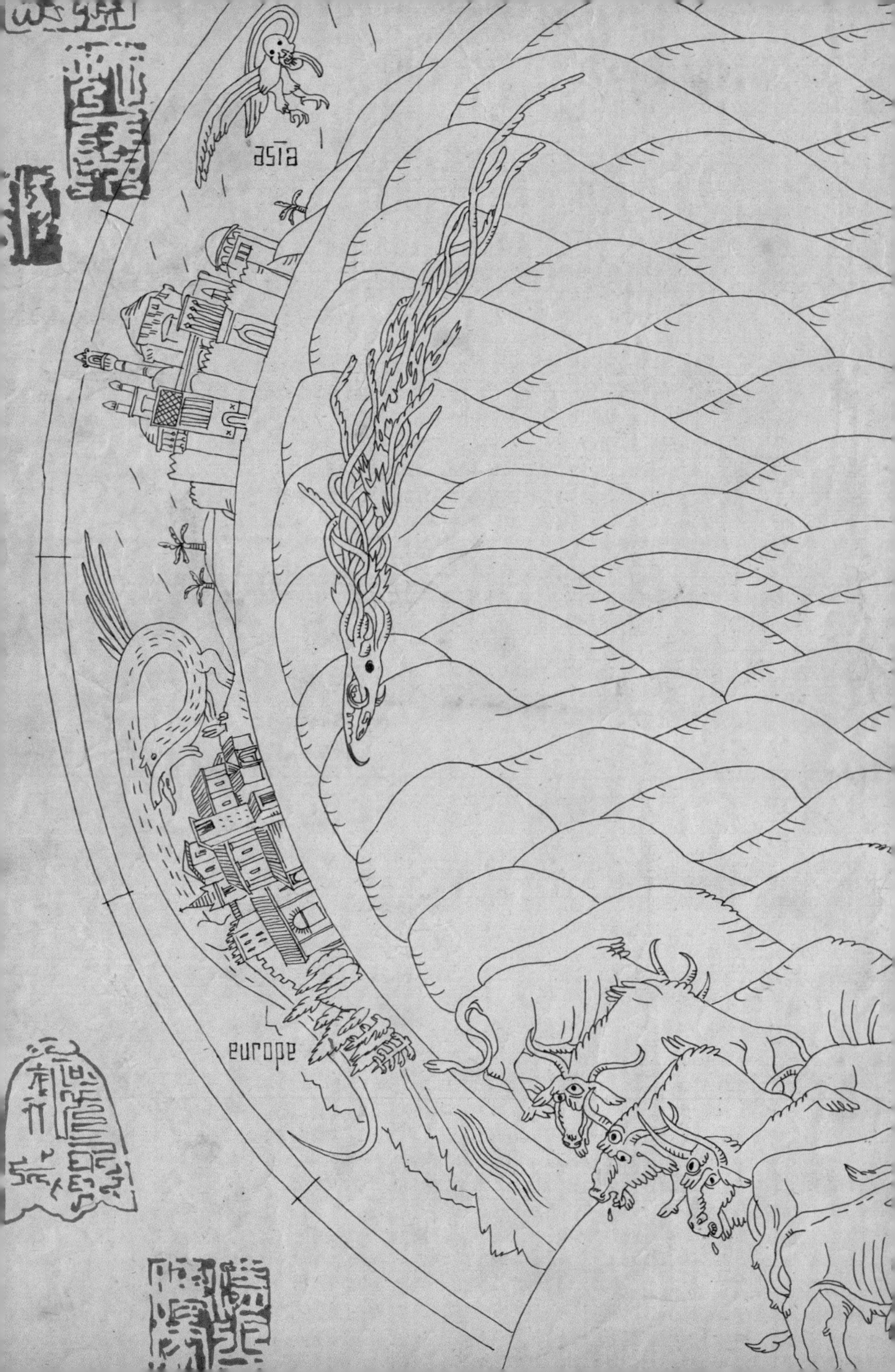

asia
europe

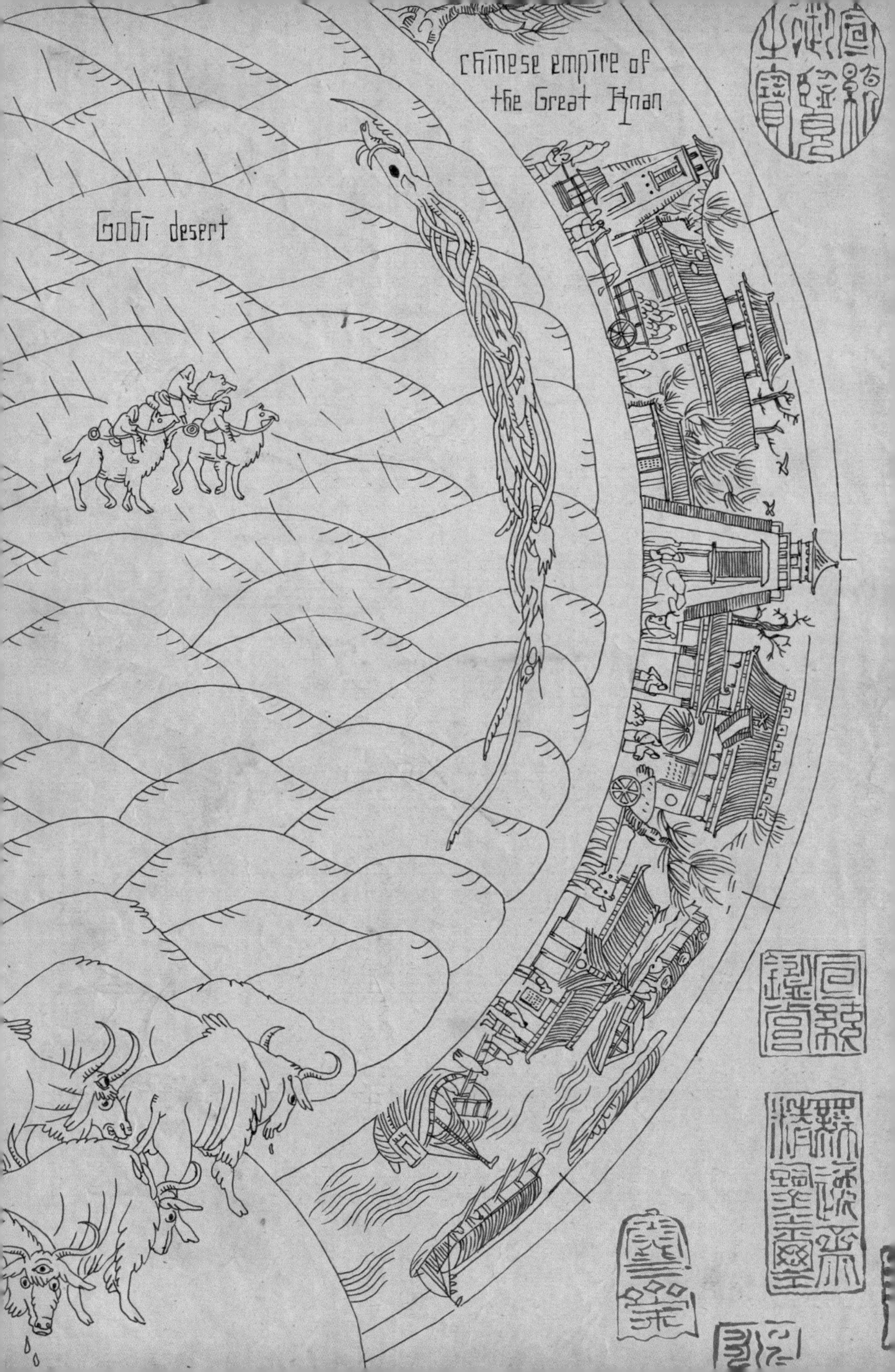
Chinese empire of
the Great Khan
Gobi desert

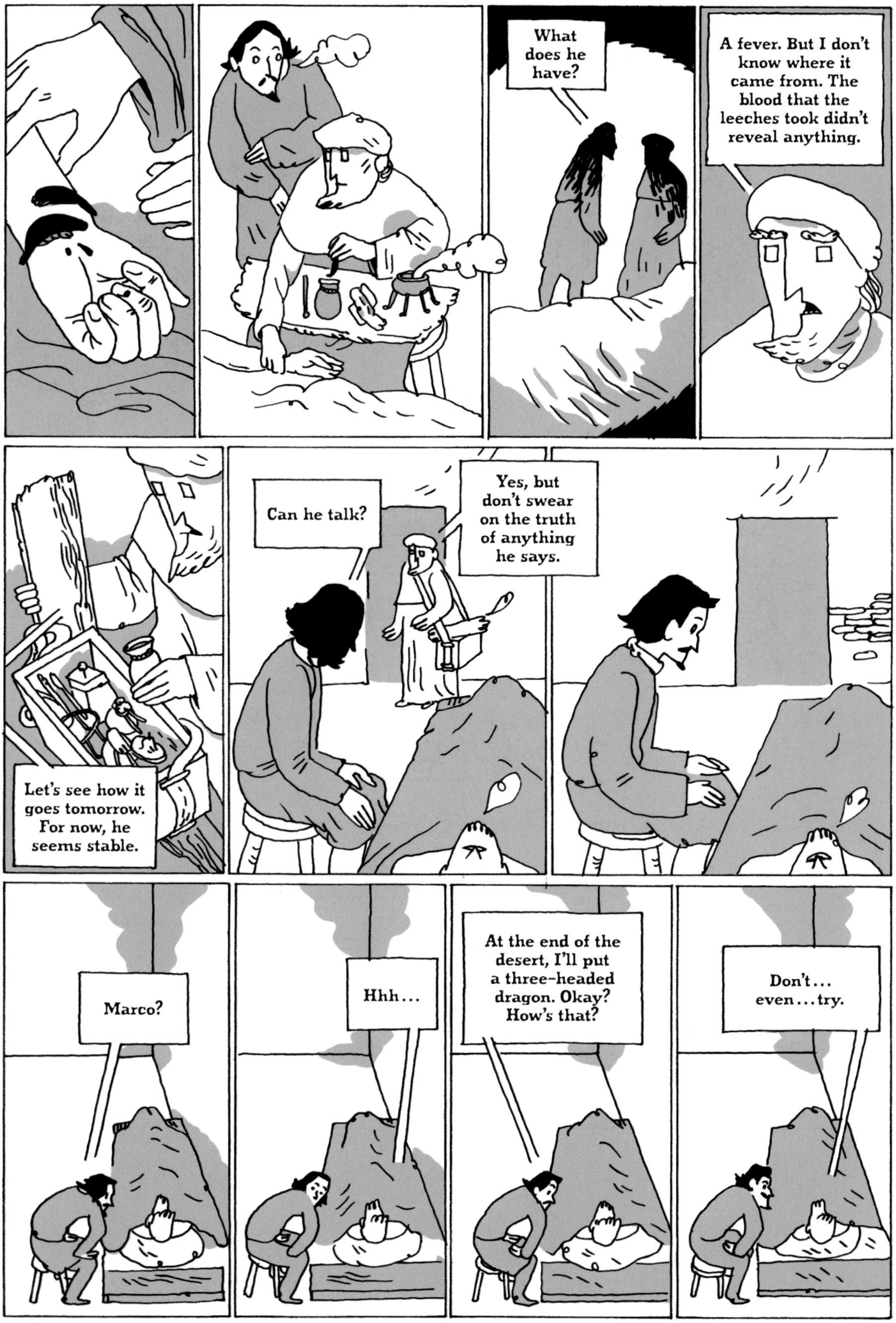
What does he have?
A fever. But I don't know where it came from. The blood that the leeches took didn't reveal anything.
Let's see how it goes tomorrow. For now, he seems stable.
Can he talk?
Yes, but don't swear on the truth of anything he says.
Marco?
Hhh...
At the end of the desert, I'll put a three-headed dragon. Okay? How's that?
Don't... even... try.

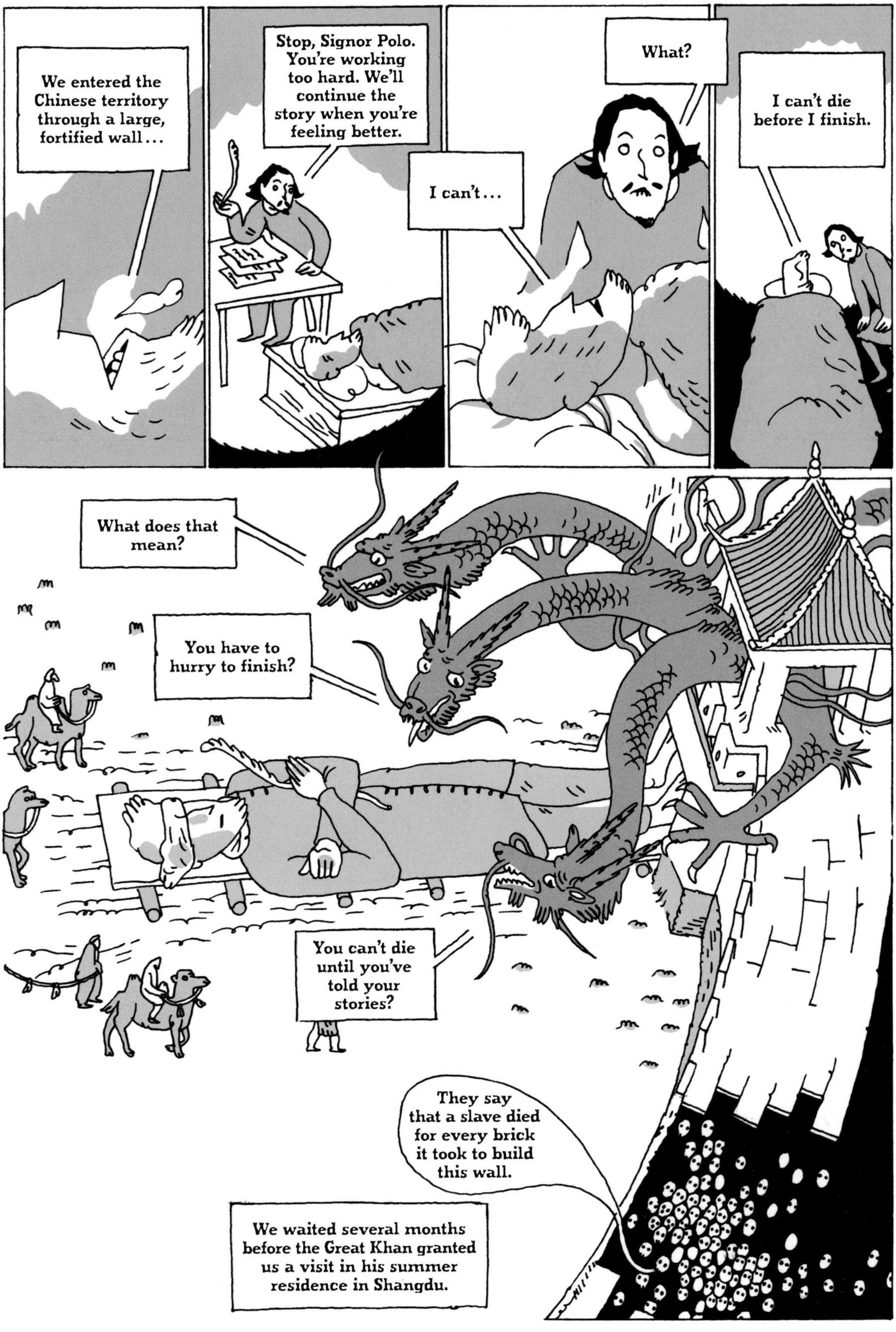
We entered the Chinese territory through a large, fortified wall...
Stop, Signor Polo. You're working too hard. We'll continue the story when you're feeling better.
I can't...
What?
I can't die before I finish.
What does that mean?
You have to hurry to finish?
You can't die until you've told your stories?
They say that a slave died for every brick it took to build this wall.
We waited several months before the Great Khan granted us a visit in his summer residence in Shangdu.

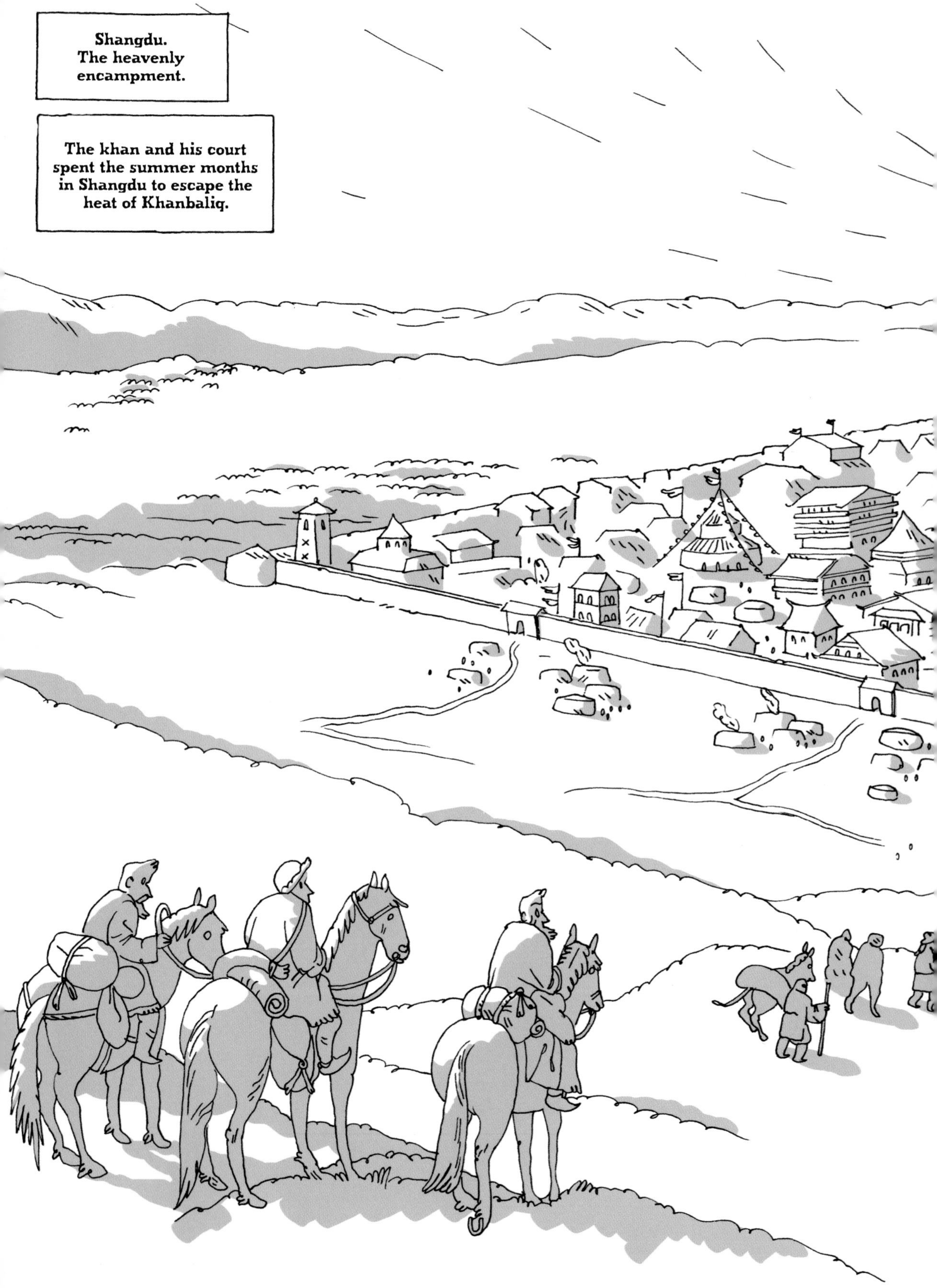
Shangdu.
The heavenly
encampment.
The khan and his court
spent the summer months
in Shangdu to escape the
heat of Khanbaliq.

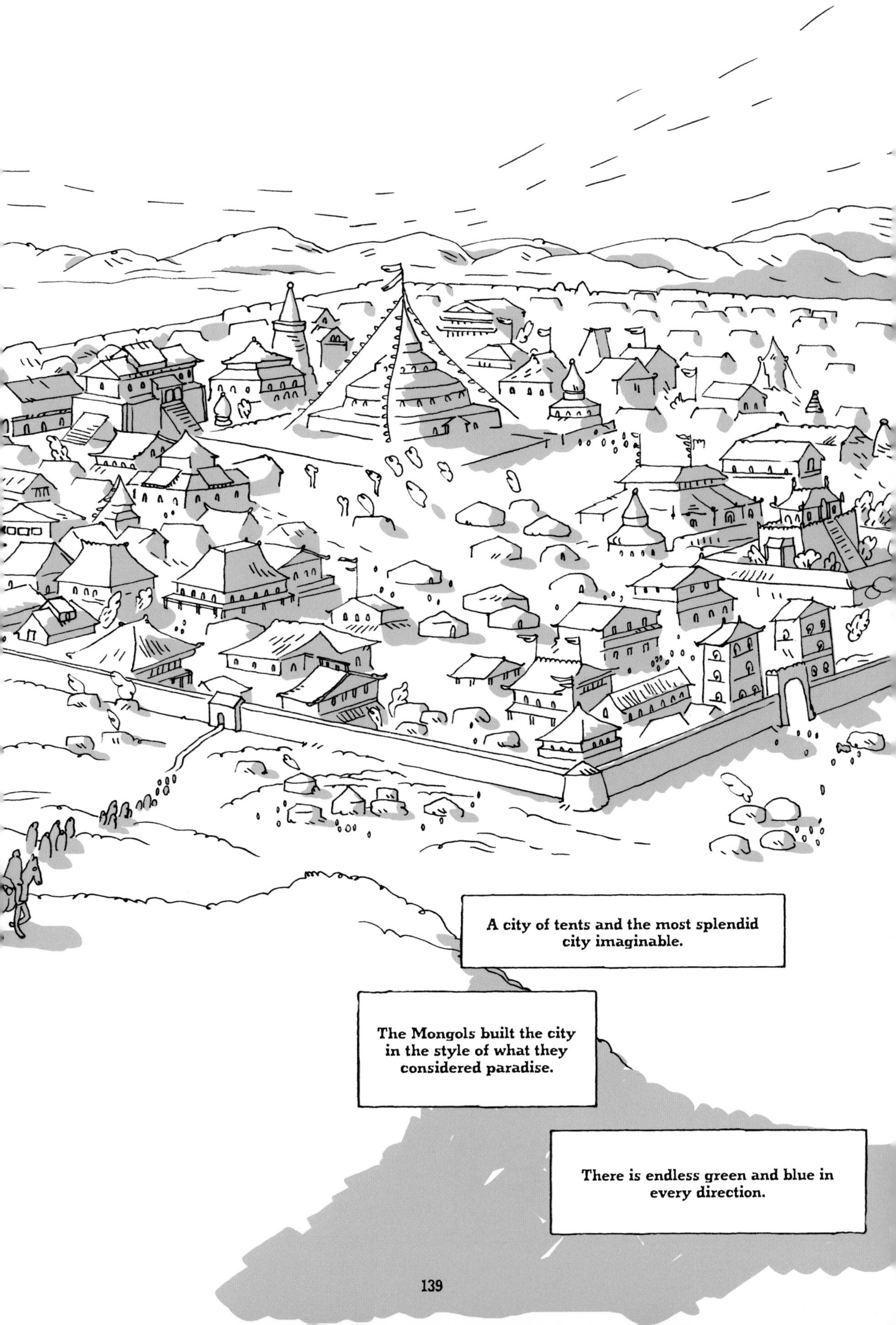
A city of tents and the most splendid city imaginable.
The Mongols built the city in the style of what they considered paradise.
There is endless green and blue in every direction.

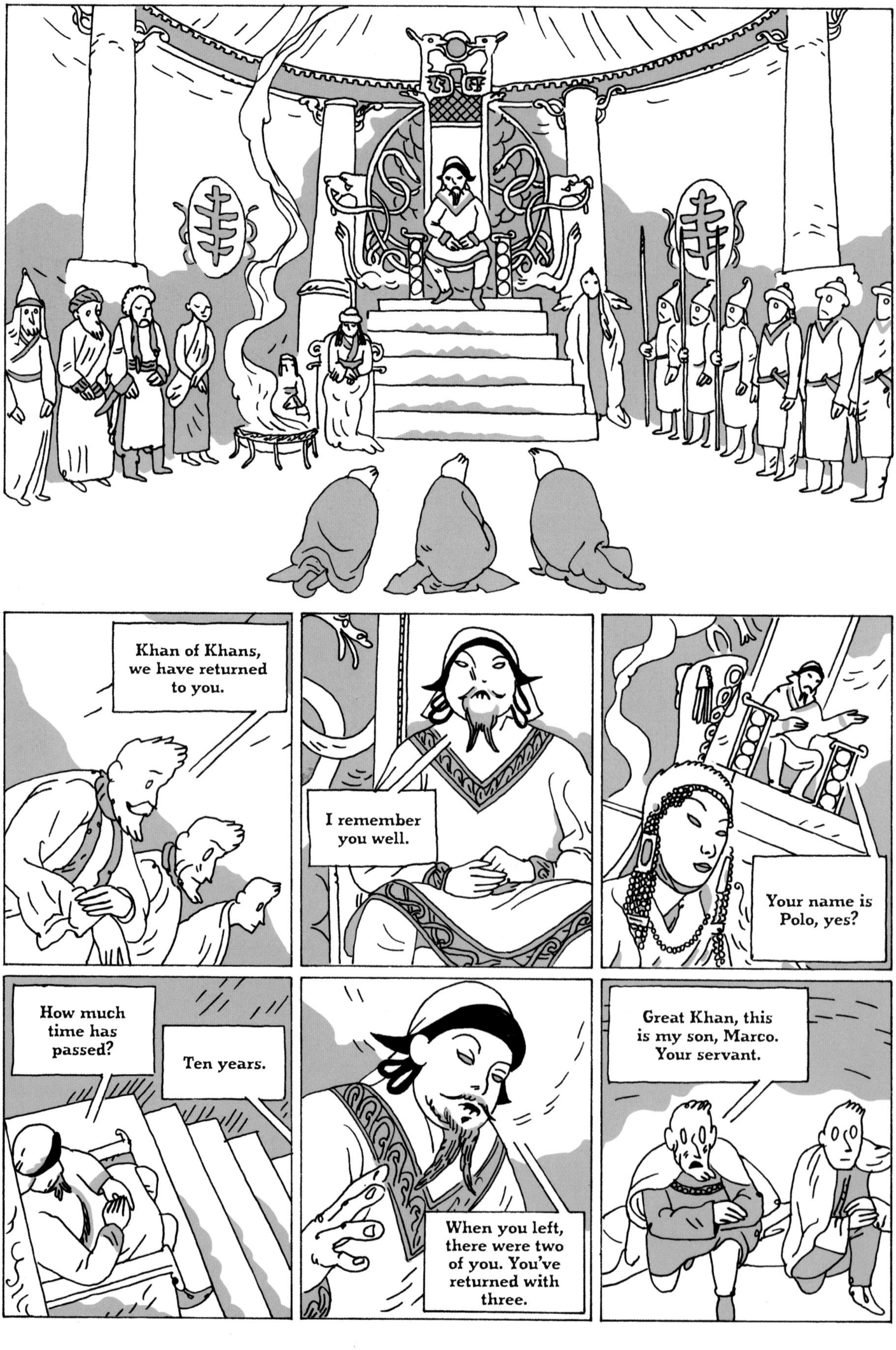
Khan of Khans, we have returned to you.
I remember you well.
Your name is Polo, yes?
How much time has passed?
Ten years.
When you left, there were two of you. You've returned with three.
Great Khan, this is my son, Marco. Your servant.

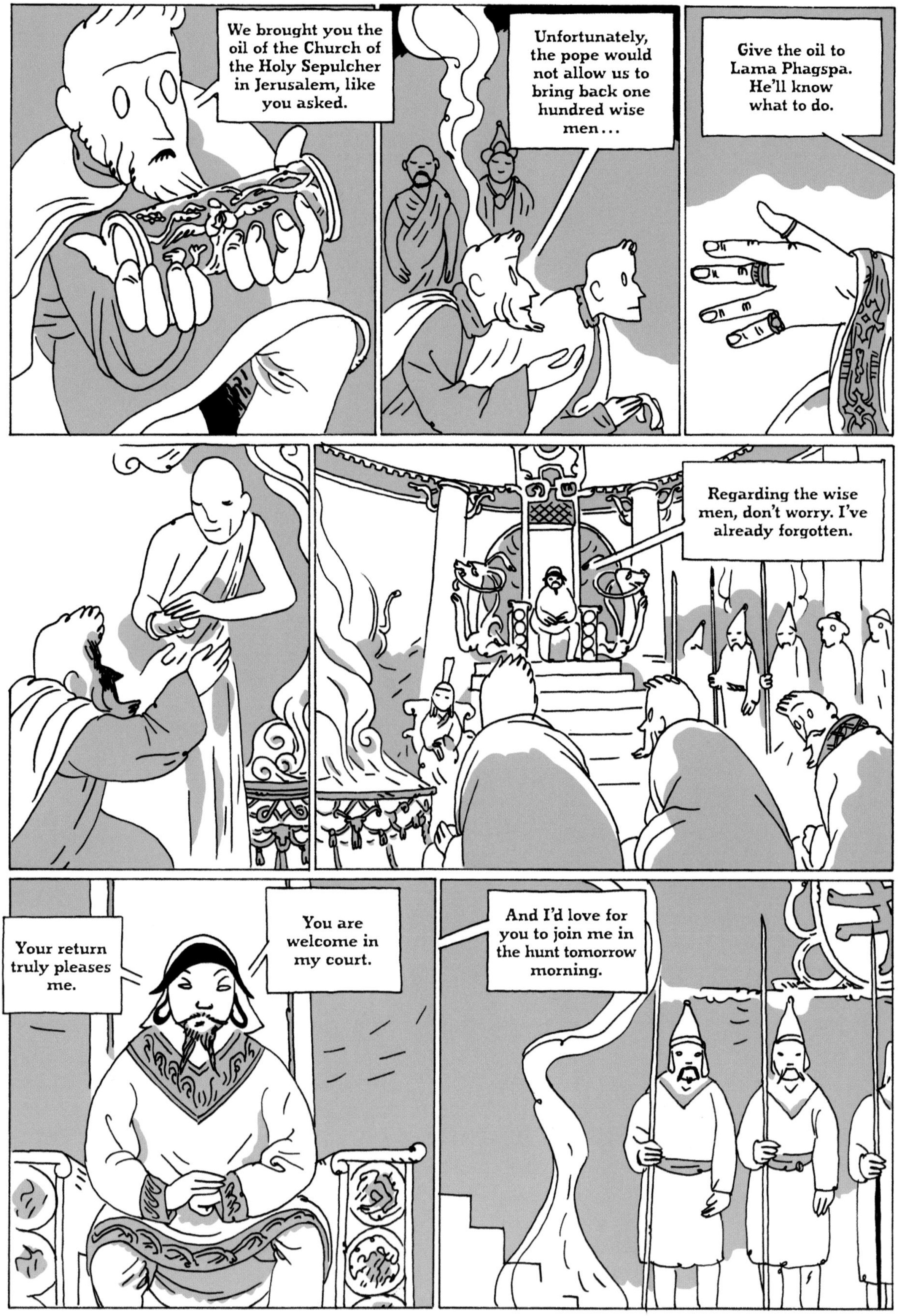
We brought you the oil of the Church of the Holy Sepulcher in Jerusalem, like you asked.
Unfortunately, the pope would not allow us to bring back one hundred wise men...
Give the oil to Lama Phagspa. He'll know what to do.
Regarding the wise men, don't worry. I've already forgotten.
Your return truly pleases me.
You are welcome in my court.
And I'd love for you to join me in the hunt tomorrow morning.

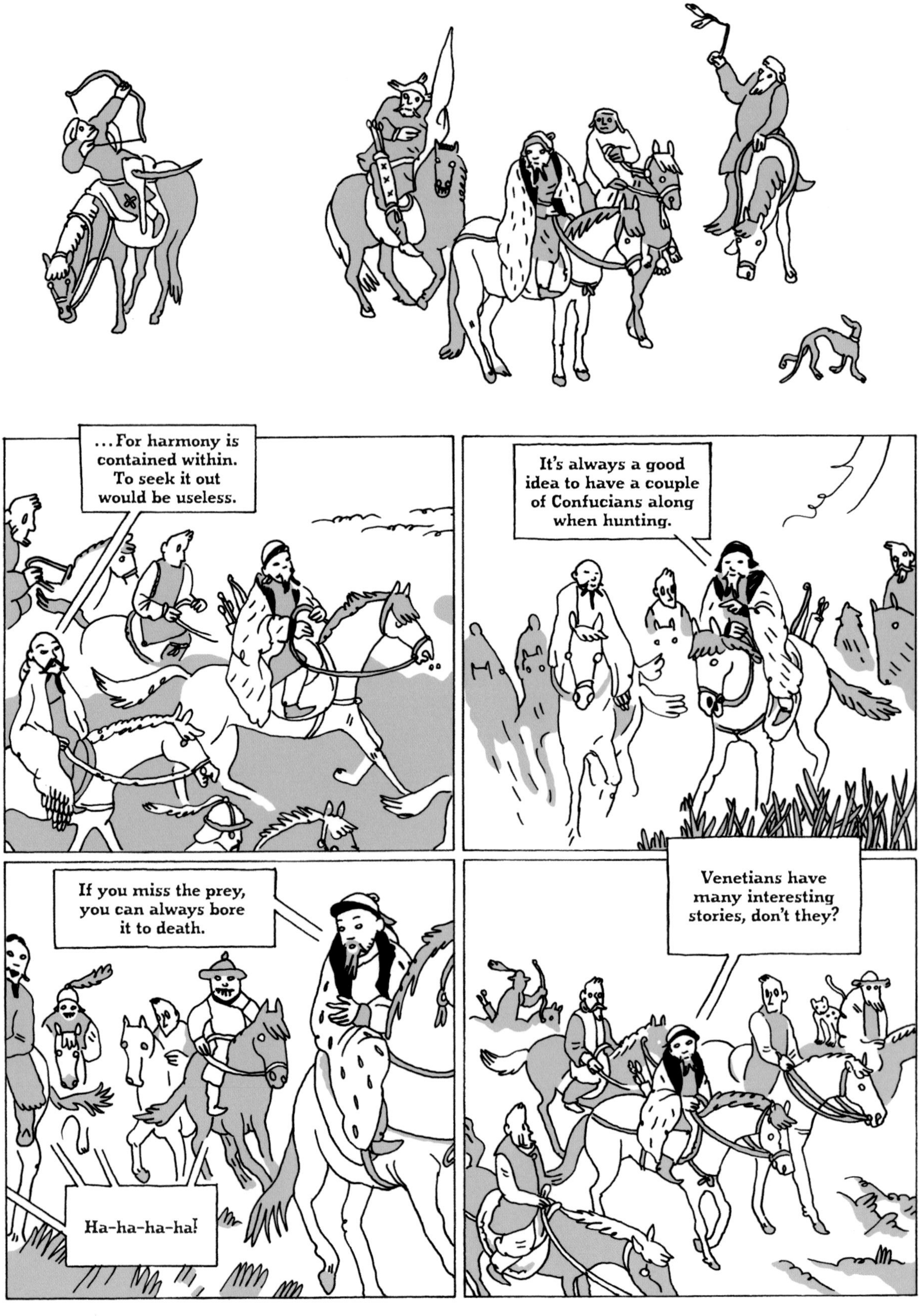
...For harmony is contained within. To seek it out would be useless.
It's always a good idea to have a couple of Confucians along when hunting.
If you miss the prey, you can always bore it to death.
Ha-ha-ha-ha!
Venetians have many interesting stories, don't they?

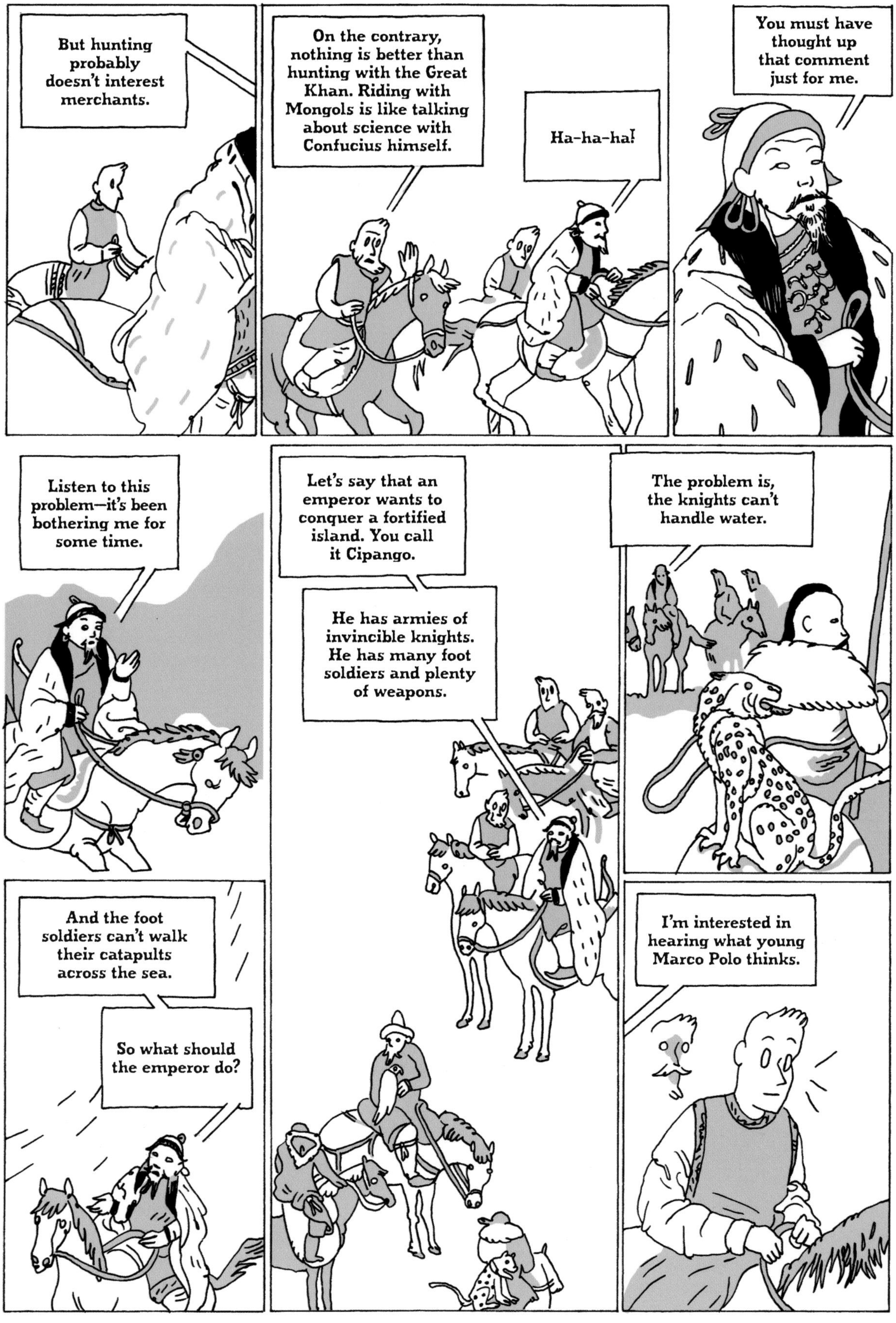
But hunting probably doesn't interest merchants.
On the contrary, nothing is better than hunting with the Great Khan. Riding with Mongols is like talking about science with Confucius himself.
Ha-ha-ha!
You must have thought up that comment just for me.
Listen to this problem—it's been bothering me for some time.
Let's say that an emperor wants to conquer a fortified island. You call it Cipango.
He has armies of invincible knights. He has many foot soldiers and plenty of weapons.
The problem is, the knights can't handle water.
And the foot soldiers can't walk their catapults across the sea.
So what should the emperor do?
I'm interested in hearing what young Marco Polo thinks.

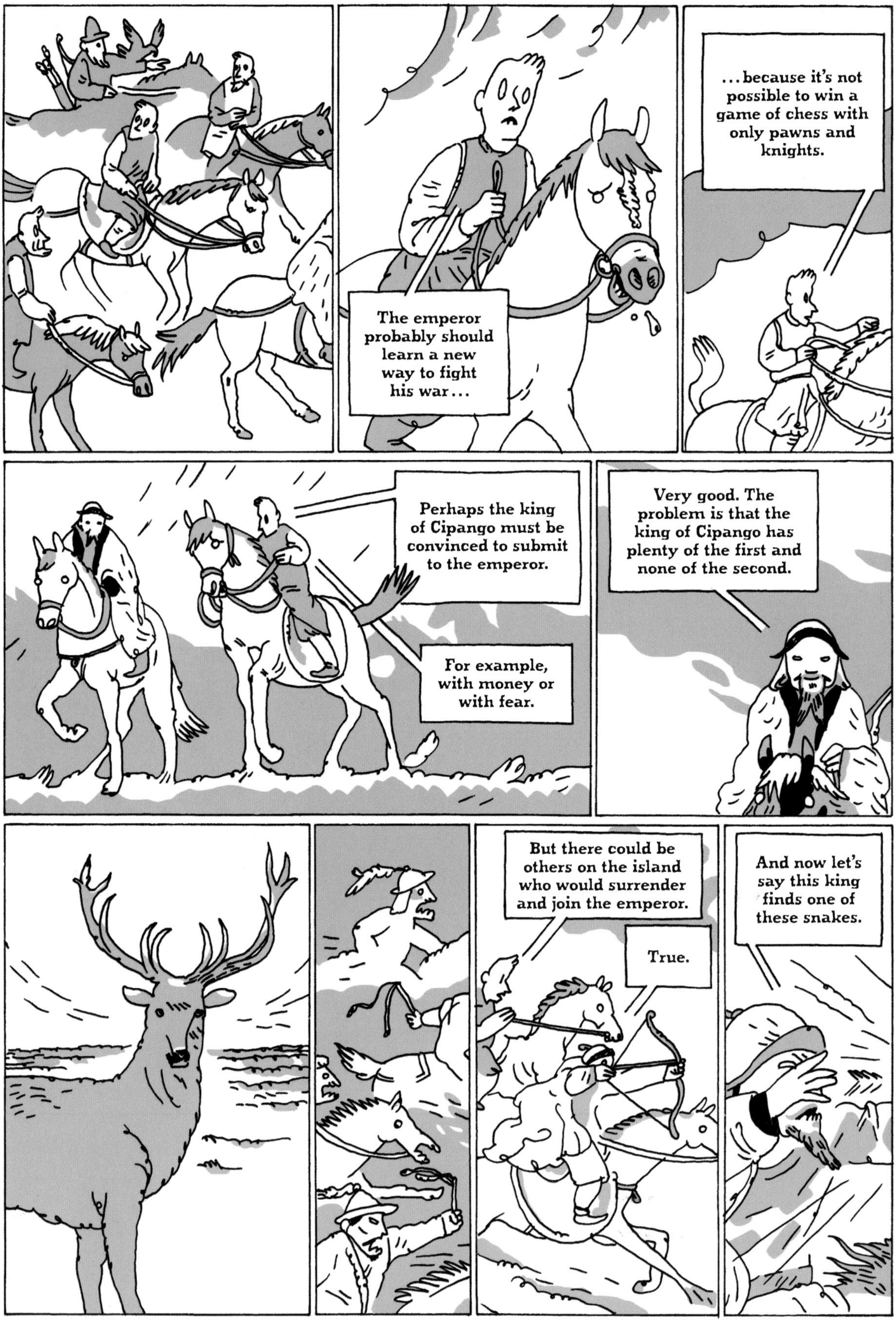
The emperor probably should learn a new way to fight his war...
...because it's not possible to win a game of chess with only pawns and knights.
Perhaps the king of Cipango must be convinced to submit to the emperor.
For example, with money or with fear.
Very good. The problem is that the king of Cipango has plenty of the first and none of the second.
But there could be others on the island who would surrender and join the emperor.
True.
And now let's say this king finds one of these snakes.

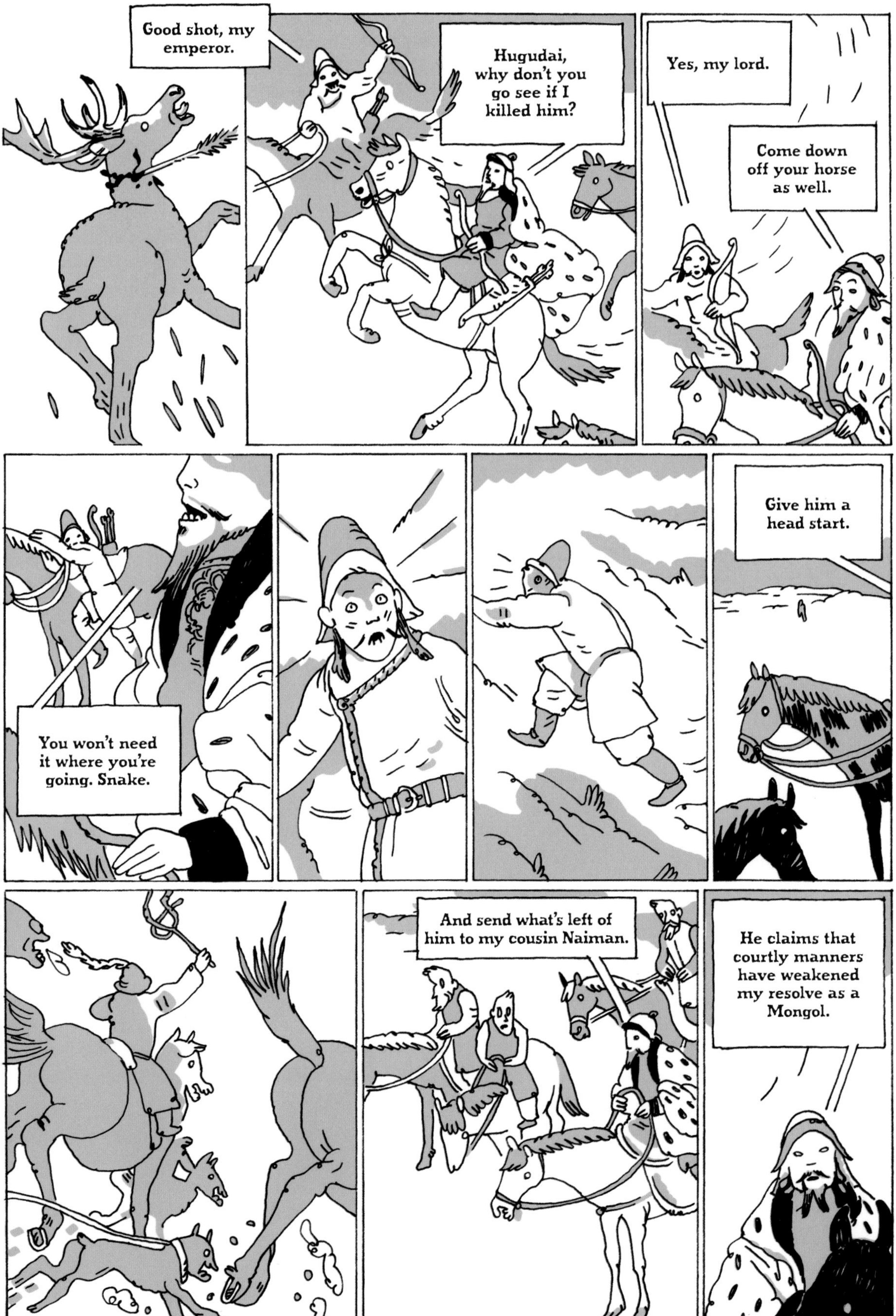
Good shot, my emperor.
Hugudai, why don't you go see if I killed him?
Yes, my lord.
Come down off your horse as well.
You won't need it where you're going. Snake.
Give him a head start.
And send what's left of him to my cousin Naiman.
He claims that courtly manners have weakened my resolve as a Mongol.

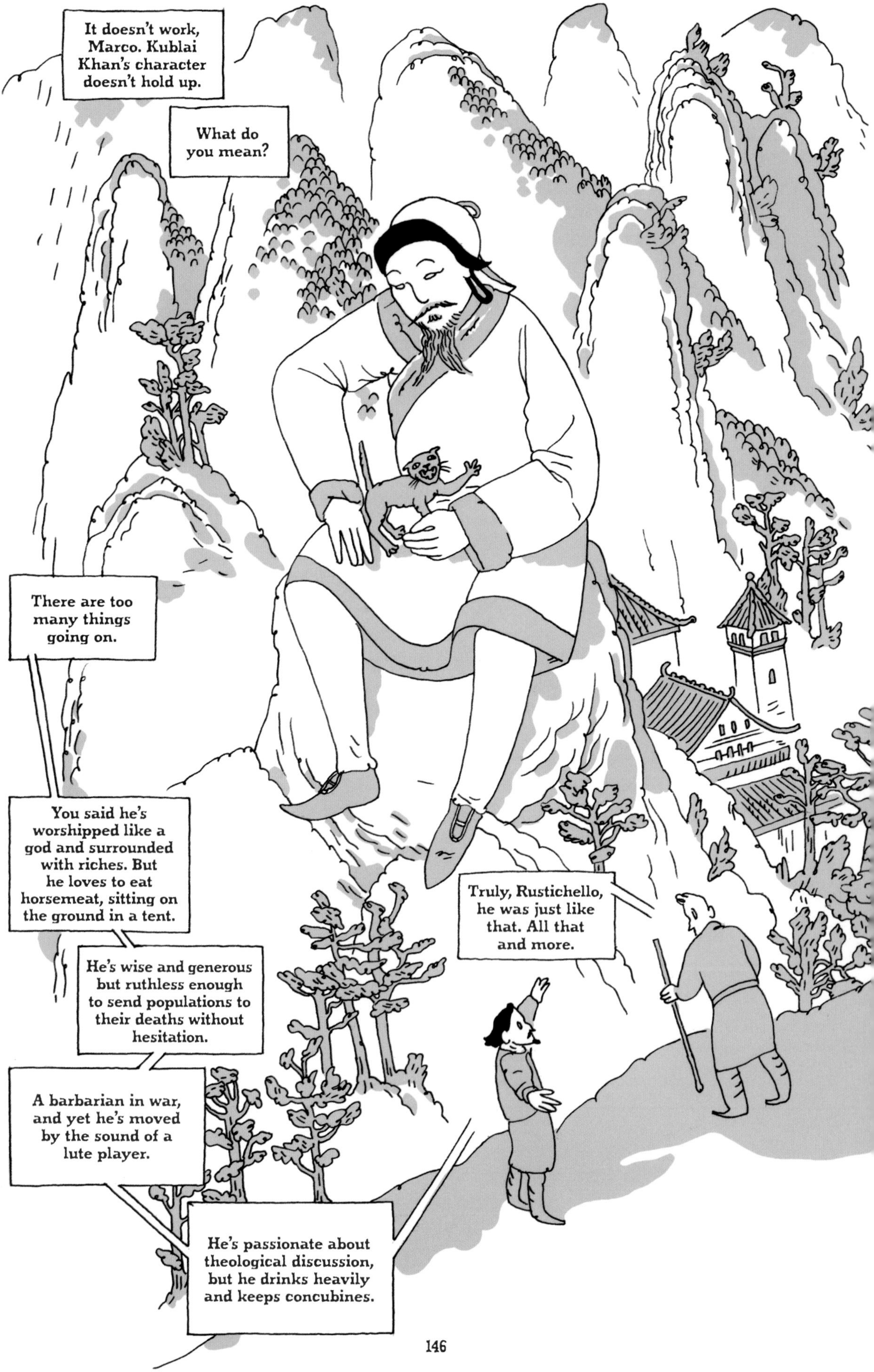

It doesn't work, Marco. Kublai Khan's character doesn't hold up.
What do you mean?
There are too many things going on.
You said he's worshipped like a god and surrounded with riches. But he loves to eat horsemeat, sitting on the ground in a tent.
He's wise and generous but ruthless enough to send populations to their deaths without hesitation.
A barbarian in war, and yet he's moved by the sound of a lute player.
He's passionate about theological discussion, but he drinks heavily and keeps concubines.
Truly, Rustichello, he was just like that. All that and more.

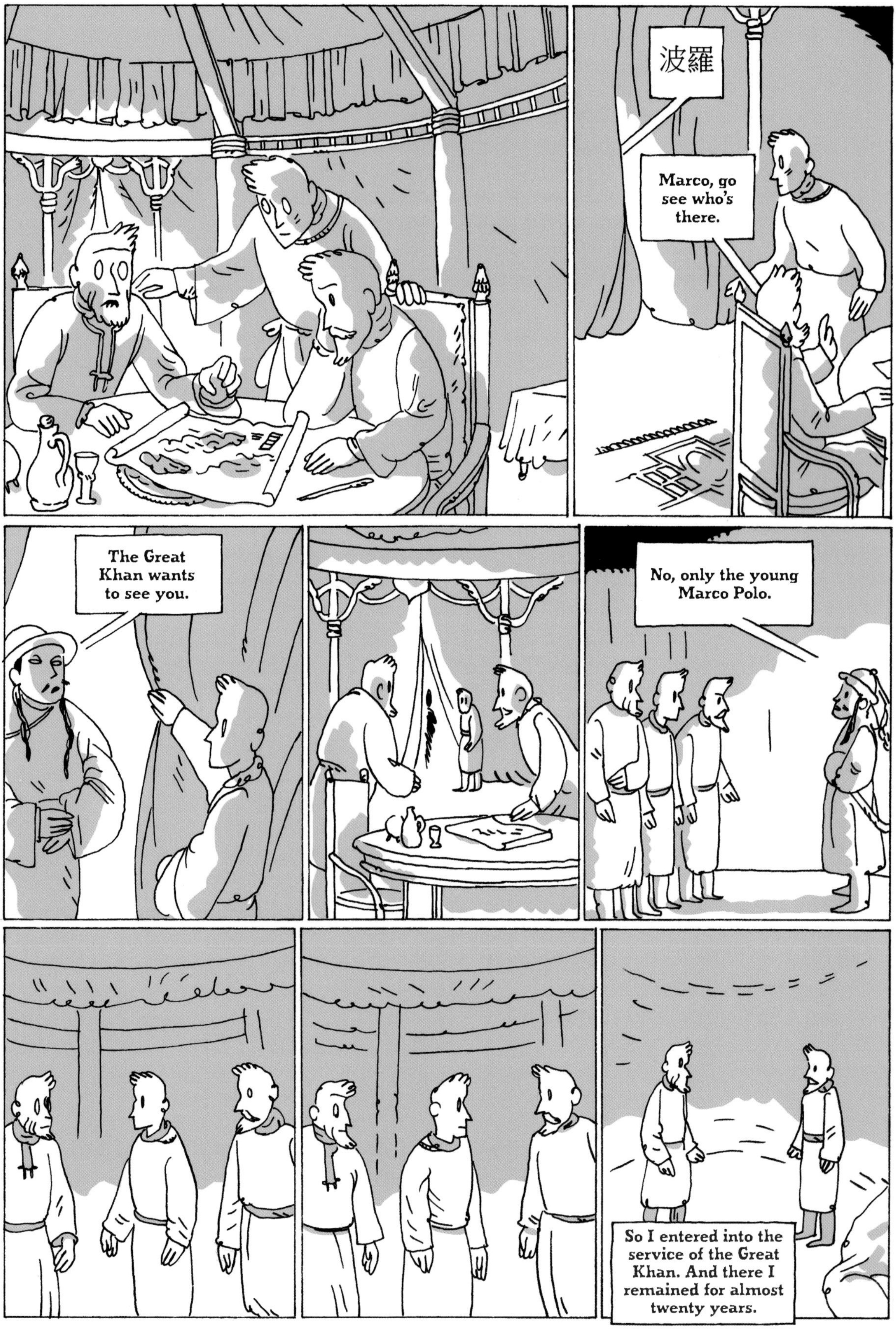

波羅
Marco, go see who's there.
The Great Khan wants to see you.
No, only the young Marco Polo.
So I entered into the service of the Great Khan. And there I remained for almost twenty years.

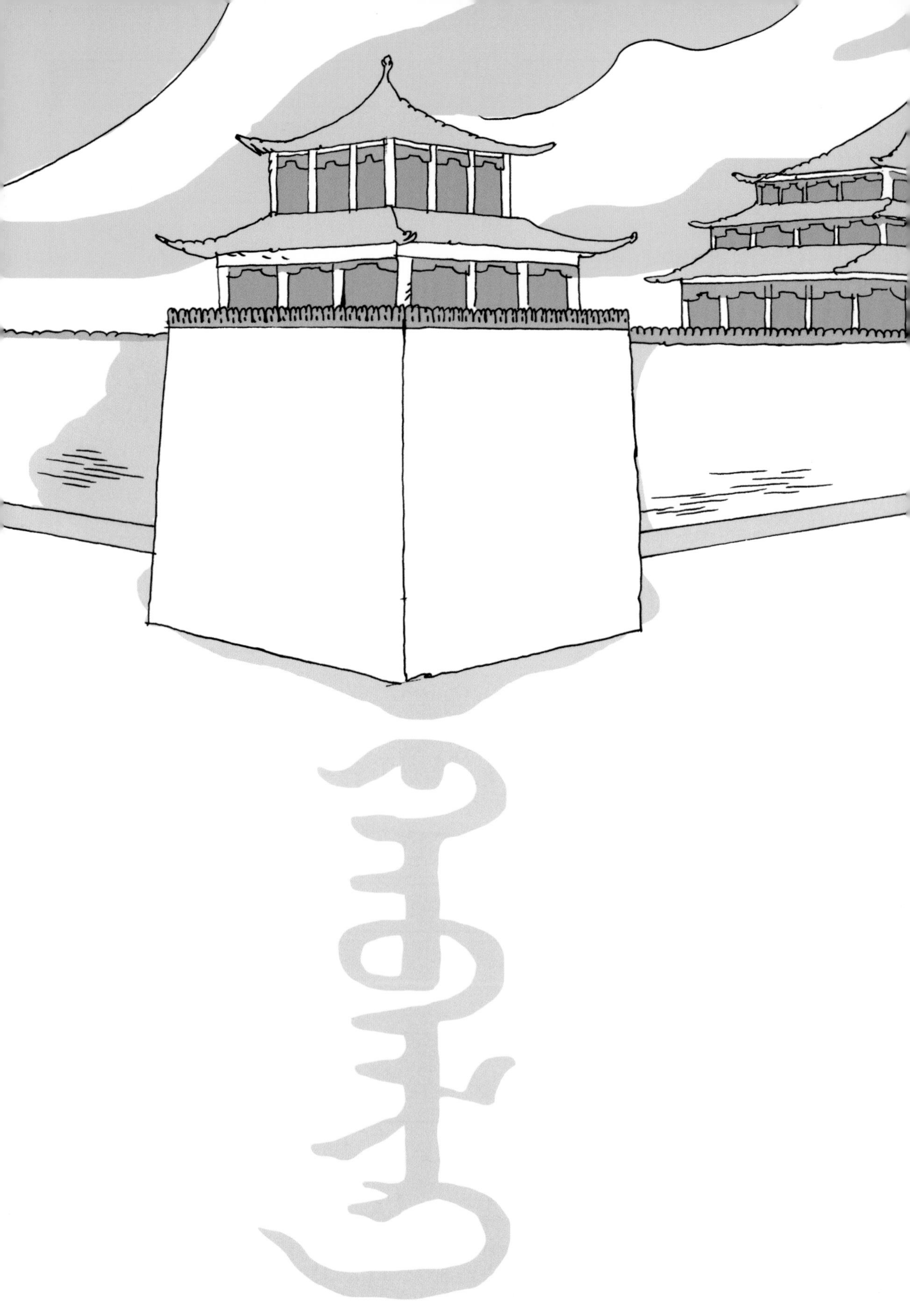

Khanbaliq.

The capital of the khan
became my home for the
following years.

Kublai sent me around the
different provinces of the empire,
but at the end of each mission, I
always came back to Khanbaliq.

I did everything for
the emperor.

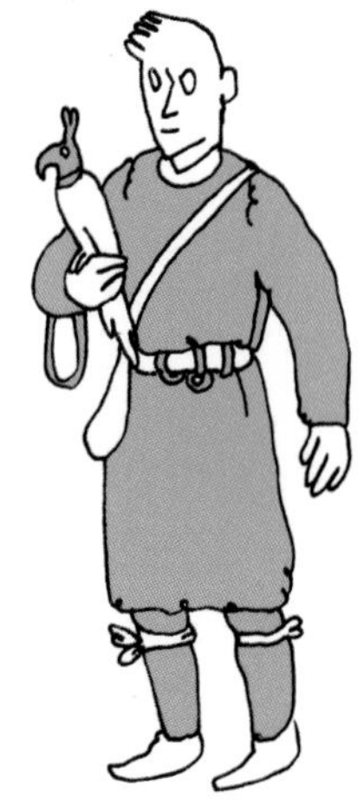

Hunting companion

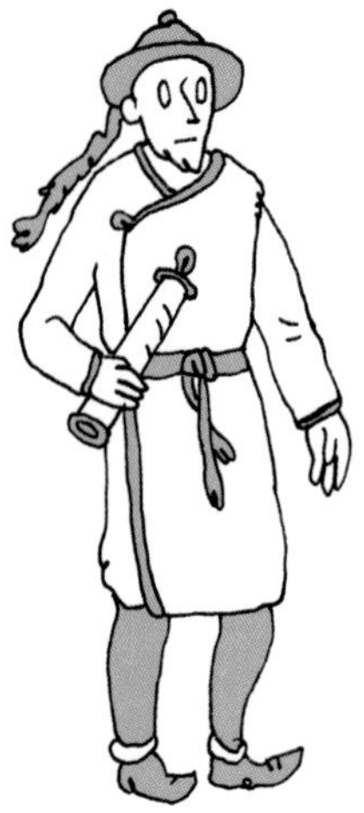

Imperial messenger

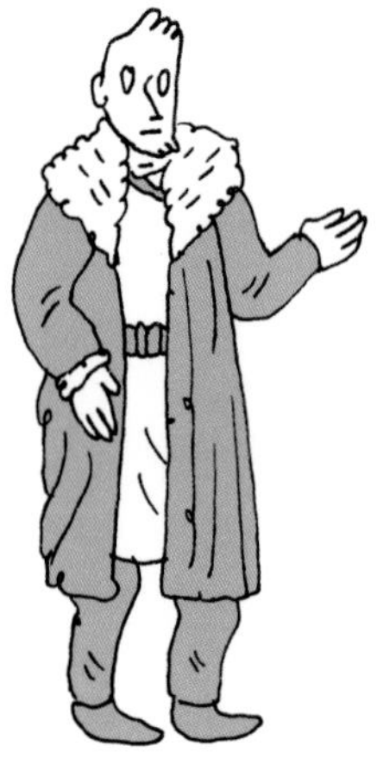

Interpreter (Persian, Latin, Tartar)

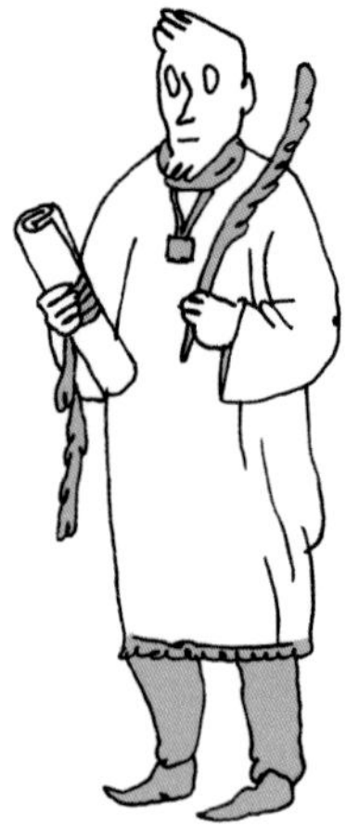

Geographer

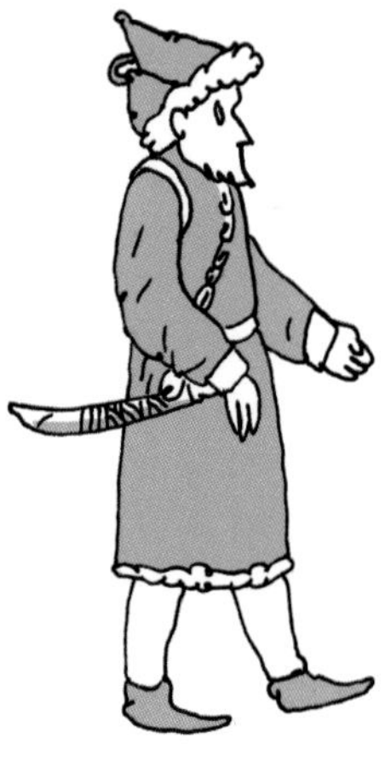

Caravan leader

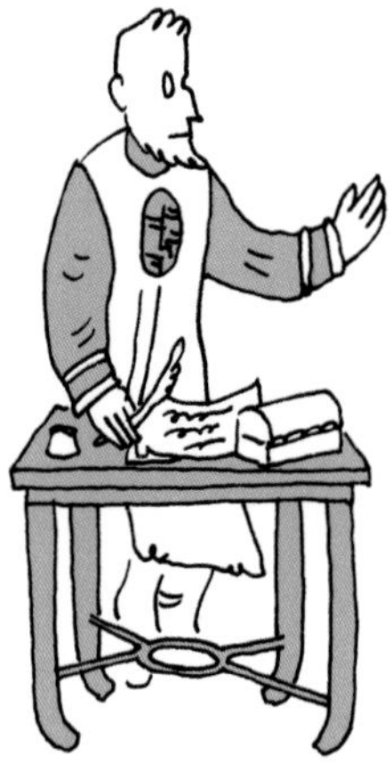

Tax collector

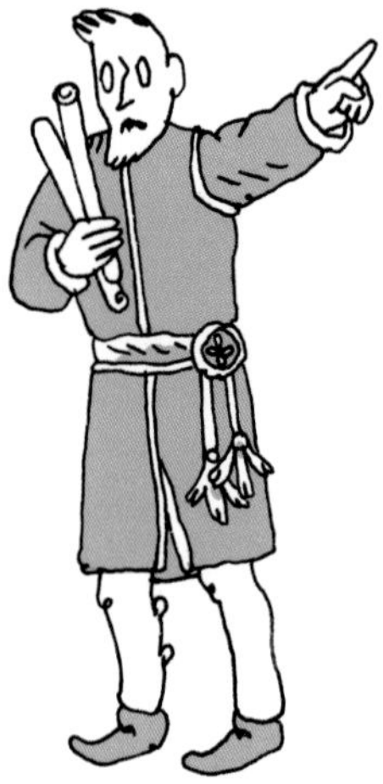

Foreman

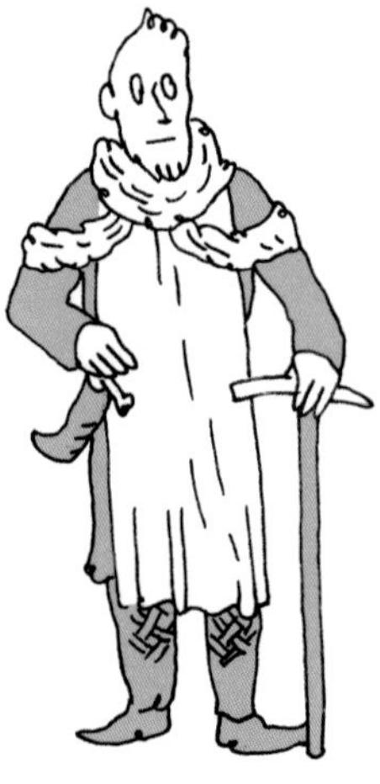

Supervisor at the mines

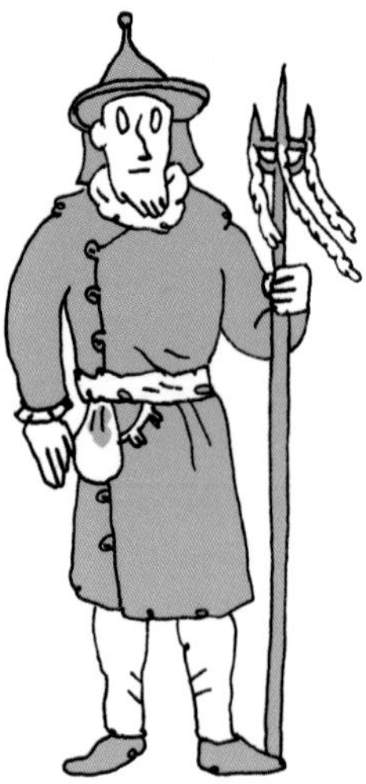

Controller of the water supply

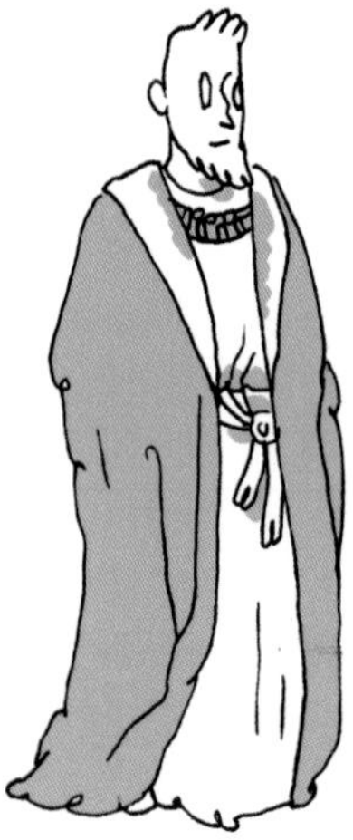

Ambassador

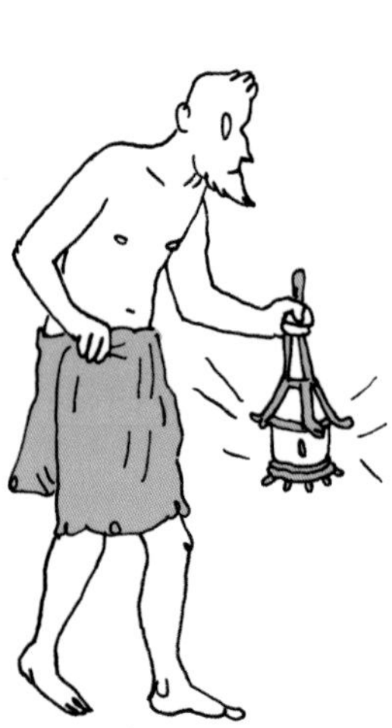

Spy

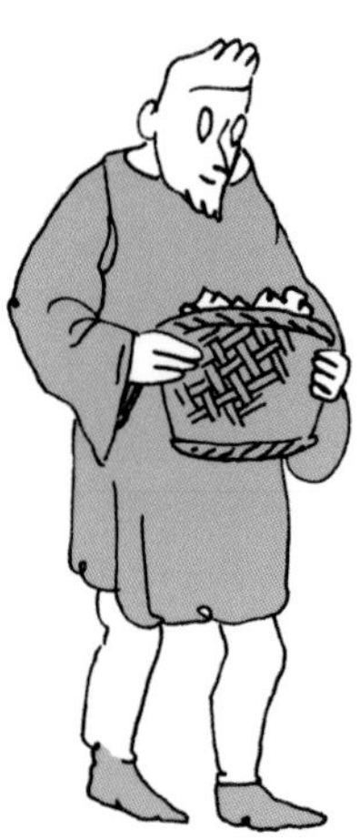

Master salt extractor

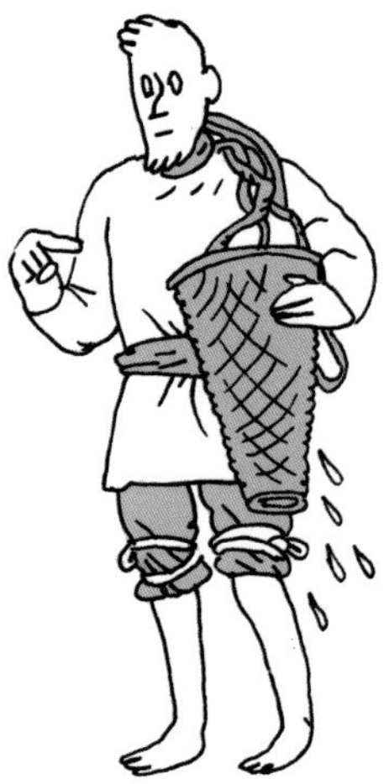

Adviser to the fisheries

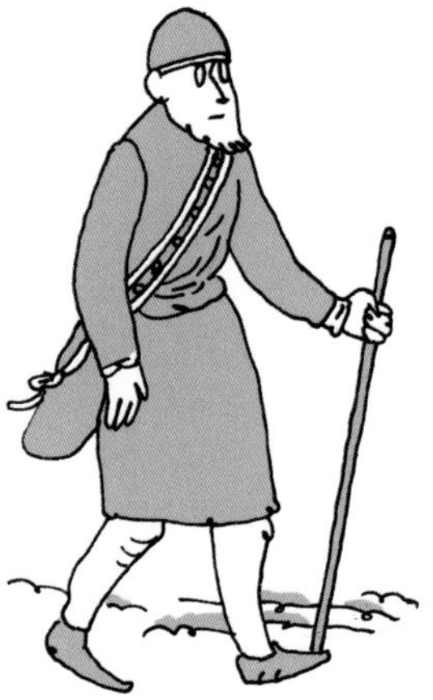

Courier

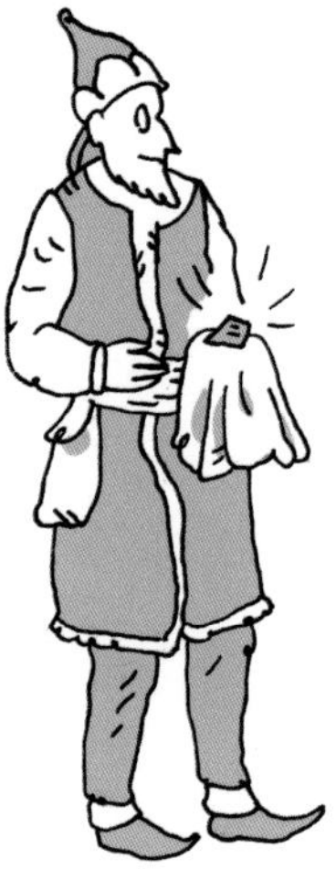

Merchant (as always)

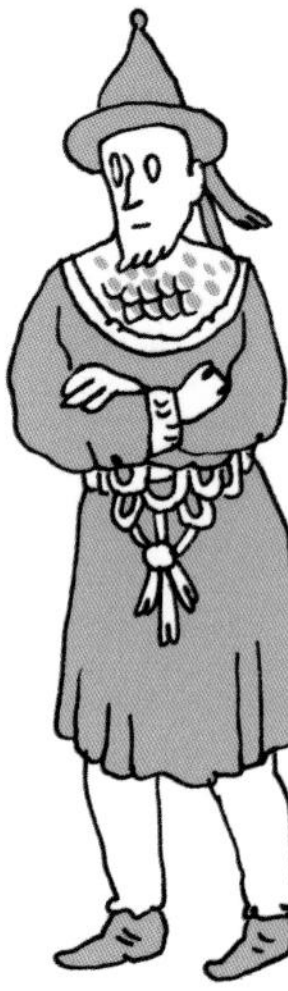

Supervisor at
the mint

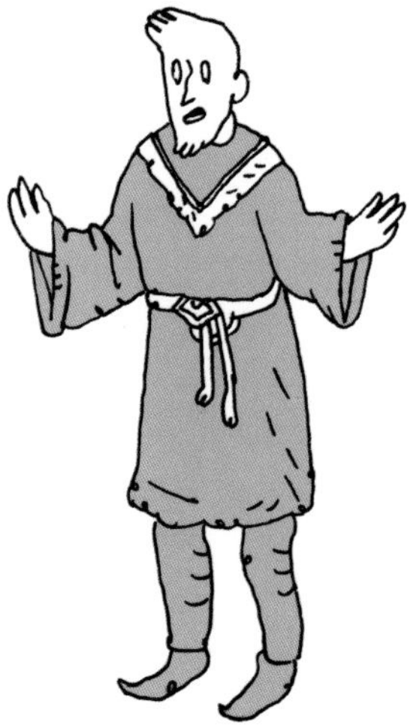

Religious mediator

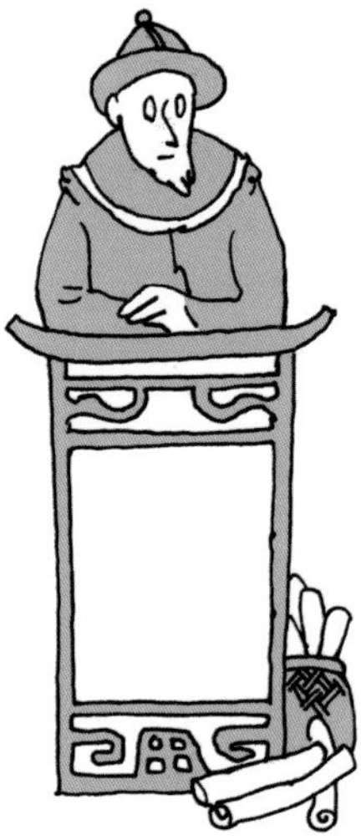

Conductor of imperial
examinations

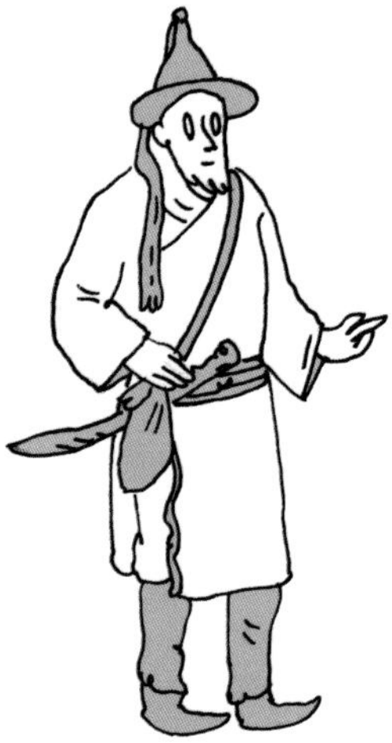

Officer of charity

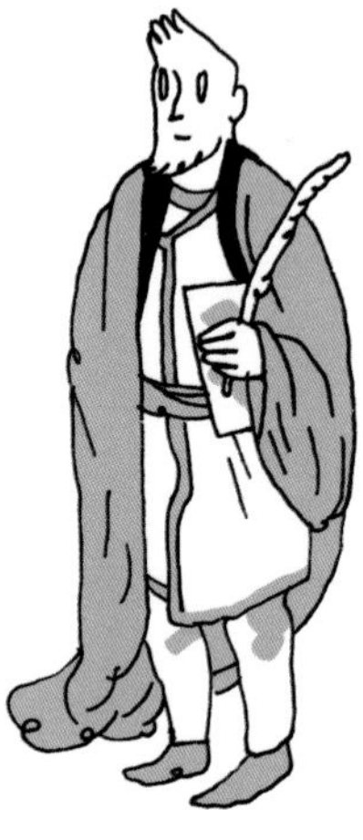

Philosopher
(improvised)

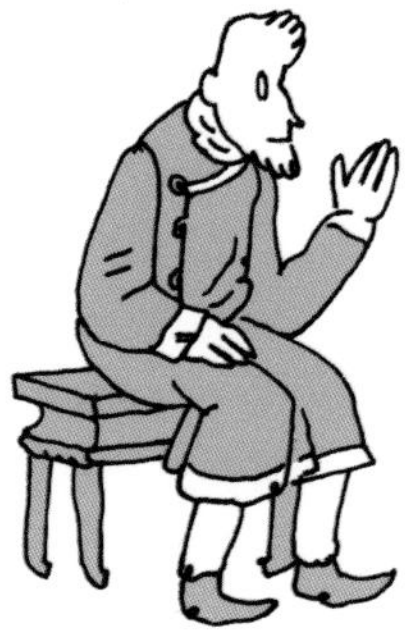

Storyteller

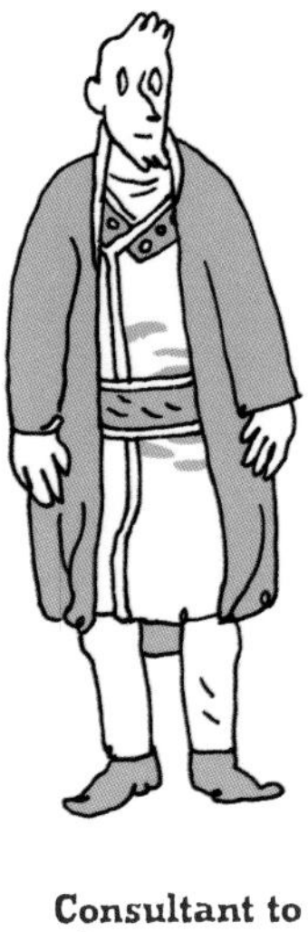

Consultant to
the emperor

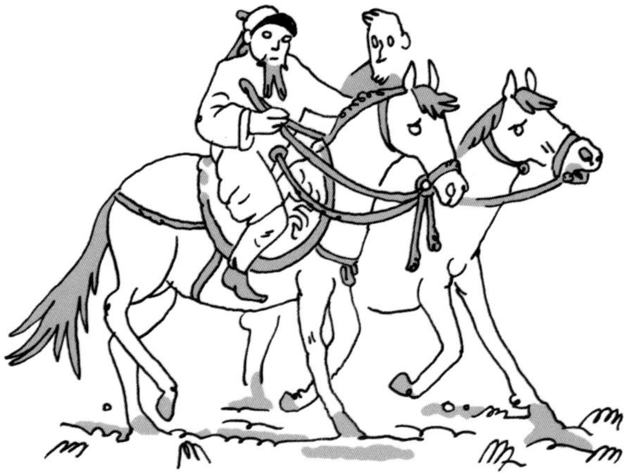

Friend

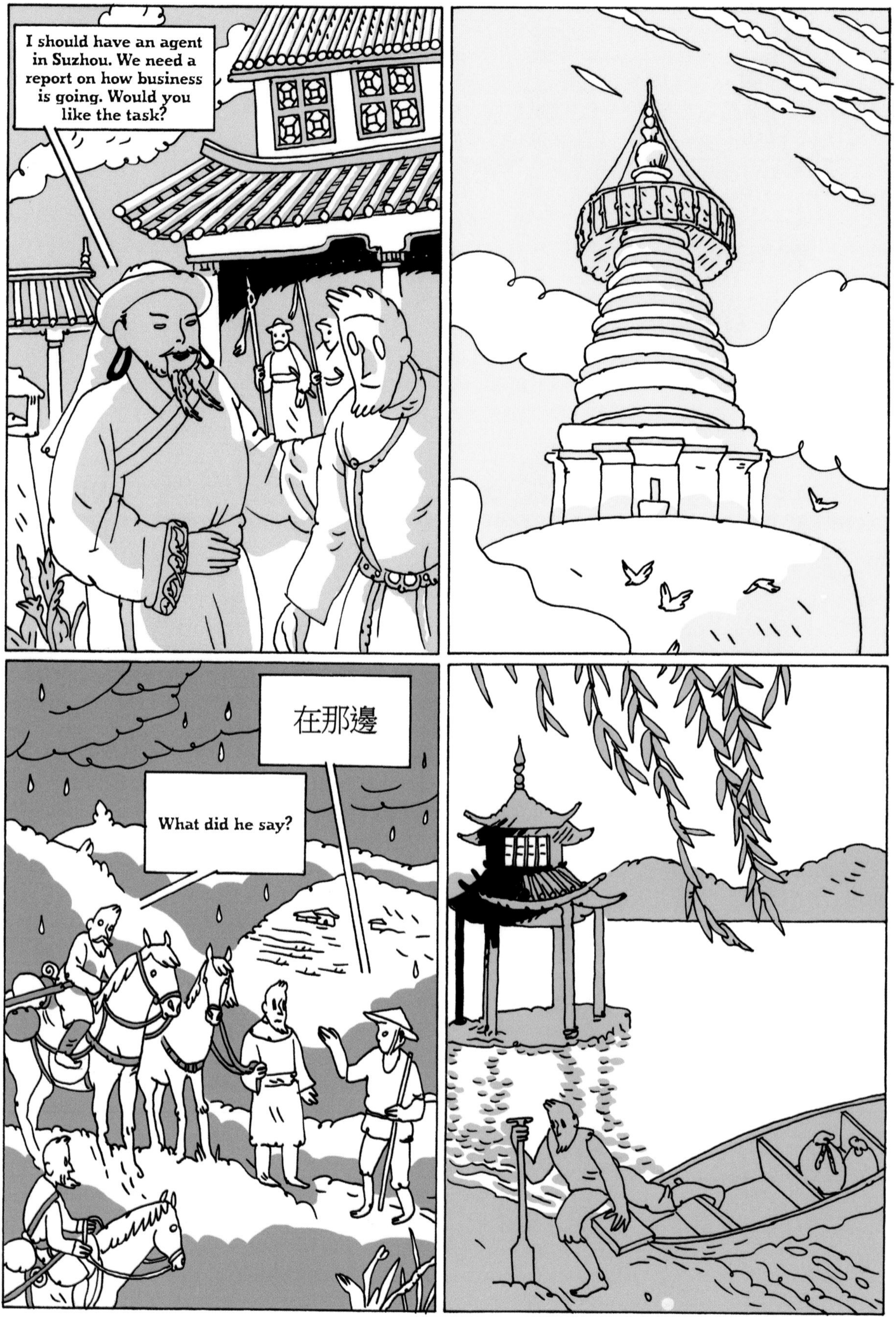
I should have an agent in Suzhou. We need a report on how business is going. Would you like the task?
在那邊
What did he say?

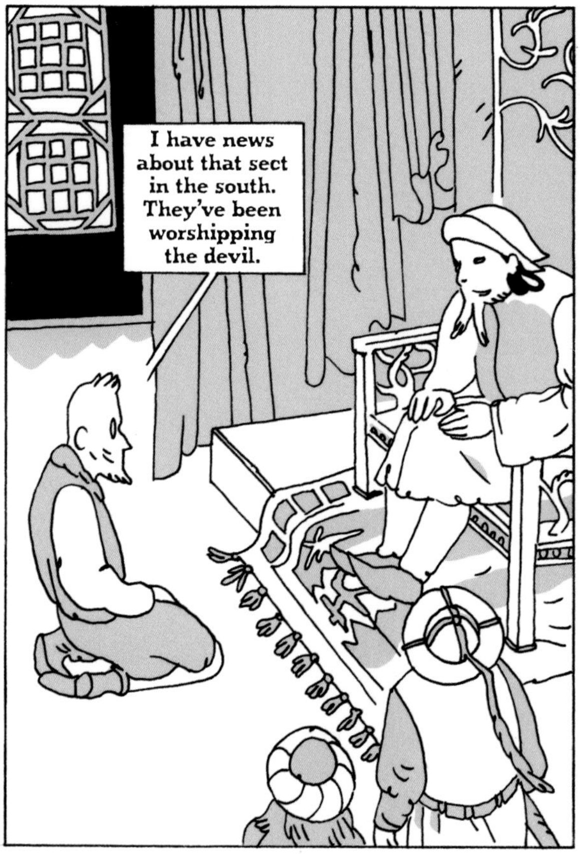
I have news about that sect in the south. They've been worshipping the devil.

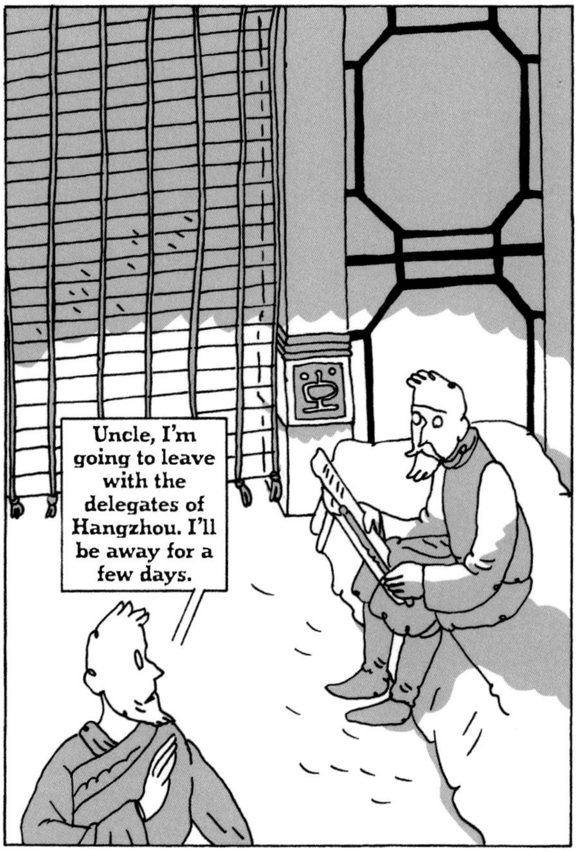
Uncle, I'm going to leave with the delegates of Hangzhou. I'll be away for a few days.

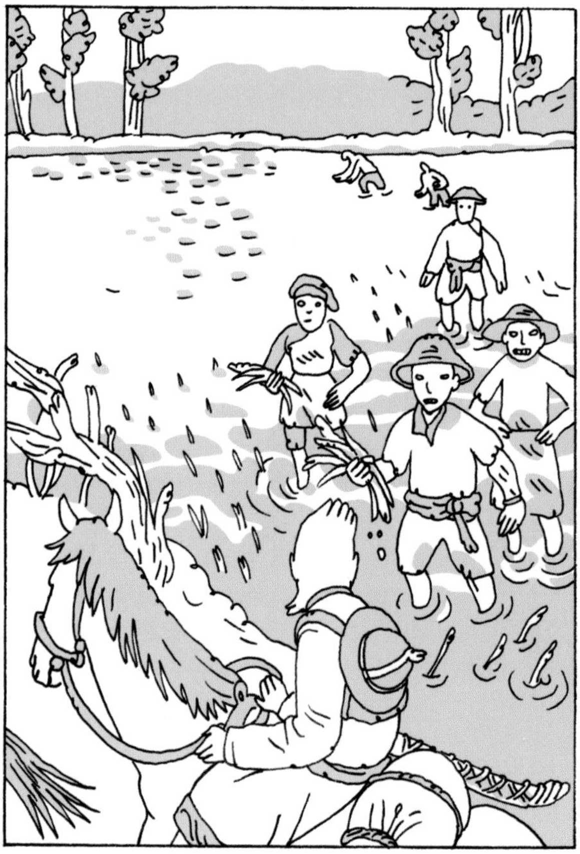

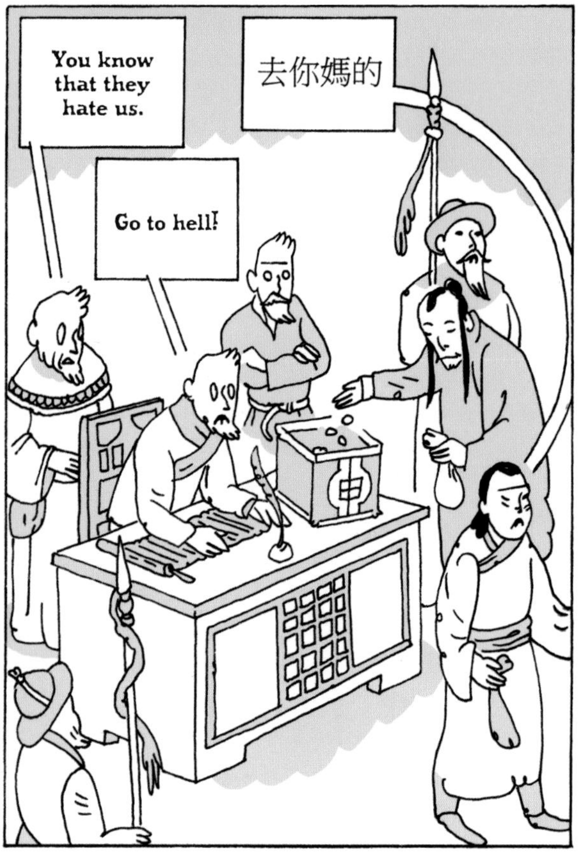
You know that they hate us.
去你媽的
Go to hell!

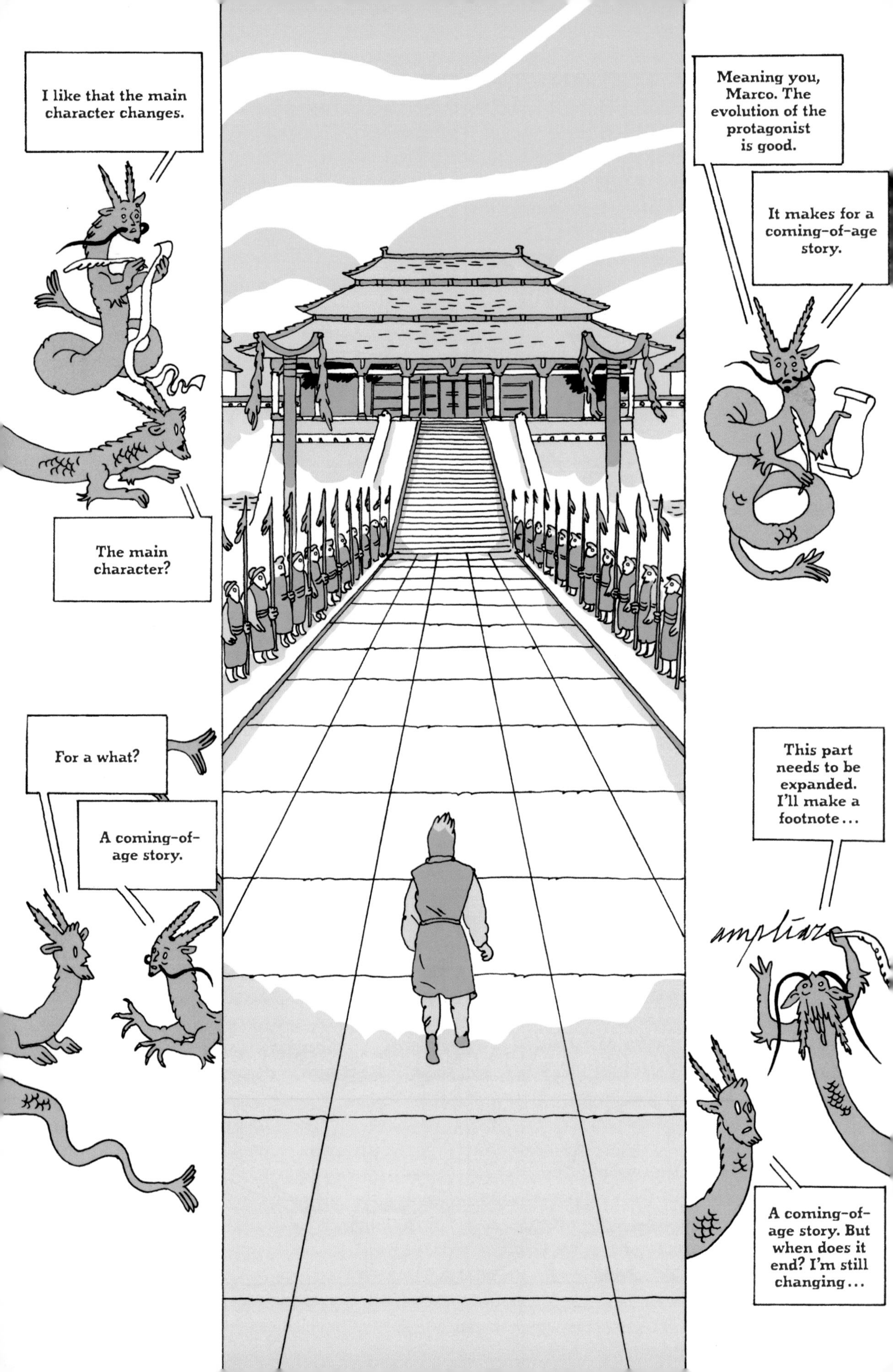
I like that the main character changes.
The main character?
Meaning you, Marco. The evolution of the protagonist is good.
It makes for a coming-of-age story.
For a what?
A coming-of-age story.
This part needs to be expanded. I'll make a footnote...
A coming-of-age story. But when does it end? I'm still changing...

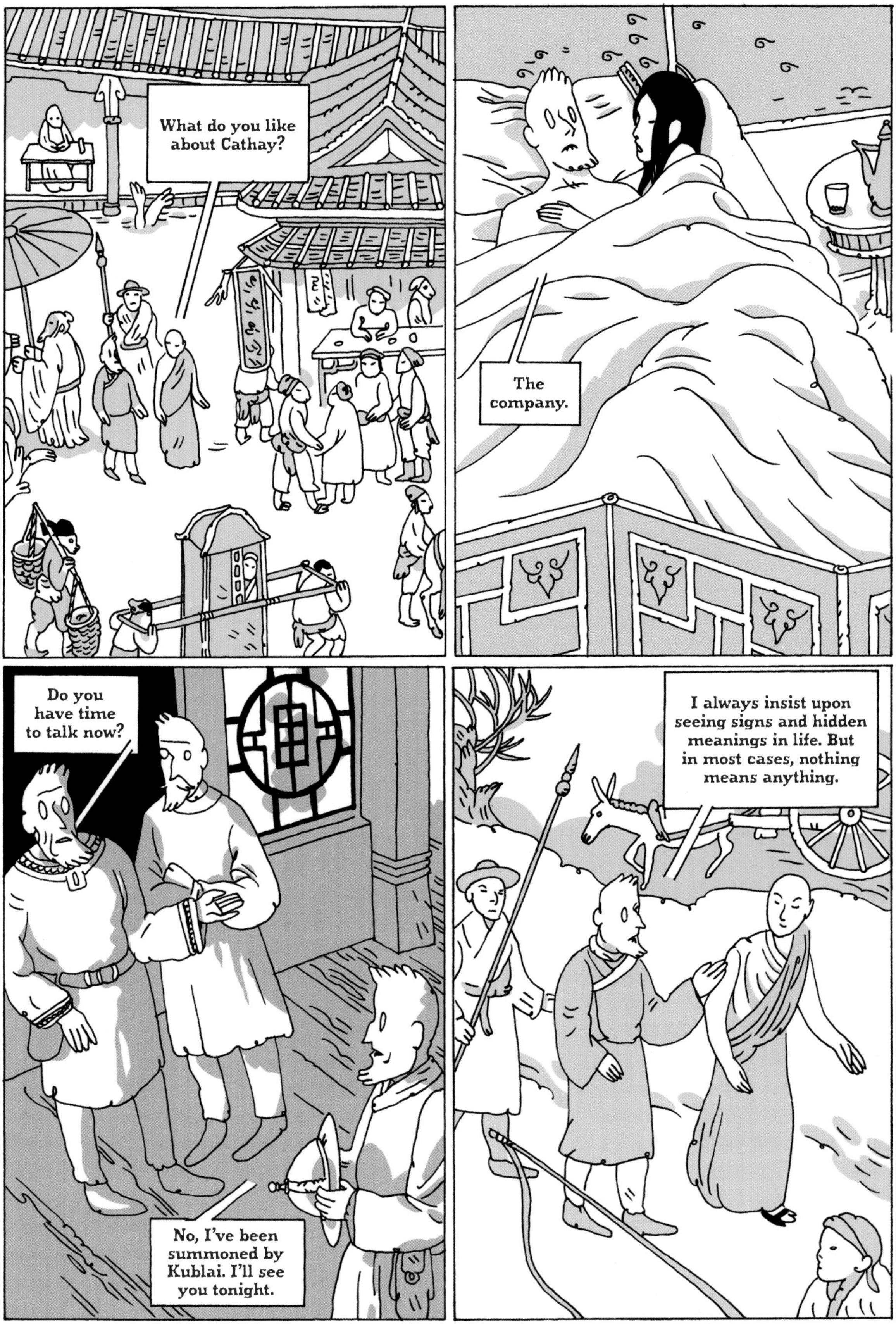
What do you like about Cathay?
The company.
Do you have time to talk now?
No, I've been summoned by Kublai. I'll see you tonight.
I always insist upon seeing signs and hidden meanings in life. But in most cases, nothing means anything.

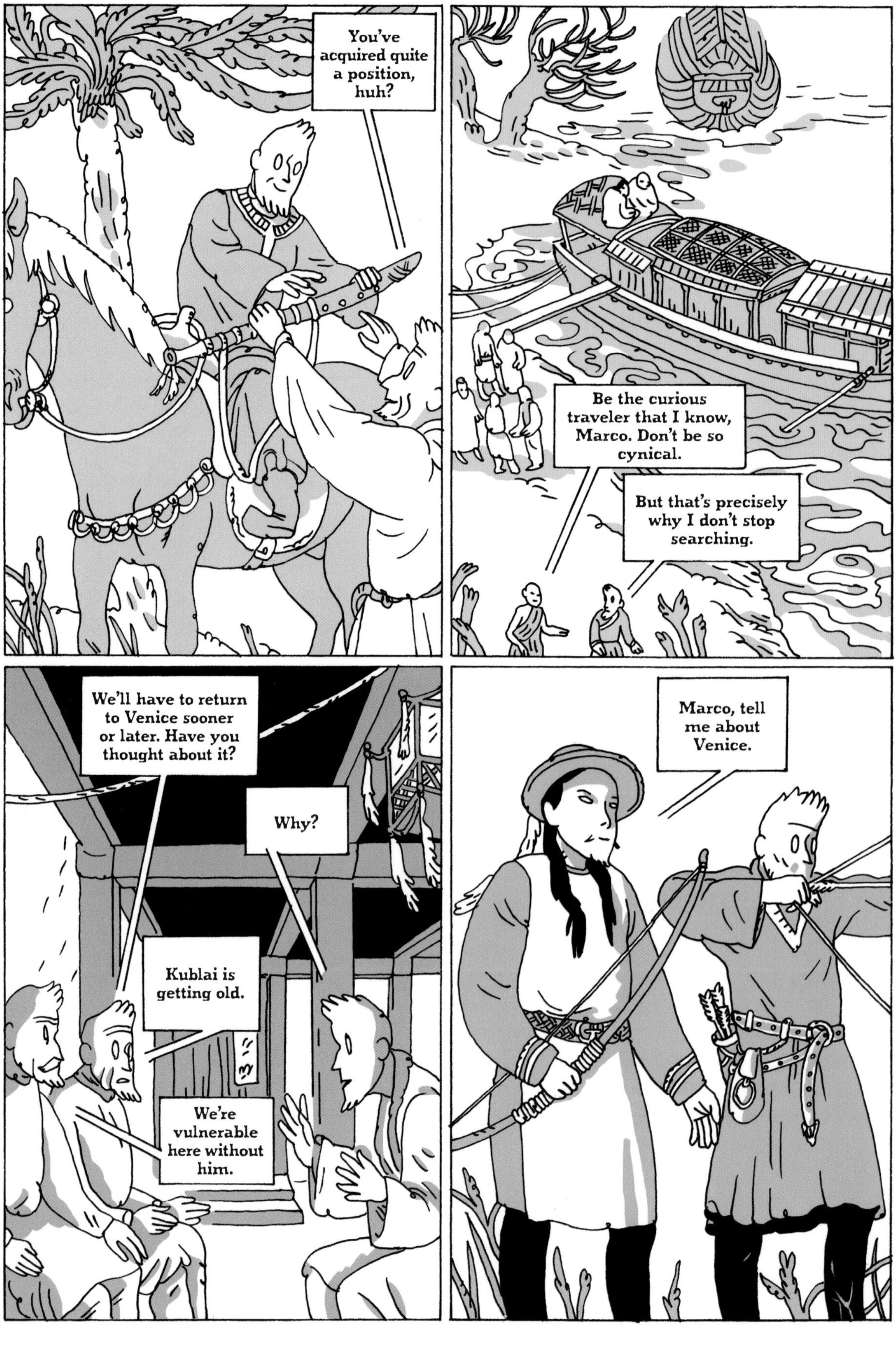
You've acquired quite a position, huh?
Be the curious traveler that I know, Marco. Don't be so cynical.
But that's precisely why I don't stop searching.
We'll have to return to Venice sooner or later. Have you thought about it?
Why?
Kublai is getting old.
We're vulnerable here without him.
Marco, tell me about Venice.

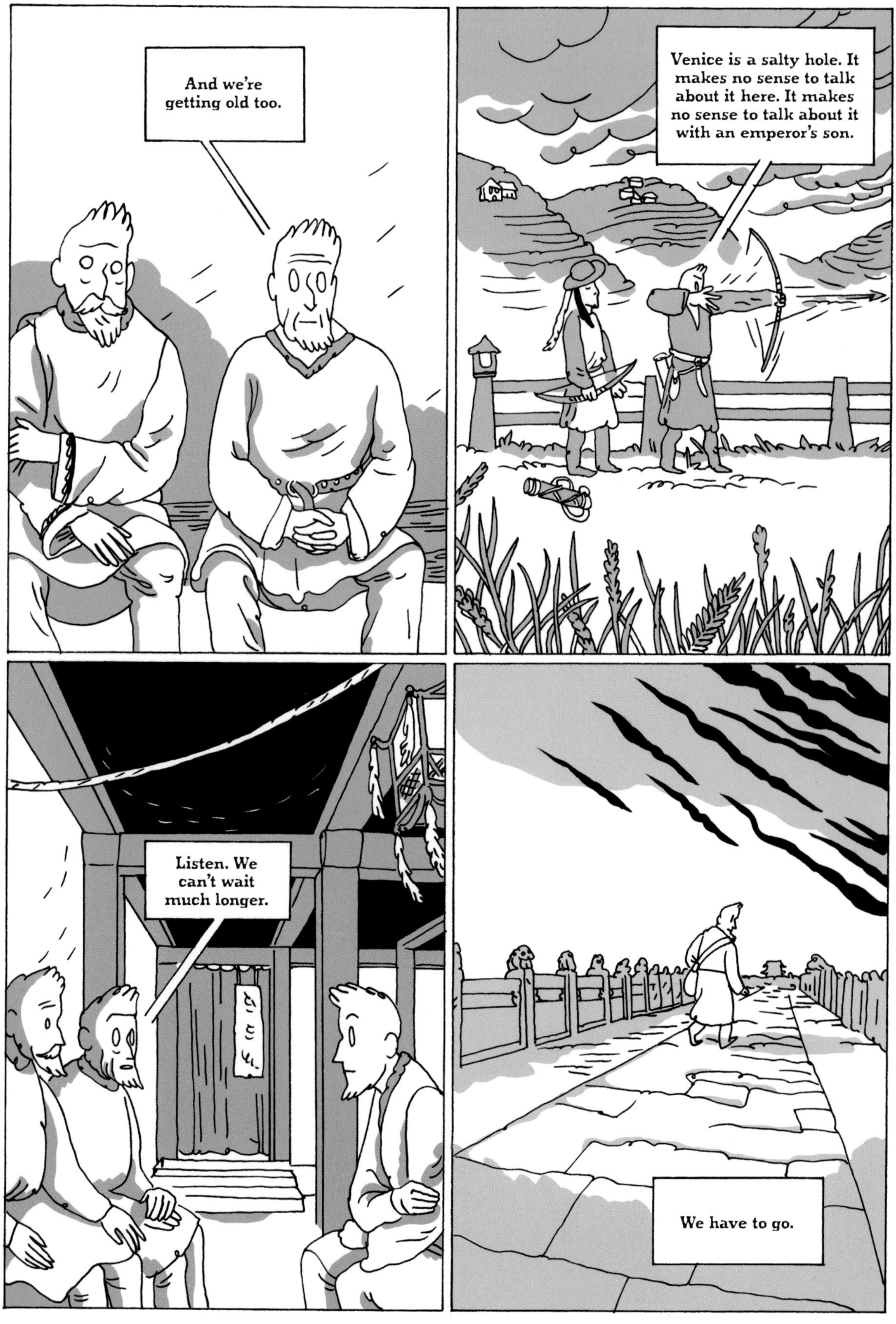
And we're getting old too.
Venice is a salty hole. It makes no sense to talk about it here. It makes no sense to talk about it with an emperor's son.
Listen. We can't wait much longer.
We have to go.

When a delegation from Persia arrived, we took our chance.

Kublai did not want us to leave. He did not give me permission.

But his cousin Arghun of Persia was a widower.

And one of Arghun's wife's last wishes was that, if he remarried, he only marry a woman of the Mongol people to which she belonged, the Bayad.

For this, the emissaries of Kublai went to the territories of the ancient tribes and chose Kököchin of the Bayad to take back to the ruler of Persia.

As the emissaries attempted a journey back, they had to give up twice because of rebellions that broke out in the heart of Asia.

So my uncle, my father, and I offered to escort them.

We were the right people for a mission like this, and Kublai knew it. I accepted the situation—reluctantly.

We left Cathay. And Persia was on the way back to Venice...

Tell me about Kököchin.

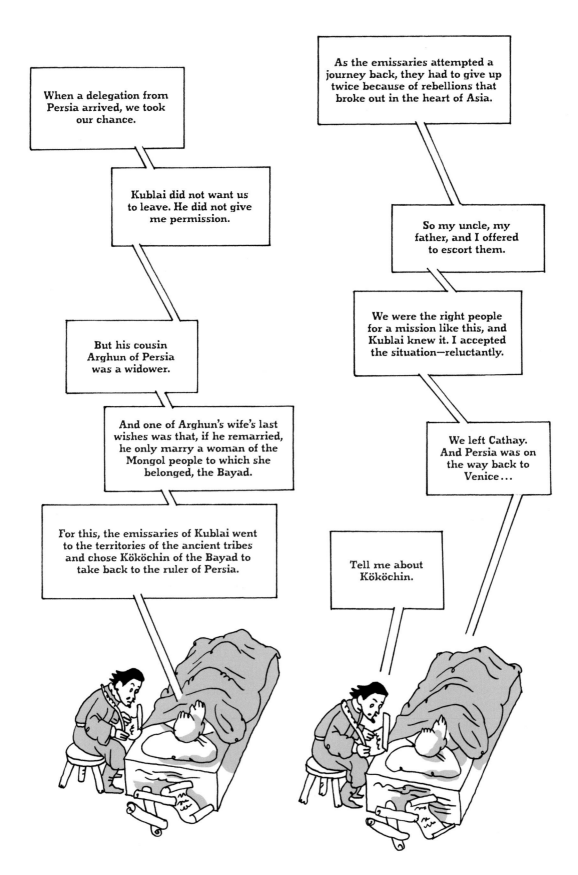

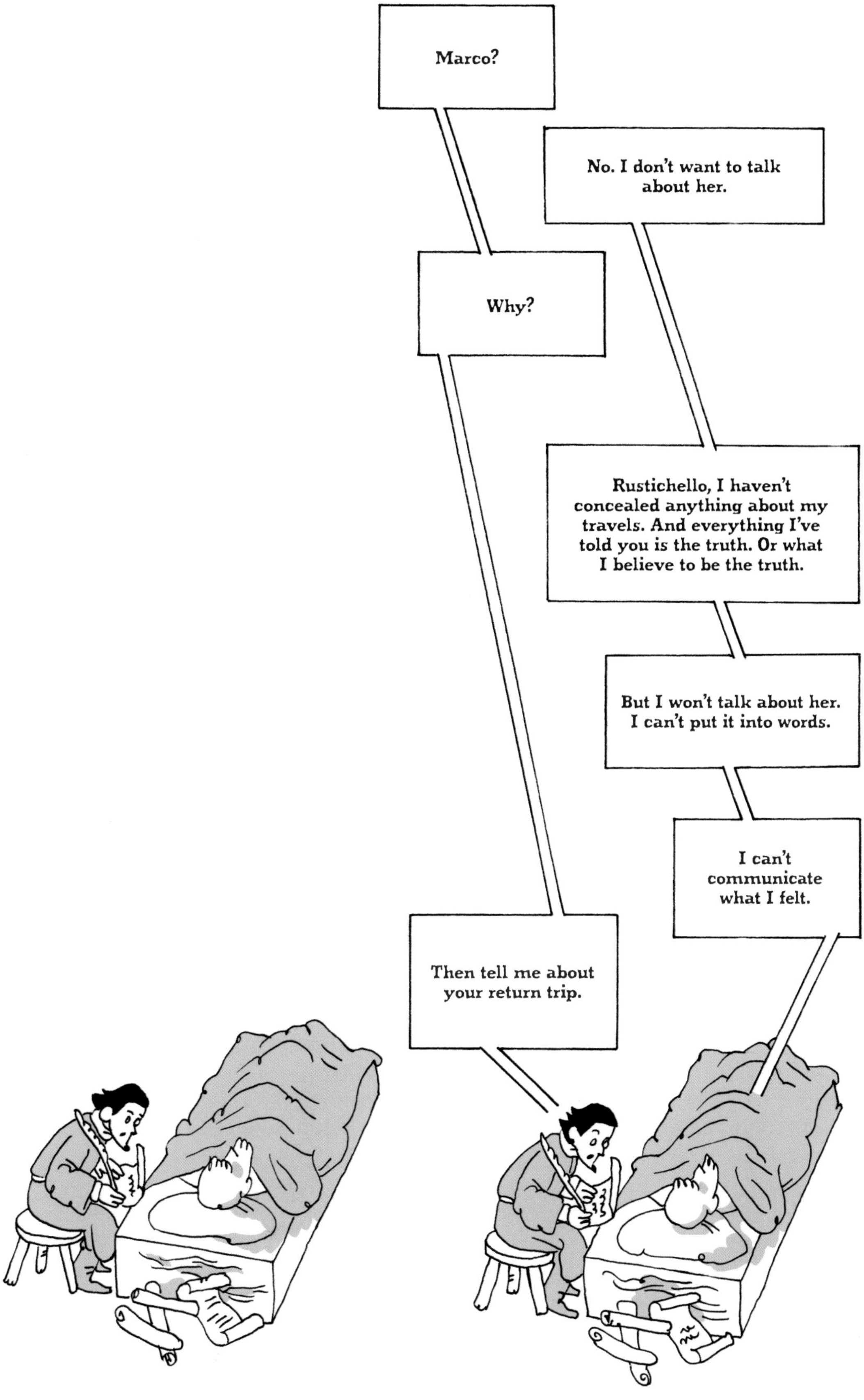
Marco?
No. I don't want to talk about her.
Why?
Rustichello, I haven't concealed anything about my travels. And everything I've told you is the truth. Or what I believe to be the truth.
But I won't talk about her. I can't put it into words.
I can't communicate what I felt.
Then tell me about your return trip.

This is the chronicle of my journey back. We started in 1290, with the aim of bringing the princess Kököchin to the sovereign of the Tatars of Persia, and ended in 1295 in Venice.

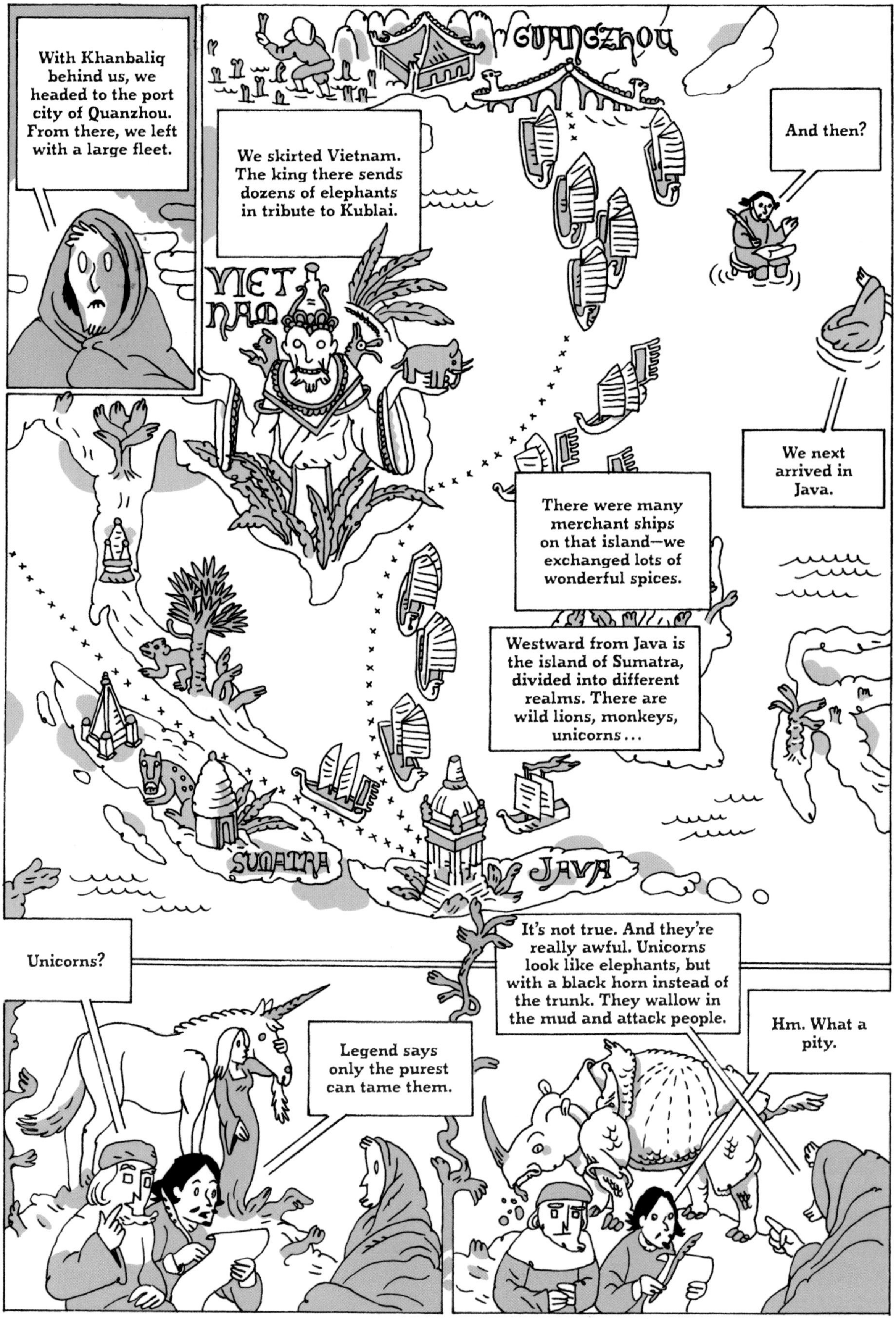

With Khanbaliq behind us, we headed to the port city of Quanzhou. From there, we left with a large fleet.
GUANGZHOU
We skirted Vietnam. The king there sends dozens of elephants in tribute to Kublai.
VIET NAM
And then?
We next arrived in Java.
There were many merchant ships on that island—we exchanged lots of wonderful spices.
Westward from Java is the island of Sumatra, divided into different realms. There are wild lions, monkeys, unicorns . . .
SUMATRA
JAVA
Unicorns?
Legend says only the purest can tame them.
It's not true. And they're really awful. Unicorns look like elephants, but with a black horn instead of the trunk. They wallow in the mud and attack people.
Hm. What a pity.

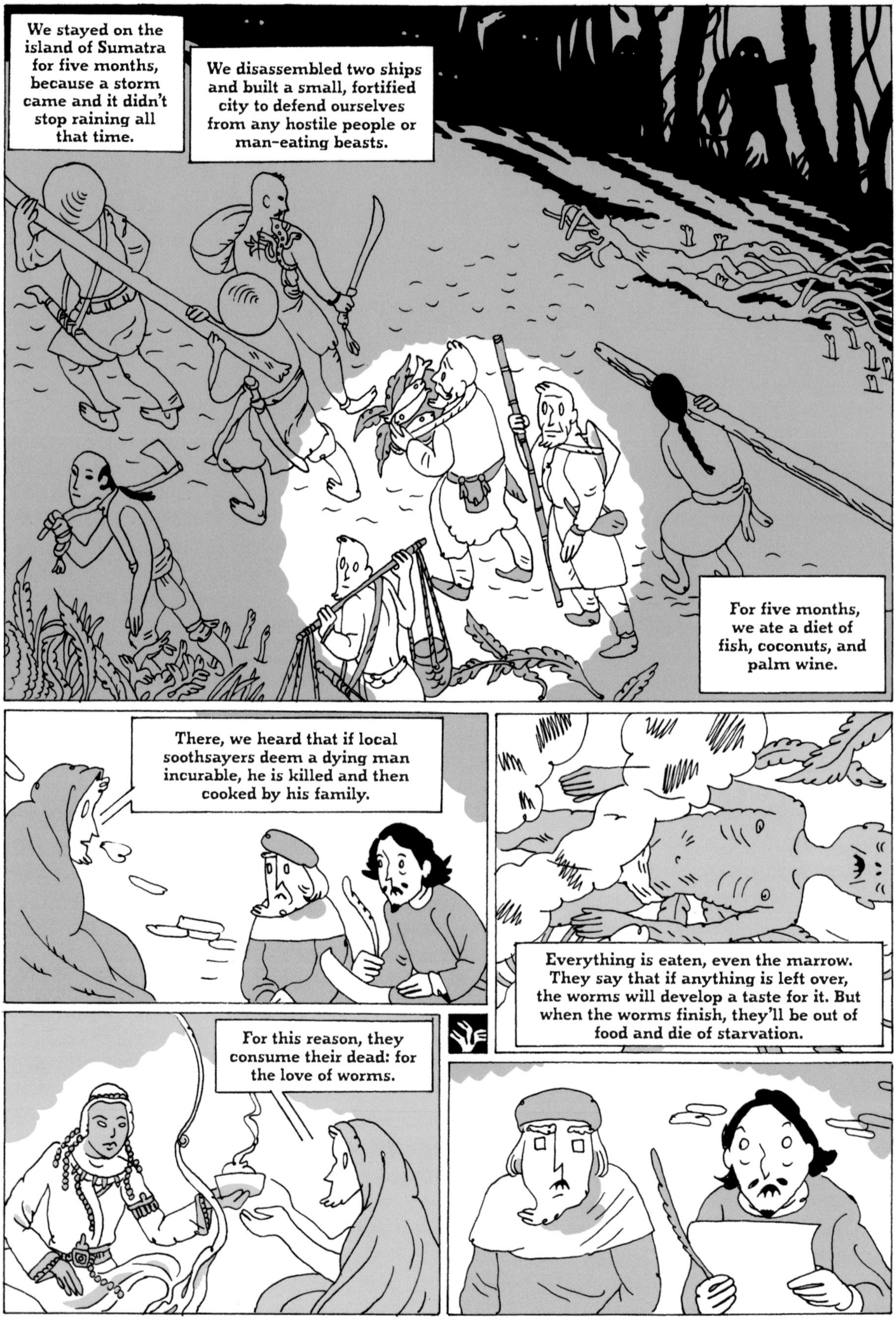
We stayed on the island of Sumatra for five months, because a storm came and it didn't stop raining all that time.
We disassembled two ships and built a small, fortified city to defend ourselves from any hostile people or man-eating beasts.
For five months, we ate a diet of fish, coconuts, and palm wine.
There, we heard that if local soothsayers deem a dying man incurable, he is killed and then cooked by his family.
Everything is eaten, even the marrow. They say that if anything is left over, the worms will develop a taste for it. But when the worms finish, they'll be out of food and die of starvation.
For this reason, they consume their dead: for the love of worms.

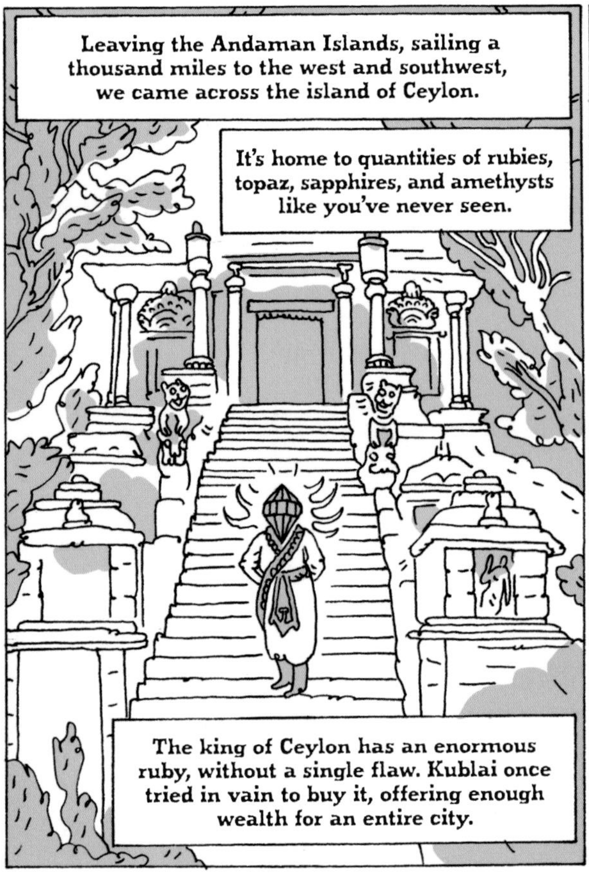
Leaving the Andaman Islands, sailing a thousand miles to the west and southwest, we came across the island of Ceylon.
It's home to quantities of rubies, topaz, sapphires, and amethysts like you've never seen.
The king of Ceylon has an enormous ruby, without a single flaw. Kublai once tried in vain to buy it, offering enough wealth for an entire city.

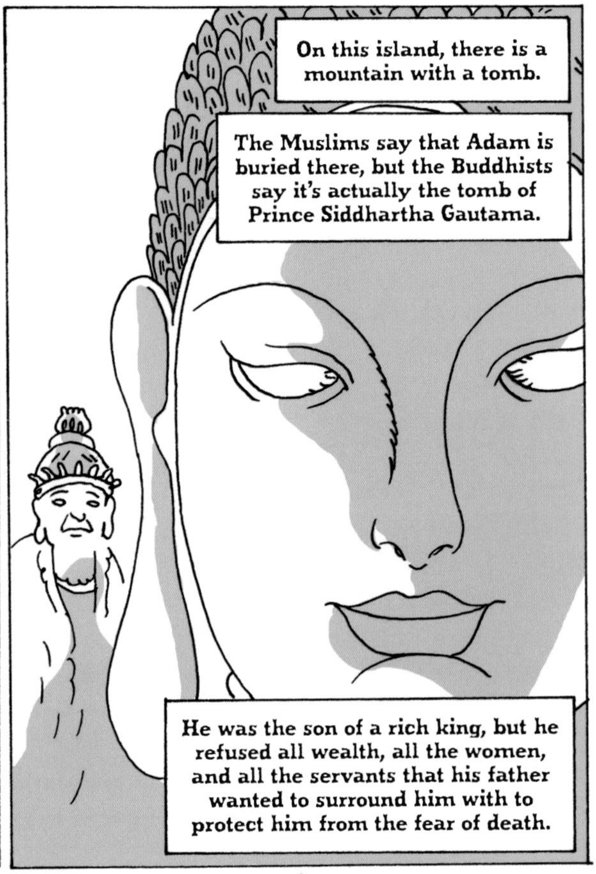
On this island, there is a mountain with a tomb.
The Muslims say that Adam is buried there, but the Buddhists say it's actually the tomb of Prince Siddhartha Gautama.
He was the son of a rich king, but he refused all wealth, all the women, and all the servants that his father wanted to surround him with to protect him from the fear of death.

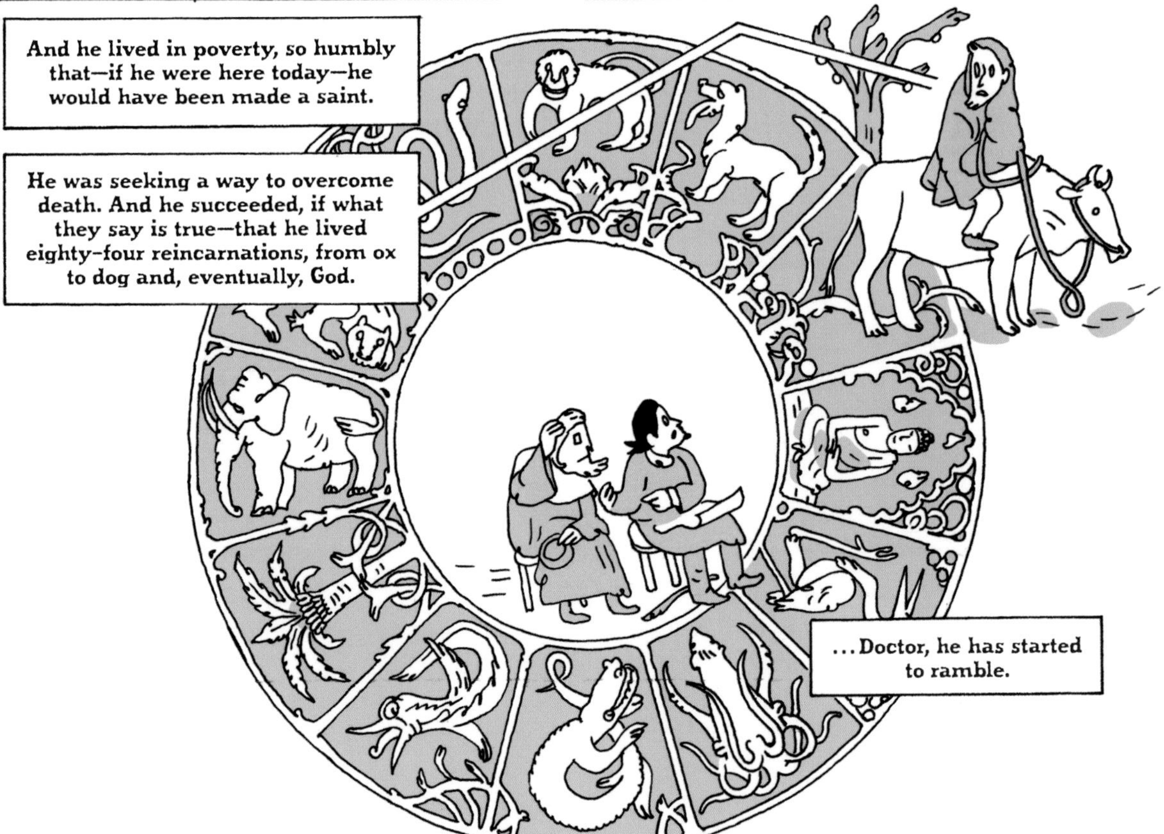
And he lived in poverty, so humbly that—if he were here today—he would have been made a saint.
He was seeking a way to overcome death. And he succeeded, if what they say is true—that he lived eighty-four reincarnations, from ox to dog and, eventually, God.
...Doctor, he has started to ramble.

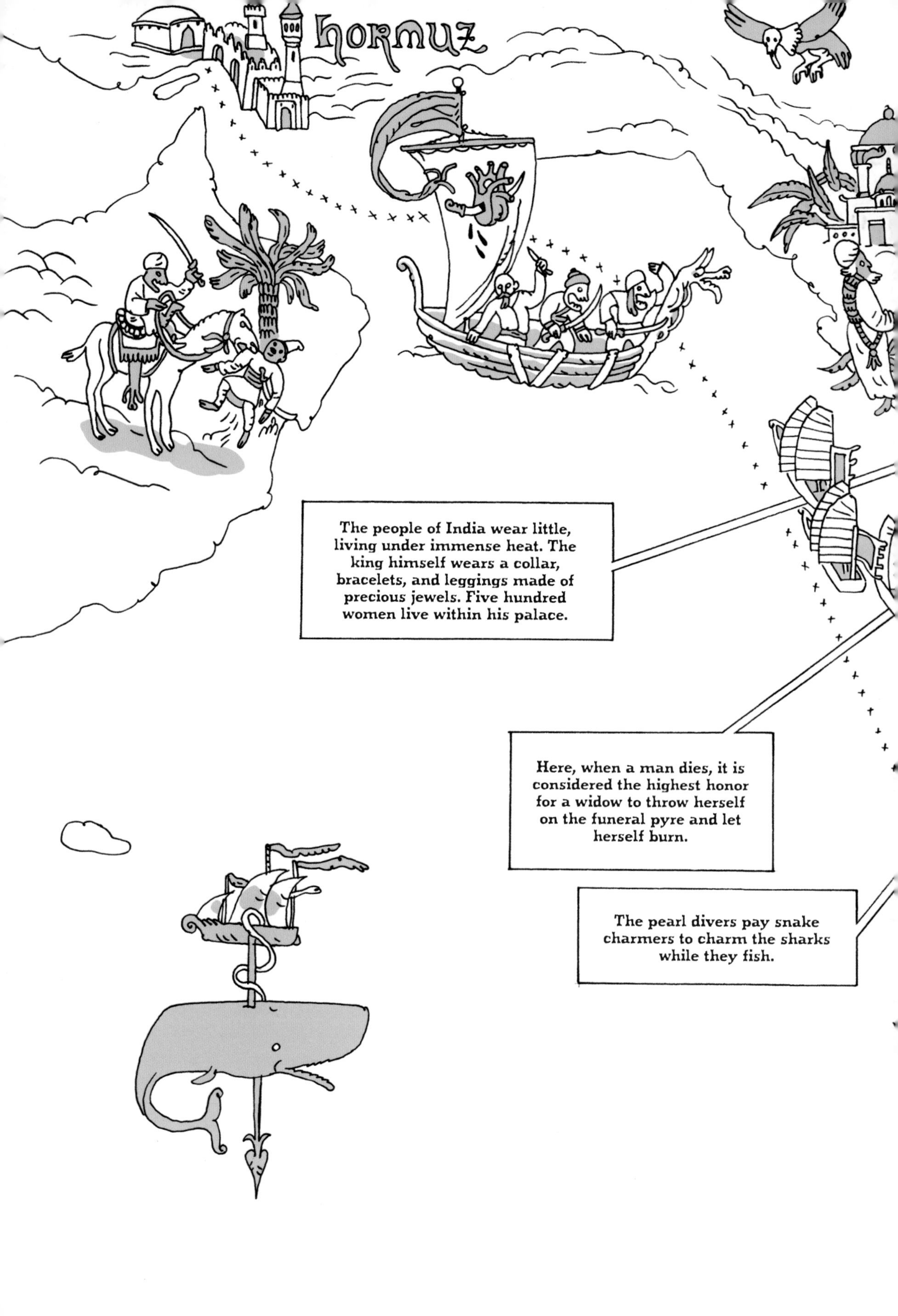
Hormuz
The people of India wear little, living under immense heat. The king himself wears a collar, bracelets, and leggings made of precious jewels. Five hundred women live within his palace.
Here, when a man dies, it is considered the highest honor for a widow to throw herself on the funeral pyre and let herself burn.
The pearl divers pay snake charmers to charm the sharks while they fish.

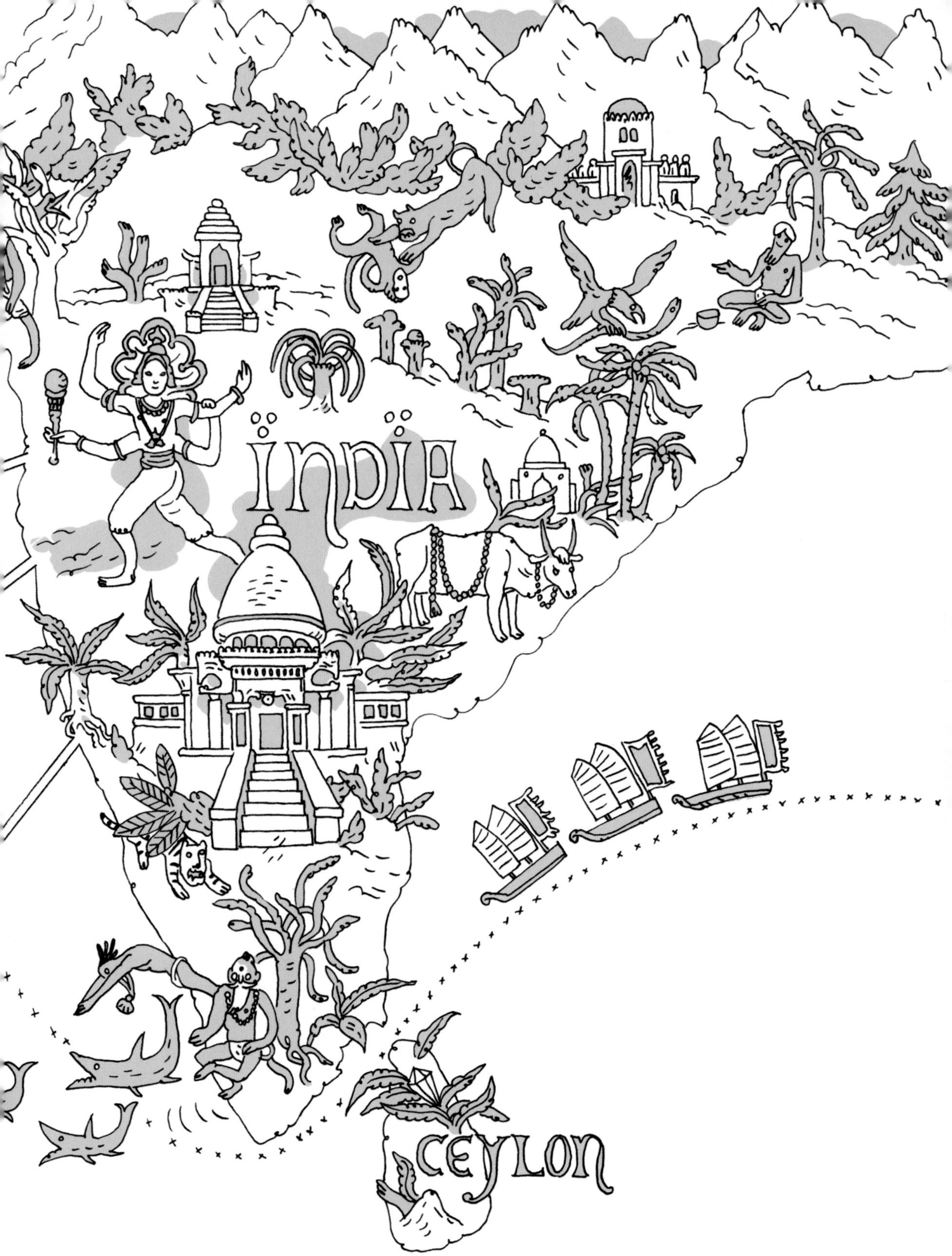
INDIA
CEYLON

Along India's west coast, we once again lost ships and men. This time because of pirates. Our numbers had already dwindled due to disease, storms, and desertions.

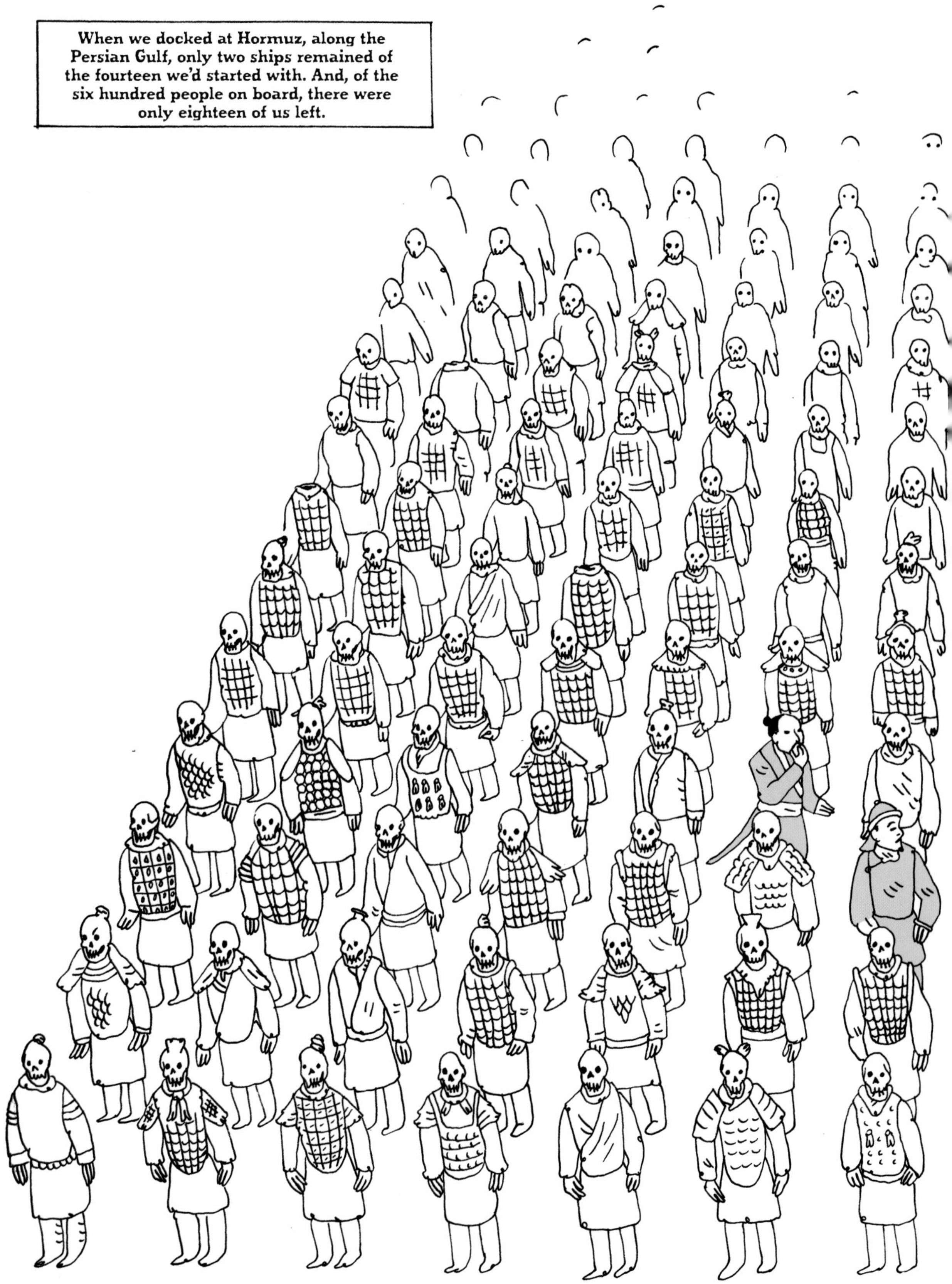
When we docked at Hormuz, along the Persian Gulf, only two ships remained of the fourteen we'd started with. And, of the six hundred people on board, there were only eighteen of us left.

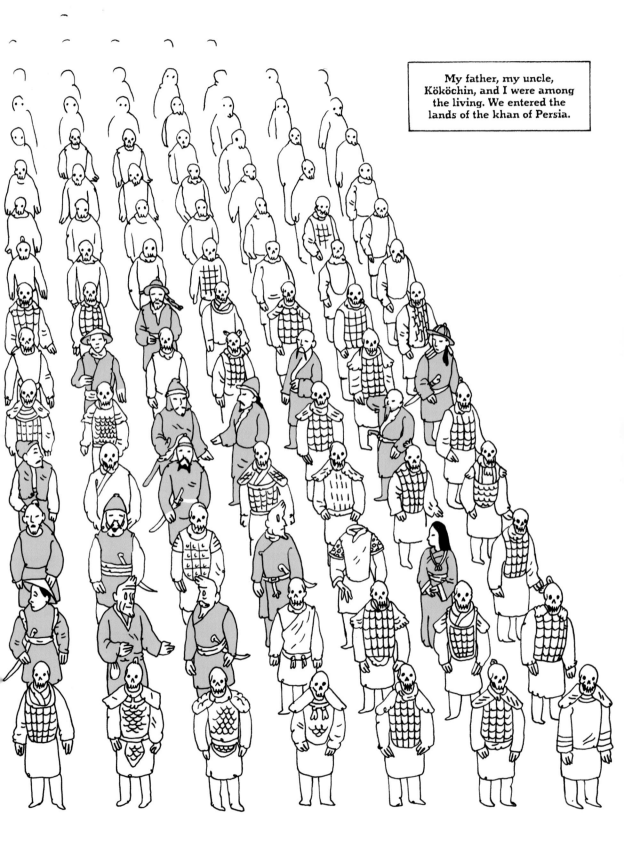

My father, my uncle, Kököchin, and I were among the living. We entered the lands of the khan of Persia.

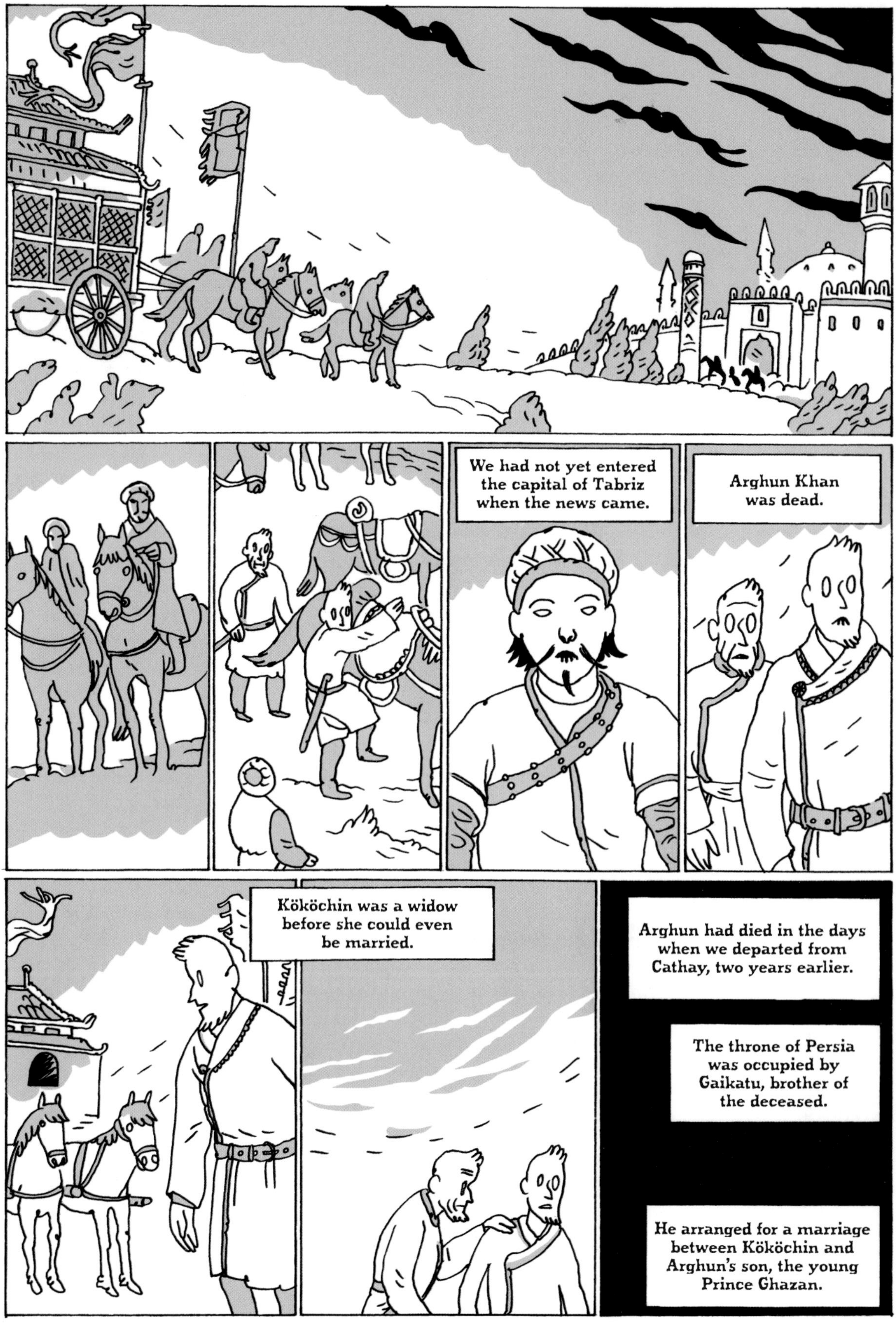
We had not yet entered the capital of Tabriz when the news came.
Arghun Khan was dead.
Kököchin was a widow before she could even be married.
Arghun had died in the days when we departed from Cathay, two years earlier.
The throne of Persia was occupied by Gaikatu, brother of the deceased.
He arranged for a marriage between Kököchin and Arghun's son, the young Prince Ghazan.

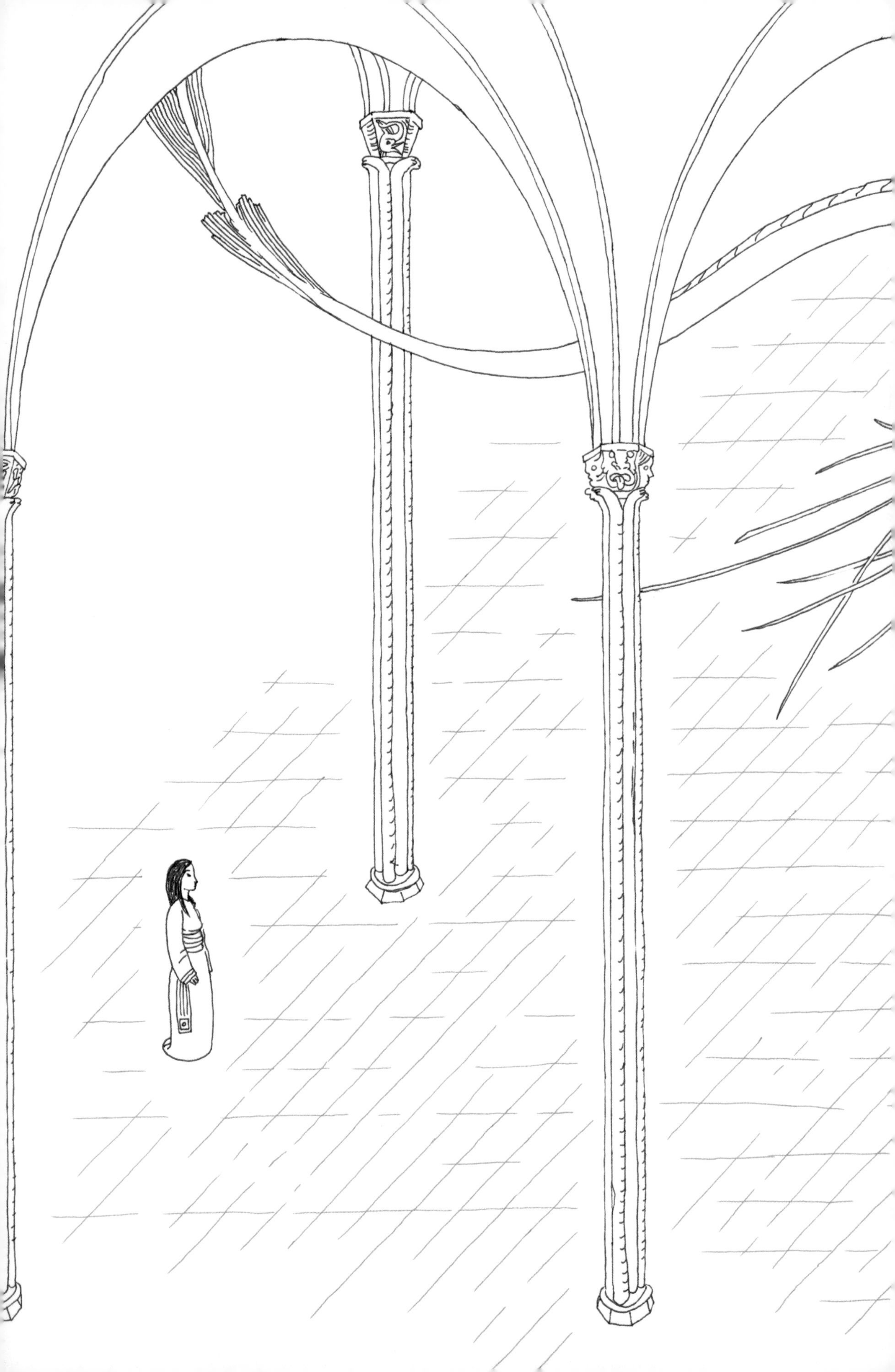

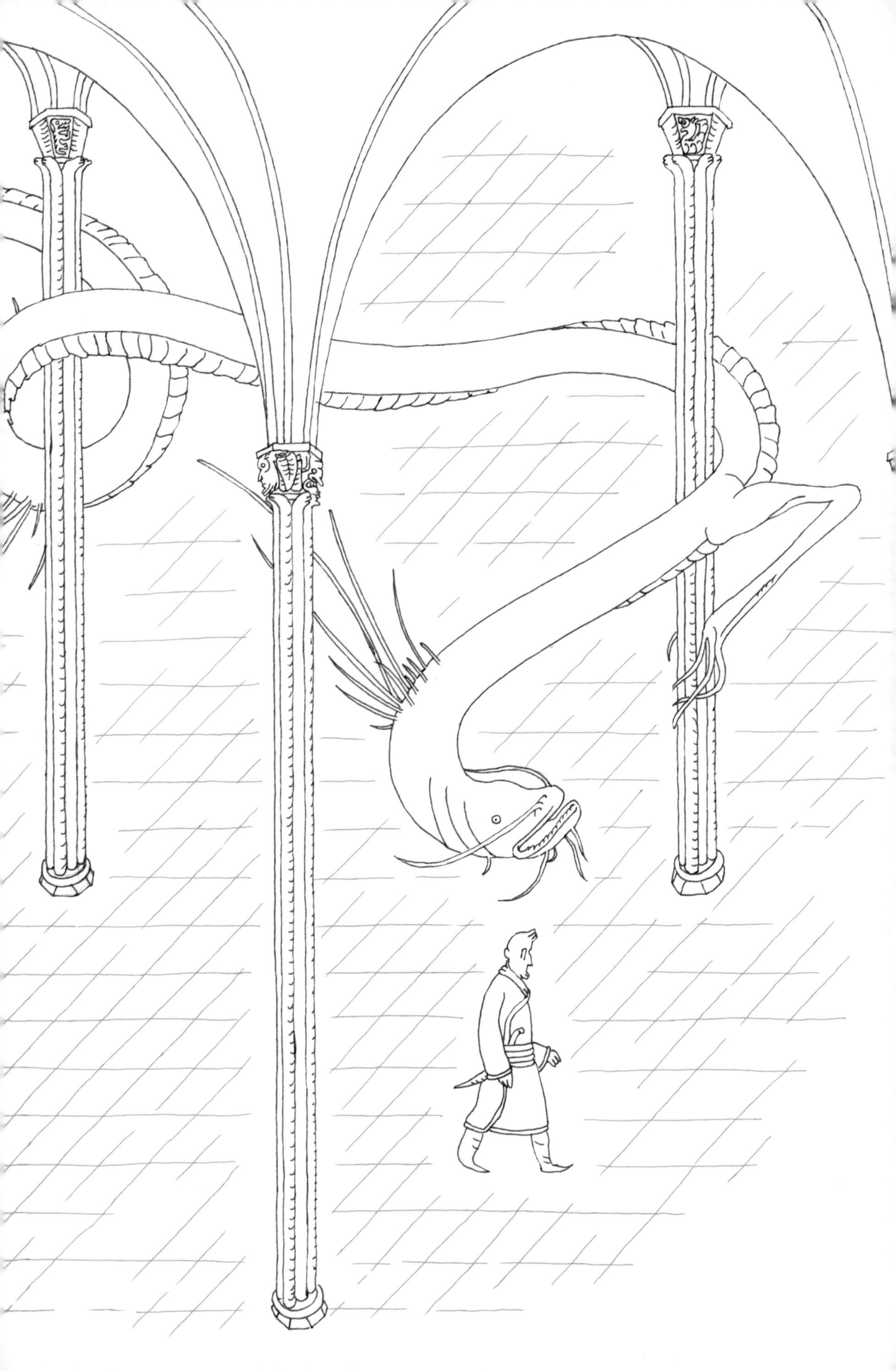

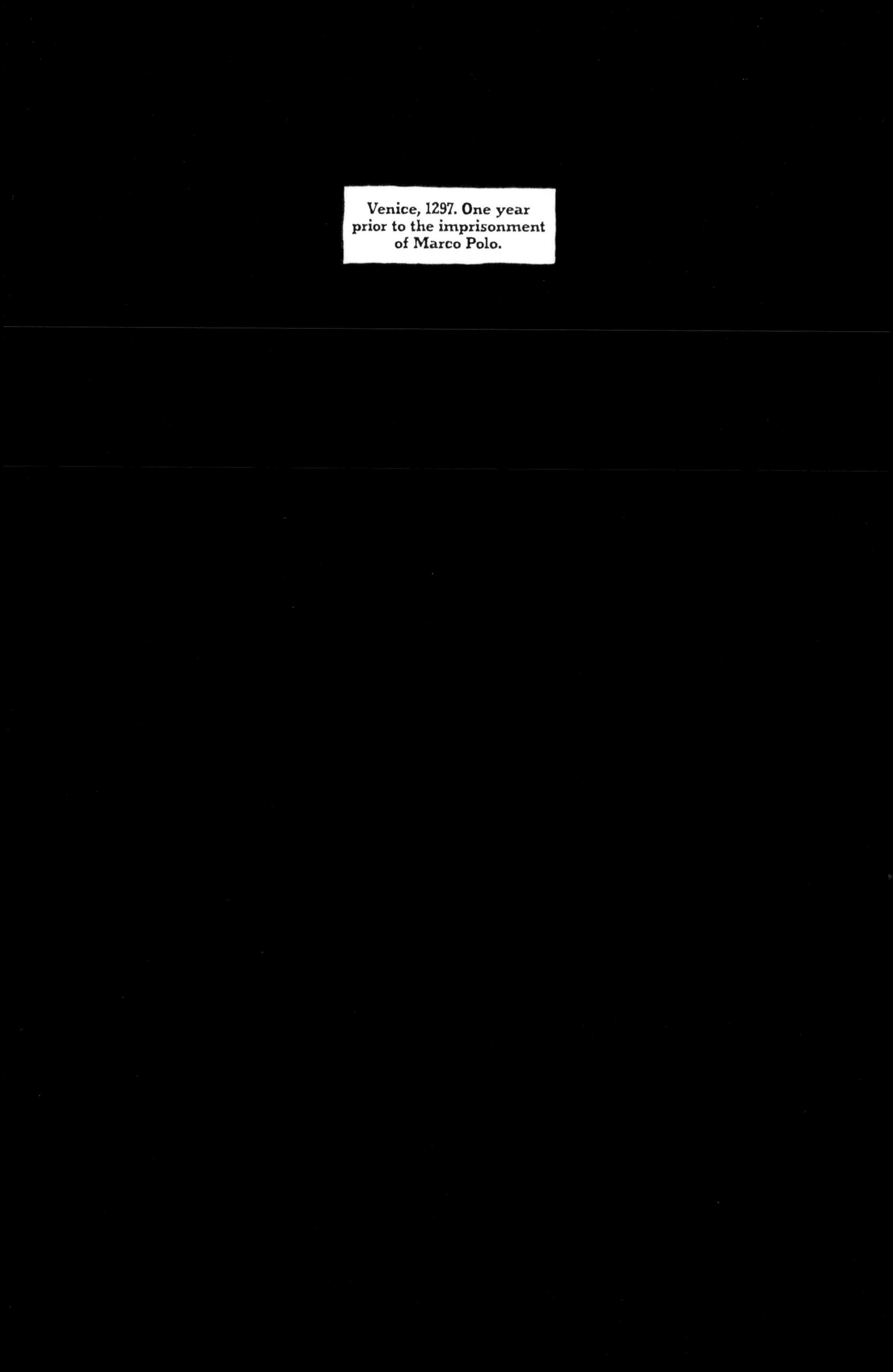
Venice, 1297. One year prior to the imprisonment of Marco Polo.

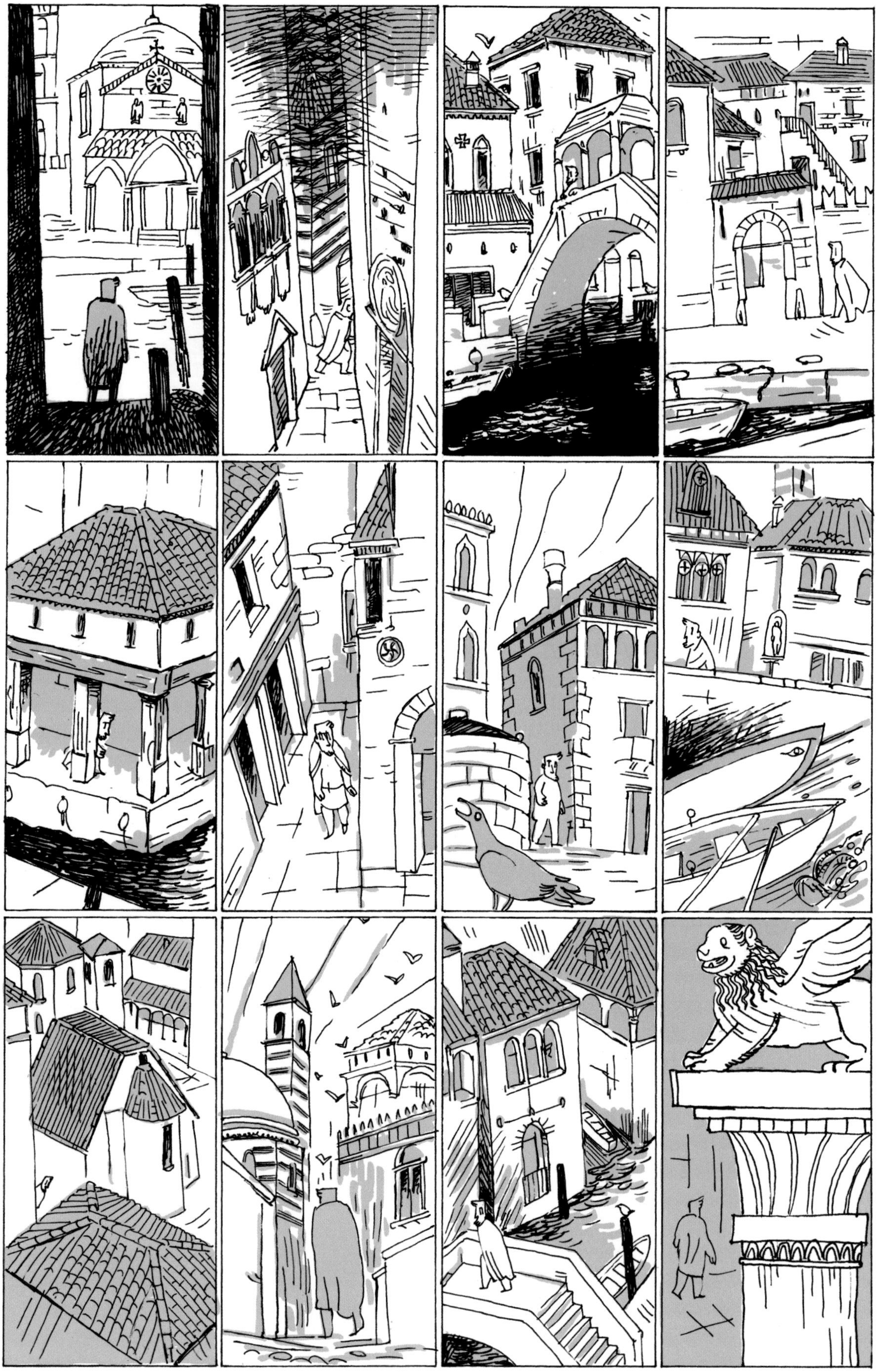

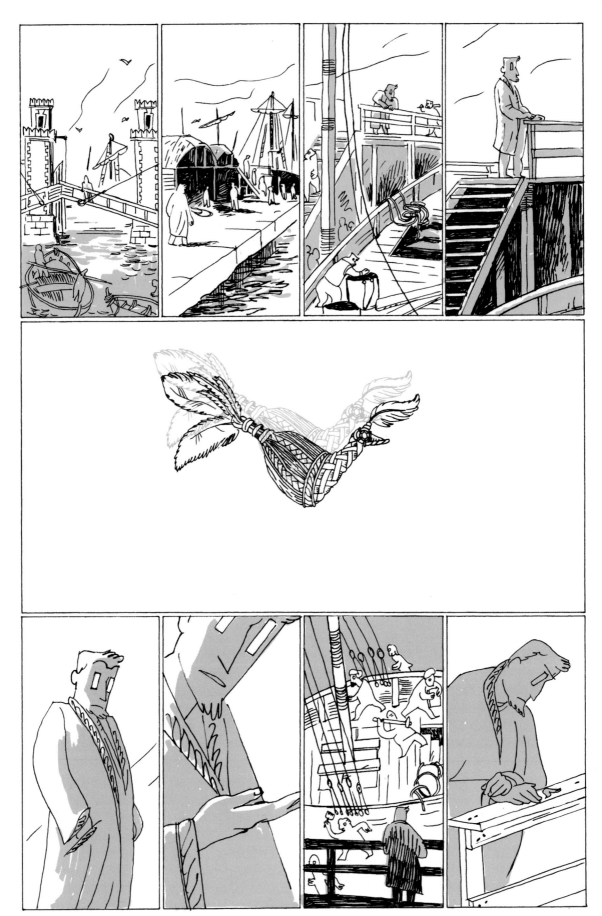

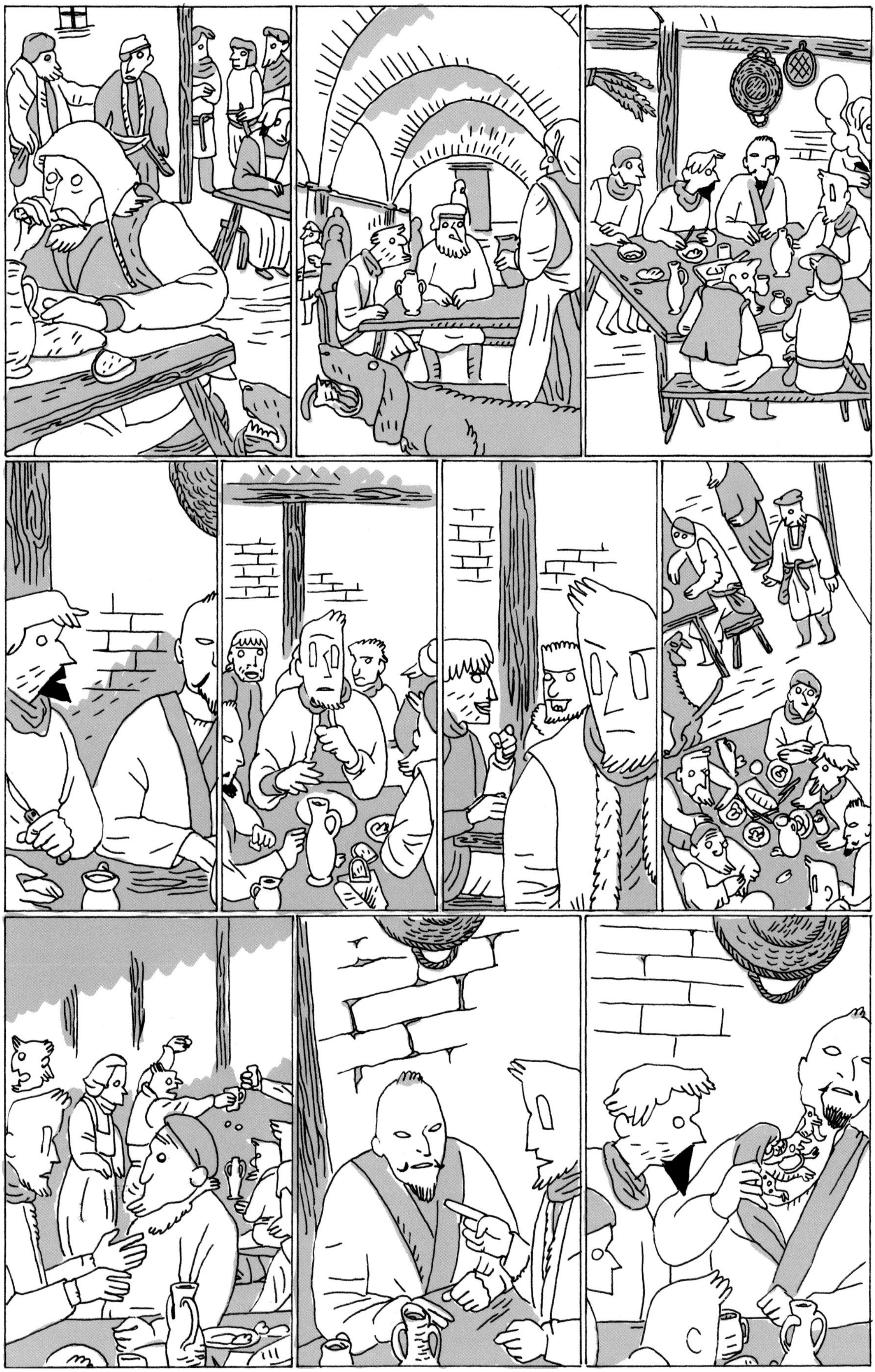

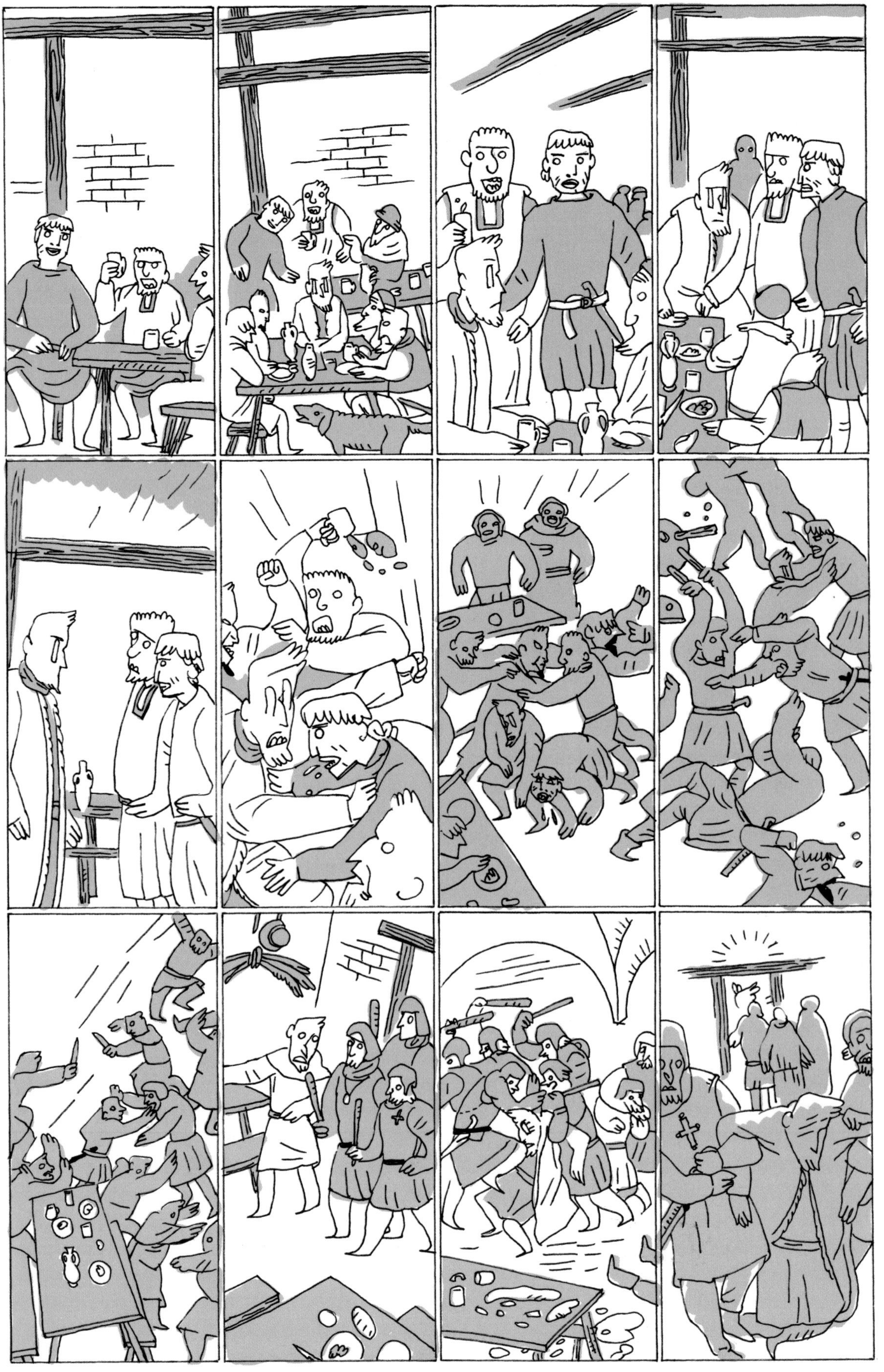

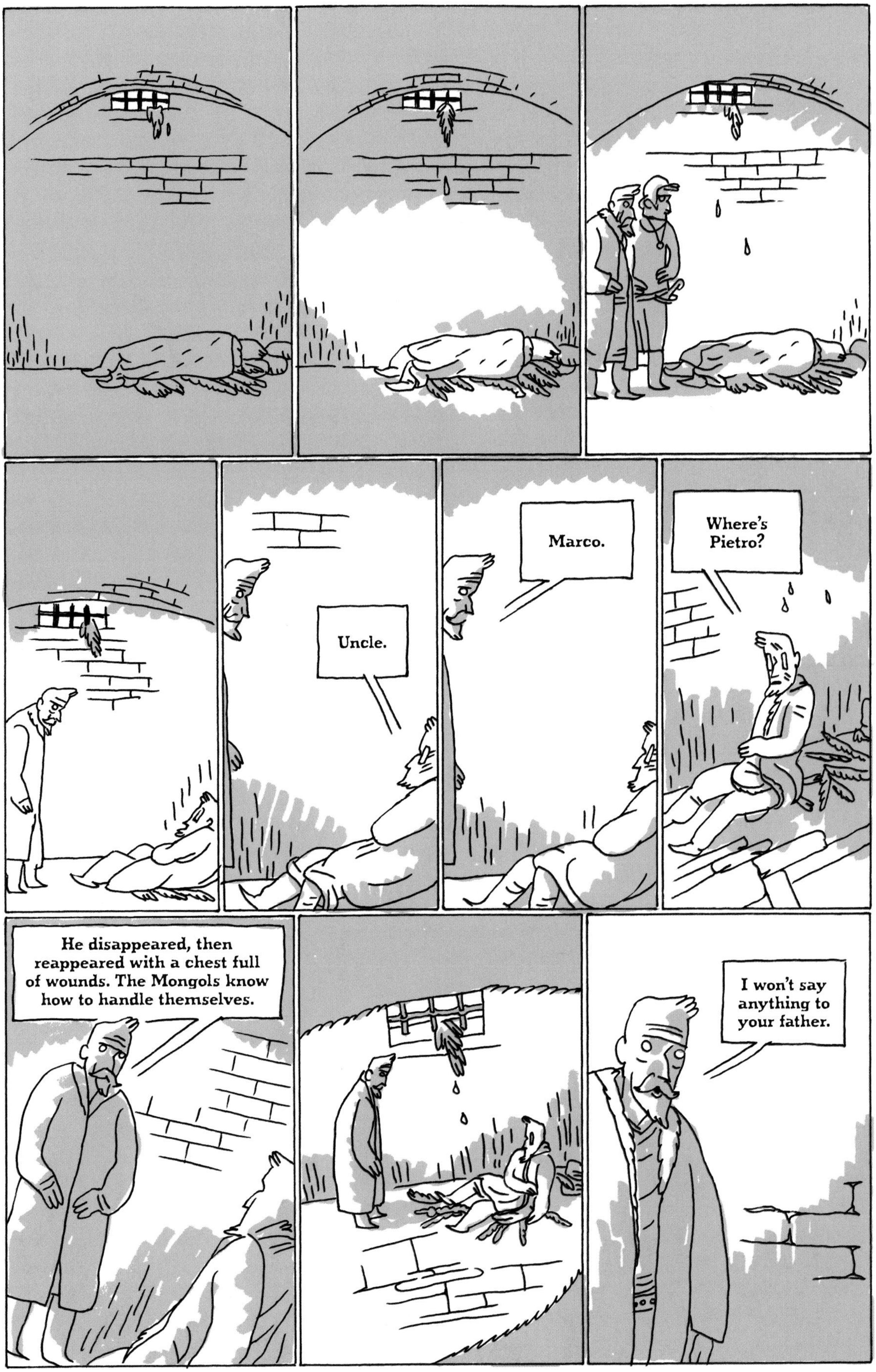
Uncle.
Marco.
Where's Pietro?
He disappeared, then reappeared with a chest full of wounds. The Mongols know how to handle themselves.
I won't say anything to your father.

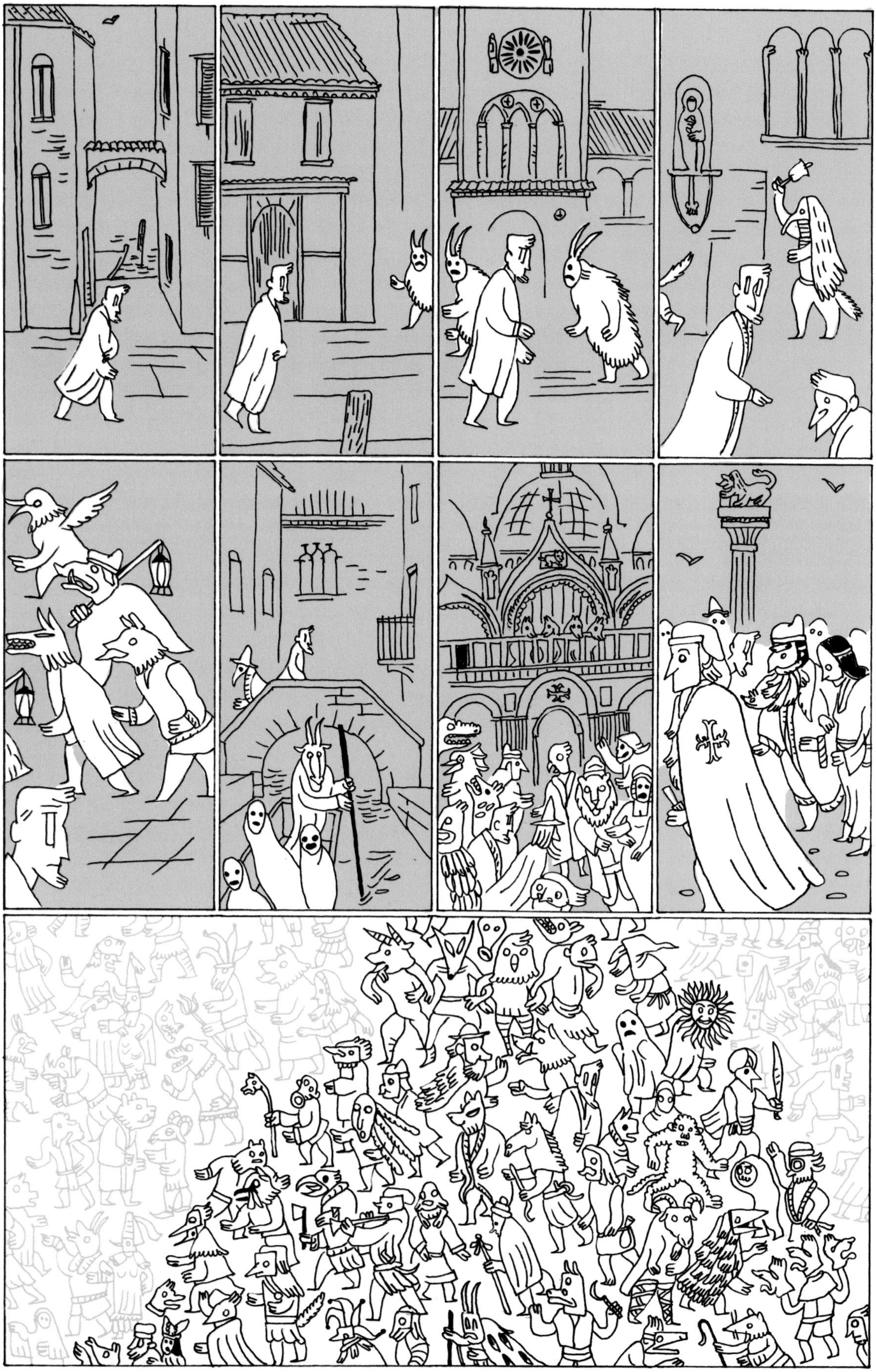

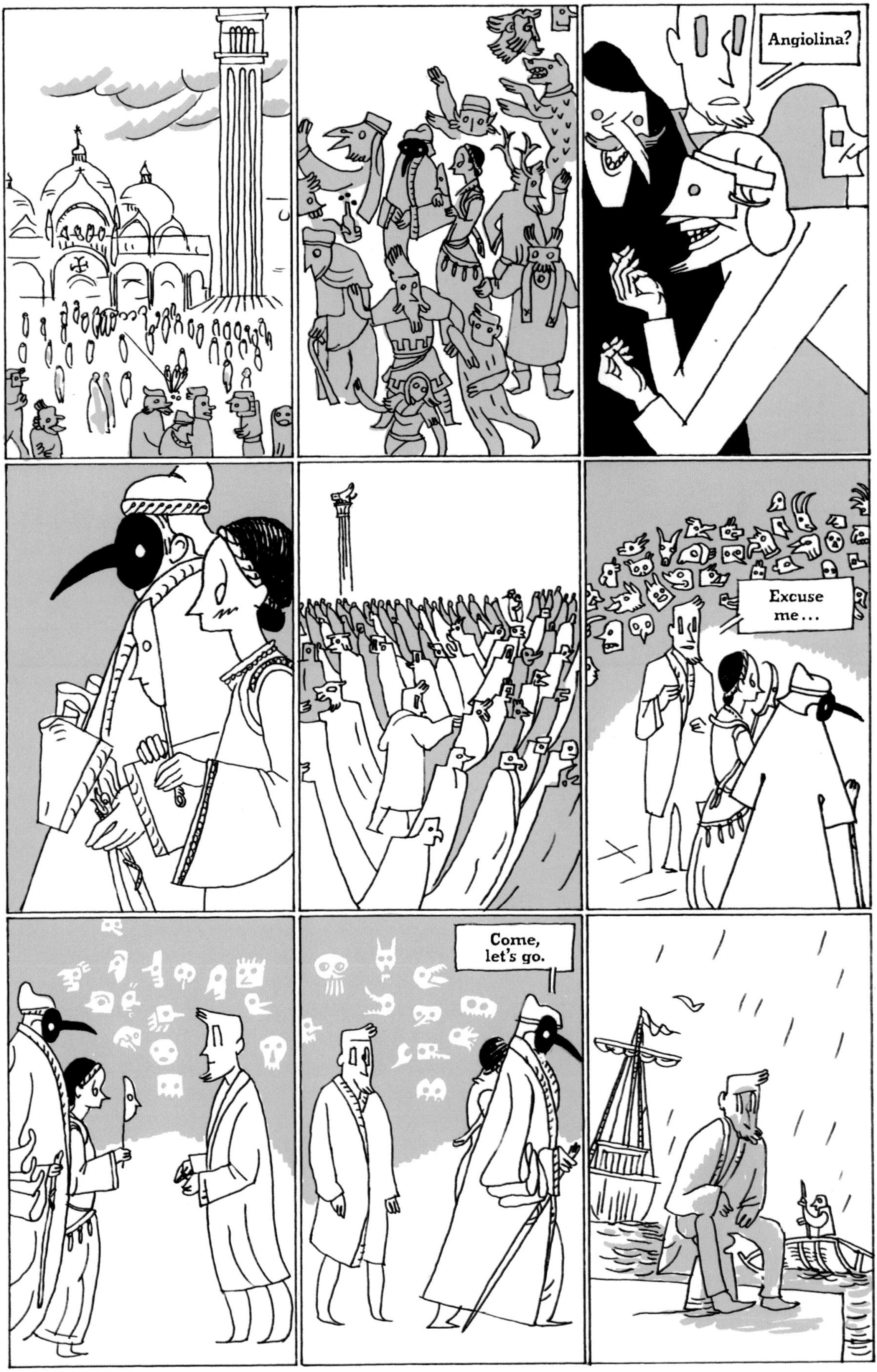
Angiolina?
Excuse me...
Come, let's go.

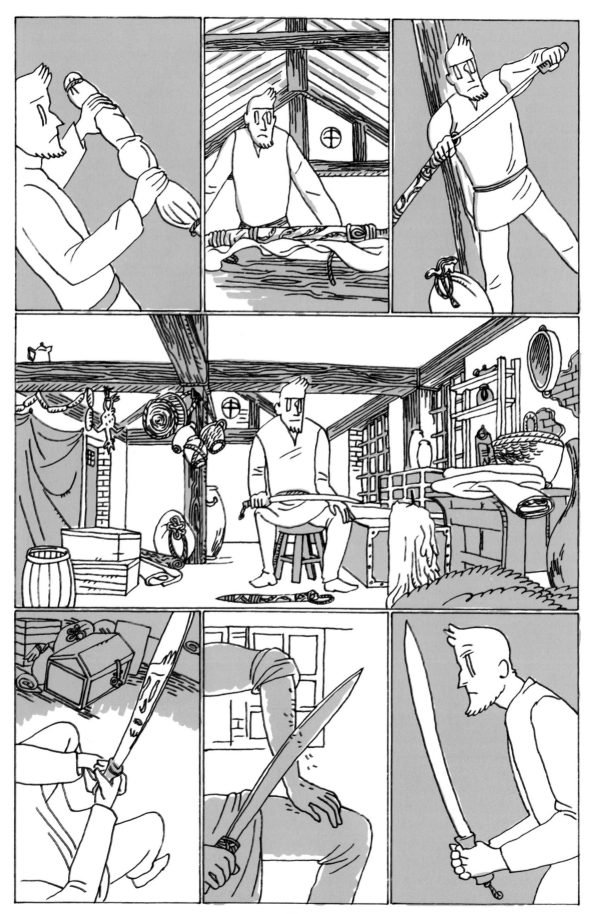

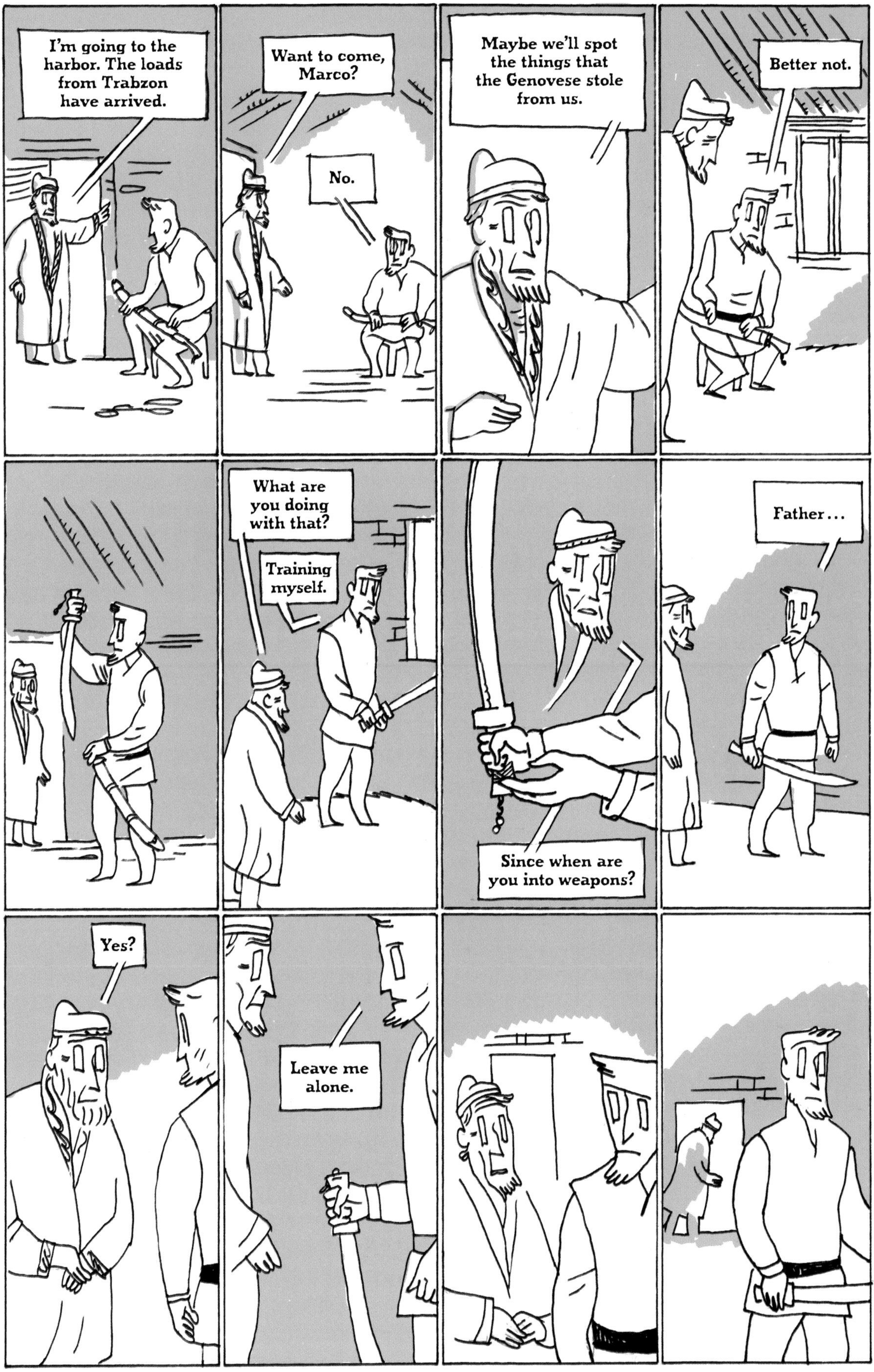

I'm going to the harbor. The loads from Trabzon have arrived.
Want to come, Marco?
No.
Maybe we'll spot the things that the Genovese stole from us.
Better not.
What are you doing with that?
Training myself.
Since when are you into weapons?
Father...
Yes?
Leave me alone.

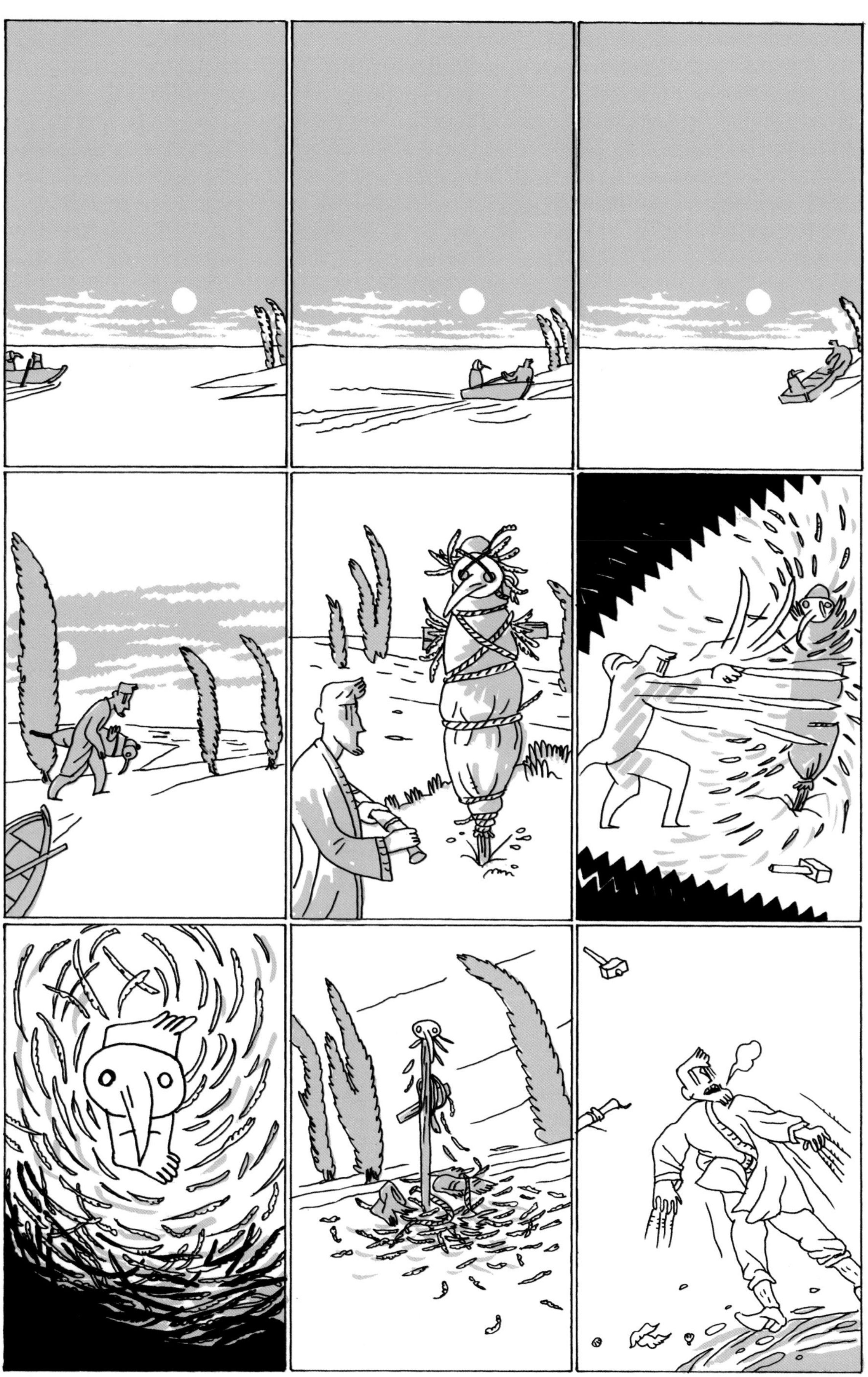

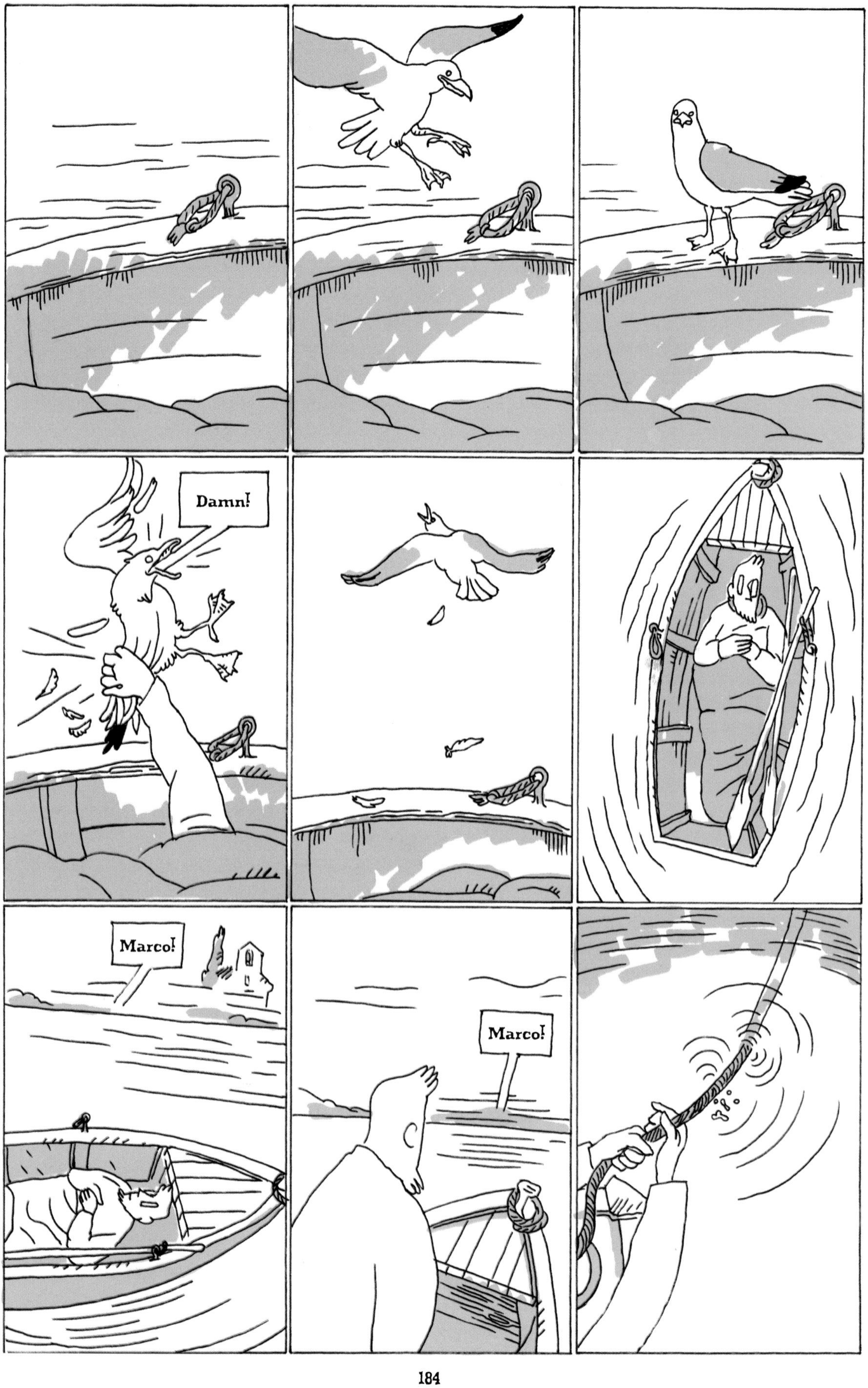
Damn!
Marco!
Marco!

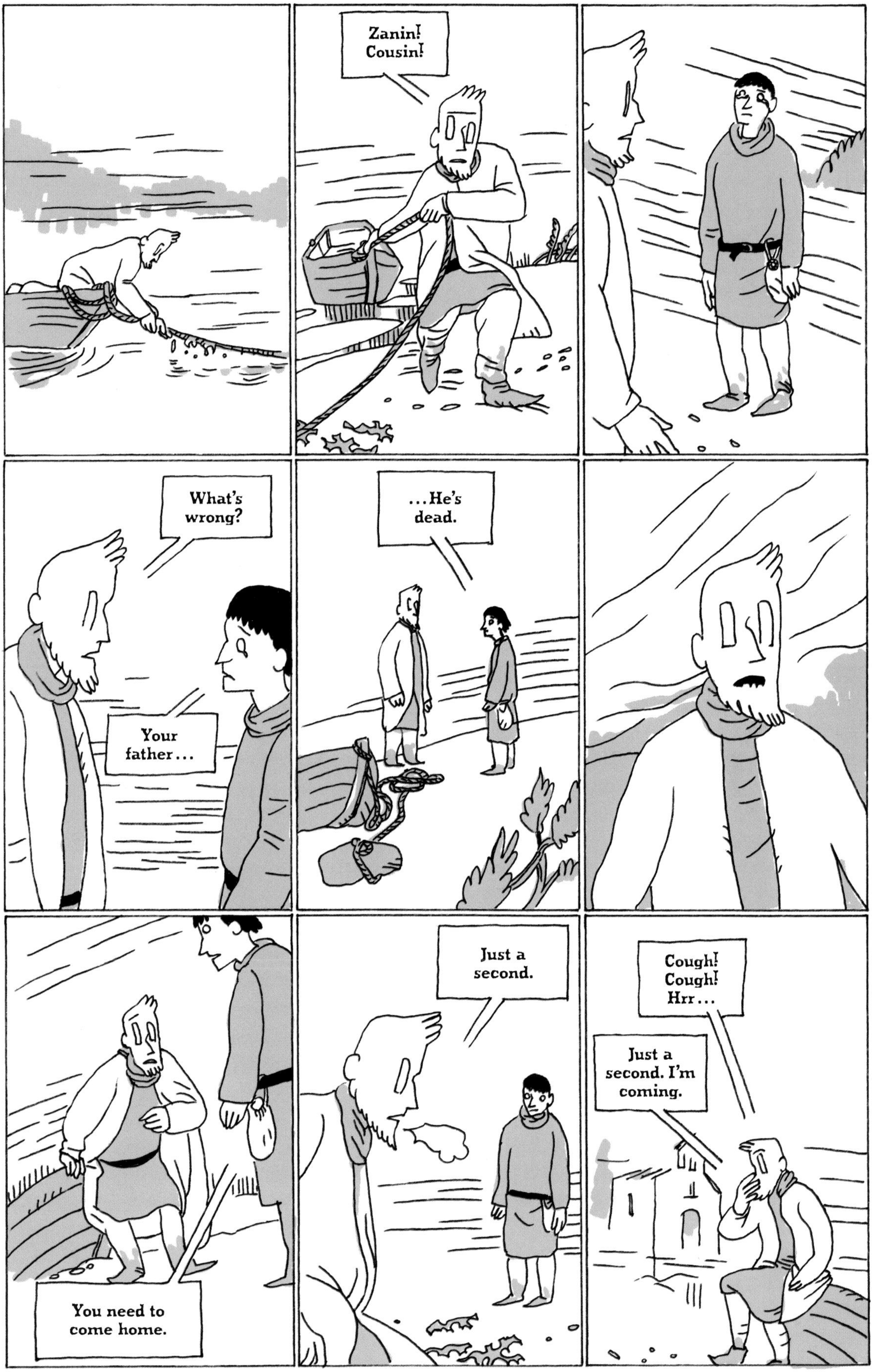
Zanin! Cousin!
What's wrong?
Your father…
…He's dead.
You need to come home.
Just a second.
Cough! Cough! Hrr…
Just a second. I'm coming.

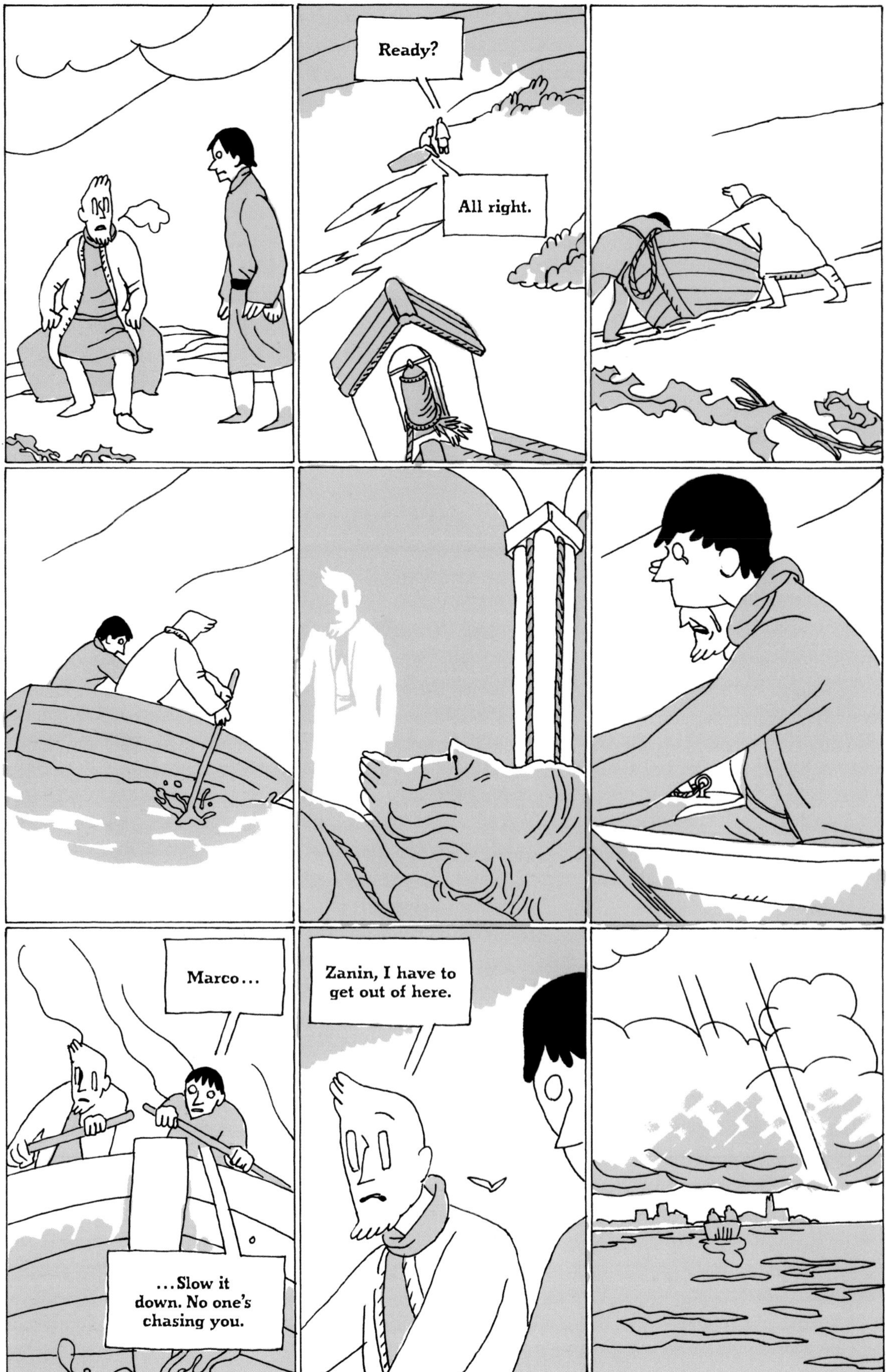
Ready?
All right.
Marco...
...Slow it down. No one's chasing you.
Zanin, I have to get out of here.

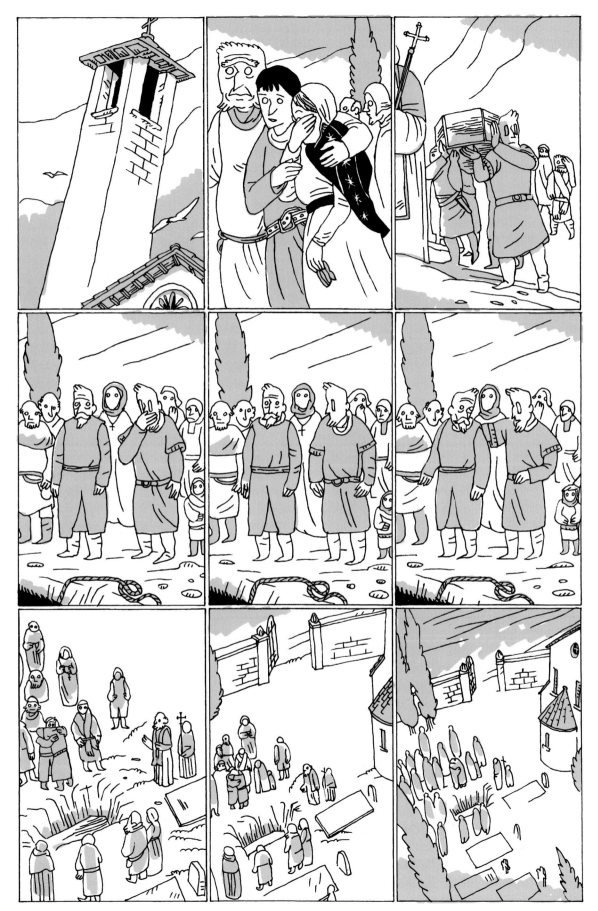

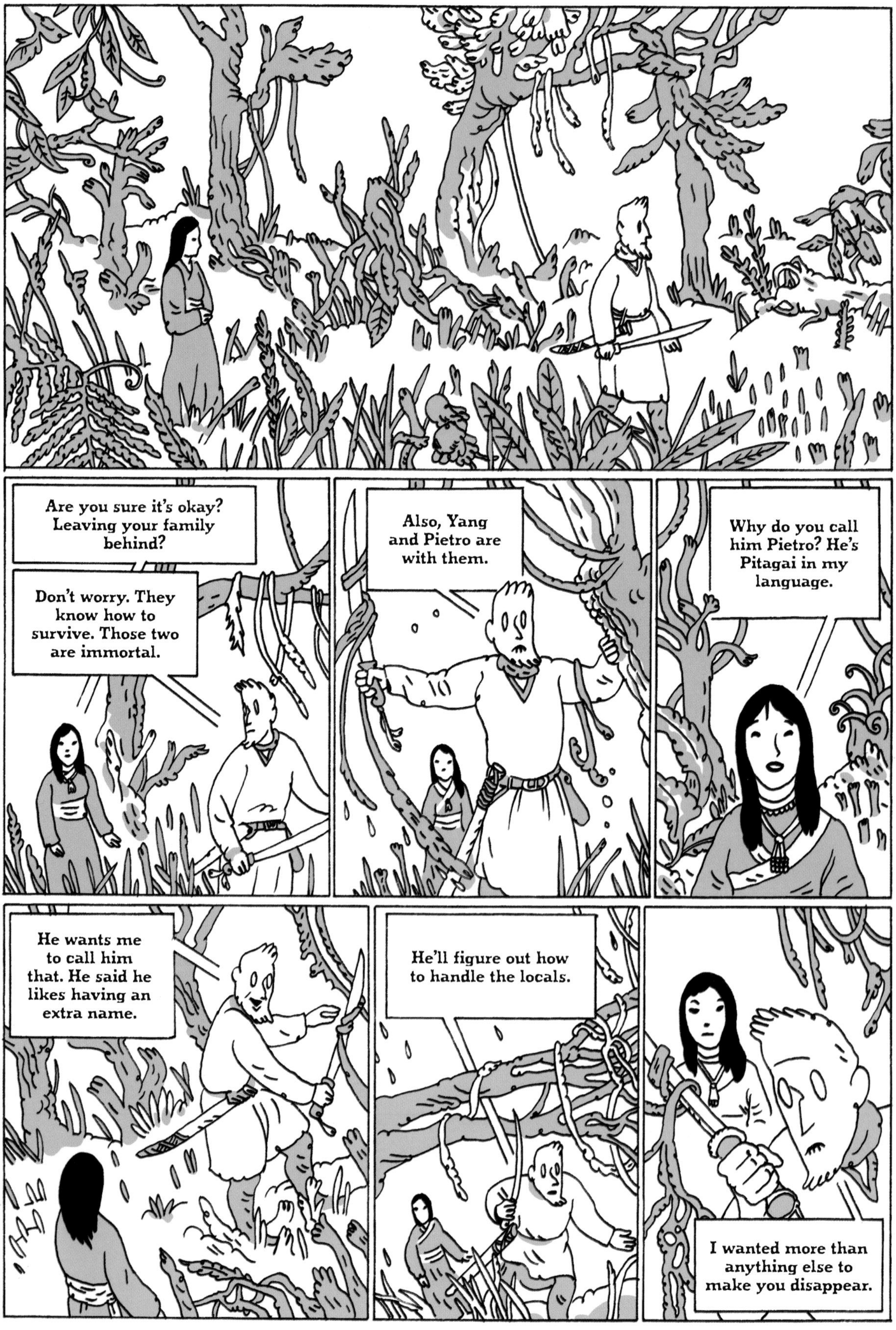

Are you sure it's okay? Leaving your family behind?
Don't worry. They know how to survive. Those two are immortal.
Also, Yang and Pietro are with them.
Why do you call him Pietro? He's Pitagai in my language.
He wants me to call him that. He said he likes having an extra name.
He'll figure out how to handle the locals.
I wanted more than anything else to make you disappear.

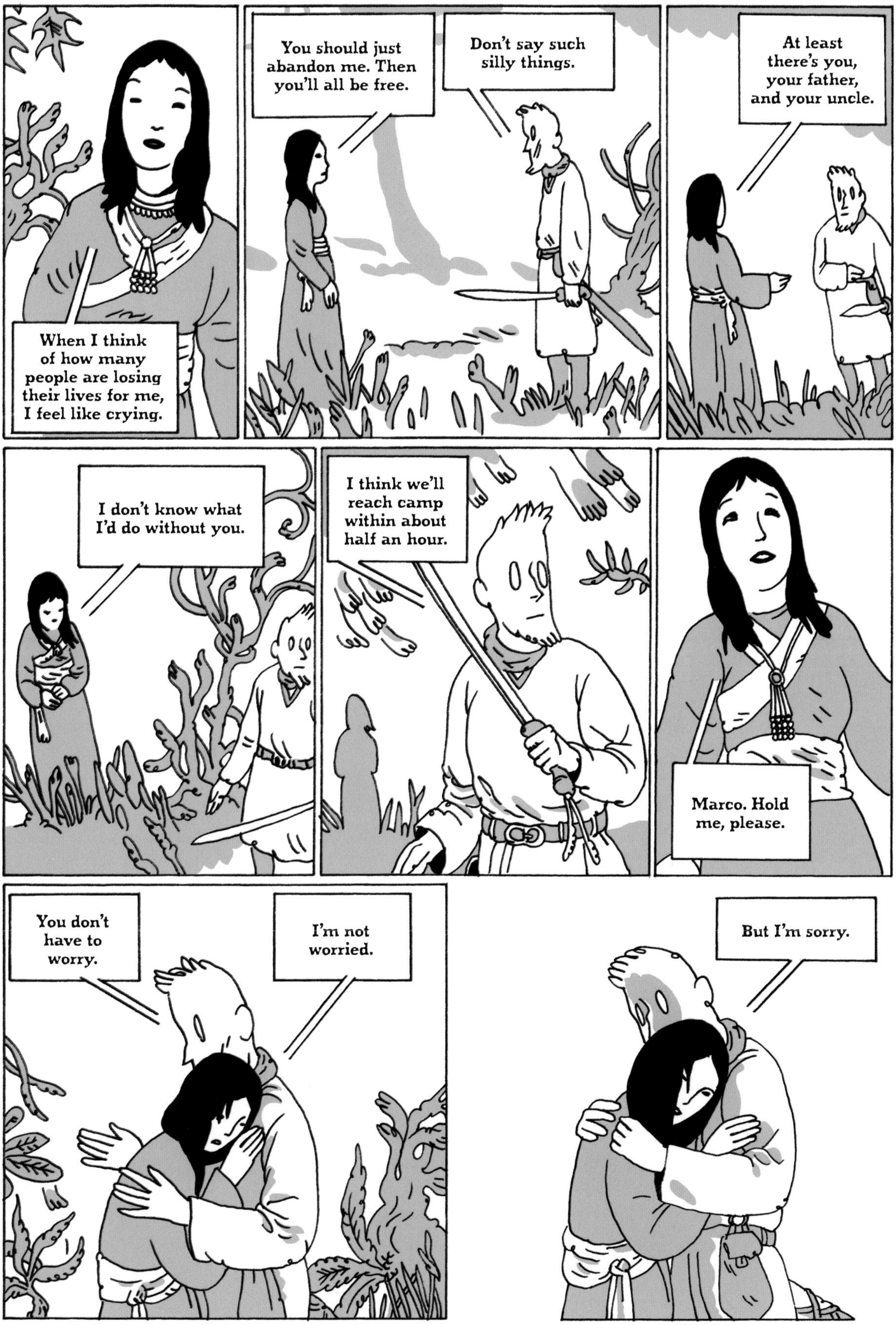
When I think of how many people are losing their lives for me, I feel like crying.
You should just abandon me. Then you'll all be free.
Don't say such silly things.
At least there's you, your father, and your uncle.
I don't know what I'd do without you.
I think we'll reach camp within about half an hour.
Marco. Hold me, please.
You don't have to worry.
I'm not worried.
But I'm sorry.

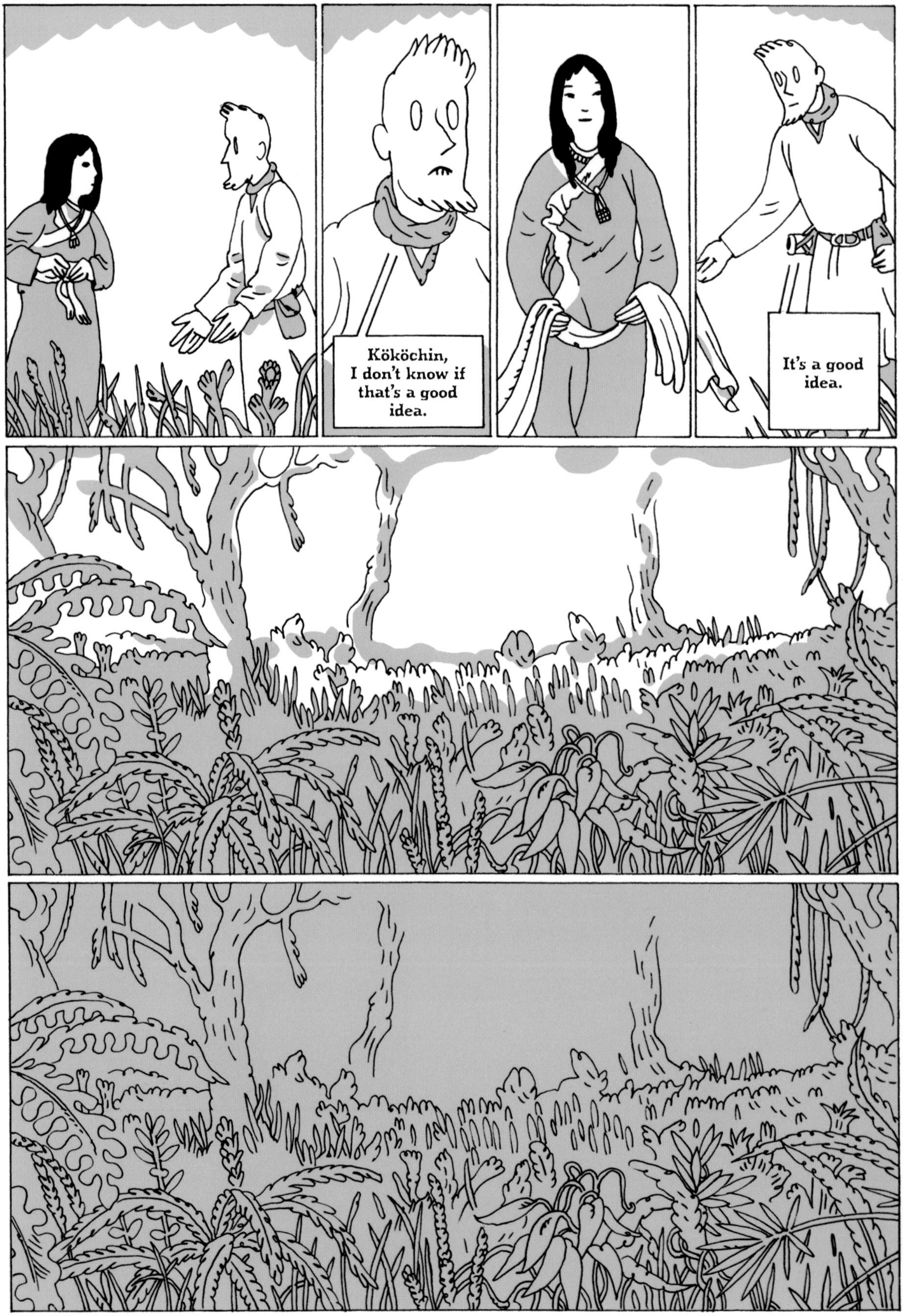
Kököchin, I don't know if that's a good idea.
It's a good idea.

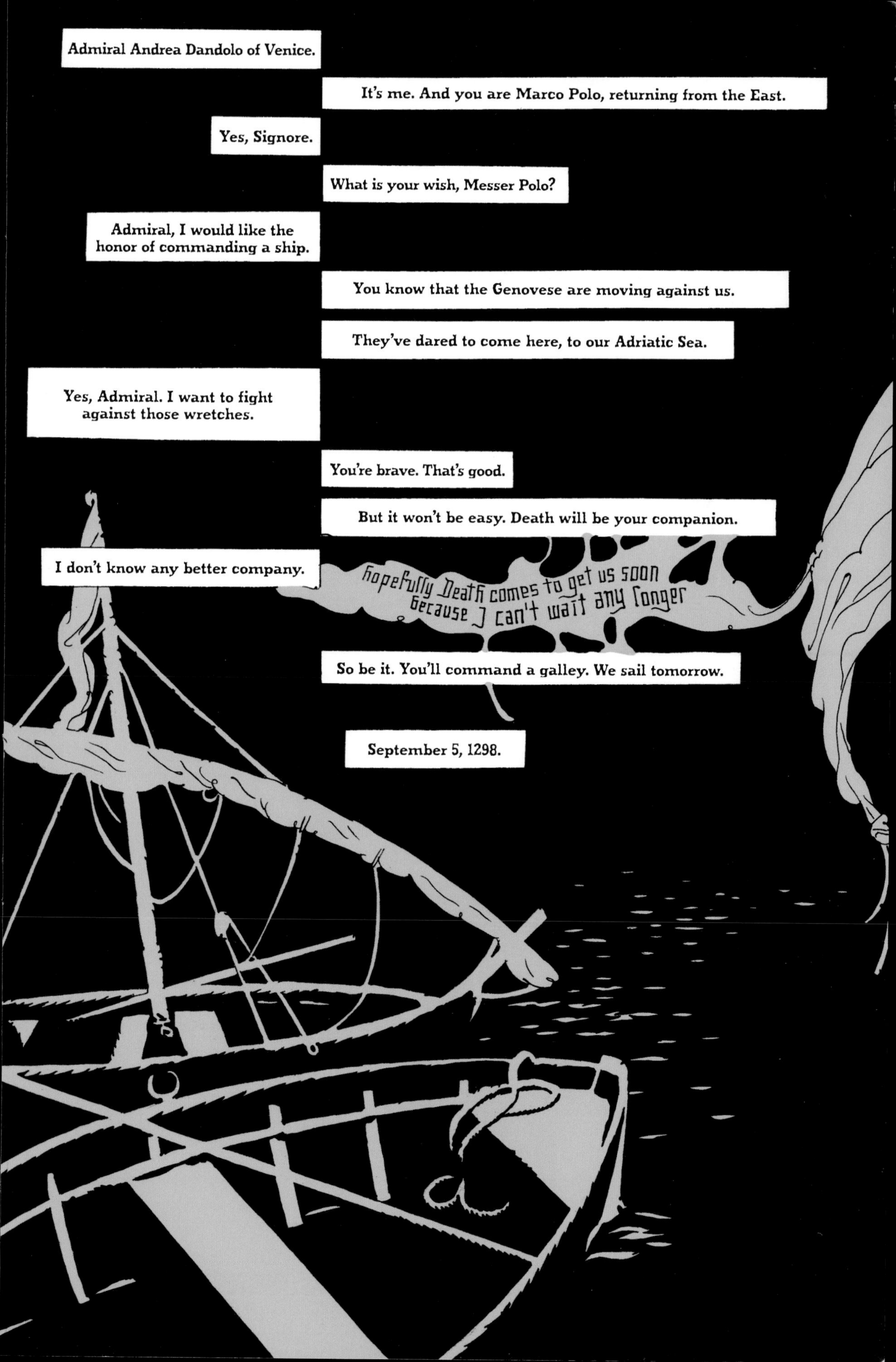
Admiral Andrea Dandolo of Venice.
It's me. And you are Marco Polo, returning from the East.
Yes, Signore.
What is your wish, Messer Polo?
Admiral, I would like the honor of commanding a ship.
You know that the Genovese are moving against us.
They've dared to come here, to our Adriatic Sea.
Yes, Admiral. I want to fight against those wretches.
You're brave. That's good.
But it won't be easy. Death will be your companion.
I don't know any better company.
hopefully Death comes to get us soon because I can't wait any longer
So be it. You'll command a galley. We sail tomorrow.
September 5, 1298.

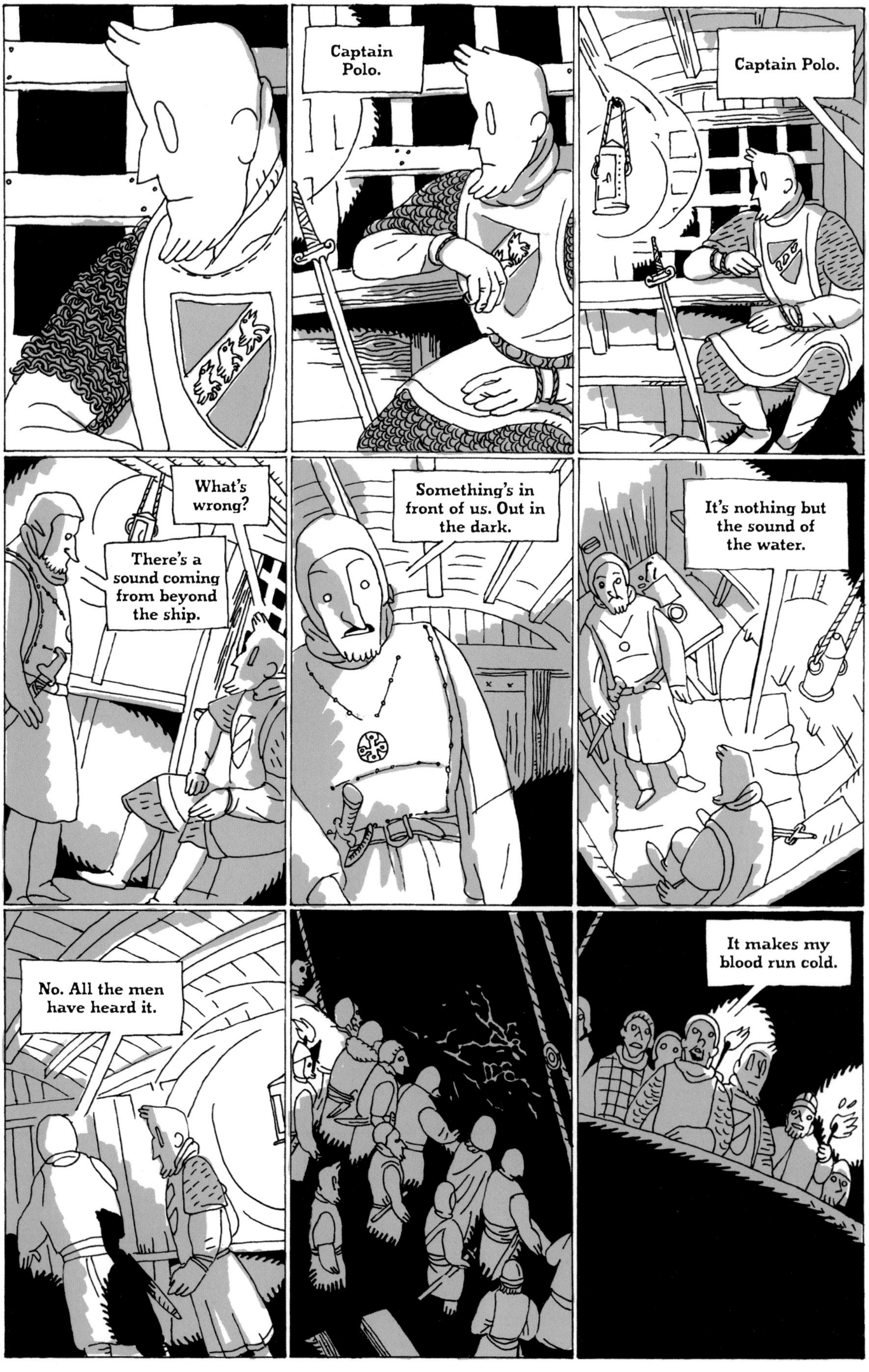
Captain Polo.
Captain Polo.
What's wrong?
There's a sound coming from beyond the ship.
Something's in front of us. Out in the dark.
It's nothing but the sound of the water.
No. All the men have heard it.
It makes my blood run cold.

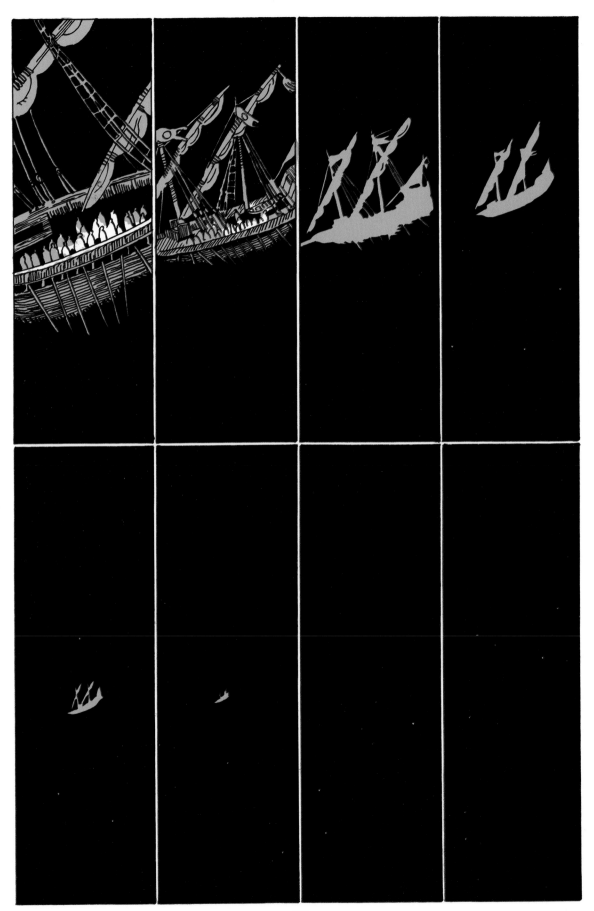

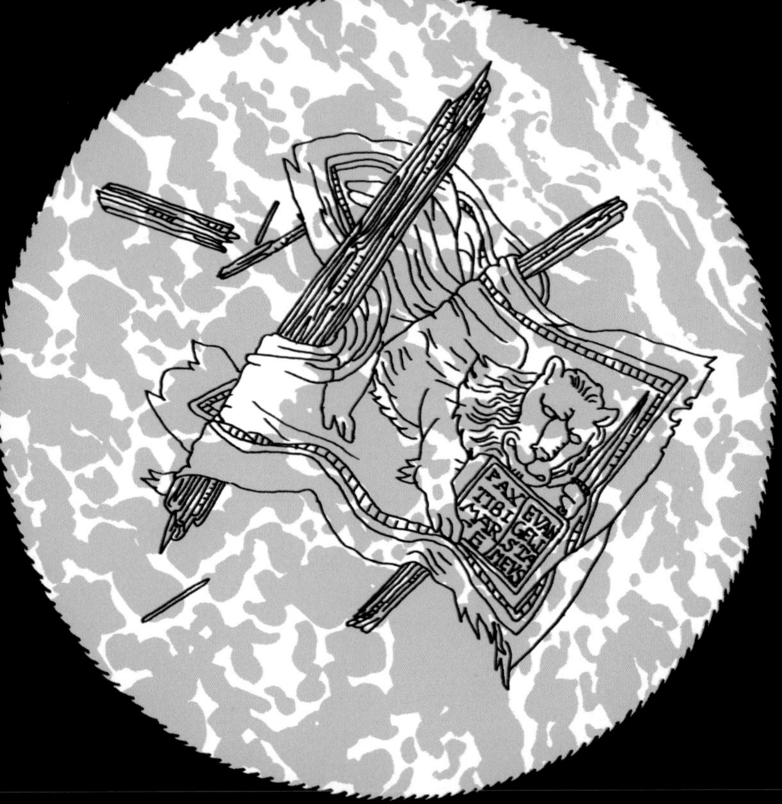
PAX
TIBI
MAR
E
EVAN
GELI
STA
MEVS

September 8, 1298

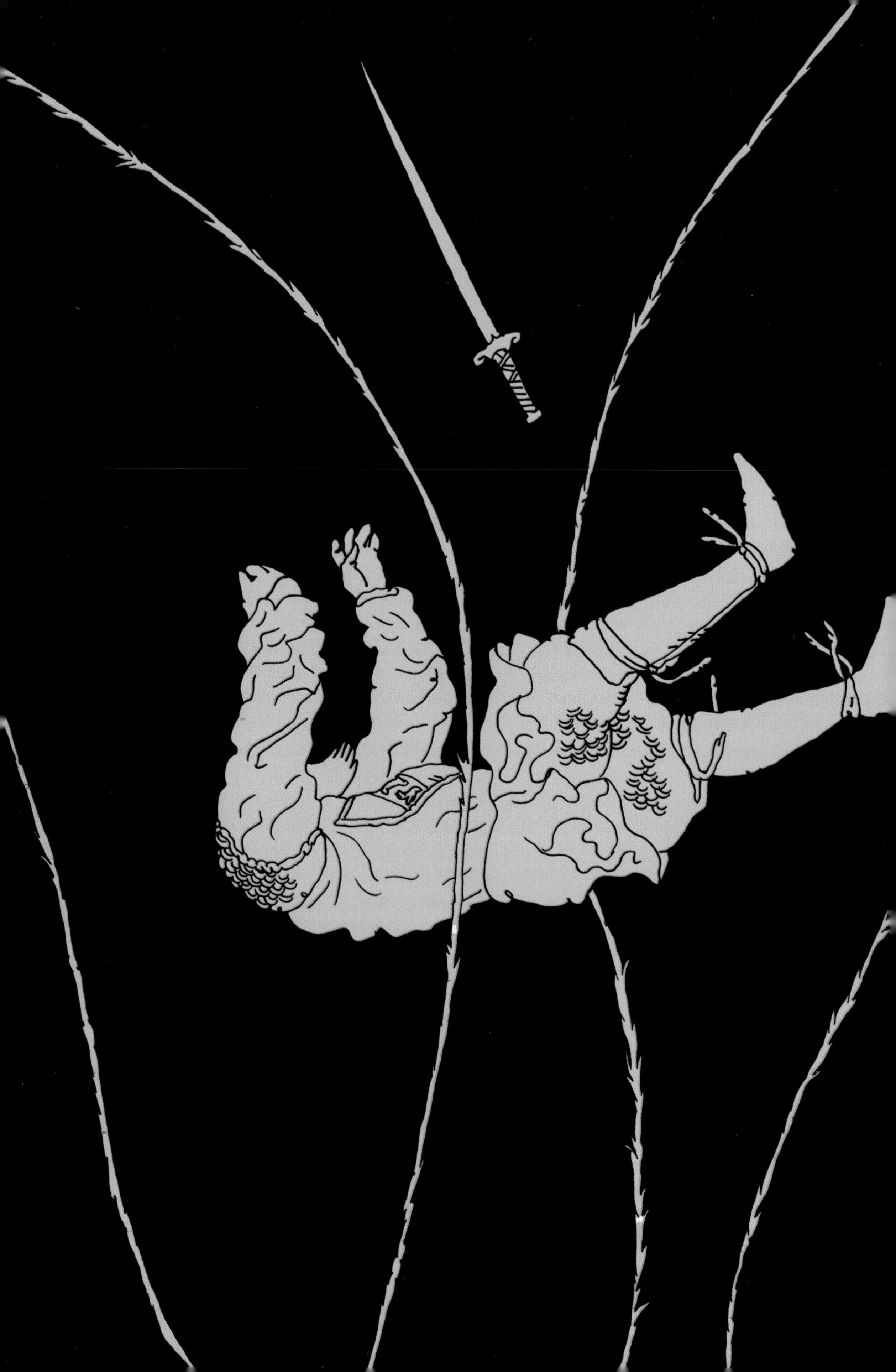

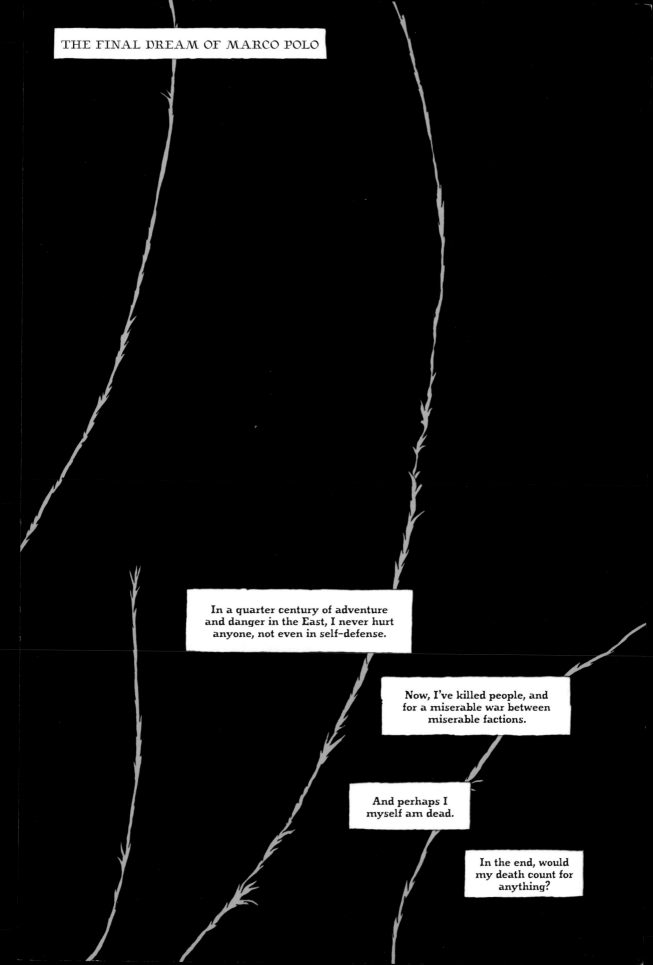

THE FINAL DREAM OF MARCO POLO

In a quarter century of adventure and danger in the East, I never hurt anyone, not even in self-defense.

Now, I've killed people, and for a miserable war between miserable factions.

And perhaps I myself am dead.

In the end, would my death count for anything?

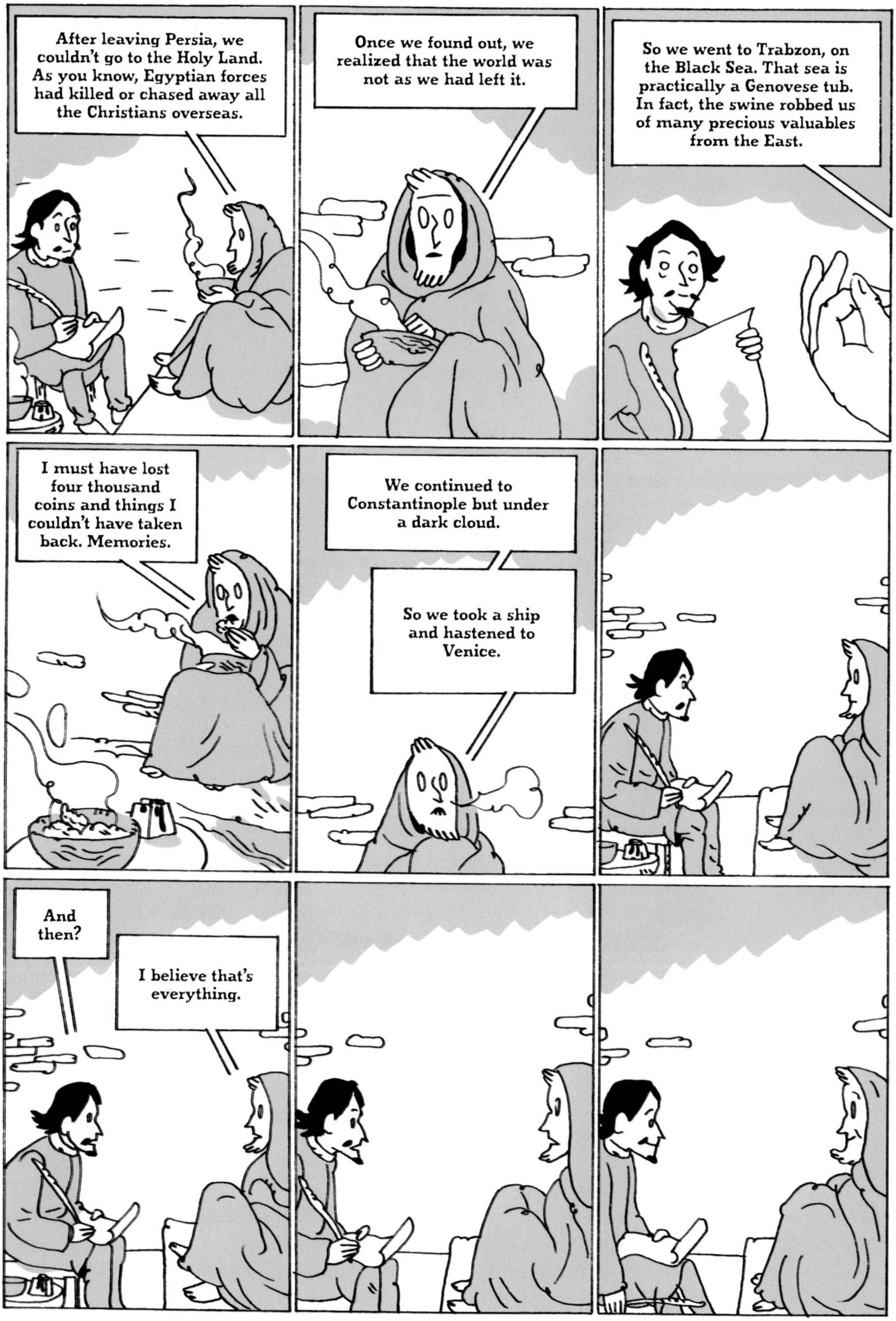
After leaving Persia, we couldn't go to the Holy Land. As you know, Egyptian forces had killed or chased away all the Christians overseas.
Once we found out, we realized that the world was not as we had left it.
So we went to Trabzon, on the Black Sea. That sea is practically a Genovese tub. In fact, the swine robbed us of many precious valuables from the East.
I must have lost four thousand coins and things I couldn't have taken back. Memories.
We continued to Constantinople but under a dark cloud.
So we took a ship and hastened to Venice.
And then?
I believe that's everything.

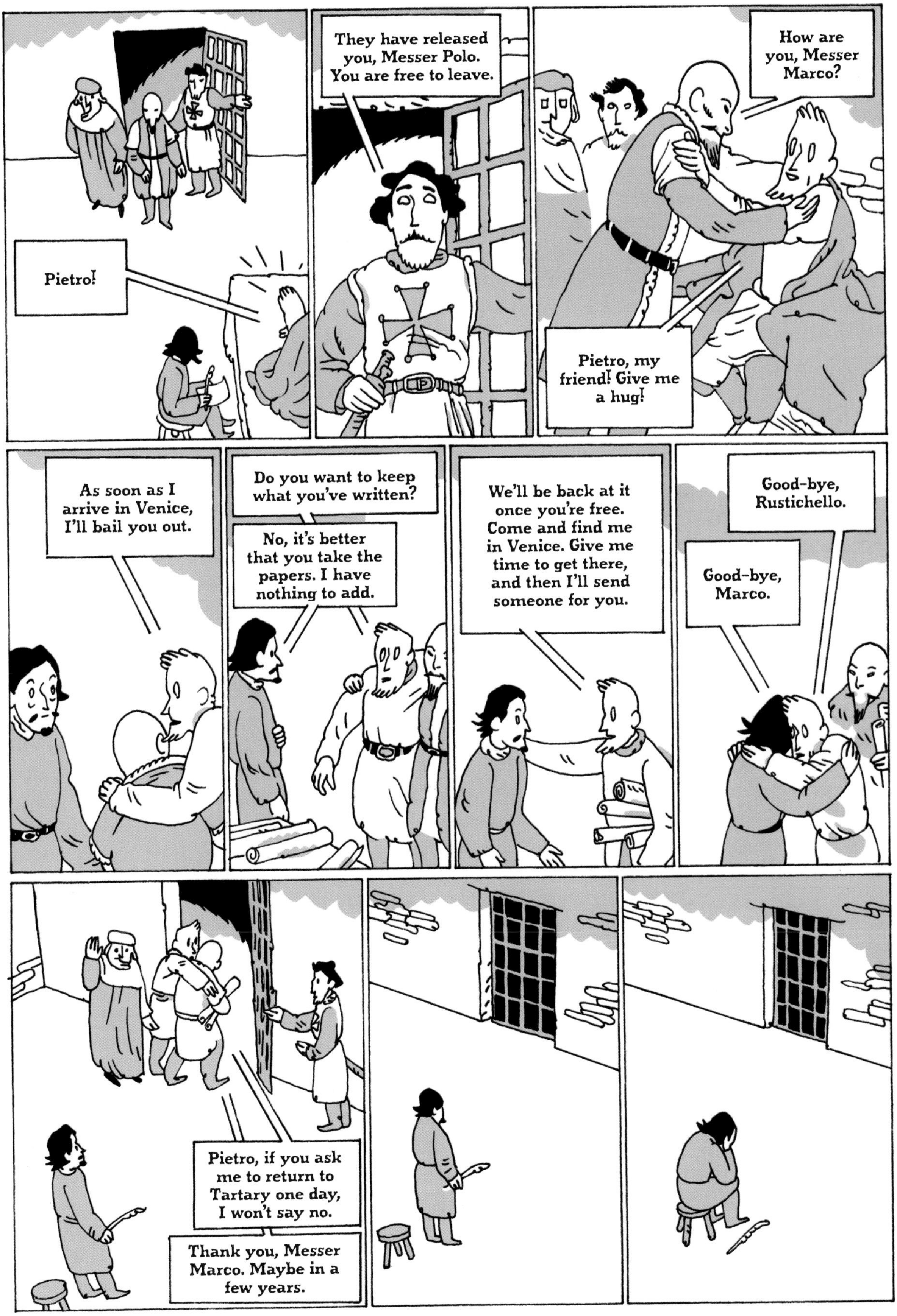

Pietro!
They have released you, Messer Polo. You are free to leave.
How are you, Messer Marco?
Pietro, my friend! Give me a hug!
As soon as I arrive in Venice, I'll bail you out.
Do you want to keep what you've written?
No, it's better that you take the papers. I have nothing to add.
We'll be back at it once you're free. Come and find me in Venice. Give me time to get there, and then I'll send someone for you.
Good-bye, Rustichello.
Good-bye, Marco.
Pietro, if you ask me to return to Tartary one day, I won't say no.
Thank you, Messer Marco. Maybe in a few years.

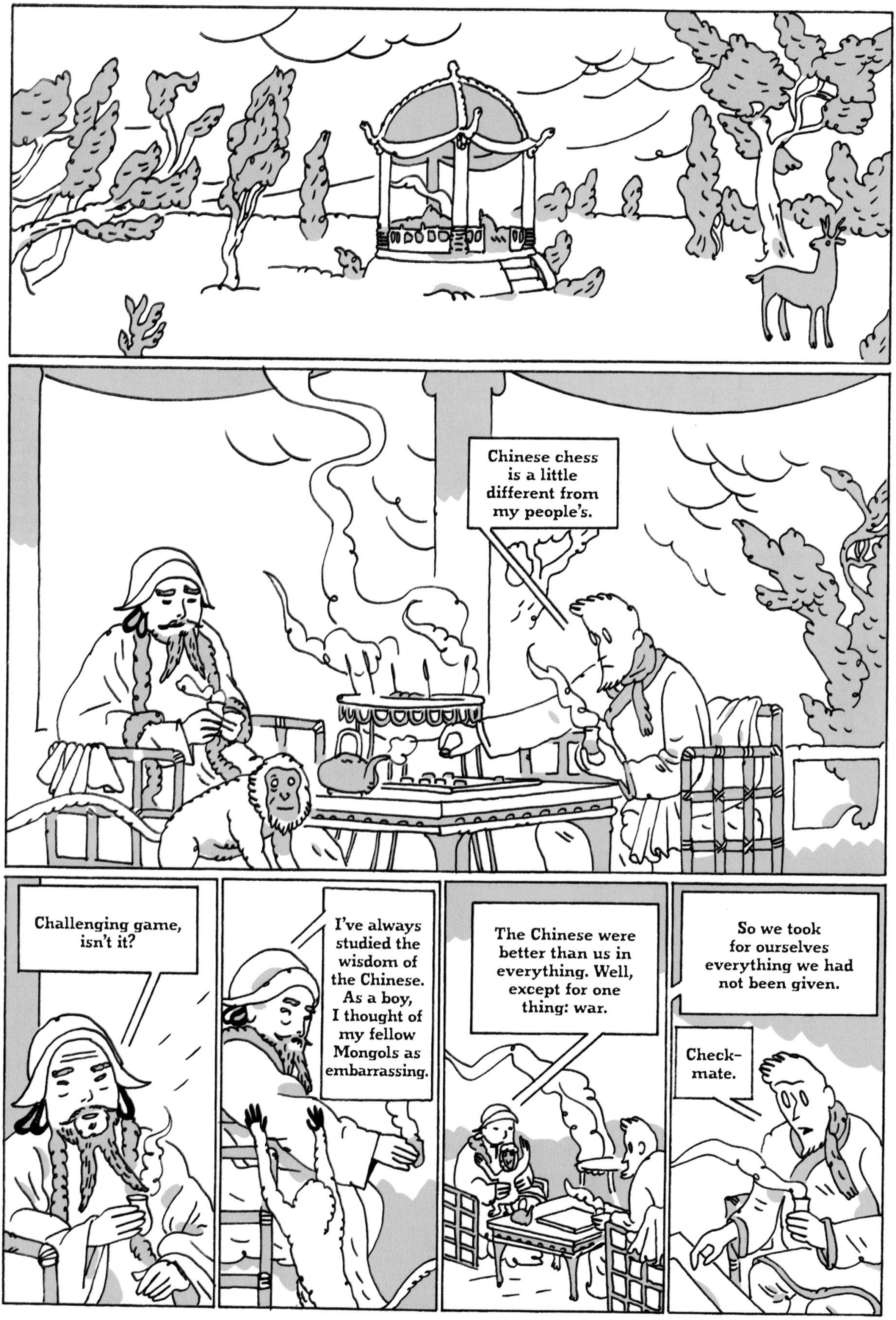
Chinese chess is a little different from my people's.
Challenging game, isn't it?
I've always studied the wisdom of the Chinese. As a boy, I thought of my fellow Mongols as embarrassing.
The Chinese were better than us in everything. Well, except for one thing: war.
So we took for ourselves everything we had not been given.
Check-mate.

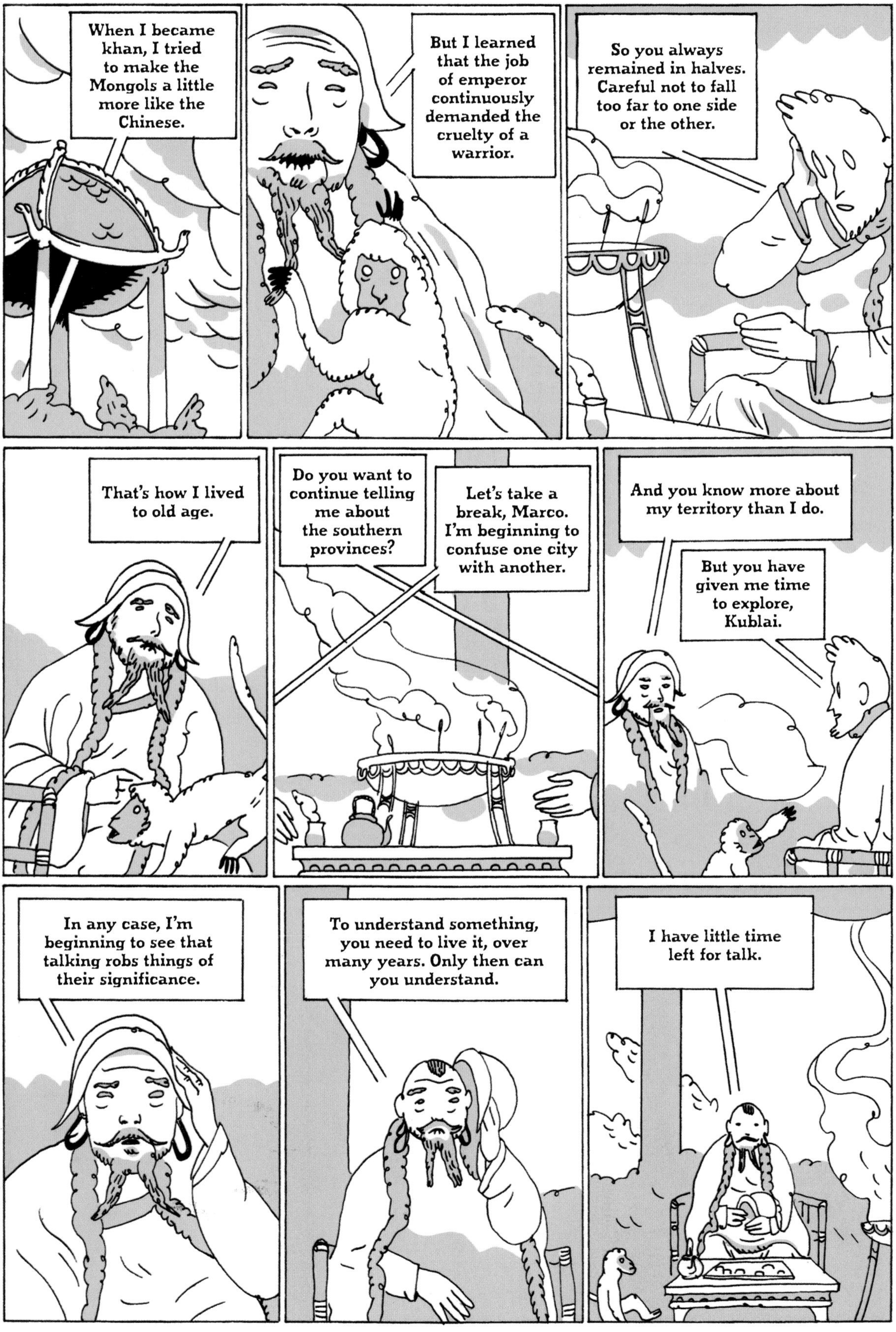
When I became khan, I tried to make the Mongols a little more like the Chinese.
But I learned that the job of emperor continuously demanded the cruelty of a warrior.
So you always remained in halves. Careful not to fall too far to one side or the other.
That's how I lived to old age.
Do you want to continue telling me about the southern provinces?
Let's take a break, Marco. I'm beginning to confuse one city with another.
And you know more about my territory than I do.
But you have given me time to explore, Kublai.
In any case, I'm beginning to see that talking robs things of their significance.
To understand something, you need to live it, over many years. Only then can you understand.
I have little time left for talk.

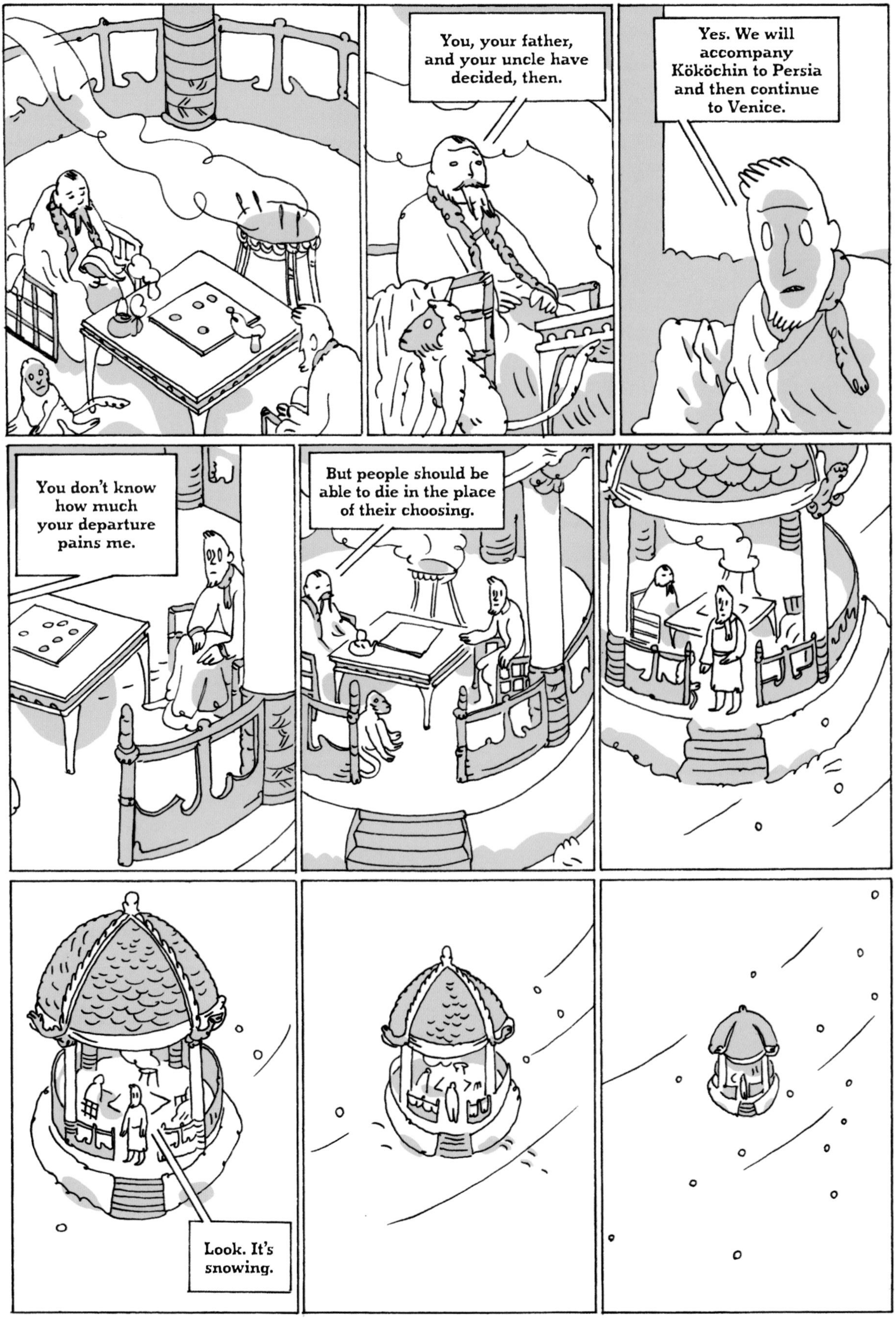
You, your father, and your uncle have decided, then.
Yes. We will accompany Kököchin to Persia and then continue to Venice.
You don't know how much your departure pains me.
But people should be able to die in the place of their choosing.
Look. It's snowing.

Marco Polo
1254-1324

A traveler, a merchant, and a diplomat, Marco Polo journeyed to China and later wrote about it in the book *Il Milione* (also known as *The Travels of Marco Polo* and *Book of the Marvels of the World*). He sought to document the cultural practices, economies, politics, and histories of different countries of the Middle Ages. Over the centuries, his travelogue has been a source of inspiration and debate for writers, travelers, geographers, and scholars.

Marco Polo was born in 1254 in Venice. At that time, maritime republics (coastal city-states) were an economic and political force in the Mediterranean. Venetian merchant ships and military ships, with their Lion of Saint Mark banners, represented power and wealth throughout the Mediterranean colonies. Each Mediterranean port included a large Venetian quarter, an enclave where the merchants of Venice practiced their trade. Separate quarters also existed for Genoa, Pisa, and other maritime republics.

Before Marco Polo's birth, the Venetian Republic enjoyed a long-standing relationship with Constantinople (later known as Istanbul, Turkey), the era's largest and wealthiest European city. However, Constantinople was also troubled by uprisings; power in the city changed hands multiple times throughout the thirteenth century. Around 1260 Niccolo and Maffeo Polo—Venetian merchants and the father and uncle of Marco Polo—were living in the town of Sudak along the Black Sea. They owned warehouses in the town's Venetian quarter. Hearing news of violence perpetrated against the Venetians in Constantinople—otherwise a natural stop on a return to Italy—they planned a trading expedition in the opposite direction, turning their eyes toward the East.

Niccolo and Maffeo made their way to Saraj, the capital of the Mongol khanate of the Golden Horde. There, they became acquainted with a delegation from another khanate, the Ilkhanate of Persia, and headed toward Kublai Khan's China (also known as Cathay). The Mongols were the dominant power in Asia at this time. After Genghis Khan united all the Mongol peoples under his command and annexed large parts of the continent, his descendants had continued the expansion, leading their forces through military conquests throughout almost all of Asia. Mongol territories extended to the edge of Europe. Over time, a political structure stabilized across the different Mongol khanates and travel along Asia's Silk Road—a network of trade routes—became easier.

Niccolo and Maffeo Polo entered into the service of Kublai Khan, the emperor of China—the most advanced and most prosperous land in the world. Kublai Khan asked them to visit the pope and to bring back a delegation of one hundred Christian wise men to serve in his court.

Tasked with this mission, the two Polo men began their return to Venice in 1265. They arrived in 1269. Marco, then in his mid-teens, met his father for the first time since Niccolo had left, when Marco was only two years old. Marco had grown up in a Venice that represented an open door to the East. Many languages echoed throughout the city's ports, and both foreign goods and amazing stories from the East were passed among the merchants. In the Middle Ages, the men and women of Europe lacked reliable information about Asia and imagined the continent as a place of wonders and monstrosities. Tall tales of the continent were common: cities of gold, men without heads, enormous-eared panotti, dogs that walked on two legs, dragons, basilisks, huge birds of prey, and sea monsters. These stores alternated between the obscene and the sublime, reflecting the anxieties and hopes of Europe during this period.

Marco Polo joined his father and his uncle on the road back to the East. The journey began in 1271. It was full of obstacles from the beginning. Between the death of Pope Clement IV and continually delayed election of a new pope, Christianity was in transition. The indecision lasted 1,006 days, the longest period to date in church history in which the papal throne remained vacant, and it culminated in the so-called fury of Viterbo. The citizens of Viterbo, a city that was then the papal seat, were exasperated by the endless deliberation over the new pope. They decided to literally lock up the cardinals in the palace, and they removed part of the roof to speed the cardinals along.

The election occurred while Niccolo, Maffeo, and Marco Polo were already en route, having reached Palestine. They made a short detour to meet Pope Gregory X, who was in St. John d'Acre, one of the crusader territories of the Holy Land. The Polos acquired the oil of the Holy Sepulcher of Jerusalem and a set of Christian scholars (not one hundred men but two Dominican friars: Nicholas of Vicenza and William of Tripoli) to take to Kublai. However, the Dominicans soon broke away from the company, and the three Polos continued onward by themselves. With help from golden coins that identified them as emissaries of the khan, they crossed into Georgia, Armenia, Persia, Afghanistan, the mountains protecting China, and the desert lands of Xinjiang. The Polos then traveled along a string of cities that led into the heart of the empire. After three years of traveling, they finally met Kublai in Shangdu in 1274. At Kublai's invitation, the Polos followed him to Khanbaliq (known in modern times as Beijing), the capital of his dynasty. Their arrival took place during a period of change and expansion for the Mongol Empire.

As the Polos began to serve the Great Khan in the role of imperial officials, Marco Polo, in his early twenties, stood out as a skilled observer and diplomat. His role grew due to his favor with the emperor. Marco traveled to the remote provinces of the khan's vast empire and to lands that had been freshly acquired. He became a witness to China's technological advancements during this period. A vast network of channels promoted the transport of goods and people, and also guaranteed rich, orderly agricultural production. The empire's many bridges and roads allowed people to move quickly between cultural centers. Its efficient economy led to abundant trade opportunities.

During the nearly two decades in which the Polos stayed in China, Marco and his relatives maintained prestigious positions in the court of the Great Khan. However, an opportunity to leave came around 1291. The khan of Persia, Arghun, a relative of the Great Khan, was a widower. He had to remarry a woman of proper lineage, from one of the original Mongol tribes stationed in the territories of Kublai. A delegation from Khanbaliq had selected Kököchin of the Bayad as the future wife of Arghun. Marco, Niccolo, and Maffeo Polo were given the difficult task of accompanying the princess and delegates to Persia. They would make the journey back to Venice thereafter.

The Polos, Kököchin, and members of the Persian khanate sailed with fourteen ships from the Chinese port of Quanzhou. In the course of their journey, they docked at Sumatra, Java, Ceylon (Sri Lanka), the west coast of India, and Hormuz on the Persian Gulf. Marco Polo's travelogues provide descriptions and observations about these places, as well as reports on what he was told about other places bordering the Indian Ocean, such as the East African coast.

Upon reaching Persia, the group learned that Arghun, Kököchin's betrothed, had died. Arghun's brother Gaikatu had seized power in a coup, taking advantage of Arghun's son, Ghazan. To avoid further problems in the area, Kököchin wed Ghazan. The Polos were able to make their journey to Venice thereafter. But new setbacks emerged: Marco and his fellow travelers were no longer able to rely on Christian ports throughout the Holy Land, because St. John d'Acre, the last of the territories controlled by European crusaders, fell in 1295 after a bloody siege by the Egyptian Mamluk forces of al-Ashraf Khalil. All Christian kingdoms in Palestine were dismantled. The Polos were forced to take a route through the area presently known as Turkey. In Trabzon, on the Black Sea, pirates—or perhaps Genovese marauders—robbed them of money and valuables. Later, they sailed through Negroponte (the island of Euboea in the Aegean Sea, a Venetian colony at the time). Marco, Niccolo, and Maffeo Polo finally reached Venice in 1295.

The three travelers found Europe changed, with a new balance of power in the Mediterranean. The upheavals in the Middle East, with Christian crusaders' strongholds disappearing, led to a more difficult trading culture. Venice also faced increased competition from Genoa, leading to armed conflict between the two Italian republics.

A formation of ninety-five Venetian war galleys took off from Venice to challenge the Genovese. One of these ships, traveling along the Dalmatian Coast, was commanded by Marco Polo. On September 8, 1298, the Venetian galleys met the Genovese fleet near Korčula, an island off the Adriatic Sea. The Genovese, though outnumbered, were able to break the ranks of the Venetian formation, at the cost of heavy casualties. The Battle of Korčula ended in a complete defeat for the Venetians. The vast majority of their galleys were sunk, seven thousand soldiers died, and at least as many were taken prisoner. Among the prisoners were Admiral Andrea Dandolo, who died immediately after his capture, and Marco Polo. In the Genovese prison, Marco Polo met Rustichello, a writer from Pisa. Rustichello may have been there since the Battle of Meloria, a 1284 conflict in which the Genovese attacked the Tuscans. The two began collaborating on an account of Marco Polo's travels.

The text, originally written in Old French, was immediately popular and sparked enthusiasm and controversy. It was widely read, transcribed, and translated, and it remains the subject of study and debate, as many of Marco Polo's claims have been disputed. Some accounts within *Il Milione* may reflect Polo's own biases or misunderstandings. Other accounts may have taken on the biases of editors or translators in the years after Polo conferred with Rustichello.

The influence of *Il Milione* can be found in the literature of later centuries. Christopher Columbus also consulted its pages in search of information about the peoples of India and China. The enigmatic title of the work could refer to the multitude of wonders Marco spoke of. *Il Milione* could also be derived from Emilione, one of the nicknames of a branch of the Polo family.

Marco Polo was freed from his Genovese prison in 1299. He returned to Venice, devoting himself to reworking and refining his travelogue. He settled into a peaceful life after marrying Donata Badoer in 1300, managing his considerable assets, and living in Venice's San Giovanni Grisostomo area. Marco Polo died on January 8, 1324.

A Traveler's Guide: Glossary of Terms

cardinal: an official of high rank within the Roman Catholic Church

Cathay: a common term in the Middle Ages for China

Church of the Holy Sepulcher: a church in the city of Jerusalem believed to encompass both the site at which Jesus of Nazareth was crucified and his burial site

delegate: a person authorized to represent the will or the position of another person; in the case of a papal delegate, the will of the pope

Dominican: a member of the Dominican Order, an organization of Catholic preachers founded in 1216 and named for Saint Dominic de Guzman

ducat: a form of currency used in Europe of the Middle Ages

friar: a member of a religious order of men, including the Dominican Order

Genovese: the people of Genoa, a seaport on the northwestern coast of Italy

horde: a group of warriors, often nomadic and traveling by horse

khan: a ruler of the Turkish, Tartar, and Mongol peoples, as well as an emperor of China, during the Middle Ages

khanate: the territory ruled by a khan, or the people within a territory ruled by a khan

Knight Templar: a member of a Christian military order

lama: a spiritual leader, often a Tibetan or Mongol Buddhist monk

Latin: in the Middle Ages, a person native to a territory within the domain of the Roman Catholic Church or a person native to a territory in which the local language derives from the Latin language

Mongol: a group of people native to eastern and central China. In the thirteenth century, the military leader Genghis Khan established a Mongol Empire across central Asia.

Old French: a language predating modern French, which was also used as a common language for elites and merchants in Europe of the Middle Ages

papal: relating to the pope of the Roman Catholic Church

Qara'unas: a Mongol people that settled in the territory later known as Afghanistan

Silk Road: a network of trade routes reaching from China to the Mediterranean Sea

St. John d'Acre: a city in Israel along the coast of the Mediterranean Sea, presently known as Acre. Control over this city was contested throughout the Middle Ages, and it was referred to as St. John d'Acre while under Christian rule.

Tartar: a member of a group of central Asian peoples including both Mongols and Turks

Tartary: a region of Asia and eastern Europe under Tartar control during part of the Middle Ages

Venetian: a person of Venice, a city in northeastern Italy

About the Author

Marco Tabilio was born in 1987 in Riva del Garda, a town in Italy's Trento Province. A cartoonist, an illustrator, and a video artist, Tabilio has been featured in group exhibitions in Bologna, Venice, Hamburg, and Berlin. His work has also been published in a variety of comics magazines. Tabilio is a graduate of the Academy of Fine Arts in Bologna. He lives and works in Hamburg.

Acknowledgments

Thanks to Alice.

Thanks to my parents, Olimpia and Silvano, and my brother, Riccardo.

Thanks to Simone and Daria.

Thanks to all the friends who have supported me at work but also before and after.

Finally, thanks to Marco Polo, Rustichello da Pisa, and to all others.